The City of Chrome and Glass

David Alan Bennett

ISBN-13: 978-1-7325794-0-8

To my family, both immediate and extended, and to Zarah for support and encouragement beyond measure.

The City of Chrome and Glass

For centuries, she dreamed of a city of chrome and glass. When she awoke, she found herself on the cold, cracked stones of a ruined tower, beneath a pale sky, amidst flurries of snow that chilled her to the bone. The memory of the dream faded quickly. The weight of shackles that she couldn't see threatened to pull her back down as she picked herself up and turned in a slow circle, her orange eyes filled with both wonder and sorrow.

Idsiyushti's dreams had turned deeply sexual when she was startled awake by someone pounding on the door of her hut. She rolled from her sleeping pallet, at once confused and embarrassed, to stand facing the door, naked.

The pounding sounded once again, shaking the door, jarring the bundle of dried herbs near the doorframe. Idsiyushti blinked and took a deep breath. She let power slide to the tips of her fingers. Outside, beyond the hut's lone window, with its painted glass that Idsiyushti had bought after saving coin from telling over a thousand fortunes, trees danced in a breeze that was no doubt hot and wet, even this early in the morning.

"Mistress!" a voice beyond the door said. "Mistress, soldiers are coming!"

Idsiyushti sighed. Beside her sleeping pallet, disarrayed with silks and furs that, no doubt, needed to be washed, the gourd of whiskey beckoned. She'd left it there last night—rather, early in the hot, night-shrouded morning—and had drifted to sleep after waiting fruitlessly for Marrah to finish her shift over at Grendl's. Marrah hadn't appeared, of course, so Idsiyushti's sleep had been filled with dreams of twists and turns, desperate gasps, burning kisses, and a deep yearning that, in those dreams, had been a talking pit of blackness that spoke to her in whispers and lies. She picked up the gourd and took a long drink, felt the whiskey burn her throat, hit her empty stomach. She closed her eyes and heard the voice beyond the door, still urgent, become momentarily muffled. Her head spun almost pleasantly. Then her eyes snapped open and she put the gourd on a table cluttered with herb cuttings and a collection of crystal balls. She threw a cloak over her thin, sweat-covered frame and opened the door.

Macon, the blacksmith's eldest son—thirty-six last harvest and married nearly twenty years—looked down at the gap in the front of the cloak and averted his eyes. He gripped his wicker hat in both hands and his face grew darker with embarrassment. "Mistress, please. The soldiers are riding for the center of town."

"I'm sure Jonath will meet them."

"Yes—yes, mistress. But we thought you should know. In case—"

"In case I need to magic the soldiers away?" Idsiyushti asked. Her head stopped spinning, leaving a dull ache behind her eyes that she had not anticipated.

"No—no! In case...yes. Sorry, Mistress. But. Soldiers. Please come." Macon turned and all but ran down the path, which was muddy in the wet heat of the morning. He didn't put his hat back on his head until he was several paces beyond her garden and into the ruined hedge maze.

The whiskey made her shiver despite the dull ache. The wind in the trees was indeed hot and wet and carried the smell of fish and spice, along with the smell of decay that was the swamp. Idsiyushti watched the dancing trees then squeezed her eyes shut until the dull ache faded into the usual warm numbness of an alcoholic buzz. She closed the door and dressed.

Jonath of the Battlefield, knighted on some nameless, muddy plain while kneeling in a puddle of fly-infested blood, stood on the wooden porch that fronted the courthouse and watched the soldiers ride their beleaguered horses through the town square. The soldiers, wrapped in rusting armor that did more to show that they had no idea how to survive in the swamp, milled about, looking confused and angry. Finally, a sergeant noticed Jonath, noticed the knight's sash across his shoulders and the tarnished chain of office around his neck. The sergeant stared and then kicked his tired horse forward.

"Looks like we just pulled you out of bed," the sergeant said.

"No," Jonath said. "Around here, wearing anything other than an open tunic and thin breeches means the heat will probably kill you before the flies do."

The sergeant spat. While dirty and unshaved, his face was pale, a face from beyond the swamp. Jonath looked at where the gob of spit had landed in the mud.

"What do you want, sergeant?"

"You have a witch in this town?"

Jonath nodded. "We do."

"Fetch her."

"I beg your pardon, sergeant?"

The sergeant spat again. The soldiers behind him sat their horses with weariness and wariness, their eyes running between the knight and their sergeant, back and forth, tired and frustrated. Jonath ran his hand absently along the edge of the knight's sash at his chest and then sat down in a wooden chair. He took a slow drink of lukewarm gin from the brass mug that had been sitting on a nearby table. His booted foot absently nudged the footman's crossbow that was leaning against the table. The sergeant's eyes followed Jonath's foot and studied the crossbow. He started to spit once again and then apparently thought better of it.

4

"Forgive me, *constable*," the sergeant said. "I have wounded men with me. I need a healer. I'm led to believe by the brown shits you call townsfolk around here that you have a witch. I need her to see to my men."

"There. That wasn't so bad, now was it, sergeant?"

"No, constable." The sergeant gave in to the urge and spat once again into the mud.

"I'm here." Idsiyushti stepped from the shadows of the tanner's shop across the alley from the courthouse. Wearing a thin cotton dress of green and blue, black hair tied back against the morning heat, Idsiyushti eyed the sergeant with obvious disdain. The sergeant returned the witch's glare, his own disdain mixed with a cruel spark that marked a man of ill manners staring at the thinly covered breasts of a young woman.

"Where are your wounded, sergeant?" Jonath asked, snapping the soldier's gaze away from Idsiyushti.

The sergeant met Jonath's eyes for several long moments before slowly turning back to the witch. "A fisher's hut at the edge of town. It was abandoned when we found it."

"Uh-huh," Jonath said, standing and hefting the crossbow. "We'll be with you shortly."

The crunch of boots through the undergrowth drew Ashakarahad's attention away from her worn field journal and her current entry. She sat, her back to the wide canvas tent she currently called home, upon a broad camp chair made of wood nearly as dense as metal. The journal was resting on a long, narrow plank table that had been propped up on two moss-encrusted tree trunks. She placed her pencil in the crease between the journal's open pages and then pushed the journal away with only a minimal tug from the invisible shackles that wrapped her tight.

"Hail the camp! Ash, you there?"

"Of course, constable. Please approach."

Jonath of the Battlefield, crossbow slung across his shoulders, stepped into the clearing. He was sweating, his tunic opened nearly to his navel. He had his stained, leather hat pushed back, revealing a high, brown forehead. As with nearly anyone she met, Jonath's eyes traveled first to Ashakarahad's wide shoulders and full breasts, covered by silk and leather despite the heat, then to the twisted horns atop her head. As with nearly anyone she met, Jonath then caught her eyes and tried to look anywhere else but directly at her.

"Care for some tea, constable?" Ashakarahad asked, trying to relieve the usual tension. The townsfolk and the farmers, fishers, and their families trying to grind out a living in the swamp had generally left Ashakarahad alone, offering vaguely kind, if not weary words when they encountered her. None, however, save the constable and the young witch, Idsiyushti, had offered

Ashakarahad deeper hospitality, not since she'd first appeared beside the creek at the edge of town and set her tent in the small clearing.

"Only if it's cold," Jonath replied. He set the crossbow down, leaning the stock against another tree stump. The demoness rose from her camp chair and pulled on a rope that led into the gentle water of the creek. The end of the rope was attached to a large jug from which she poured blue-black tea into two mugs. The constable raised his mug towards her out of politeness and Ashakarahad returned the gesture. The tea wasn't cold per se, but it wasn't hot, wasn't really even warm. It tasted of cinnamon and earth and made the tongue and lips tingle and go cold regardless.

"Soldiers passed through," Jonath said, smacking his lips. He perched himself on the trunk next to the crossbow.

"I believe I heard the commotion, even here," the demoness said, returning to her camp chair.

"They had wounded and heard that Idsi might be able to heal them."

"Did she?"

"More or less. She doctored them up pretty nicely, put new, good bandages on them where needed, gave them some sort of medicine, but I doubt she used any magic." Jonath sipped his tea and looked around at the heavy foliage surrounding the clearing. "I don't think she liked the way they kept leering at her, to be honest."

Ashakarahad simply nodded.

"Their sergeant—an ass of a man—said they were originally on the trail of some trolls when they were set upon by a group of the dead in the swamps."

The demoness leaned forward. "Really?"

"He didn't say how far from here, but they looked exhausted and their horses looked ready to drop."

"In this swamp, soldiers and horses could go less than a mile and look like they'd been traveling for weeks."

Jonath laughed, clear and loud. "Yeah, that's true."

"Where are they now?"

"Ortes's old shack on the other side of town. I told them to move on as soon as they could."

"They're imperial soldiers," Idsiyushti said. "Can you do that?"

"I'm the constable here and that's how being constable works," Jonath smiled. "Besides, we're not at war, at least not on this side of the empire."

"Still—"

"Yes. Still. I thought you should know. Soldiers, trolls, the dead crawling around the swamp."

"Soldiers at least. Did they say that any of the undead survived the attack?"

"The sergeant wasn't certain. Apparently, they hadn't had much experience with the dead were they came from. Troll hunters, he said. All they really knew about." Jonath sighed. "And I doubt they know that much about trolls to begin with."

"Thanks for the warning."

"You should come into town," Jonath said. "We're going to try to get word to all the families on the outskirts. Try to get them to come into town until we've had a chance to scout the area a little better."

"And until you're certain the soldiers have moved on."

Jonath smiled.

"I'll be fine out here, constable. Really." Jonath's eyes once again traveled to Ashakarahad's broad, leather-covered shoulders. He did a remarkable job of not letting his eyes wander to the massive, bladed staff of polished wood she had hanging from a post just inside the tent itself.

Instead, the constable laughed again. "It's not you I'm worried about, Ash. It's the townsfolk. If something happens, I could use you. We only have a few veterans in town—and some of those I'll need to scout the swamp."

"I appreciate the offer, constable," Ashakarahad said. "And I will come in if it becomes urgent. Tell you what I'll do in the meantime, though." Jonath finished his tea and stood. He placed the mug on the table before the demoness and waited. She said, "I'll take a look around the swamp. Scout it for you. Bring in as many of your people as I can. I'll check in on anyone I come across. They aren't that hospitable but they don't run from me. Well, anymore." Jonath frowned at that. Ashakarahad laughed, a great, deep-throated laugh. "And I've dealt with trolls before. And soldiers."

"And the dead?"

"They're technically why I'm here," she said. "The presence of any sort of undead here in the swamp, if true, would mean that I'm closer to my goal than I've been in a long, long while."

"Your goal," Jonath said. "Researching the old ruins in the swamp."

"That's not my goal, constable. That's just how I'm going about it."

"All right," Jonath said after a time. "I appreciate it." He picked up the crossbow. "Just make sure you come to town if it gets rough out here. And thanks for the tea."

Ashakarahad nodded and smiled. Jonath glanced quickly away from her teeth.

Grendl went down into the dank basement, which had been carved out and shored up with brickwork by his very own hand. He dusted off three large casks and rolled them as gracefully as a one-armed dwarf could to the freight platform. He checked the thick ropes connecting the platform to the winch system on the floor above. Satisfied, he rang a bell that was on a hook near the narrow stairs and one of the girls began turning the winch's hand-crank. Gears rattled and the cask-laden platform began to ascend towards the broad hole in the ceiling. Grendl took the lantern in hand and climbed the stairs, blowing out and depositing the lantern on its hook by the upper landing.

Chrona, a stern lass with strong arms, was working the winch, pausing periodically to wipe sweat from her brow with her apron. Grendl favored her to help him raise and lower the platform and bring supplies out to the tavern floor. And since she refused to work on her back upstairs, working the winch made even more sense.

"This'll be enough for the soldiers?" Chrona asked as the platform reached floor level and she locked iron safety catches into the gears to keep the platform in place. Grendl had always been impressed by the young woman's quick grasp of the machinery. He suspected that she applied herself diligently to studying and working the winch system to augment the air of superiority she surrounded herself with. Which suited Grendl just fine. He gave her a little extra each week for helping him with the platform and winch, and for helping him keep up with the inventory and daily totals.

"I doubt we'll need even one of these casks," Grendl said. "Jonath kicked the soldiers out of town. But they might linger—I doubt they like being rousted by some knight twenty years their senior and with the wrong color skin. Always pays to be prepared."

Chrona's dark eyes flared. "He's the constable. If they disobey him, he'll arrest them, doesn't matter if he's from the swamp."

"He'll try," Grendl said. He began rolling the casks off the platform and Chrona eventually moved to help, as if what she needed to be doing had only just occurred to her.

"Will they put up a fight?" She asked.

"I don't know, but I wouldn't put it past them. Don't worry about it, though. I said that Jonath would try to arrest them, but if they put up a fight, I suspect that he'll be burying more than one of them in an unmarked grave."

"I'll help him," Chrona said, lugging the last cask to its place. "They didn't look like they had any manners."

Grendl eyed the girl. "Help him fight or help him bury the bodies?"

"Maybe both. Wouldn't you?"

Grendl laughed. "I don't mind rousting drunks, but 'round here the drunks are all my neighbors. Soldiers though…. Besides, I hate throwing out paying customers."

"Maybe that demon will come into town and help."

"Now that'd be a sight to see," Grendl said. He led the girl back out to the bar. It was still early afternoon and only a few townsfolk were left, lingering over the remains of lunch and the thick beer that Grendl was famous for serving. Marrah was behind the bar, wiping it down with a dirty rag. Sek and Caeri were probably upstairs, still asleep. It was a small town, but his whores were generally kept pretty busy. Grendl walked out front and sat in one of the chairs that lined the porch. The air in the town square was hot and wet, the square itself more or less empty. Soon, however, despite the heat, the square would liven up with farmers and fishers and their families wandering into town for food and supplies. Many of them would eat at Grendl's. Afterwards, the women would tend to the shopping, the children to running in the hot streets, and the men would gather on Grendl's porch and smoke and gossip. A few would go upstairs. Grendl thought about hiring a minstrel, about trying to lure the men to stay inside the tavern after their meal—probably lure many of the women back in too—but it was too hot to be cooped up and paying a minstrel to play for an empty room was pointless and bad business. Besides, get the wrong minstrel and he'd turn his place into another queer joint like Jak's, and he'd be damned if that was going to happen.

He looked out at across the town square, at the daub and wood courthouse, let his eyes crawl up to the useless bell tower. Maybe he should talk to Jonath, Marin, and the other merchants about hiring a bona fide, non-queer minstrel to play outside, in the evening, center of the square at the foot of that damned standing stone. Grendl sat back in his chair and nodded. He could probably convince the constable to let his girls carry out trays of beer and sell them to the crowd.

He eyed the square again. There wasn't a soldier in sight.

Idsiyushti was crouched in the branches of a kudzu-covered tree when Ashakarahad stepped out of the brush, bladed staff slung over her wide shoulders.

"Hello, little witch," Ashakarahad said. Idsiyushti blinked at that—she'd concealed herself with magic and was certain no one could see her. "Don't worry," the demoness continued, "No one else is liable to be able to spot you."

"So you can read minds too," Idsiyushti said, crestfallen and confused.

Ashakarahad laughed deeply. She slung the staff from her shoulder and leaned against it. "No, little witch. But I can see you and I can tell that you didn't want to be seen. I've been around long enough to know that when mages of any sort don't wish to be seen—and you can see them—they often think the same thing."

Idsiyushti leaped from the branch and landed on the soft, swampy earth. She adjusted her dress and absently, almost sensually, squished the weeds and muddy soil with her toes. "I'd usually be angry at being called 'little,' but, in your case, Ash, you can call everyone little and you would be speaking plain truth."

The demoness laughed again. "I hear the soldiers will live, thanks to you." There was a gleam in Ashakarahad's orange eyes that Idsiyushti hoped meant the demoness was just being playful.

"If it helps get them out of the swamp, then —"

"Indeed. What brings you out here?"

"Jonath said he talked to you, that you said you were going to scout the swamp," Idsiyushti said. "He said that if you found any of the families out here, you'd suggest they come into town until the soldiers leave and we are sure there isn't anything more dangerous lurking in the swamp this close to the town."

"That's true."

Idsiyushti nodded. "Then I'll go with you. I want to see if there's anything dangerous too and you will need my help with the swamp families."

"Oh?"

"They know me." Idsiyushti recognized the petulance in her own voice, but the numbness of the whiskey she'd drunk before leaving town pushed her beyond caring. "And I can very much take care of myself."

"Who is going to take care of the townsfolk while you're gone?"

"Thome's fever broke two days ago. The Genson twins are feeding just fine now, no more coughing and no more runny shits. Delise's leg is mending fine—even though she won't stay off it. And if there are monsters in this swamp, near the town, I want to know about it."

Ashakarahad studied her for a long time. Idsiyushti found herself standing tall and proud under that gaze. She balled her fists and raised her chin even higher. The demoness smiled, showing sharp teeth. Ashakarahad hefted the bladed staff and slipped its leather strap back over her shoulder. She indicated the trees. Idsiyushti adjusted her own belt of pouches and small sacks and they slipped together through the brush.

"How long have you been the town witch?" Ashakarahad asked when they stopped at a wide clearing and studied traces of the soldiers, looking for tracks of trolls or anything else.

"Since I was fourteen. So four, going on five years, now."

"When did you come into your power?"

Idsiyushti looked up at the demoness and said, "I was born with it. I don't remember not having it. But I had no real teacher until I was six or seven. Then an elf taught me more. I basically sat at his feet until he sent me away. To be town witch. He talked and I listened and I tried to learn."

"This was in the swamp?"

Idsiyushti nodded. "I was born at the edge of the swamp, way on the other side of the deep dark."

"What about your parents?"

Idsiyushti raised her chin again. "They left me in the woods when I was just old enough to walk. I don't remember how I survived. I don't remember much except crying and stumbling and dreaming. But I lived. And the fey found me. Taught me and raised me until they took me to the elf."

"I've not seen any signs of the fey."

"They were a traveling band. They stayed with me for several years, even while the elf taught me. They aren't around anymore."

Ashakarahad nodded. "From what I've seen, you should've been trained in a wizard tower somewhere."

"There are no more wizard towers. Not here, not in the swamp. There's just the ruins of wizard towers here. Those old things that don't really look like towers at all."

"I know. They are the ruins I'm studying."

Idsiyushti lowered her chin, relaxed her fists. She watched the demoness bend down to study the ground. Idsiyushti felt a twinge of guilt for lying but figured that was just the whiskey again. She actually did remember what happened after her parents had taken her into the woods and abandoned her, terrified of what she was, what she might become. She had cried, that was true. She had slept fitfully, dreamed. She had hidden from the dead that rose up and wandered out of the deep dark. The fey had found her almost immediately, probably pure luck but maybe because they'd been drawn to her burgeoning power. She'd survived by eating plants pointed out to her by glowing, flitting fey, caught and cooked small animals under the tutelage of tree spirits and gnomes. Some of the fey watched over her and pulled her hair until she woke if danger was near—others tried to chase the danger away, but not everything was susceptible to the illusions and pranks of the fey or the complex machinations of the gnomes who guided her. The spirits and fey had tried to show her how to perfect her magic, control it, so she could survive. But they were not human and could not teach her human magic—her efforts became a form of corrupted fey magic at best.

Finally, the clan leader, an ancient gnome, had led her to a rocky spur that overlooked a broad, fog-shrouded patch of the deep dark. Atop the spur sat a silver-haired elf, so motionless that she thought the elf was a statue. The gnome clan leader told Idsiyushti that she was actually a danger to the fey and spirits, that she was a danger to herself and to the land because they could not teach her how to properly use her magic. He had gone to speak with the elf, an old, old friend, and had convinced the elf to teach Idsiyushti how to wield her magic, how to be even stronger. The elf had looked at her then, with yellow eyes that looked like they belonged to a falcon, eyes that seemed to see through her, see all of her, her life expanded outward from that point. And for a moment, she thought she'd seen those eyes fill with tears.

Perhaps sensing there was more to the story, Ashakarahad asked, as they left the clearing behind and followed the soldier's tracks, "How did an elf know how to teach a human how to do human magic?"

Idsiyushti looked up at the demoness and shrugged. How indeed? "I don't know. Maybe he'd learned the ways of human magic before. He seemed old, although it wasn't easy to tell—maybe he'd seen the wizard towers before they were ruined? Maybe he'd studied in them? Perhaps even helped build them?"

"Or tear them down."

"Or that. I've no idea and I never thought to ask." That part was also true. "What are you looking for in the ruins?"

Ashakarahad was quiet for a time. Then, "Answers. I actually do remember the ruins before they became ruins. Well, to an extent. I was summoned to this world by the mage-lords, kept as a sort of slave for I don't know how long."

Idsiyushti gaped. So the tales of demons summoned by wizards were true! But a slave? She blinked, trying to figure out how to respond. Finally, she settled on, "But if you knew the ruins back when they weren't ruins, if you knew the ancients, why study them now?"

"Because I don't remember much of my captivity. In truth, I don't remember any of it. I remember the summoning—I had been traveling through a forest of glass on a world with three suns, and I suddenly felt this compulsion, an irresistible urge. I should have known what it was. My people have countless tales of summoning. But I was distracted and not thinking. So I turned and followed it and then I wasn't on that world anymore. I was in some sort of magic circle. On a brick floor. I couldn't see beyond the circle—just dancing lights. And then I don't remember anything else. When I finally came to my senses, I was lying in a ruined tower far from here. That was a long time ago and I've been studying the ruins ever since."

"A forest of glass?" Idsiyushti's head was spinning. She had so many other questions.

"My people have the ability to travel to many worlds. It is part of our culture. We explore, learn, trade, and sometimes we conquer."

"But why are you still here?"

Ashakarahad shrugged. "I can't leave this world and I don't know why. Which is why I spend my time researching the ruins."

The mint crushed up and marinating at the bottom of the goblet was a cold counterpunch to the whiskey's smooth burn. Jak sat back, the wooden chair creaking. Sitting on the whitewashed banister, framed by square porch columns, with a backdrop formed from thick trees and kudzu and the edge of the tall barn Jak had built four or five years ago, Peler played a Cherrywood mandolin. Peler was handsome, young, strong-willed and determined to be a minstrel despite his father's determination to make a swamp fisher out of him. Peler looked at Jak and smiled that smile, winked that wink, and Jak smiled back, sipped more mint-muddled whiskey, tried not to notice the too-sharp notes and broken rhythm.

Peler stopped trying to play and turned at the sound of a horse. Jonath rode into the yard, emerging from the trees along the path that led into town. Peler glanced back at Jak, who shrugged. Peler might not remember, personally, a time before Jonath had come back to the swamp from his many adventures and battles and been appointed constable. But no doubt the men and women drinking at Jak's mahogany bar, some in drag, some barely clothed at all, had told the boy about how old constable Skex would ride out with several men from the town, drunk, angry, looking to raise a veritable ruckus.

"Constable," Jak said.

Jonath tipped his leather hat and dismounted.

"Peler, see to the constable's horse," Jak said.

"But—"

"Peler," Jak repeated, sipping mint and whiskey.

The boy glared, tossed his black locks and leaned the mandolin carefully against the porch wall. Then he climbed down and led Jonath's horse out of sight, in the direction of the barn. Jonath climbed the steps of the porch. He had a crossbow slung across his shoulders and his tunic open in the heat. Jak took another long sip of mint and whiskey, relished the cool burn.

Jonath indicated an empty chair nearby and Jak nodded before taking another goblet from the silver tray, tarnishing already despite last night's polishing, and poured mint-muddled whiskey from a wide-mouth bottle. He handed the drink to Jonath who stared at it for a moment and then drank long and hard, eyes closed. The constable sat back and looked out at Jak's yard, the trees beyond the barn.

"Not sure which I needed more," Jonath said. "This or Ashakarahad's tea."

"Drinking tea with a demon," Jak admonished.

"And whiskey with a queer," Jonath said, "who sells that whiskey without the town council's approval at a bar in his own living room."

Jak wondered whether or not he should bristle but decided against it. He'd spent too long, when he was younger, bristling at other peoples' words and deeds. He'd grown up bouncing on the knees of his mother's whores, sucking at their tits when they had children—and milk—of their own. Grown up in the shadow of his mother's rituals and arcana, the chants and incense and forays into circles to traffic with things from the abyss. (He'd seen creatures like Ashakarahad called forth, seen them polite, like Ash, but also seen them wicked and evil and violent, the reason he looked at Ash askance whenever the demoness entered his field of vision. Why Ashakarahad was in the swamp, who had summoned her in the first place, why they had—those were all things he didn't know. She acted indifferent, as if called forth and then set loose and, as of yet, she hadn't bothered to tear them all apart.) Then he'd traveled and fought and loved, even whored himself out when he needed to. And all along he'd been ridiculed for being an overly dramatic storyteller, a liar, a passingly decent singer, a sword fighter, a thief, the son of a whore, the son of a necromancer, a killer, queer.

Then he'd thrown all that away when he had inherited a swamp ranch out in the hot, wet sticks, somewhere within spitting distance of the ass-crack of the empire, from a dead cousin three, four times removed with, no doubt, an incorrigible sense of humor. Jak also had no doubt that his mother had been at the heart of the matter, wanting him far away from the red-lit streets of Drilithae and her taverns and brothels and places of power. Jak had no idea why his mother would want him gone—although he had a few ideas, slick, wet, and politically embarrassing, all of them—but she'd seen him off, wrapped in a cloak of ermine, surrounded by several of her favorite novitiates in the arts of sex and black magic. She'd handed him a wrapped amulet made of cold iron as a parting gift, warned him about closed-minded hicks and vengeful dead—as if he needed that warning—and turned and left, her whores and mages casting only cursory glances backward. The amulet had runes and glyphs that Jak recognized as necromantic and he'd left it wrapped and bundled in his saddlebags. When he'd finally arrived in town and seen the jagged, gap-toothed cemetery with its raised sarcophagi and drunk-angled urns beside the tumbledown temple to the fish-eyed, tentacled swamp gods, he'd dug the amulet out and stared at it. Now it rested on a shelf behind the living room bar, among a collection of yellowed and tarnished "relics" that he dazzled his customers with.

"What do you want, constable?"

"Soldiers came through town. Rough lot," Jonath said.

"You sent them my way, of course," Jak said, refilling both their goblets from the wide-mouth bottle. "Or did they go off to fuck Grendl's sloe-eyed whores?"

Jonath sighed. "I sent them on their way after Idsiyushti saw to their wounded. But they may stick around."

"Well, I did get a new shipment of rum in," Jak said. "So we should be fine."

"They say they were attacked by the dead," Jonath continued.

"Ah. They say."

"Yes."

"Were they? Attacked by the dead?"

Jonath shrugged. "Don't know. But I aim to find out. I'm riding out and telling folks that they might want to come into town, camp in the square if they don't have anyone to stay with."

"Why? I'm not from around here, but I don't think most of these good swamp folk would like the idea of leaving hearth and home to camp out in town if it isn't a fair or a festival or something. Soldiers passing through, I doubt folks'd bat much of an eye."

Jonath nodded. "Agreed. But this story about the dead, and the fact that several soldiers were actually wounded and needed a witch's attention. That's something. Maybe they'll move on, but maybe they'll stay around, mucking about in the deep dark, cause trouble for folks. *Someone* beat the hell out of them, or at least some of them."

"You don't really think the dead did it, do you? This close to town?"

"I don't. Nor do I think it was trolls—that's who they say they were actually hunting when the dead attacked them. But I would hate to be wrong."

"Uh-huh. Soldiers, trolls, and attacking dead," Jak said. "And I was just telling folks last night over shots of some of Miq's fine, old-fashioned moonshine whiskey, that I thought this town was boring as shit."

"I can't tell you how to live your life, Jak," Jonath said. "I can't tell you to pack up and join us in town—"

"Because no one would want to share a tent with me and my Legion of Queers?"

Jonath finished his drink, ignored the question. "But I worry about the folks that come out here to drink and...fraternize. Good men and women who make the long walk—"

"It's not that long."

"In the night, drunk, with soldiers and trolls and the dead about?"

Jak stared at Jonath for a long time. "Point taken. I'll think about it, constable."

Jonath nodded, rose and went to go find his horse.

The trail left by the soldiers as they wound their way through the swamp was wide and meandering. The wounded that Idsiyushti had tended appeared to be able to sit their horses, although it also appeared that they were slowing the troop down. The witch and the demoness followed the tracks for nearly two days, mostly out of concern that the troop's winding course threatened to double-back towards the town, or move to circle it. But the tracks merely twisted through the swampy undergrowth as if the troop were either searching for something or were simply uncertain of the exact path to take. Idsiyushti commented early on that the paths that led through the swamp were generally obvious, marked by old stones in many places, half-rotted plank bridges in others. But when the soldiers followed those paths, they followed them only for a short time.

"They are either continuing their search or trying to look like it," she had said. "Because otherwise, they are daft. They've had to turn aside or double-back simply to avoid the water and mud and trees more than once."

"Like you said, perhaps they are trying to make it look that way," Ashakarahad replied. They hadn't spoken much in the last day or so, and when they had, it was mostly the young witch trying to coax details of Ashakarahad's background out. But the demoness, although full of interesting stories of places she'd seen, been, or read about, had been tight-lipped about her past.

"Perhaps the soldiers still think there are trolls about, or maybe they are trying to throw off an ambush of the dead," Idsiyushti suggested.

"Maybe," was all that Ashakarahad had offered in return.

The tracks of the troop tended to avoid farmsteads and fisher's huts, although it appeared that the soldiers had stopped and made a brief camp at Miq's place. The old man was solitary and, while rude, not usually hostile. He was also well known for his several stills and his homemade liquors. Miq eyed both Idsiyushti and Ashakarahad with suspicion as he told them that the soldiers had paid him a less-than-fair sum for small barrels of the stuff. He had balked at the price but it was clear that the soldiers were not going to be denied, so Miq had agreed.

He had been preparing to pole his small barge away from the dilapidated dock out behind his hut, aiming on heading towards town to complain about the soldiers to anyone who would listen, when Idsiyushti had hailed him.

Ashakarahad, although she had never met the hermit, passed Jonath of the Battlefield's warning on, suggesting to Miq that he stay in town just to be safe. The old man spat into the murky water beyond the edge of the barge, said that he was only interested in going to town to try to pick up some more grain and to curse the soldiers. He'd be damned if he was going to stay away and let the soldiers come back and steal the rest of what he owned.

Idsiyushti mentioned that the soldiers had said they were on the trail of trolls and had been set upon by the dead. The old man, leaning on his barge pole as it stuck out of the water, merely laughed. He spat again, eyes narrow, and offered to trade Ashakarahad liquor for her bladed staff. The demoness politely refused and when Miq finished spitting once more, with what looked like customary disgust, Idsiyushti offered to trade some herbs and medicines from her pack for a jug of whiskey. The old man looked out at the murky water and the trees surrounding it, then up at the sky. Then he nodded and climbed back off the barge.

Idsiyushti tied the earthenware jug to a strap and slung it across her shoulders, a counterpoint to Ashakarahad's staff, and they watched the old man pole his barge away from the rickety dock. The tracks of the soldiers showed they'd worked their way to a narrow plank bridge that crossed from tiny island to tiny island until they'd encountered a rope-guided barge. The barge was unmanned yet oddly in good repair—townsfolk and swamp-dwellers often came out to maintain some of the bridges and barges that dotted the landscape. It appeared that the soldiers had used the barge to cross the water three or four at a time, along with their horses. Their tracks churned up the damp earth on both sides of the crossing.

The witch and the demoness departed from the path to visit the small homesteads and huts in that region of the swamp. Several of the families scraping out an existence there refused to leave, but others heeded Idsiyushti. After she gave nearly every family member, sharecropper, fisher, and, in one case, a massive, beloved pig, a quick examination—doling out herbs, salves and quick incantations where needed—many began to pack their mules, carts, or small boats for the trip into town. Between visits to the ramshackle huts, tumbledown barns, and lean-tos, Idsiyushti and Ashakarahad returned to the soldiers' trail but there was no sign of the soldiers themselves.

"Where do these soldiers come from?" Ashakarahad asked at one point when Idsiyushti stopped to gather the leaves of a thick, thorny bush that grew from a gnarled, rotten tree whose dead roots vanished into dark water.

"Don't know. Probably Esgen. It's the largest city around here. 'Bout a week and a half's hard ride from here. It's supposed to be a port city, sits on the delta. Been there?"

"No," Ashakarahad said.

"Oh," Idsiyushti said. "Me neither."

"There aren't closer garrisons of soldiers than that?"

"Probably," Idsiyushti said, spreading the leaves she gathered on the turf a few feet from the tree's roots and the water's edge. She held each leaf up to examine it closely, smell it, rub it between her fingers. "There are other villages nearby."

"I've passed through a few," the demoness said, sounding unimpressed.

"Yeah, well, there's probably soldiers there, at one of them. Just a guess though." Idsiyushti chose several leaves and wrapped them in a cloth. The cloth was then placed into her pack. Idsiyushti uncorked the jug she'd traded from Miq and took a long drink from it, wiping her mouth after gasping away the tears that suddenly watered her eyes. "Ugh. That's a bite," she breathed. She held the jug out to Ashakarahad, who was leaning on her staff, studying the dark water. The demoness shook her head and Idsiyushti shrugged, recorked the jug.

Grendl stepped from the hot interior of the tavern to the hot night air of the tavern's wide front porch. Bonfires and cookfires had been lit throughout the square, and families from the outskirts had set up tents all around the remains of the tall standing stone that squatted there. Behind Grendl, at the long bar and at the many tables, patrons sat and drank, talked and laughed, gambled and, upstairs, fucked his whores. Grendl breathed deeply, drinking in the hot, wet air and the sudden explosion of nightlife that went far beyond the men who spent the evening on the porch, smoking and drinking, beyond their womenfolk who spent the evening shopping and gossiping. In more than one place, instruments were playing, the simple instruments of the sharecroppers and fishers, not the minstrels that would sometimes arrive for the harvest fair that was several weeks away. But money was changing hands and business, not just Grendl's, was good.

"Perhaps we should have soldiers scare the constable more often," Grendl said.

One of the men sitting on the steps before him, smoking a long pipe and fanning himself with a stiff linen hat, turned and said, "What's that, Grendl?"

"Nothing," the dwarf replied. "Just commenting that it's a grand night."

"That it is," the man said and turned back to watch the families in the square as they cooked food and tried to make themselves comfortable in the heat of the night.

Grendl saw Jonath of the Battlefield climb the few stairs to the porch of his office on the other side of the square. Jonath turned and looked back. His crossbow was slung casually over his shoulder. He tipped his broad leather hat back and when he saw Grendl, gave a brief wave. Grendl grunted and went back inside.

Jonath hung his hat from a stand in the corner and then poured water from a pitcher into a wide bowl. He was toweling his face with a smudged rag when the wooden door to the office opened and the sounds from the square became louder. Marin of Etrusq, knight's sash embroidered and fine and slung across a rich, loose tunic, stepped into the office and closed the door behind him. The old knight limped his way across the office to the sideboard.

"Judge," Jonath said.

"Jonath," Marin responded, pulling the stopper from a bottle of port and pouring a large measure into one of the few crystal glasses that Jonath had on hand. Marin sipped the port and smacked his lips.

"Help yourself," Jonath said.

The old knight smiled. "What happens when the soldiers plunder all the empty farmsteads while the farmers and their families sleep in the town square?"

"I doubt that'll happen but it's better than plundering the farmsteads *while* the families are present."

"Maybe," Marin said. He took a seat opposite Jonath, at a broad, ancient desk. "But what will they have to go back to? Razed crops? Stolen livestock? Burned down huts?"

"That's rather pessimistic."

"They're soldiers, Jonath! What do you expect them to do?"

Jonath wiped his brow with the smudged rag he'd toweled himself off with earlier. The presence of Marin made the air in the office even heavier, the few lit candles flickering as if through a haze. The old knight smelled of onions and liniment. "I expect them to take their wounded and move on. They aren't a raiding party and they weren't hurting for supplies."

The old knight's dark, wrinkled brow wrinkled further. "You're not that naïve," he said. "Not you, Jonath *of the Battlefield*." He sipped port. "Say, why 'the Battlefield?' Why not just give you the title of the nearest town or village?"

"Ask the emperor," Jonath said. "It was the Desadian Chaos. He'd just won the empire but I doubt he knew the names of any of the nearby cities, much less a village." Outside, someone began playing a doleful tune on a reed flute.

"Ask the emperor," Marin chuckled. He finished the port and put the glass on Jonath's desk. "Well, I'm sure we'll have plenty of fines by the time this is all over. Raise the town coffers a little. We should probably tax Grendl for something or other. And the queers out at Jak's."

Jonath laughed. "Probably."

Marin of Etrusq rose stiffly, straightened his sash and tunic. "I just hope it's not soldiers we're fining. I don't recall soldiers taking a liking to paying fines or spending the night in a tiny, backwater cell, sleeping off a drunk. But I'm an old man, my memory isn't what it used to be."

"'Night, judge," Jonath said as the old man hobbled out the door. Jonath stood and carried the old knight's used glass back to the sideboard. He unstoppered the bottle of port and poured himself a measure using the same glass. He downed the drink without savoring it or thinking about how he could still smell the judge's thick breath on it.

W here are they headed?" Ashakarahad asked. The churned prints of hooves and boots had begun to follow a recognizable track that showed someone had once tried to pave a way through the swamp.

Idsiyushti uncorked the whiskey jug and took another sip before stepping onto the track. She looked to either side then turned right, began following the road. Ashakarahad's long, pointed shadow appeared as she stepped onto the road and watched Idsiyushti. The witch walked only a short distance, her feet still bare, the whiskey in the jug slung across her shoulder sloshing, joining the constant whine and whisper of life in the trees. She bent at what looked like a short, carved stone. A mile marker. Ashakarahad followed, and Idsiyushti sat down on the marker, rubbed the dirt and sweat from her face with the hem of her dress.

Looking back the way they came, Idsiyushti said, "There's another town that way, couple hours down the road. Folks call it Baker's Beans. If the soldiers stick to the road, they'll find it. Didn't know there were any trolls there."

"Perhaps they're hoping for a friendlier welcome than what they received from Constable Jonath."

"Dunno," Idsiyushti said. "Maybe."

"You don't believe the soldiers are looking for trolls," Ashakarahad said. She adjusted the strap of her staff and slipped a piece of jerky in her mouth. Idsiyushti looked up at the demoness and grunted.

"There aren't any trolls in the swamps. Not in these parts, anyway. Way out there—" she waved at the trees

"—out in the deep dark…maybe. Trolls. Hags. Other things. The dead. But here?"

Ashakarahad chewed the jerky. It was salty but otherwise flavorless, with a tendency to stick between her sharp, jagged teeth. She couldn't name what animal it had come from. "You don't think they were attacked by undead, either?"

The young witch took another sip from the jug. Ashakarahad hadn't seen her drink any water since they'd traded herbs for the whiskey the day before. Just whiskey, along with a few scattered puffs on a gatflower pipe she'd pulled from a belt pouch. Idsiyushti wiped her mouth with the back of her hand, no longer wincing as she swallowed. "I don't know. Maybe if they were trudging through the deep dark. I've spent time out there. Hunted there, hidden there. Seen things. Tracks, the dead, monsters."

"You ever fight anything out there? The dead, trolls?" Ashakarahad asked, hawking jerky spit into the trees.

"Not if I can help it," Idsiyushti laughed. "But yeah. Anyway, I've never seen anything come near the towns or the trails that aren't out in the deep dark. People hunt monsters and outlaws. Around here, I mean."

"Like a militia?"

"Yeah. But nothing's come crawling out of the deep dark in the recent past. Not since I've been here." The swamp buzzed around them, hot, wet, thick, smelling like decay, old shit, and spring flowers.

"So where does this lead?" Ashakarahad asked, indicating the road leading away from Baker's Beans.

"Eventually back to town. Our town. The soldiers took the long way around to get here. Really long. Town's not more than half a day from here. Maybe less."

"Something attacked those soldiers," Ashakarahad said abruptly. "You healed them. You saw. I didn't see them, but you did."

"Yup." Another sip of whiskey, sipped smooth like drinking cool water.

"Unless they started fighting among themselves," Ashakarahad said. "Hacked each other up before deciding to stop and lie about it." She shook her head. "Either way, something hit them and I can't imagine it was any of the townsfolk."

"Yup," Idsiyushti said again. "And if people had attacked them, I imagine the soldiers would've said. Been even less friendly."

"And probably tried to get Jonath to raise your militia and ride out with them," Ashakarahad said. There was something about Idsiyushti. A jagged something, young, hot, and feverish, hidden just below the surface. Ashakarahad watched the girl drink again from the whiskey jug. She'd seen mages convert wine to water, heard of mages who could do the same with poison. Among her own people, there were those who could convert, through a sort of internal alchemy, one substance into another inside their own body, using it as a sort of fuel for life, sex, magic. But that was only whispered about in this place. The fey, for example, diminutive and wild, were said to drink fermented honey and herbs from bowls made of buttercups and tulips, converting the drink to potent sorcery and reckless abandon. Ashakarahad could all but smell the fey coursing through Idsiyushti's magic.

The witch burped long and loud and said, "Unless they thought we might be in on the attack."

Ashakarahad shook her head. "Then they would've attacked the town. Or worse."

"Yup." Idsiyushti stood. There was a slight wobble in her stance, but it was fleeting and Ashakarahad didn't see it again. "So, 'the dead.' All right. Fuck the soldiers. Let's go back and take a look."

The old hut where the soldiers had holed up and Idsiyushti had tended their wounded was a tumbledown wreck, the remains of a garden on one side and a rotten lean-to barn on the other. The mud and earth were churned by horse hooves and heavy boots, and the interior of the hut was a mess of cast-off bandages, left-over rations, and the stink of unwashed men in armor.

The path that had brought the soldiers to the hut cut around and through fields and patches of standing, murky water surrounded by thick-rooted trees and loud, unseen wildlife. Idsiyushti insisted on checking the few small, abandoned homesteads they encountered along the way. She searched each meticulously but found little to indicate anything other than that the swamp folk had left in a hurry. In some cases, the witch stopped to feed livestock left behind in dilapidated pens and barns, finding small supplies of grain and suet nearby.

"I'm surprised that so many would leave their homes and property on just the whisper of danger," Ashakarahad said at one point as Idsiyushti tossed grain to a collection of chickens who tumbled over each other for the chance to eat.

"We take care of ourselves out here," Idsiyushti said, "but we aren't stupid or foolish. We know sometimes it's best to go into town and stay there, find safety with the others."

"The soldiers didn't come here but passed by very close. Could probably see candles in the windows."

"And could probably be heard clomping around out there." Idsiyushti put the grain sack away and took a drink from her sloshing whiskey jug. "Like I said, we aren't stupid."

The demoness shrugged and led the way back into the trees. Eventually, the homesteads were left behind and the trail wound deeper into the swamp, cutting through standing water that would have made crossing difficult for all except the horses. Ashakarahad was forced to carry Idsiyushti on her shoulders, an easy weight to be sure, but after each crossing, both were wet and reeking of the stagnant water and muck. They set camp twice and Idsiyushti disappeared into the trees and returned with small game that Ashakarahad cooked on a tiny fire she'd lit with wet, smoky wood.

The witch also gathered herbs and small stones, smoked gatflower, sipped from the whiskey jug and not once drank water, even with her meals. Ashakarahad watched Idsiyushti, and the young witch knew it, could feel the demoness' eyes. Out of boredom, Idsiyushti began to cast smiles up at Ashakarahad but the demoness didn't flirt back, simply just continued to watch.

Ashakarahad only drank water from the murky swamp, first mixing it in a gourd with a powder from her pack, then drinking long and deep. She didn't sweat, even in her leather and silk, but Idsiyushti didn't know if that was something unique to Ash or to her kin as a whole. The thought of traveling with a demon, a creature so clearly not from this world, didn't bother Idsiyushti. Sure, when she'd first met Ash, Idsiyushti'd had to master a racing panic at the base of her spine, a desire to hurl spells and try to send Ashakarahad back to the abyss using techniques she barely remembered from the old elf's lessons. But Ash had been nice and weary and careful and, to be honest, sexier than even

Marrah—a thought that made Idsiyushti's heart twinge with guilt. Sure, Ashakarahad was nearly two heads taller than the tallest of the townsfolk, sure she was huge and muscular, with horns and weird eyes and skin that looked, in a certain light, like it was actually made of tiny scales. But Idsiyushti had found her thoughts racing at times, late at night, sometimes wrapped in Marrah's arms or with her face buried between Marrah's legs. She'd think of Ash then, maybe touch herself or lay back and let Marrah do it with nimble whore's fingers, sweet and practiced and delicious.

Idsiyushti also knew the demoness was concerned about her whiskey-drinking. But the whiskey fired Idsiyushti and the subtle headache that accompanied it was a gentle reminder of who she was, what she was doing. She knew the spells of conversion, learned from the fey and the solitary elf—spells that let her survive and draw energy, power, and sustenance from liquor the way she could from sleep or food or even sex. But she didn't know how to distill the fey's sweet nectar. So she used whiskey and gin and, in a pinch, thick, greasy wine. The dim buzz she experienced after drinking the whiskey and then converting it, inside, to something to keep her alive, from dying of thirst, from growing sick with pained kidneys, the magical heat that flushed her entire body and made the wet decay of the swamp more bearable, was all worth it.

She slipped her belt to the ground, followed by her pack and the whiskey jug. She slipped her dress off and walked naked between the roots to the dark water. She scrubbed her dress—changing her own smell for the smell of the rotting swamp—and then slipped under the water herself. She scrubbed herself and then stood and looked back through the roots. Ashakarahad was cleaning her staff with a rag and some polish from a small, round tin. Something squirmed against Idsiyushti's bare foot and she laughed. Long ago she'd learned the charms to keep leeches, snakes, and biting fish away while she bathed.

She climbed from the water and dripped her way to the smoky fire, the demoness glancing only once at her nakedness. The buzz of the whiskey, the subtle headache, made Idsiyushti smile as she sat down, knees drawn up, to stare into the flames. Then she looked up at Ashakarahad and wondered what it would be like to fuck the demoness, or be fucked by her, thoughts of Marrah pushed momentarily aside. Ashakarahad, as if sensing Idsiyushti's thoughts, glanced back across the fire, let her eyes settle on the dark triangle just past Idsiyushti's small, brown feet. The demoness frowned and shook her horned head. Idsiyushti laughed again, took another sip of whiskey, and pulled her wet dress back over her head, the smell of swamp water engulfing her. A single snap of her fingers and a word or two and the dress would be dry—would be clean, if she desired—but Idsiyushti liked the smell of the swamp wrapped around her. And the wet dress was cool on her skin. She looked at Ashakarahad's broad, leather-covered back and smiled to herself.

Despite her magic, the insects finally began to get on Idsiyushti's nerves. She stopped to strip her dress off again, not bothering to glance up at Ashakarahad, who merely grunted. Idsiyushti rubbed a salve all over her body, her arms and legs and small tits now glistening in the wet heat as if she had been oiled for dinner. The buzzing, biting insects still lingered around her, but no longer tried to land or buzz her ears, tried to fly up her nose or piss in her eyes. She still had the charms, but now they would draw less from her whiskey-distilled reserves. Idsiyushti finally looked at Ashakarahad as she pulled her dress back on. The demoness was purposefully looking into the trees, staff slung horizontally across both shoulders like she was carrying buckets from a well. The insects didn't seem to bother Ashakarahad at all, didn't linger near her, didn't bite her. Idsiyushti wondered if it was something that the demoness wore or if her kind just weren't of any interest to the gigantic swamp flies and mosquitoes.

Strapping her belt and pack back on, taking another sip of whiskey and feeling her head spin slightly at the burn down her throat, Idsiyushti said, "You don't like girls."

Ashakarahad's orange eyes slid sideways and down to lock onto Idsiyushti. "I like them just fine."

"I mean like to fuck them."

Ashakarahad frowned. She stepped close to Idsiyushti and reached down with a massive hand. She grabbed one of Idsiyushti's nipples through the front of her dress, twisted. Idsiyushti gasped, rose on her bare toes, a different kind of fire suddenly burning in her throat, between her legs.

"I like to fuck them just fine," Ashakarahad whispered. She twisted harder and Idsiyushti heard herself squeak, tears blurring her vision. "But I'm one of the Eld. A demon. I'd break you, little witch."

Ashakarahad released Idsiyushti and stepped back. Idsiyushti rubbed her nipple, felt claws of heat racing up and down her spine. Her mouth watered. She took another sip of whiskey. But she was damned if she was going to back down now. "Then why do you look away?"

"So I'm not actually tempted to break you."

Idsiyushti rubbed her nipple again, willed her breathing to return to normal. "Have you ever been out to Jak's, back in town?" she asked out loud.

Ashakarahad studied her for a time. "No. Why?"

"It's a place where—" Idsiyushti stopped and sighed. "Never mind."

The demoness turned and continued into the trees. By the time Idsiyushti caught up with her, Ashakarahad was studying rows of desiccated sugar cane, staff still across both shoulders. Idsiyushti came to a halt beside her, felt herself wobble slightly.

Ashakarahad looked down. The fierce look she'd had earlier was gone. "Why do you only drink liquor, not water?" It was a question that Idsiyushti was certain the demoness had wanted to ask for some time.

"I can turn the whiskey to the same function as water, or food, sleep, whatever. It's something the fey do all the time."

"Which might explain why the fey act like drunk children. I meant that we have plenty of water to drink and more than enough to eat—although the variety does lack. Why bother converting whiskey? Why not conserve your strength, your energy?"

"You've met the fey?" It hadn't occurred to Idsiyushti to ask before. It did occur to her that she was avoiding answering Ashakarahad's question.

"I've met all sorts, little witch."

Idsiyushti felt her jaw tighten. The silence was finally broken when she said, "Practice. I like to keep in practice."

Ashakarahad stared down at her. After a while, the demoness sighed, a melodramatic sigh that was a little too human. She changed the subject. "Sugarcane planted in rows. Is there a plantation near here?"

Idsiyushti shook her head. She uncorked the whiskey jug again but ground her teeth instead of drinking. She recorked the jug and said, "No. Well, there used to be. I think so, at any rate. The swamp has seen a lot of years. Large farms and plantations used to be all over the place. I actually live near an old, abandoned mansion."

"Who lives here now?" Ashakarahad indicated the cane rows with a jut of her chin.

"No one? Maybe hermits, small-time farmers who never come into town? I dunno. Goblins, maybe?"

"Goblins?"

"They often worked as field hands and servants on the plantations in the old days. But it's been a long time. They rarely come into town. They aren't welcome."

"Are they violent?"

"Not that I know of. The townsfolk just don't like 'em."

Parting the sugar cane, they found the path of the soldiers. The cane whispered in the wet air, closed in around them except where it had been trampled by horses and men, a path that was wide and winding. Overhead, the sky was nearly cloudless. Birds could be seen through the movement of the cane stalks, distant dots, while others were close at hand, circling.

They smelled the tiny village with its rotting corpses and burned out hovels long before they found it in a wide clearing surrounded by dead sugar cane.

****

Jonath was uncertain which had been more disturbing: The sight and smell of the mutilated goblin corpses lost within the sugar cane fields, or the sight and sound of Idsiyushti sitting cross-legged atop a column of swirling dust, riding the column into town. He'd stood wide-eyed on the porch of his office and watched her step down from the column as it swirled away into tiny dust clouds that vanished into the earth of the square. She'd told him of what she and Ashakarahad had found in the cane fields, following the soldiers' back-trail. He'd shaken himself loose after several moments to gather several of the townsfolk still staring wide-eyed at Idsiyushti, as well as a few of the shopkeepers, and the grumbling militia members drinking and playing dice in Grendl's.

They'd ridden in a long column of horses, mules, carts, and wagons out to the fields—taking the roads and crossings rather than the twisting trail of the soldiers. Then the townsfolk and militia had hacked their way through the cane with axes and knives, following Idsiyushti's directions.

Mounted behind Jonath, Idsiyushti smelled of herbs and sweat, swamp water and whiskey, her small breasts rubbing against his back through the fabric of her thin dress and his tunic. Jonath rode with his crossbow ready, trying to lose the sensation of her over-hot closeness in the whisper of the dry sugar cane, the excited talk of the townsfolk, the hacking of cane stalks, and the sloshing of whiskey in the jug slung across Idsiyushti's back. The memory of watching her ride into town atop a dust whirl pricked pins into Jonath's neck and warred with the sudden guilt he felt at the fact that when he called on Grendl's whores, Marrah was the only one he ever chose.

The goblin village—if you could call it that—was indeed in a broad clearing nestled amongst the cane. Tendrils of smoke rose from burned out huts and were carried away by a wet wind that made the cane sway as if in mourning. Bodies and body parts were strewn across the churned ground.

Jonath pulled his horse to a stop at the edge of the clearing. The smoke and carnage raised nightmares from his memory—dragon flights streaming fire, the air filled with terror and magic, blades, blood, and the screams of far too many children. The Desadian Chaos had been accurately named. Jonath shook his head and swallowed bile. He gripped the crossbow tight and kicked the horse forward, Idsiyushti's closeness all but forgotten.

The townsfolk were repulsed and intrigued all at once. Jonath, pushing his memories deep, directed the wagons, horses, and mules to circle the clearing, not to trample the dead until he'd had a chance to search the place. Ashakarahad stood in the center of the clearing, staff across both shoulders, and Jonath carefully walked his horse through the carnage to her side. He swung Idsiyushti down and then followed. His horse was unfazed by either the presence of the dead goblins or the demoness and, instead, immediately bent down to munch a patch of stumpy weeds. Jonath fought down a wave of nausea.

Without preamble, Ashakarahad pointed to several spots across the clearing, towards the sugar cane stalks rustling the in wind. "The soldiers entered the clearing, near as I can tell, from four spots. Fired bolts first, then rode in hard. Looks like the goblins put up a good fight, but it didn't last and did them no good."

Jonath's stomach was still churning. He accepted one of the rags that Idsiyushti had dipped in cloves and spice, which she was handing out to the townsfolk who were finishing up vomiting their last meals and drinks. He tied the rag around his head and covered his nose and mouth. A cool, herbal smell clawed its way up his nose and down his throat and he shivered despite the wet heat.

His tongue thick, he asked, "You're certain that the soldiers did this?"

Ashakarahad shrugged. "Heavily shod hooves. Heavy boots. Cuts from well-made weapons. And while it looks like they took nearly all their bolts with them, a few were left behind. Military grade." She used the toe of her armored boot to nudge three, cracked bolts sitting in the bloody soil.

Jonath bent to study them. "Military grade," he agreed. He rose, pulled the bolt from his own crossbow. Not military grade. Made by Drag, the town blacksmith. He slipped the bolt in the quiver at his belt, released the tension in the crossbow's string, slung the crossbow across his back. He pulled his hat from his head and fanned himself. He walked carefully through the carnage, noticed that most of the townsfolk stayed back, passing jugs of liquor around. He watched Idsiyushti partake, despite the whiskey jug slung across her back. He stopped and bent down to study an iron sword, crudely made, that was still gripped by bloody goblin fingers attached to a severed hand. The nearest mass of body parts was five or six feet away. His vision swam and he closed his eyes for a long time.

"Are these the 'dead' the soldiers fought?" he finally asked.

"The goblins do appear to have put up a fight," Ashakarahad said. "So unless the soldiers also fought the dead before attacking the goblins…. Either way, I'm going to follow the back trail even further for a bit. If it doesn't look like the soldiers had wounded with them, like it did when they left this clearing, then we'll know."

Old Marin stepped carefully across the field of corpses, scented rag held firmly to his mouth and nose. "This smell doesn't bother you?"

The demoness shook her horned head. "I've smelled worse." Her mouth twisted into a slight grimace that displayed jagged teeth.

Marin stared, finally forced his old eyes away with a shiver. "What do you make of it, Jonath?"

Jonath turned a slow circle, letting the cool bite of the herbs in the rag at his mouth and nose wash over him. He wanted to close his eyes again, just luxuriate in the cold scent. Maybe he'd ask Idsiyushti to make up some more rags just so he could sit on his porch, feet kicked up, smelling cold and forgetting.

"Appears the soldiers lied, judge," he said.

"No shit," the old knight laughed, a rattle in his chest.

"Why would they lie?" Ashakarahad asked. She was eyeing the distant edge of the cane field.

"Because putting down the dead isn't against the law here," Marin said. "Slaughtering goblins, peaceful ones at that, despite their shit-colored blood, is. Even for soldiers."

Jonath walked over and took the jug of liquor from the flour-covered hands of Cornal, the miller's apprentice, who protested by dry heaving at Jonath's boots. Jonath looked away, pulled the cork, and took a long, burning drink.

****

Grendl gathered up the coins from the dirty hands of several children before filling their clay bowls with small beer and watching them squeal and laugh their way out the door into the town square. He tossed the coins into the chest on a shelf behind the bar.

"You must be loving this," someone said. Grendl turned back to the line of townsfolk seated at or leaning against the bar. Ned, one of three brothers who owned the mercantile next door to Grendl's tavern, made eye contact and indicated the children jostling each other out the door, spilling small beer onto the sawdust and rushes. "First, folk were scared of soldiers, so they flocked to town and spent their money here. Now they're scared of dead gobs out in the cane fields and they stay in town, spend their money here."

Grendl refilled Ned's brandy as the ferret-faced man tapped a coin on the bar top. "Not hurtin' your business either." Ned laughed and raised his glass and swallowed the brandy in two long gulps. Then he patted the shoulders of the man next to him and left the bar, weaving his way up the stairs, looking to spend some of his newfound coin on one of Grendl's girls.

"You shoulda seen it, Grendl," Macon, the blacksmith's son, said. He was drinking from a tall mug of the thick, black ale that Grendl brewed in a shed out behind the tavern.

"I've seen it," Grendl said. "Seen plenty of dead gobs. Dead ones are only slightly more disgusting than live ones."

"You're a hard man, for a bartender." Macon swayed slightly on his stool.

Grendl said, "Dead gobs are one of the things my people do."

"But not 'round here. These gobs were peaceful. They were massacred."

Grendl leaned in close. Macon smelled of forge-smoke, piss, beer, and something stale that Grendl couldn't identify. "Dead gobs are dead gobs. Better off for all of us than live gobs. But just because we can't hunt them here, doesn't mean one dead gob looks any different than any other dead gob. Massacre or no massacre."

"Fuck, you're a hard ma—dwarf," Macon slurred.

"You mean he's just like any other dwarf," someone further along shouted. Laughter rippled up and down the bar.

"Gobs always trying to steal dwarf gold, ain't that right, Gren?" a voice asked.

"Always trying to take your mines and rape your women!" another shouted.

"End up raping the men too, because gobs can't tell a man dwarf from a bitch dwarf," another said. "That how you lost your arm, Gren?"

Grendl smiled wide at the laughter that followed. He made eye contact with the last speaker, a young, ruddy-faced foreigner he didn't know well who lived out in the swamp and worked land with a few others. Grendl kept his eyes locked on the boy until he closed his mouth. The boy staggered back from the bar. He was swallowed by the crowd and pipe smoke and Grendl turned to refill someone else's drink.

Set, the candlemaker, tall and skinny and bald, leaned across the bar and ordered a tawny port in a tall, clay tumbler. "Why didn't you go out there with us, Grendl? Figure someone like you would be good looking around at gobs."

Grendl scooped Set's coins off the bar. "Idsiyushti said the gobs were dead, nobody was around. Jonath told me to stay behind. Said he needed someone here who could kick the shit out of anybody who thought to show up and cause trouble with the militia gone out to the cane. And like I said. I've seen dead gobs. Don't need to see more."

Set, like many of the townsfolk who had followed Idsiyushti and Jonath out to the fields, looked tired, eyes distant, like he was staring at something that was superimposed on what was right in front of him.

"I seen a lot in my time," Set said. "Did some caravan work when I was younger. But I'll be damned if those dead gobs don't take all." He took a sip of his port. Grendl started to move on, but Set spoke again. "Figure you'd not only be happy about the money coming in right now but also be happy that them gobs're dead."

Grendl leaned back in. "I hate gobs. They stink and they scurry about like rabid squirrels. They gather in a horde and—well, you don't want them gatherin' in a horde. A dead gob is better than a live gob, like I said, but I don't give a single shit that these particular gobs are dead."

"Just figured you'd be wanting to reward them soldiers or something, that's all," Set said.

"Why? You know those soldiers?"

"No, I—"

"Then shut up. I hate gobs, but I also hate soldiers who kill something that was just minding its own business without any cause. You get soldiers runnin' around just killin' to be killin' and you might as well have a gob horde for all the difference."

"I'm sure those gobs attacked first," someone else shouted.

"That's not what the demon said," Set supplied. "She said it looked like the soldiers'd surrounded the gobs and then let loose with crossbows 'fore attacking on horseback."

"Well good!" another voice said. "Ain't that right, Grendl?"

Grendl ground his teeth and scooped more coins off the bar.

****

The cane stalks whispered incessantly.

Ashakarahad, eyes on the churned earth left by the hooves and boots of the soldiers, moved slowly. Behind her, curling into the humid breeze, the greasy smoke from the pyre engulfing the dead goblins rose, like the murky tendrils of a bubbling cauldron about which the sugarcane danced and weaved, an army of whispering witches. The trail of the soldiers as they'd approached the goblin clearing was trampled enough that she hardly needed to cut her way through. There was also no sign that the soldiers had been dragging wounded with them, unlike when they'd left the clearing. Anger rose up, but she was uncertain if the anger was due to the soldiers attacking the goblins or the fact that they'd lied about the presence of undead.

She'd chosen to camp outside the town because the dead were said to inhabit the swamp, densely congregating around the standing stones and tumbledown ruins of the mage-lords. She'd seen the ruins and standing stones—the town square was built around one. But she'd not found the cursed dead despite the tales. She'd sensed no power flowing from the stones and the ruins, power that, at turns, was said to compel the dead—as she herself seemed compelled—and to force them away like an unguent used to drive flies away from old meat.

The sugarcane ended abruptly and Ashakarahad found herself once again among trees with labyrinthine roots that reached into dark water. Insects buzzed but left her alone. Across a stretch of water, she could see more wilderness, thick and green and hanging with moss and vines. The soldiers had made camp before entering the cane field, but they'd left very little trace other than the remains of their fires and a few cast-off pieces of cloth and leather. The sun was turning the sky red, so Ashakarahad set her own camp among the remains of the soldiers' camp. She sat and stared and chewed jerky from her pack. She cleaned the bladed staff and her long knives before making a few notes in her journal. Then she leaned herself against a tree and slept.

In the heat of the morning, she forded the wide, dark water, and entered the forest beyond. Whispering trees, dark and gnarled and overgrown with sickly-sweet honeysuckle. Tall grass where the ground wasn't choked with leaves and rocks. She found the trail of a lone soldier after wandering the water's edge for nearly an hour, and she followed the trail deeper into the woods. She found wild sugarcane and flourishing grapes ripe on their twisted vines. She found the remains of orchards and, eventually, the remains of homesteads and farms, long gone to dirt and seed. The trail of the scout found those places too, sometimes resting, sometimes rooting about, perhaps looking for forgotten treasure. The trail crossed other trails, more solitary soldiers, and she could tell the scouts stopped and chatted and smoked before going their separate ways. Finally, the trail entered another overgrown clearing and stopped at a ruined kiln made of uneven stones and mortar. The soldier had sat with some of his fellows near the old kiln for a long time, drinking and smoking. Ashakarahad sat there too.

She'd seen many places like this in the wilderness of the swamp. Places where men had come and gone and will again at some point, an endless cycle of homesteading and abandonment that left the landscape dotted with gnarled trees planted in eerie rows, burned out foundations, and black, yawning shells of houses, made of stone, brick, and wood. In some cases the houses were nearly preserved save for the overgrowth of kudzu and the hint of wood rot, empty and dirty, sometimes with household items still inside as if the owners had simply forgotten to return.

Of course, the ruins of the mage-lords were present too, although often difficult to spot in the overgrowth and with the weathering of time. It was not uncommon to find a set of old tower stones among the silent, preserved remains of an empty farm or collection of ramshackle huts hobbled together and still, somehow, standing.

But there was just no evidence the power of the mage-lords was still there, buried in the earth or under layers of kudzu or lost in the trees or sunken under the water. Nothing but the standing stones or circles or the decayed touch and mocking whisper of the wind as it sang through the trees in a way that suggested rumors of power long vanished.

It had been decades since she'd come to her senses on the frozen floor of a broken tower far to the north. But how long had she lain there, how long since the ancient wizards had summoned and bound her to their service? She had no way of knowing. Now her search for the power that kept her bound to the world seemed doomed to fail.

She sighed.

She leaned with her back against the remains of the kiln and looked at the trails of the scouts around the clearing. They had been on foot, the main part of the squad elsewhere. Was it worth trying to find another camp? The soldiers hadn't discovered anything other than what Ashakarahad had already found in her forays into the trees, except the goblins. They had said they were hunting trolls, but she had found no sign of trolls either. So why lie about the goblins? Why say they were attacked by undead?

Ashakarahad looked beyond the clearing. The thick trees danced. Dark and foreboding despite the midday sun. The clearing was lonely and desolate, the kiln a jagged reminder of loss and abandonment. Ashakarahad sighed again. She climbed to her feet and hefted the staff. She took a drink of water and vanished back into the trees.

The Winall House simultaneously overlooked a portion of the town and a portion of the swamp beyond. Made of blackened stone and rotted, charred wood that suggested a decades-old fire, the House stood in an overgrown meadow atop a sharp rise of stone and earth. Nearby were the remains of a rock-walled well and the falling-down husks of a barn, stables, and what might have once been servants' huts and a smoking shack. Kudzu, weeds, and wildflowers claimed dominion there now, although it was said that, late at night, lights could be seen in what used to be the largest room in the House and distant, whispered music could be heard dancing on the wind.

Idsiyushti's hut and herb garden lay in the shadow of the desolate House, in the remains of a hedge maze with broken statuary. She had chosen to live there when she heard the tales told by the townsfolk of the House, its former occupants, and rumors of lights and music. But she had found no ghosts, only small animals living in the house and the meadow. At night, she liked to climb the rickety stairs to the burned-out third floor and watch the lights of the town dance and weave through the tops of trees swaying in the hot winds. She had searched the house and the barn and the empty huts and found no real evidence of the former inhabitants. They had obviously been wealthy landowners—Jonath had even told her that it was assumed that they had started the town itself long, long years ago, years lost to memory and given over to myth. She had asked why no one had ever gone to live there again and neither Jonath nor anyone else could give her an answer. So Idsiyushti called the place home, and if, late at night, she found herself drifting to sleep with gatflower in her pipe and the hints of music and laughter, shadowed and thin, coming from the house, she never bothered to tell anyone.

She sat in her herb garden, high on gatflower and watching bees flit from flower to flower, the sky overcast but still hot. She drank tea from an earthen cup and let the day's heat and the buzz of the bees and the whisper of hot wind through the black, empty windows of the House dissipate the whiskey in her system. She closed her eyes. Her legs were crossed, and she breathed in the tea, only vaguely wondering what Ashakarahad was doing now, still out in the deep dark. Wondering, with almost the same thought, if Marrah was busy with someone at Grendl's, what wild delights they were paying her for, whether she was fucking them or they were fucking her.

A boot scraped somewhere below the edge of the garden. She opened her eyes and took another sip of tea.

Purging after subsisting on liquor alone was a delight in and of itself. It made her feel strangely alive and disconnected from the world around her, allowed her mind to drift into a form of nothingness that was welcome, like a waking sleep that left her energized and hungry. A stew was bubbling in an iron pot over a fire on the other side of her hut.

Marin of Etrusq made his way slowly along the remains of the path that led to her garden. He walked with a heavy cane in one hand that he used to lever himself along every fourth or fifth step, like a slow, black barge moving along a river muddy and thick. His clothes were tight and looked warm, and a wide-brimmed, fur hat covered his head. He stopped to stare up at the remains of the House before continuing on, looking wrapped in memories that were not entirely pleasant.

"Mistress," the old judge said as he came to a stop at the open garden gate.

"Judge."

He came forward and levered himself onto a stool she indicated with a wave of her hand. She proffered a mug of tea which he accepted with a smack of his lips and a smile.

"I got lost in the hedge maze here when I was a boy," he said. He looked around. There was nothing left of the hedge maze beyond her garden now save for broken statues and twisted clumps of shrubbery that only hinted at care and arrangement. "My gran used to bring me here for parties. I was so young then. The house seemed even larger than it is. Alive. Still seems that way now, but it frightened me differently back then. Scared me because it was full of laughter and people and I'd want to run and hide in the hedge maze while other kids made a game of trying to find me. Now it just frightens me because, well—" He laughed. "This is good tea."

"Thank you." She glanced at the ruined house. "It's a long way to walk for just a cup of tea and memories."

He removed his hat, revealing tight white curls, and wiped his brow with a rag he pulled from his doublet. He pulled a pipe from his belt and filled it from a pouch. He held the pipe out to her, his bushy white eyebrows raised. She took the pipe and touched her finger to the bowl. There was a spark and then she breathed in the tobacco. It was good but not local. She handed the pipe back and she leaned forward to light it for him. He nodded.

"We went a long time without a witch here in town," he said. He held the pipe aloft. "I miss the old ways."

Idsiyushti shrugged. "My ways are my ways. And the ways of the fey," she said. She found a stick nearby and lit it with her fingers, handed it to him so that he could keep the pipe lit. The tiny spell tingled along her spine, fingers, and toes.

"I could tell you I came because of the goblins," Marin said. "That their killing scares me—well, that someone

63

would do that, soldiers it seems, close to our town. That it's put the town on even more edge than when it was just the threat of the soldiers doubling back and causing trouble."

Idsiyushti closed her eyes, leaned back against the hut's door jam. She felt the judge's old eyes on her.

He continued, "But it's not. Oh, I'm concerned that the soldiers have broken the law — as much as soldiers can, and that's not an easy point, trust me. No, what scares me is out there in the deep dark. Something waiting, watching, lurking."

She opened her eyes.

"That's what it feels like, anyway," Marin said, blowing a lopsided smoke ring. Idsiyushti noticed the wrinkled, long-fingered hand holding the pipe was shaking slightly. "It's like a dread of some kind. Creeping along the ground. Heading right for us. And we're worse for it, or will be. Folks are already too on edge now. And this will make it so much worse."

Idsiyushti sipped tea, slurped it without noticing. "Do you mean the dead?"

Marin blew another smoke ring and watched it hang in the hot air, watched it slowly drift apart, strand by strand, like it was being unwound by a tiny, invisible hand that was both patient and tenacious. "I don't know what I mean." He sipped his tea and watched the shadows of the ruined House. His hands were still shaking. Finally, he said, "I like the old ways. All of them, but times change.

"When I was a boy, when I used to come up here, our witch lived out in the deep dark. Folk would go to her and once or twice a week she'd come to the edge of town and doctor up the sick if needed. She was an old woman who lived in a hut that stood on nine legs, reached her front door by crossing a rope bridge. Believe it or not, she was even tinier than you are—but she was no gnome or dwarf, don't get me wrong. She used to carve little figures out of clumps of dried tobacco leaf and us kids'd go out and fetch 'em and sell 'em in the square. Then we'd take the money and buy sweets. She never demanded we take her anything other than more leaf and liquor and, sometimes, a pastry.

"But she was something, out there in her hut—some said that it even walked about on those nine legs. Ha! But she never came into town. She never made a spectacle of herself." He looked at her then looked away. "Anyway, she was long gone—her hut too—by the time I was a grown man, a veteran, a knight, and came back here to be judge. Long gone, but we all remembered her."

Idsiyushti was sitting rigid and tight. "I don't understand—"

"I know about you and Marrah, but I don't care who you fuck out here in this ruin. I don't care if you go to Jak's, I don't care if you drink nothing but moonshine liquor that I'd jail any other person for. But you rode into town on a cyclone yesterday. A damned cyclone, Idsiyushti! Folks are scared enough! We've had fights, now. Lots of shouting and carrying on. One of Grendl's girls was even stabbed —"

Idsiyushti felt like Marin had struck her across the temple with his cane. "What?"

He waved her back. "It was only a scratch and she refused to come out here. And it was Sek, not Marrah. Don't worry. We did have a hard time keeping Grendl from knocking heads in, and we couldn't figure out who had done the stabbing. Sek refused to give the man up — but Grendl used to be a constable a long time ago, or so they say. Back east or northeast or somewhere. Anyway, Jonath and I talked him down, but that was no easy task."

Idsiyushti leaned back. Grendl a constable? Whores being stabbed and refusing to name their attacker?

"This dread, this thing that I feel, out there, in the deep dark," Marin said. "There's already enough trouble. We don't need more. We don't need brash spectacle. Not this close to town." He looked at her through a haze of pipe smoke.

"I understand," Idsiyushti said. "Don't worry. I won't ride into town on a cyclone or a golden dragon or a fiery gator and flaunt my bits at the other girls or turn all the straights queer with a wave of my magic tits."

Marin held up his hands as if to ward her off, but he laughed, deep and rich. Idsiyushti rose and went into the hut. She returned with a small pouch and tossed it to the judge.

"Here's the mixture for your joints. So you don't have to come back up here next week. Now, if you'll excuse me, I have a stew to eat."

The old judge rose, stiff, and put on his hat. He shook out his pipe and tucked it away. He looked down at her and then hobbled out the gate and back up the path, his laughter gone, his fear murky and circling.

The streets of the town were a mix of packed dirt and cobbled stone, still hot in the thick evening air. Jonath walked the rutted back streets, avoiding the town square, watching shadows, and glancing at candle-lit windows, his chain of office a burden that seemed to be growing with each step. He'd exchanged his crossbow and broadsword for a truncheon and a pike because it was his own townsfolk riled up at each other—heads needed knocking, not removing. Fistfights were now a common thing, although Grendl's lightly-knifed whore was evidence that the riling-up could get much worse.

The sounds of the night, with new layers brought on by the arrival and departure of the soldiers and the discovery of goblin village, were distinct and driven, like an old-timer newly awakened from a long nap, stiff and aching and loud even though no one was listening. Boisterous laughter echoed off wattle and daub walls, off wood and brick, shingle and thatch, coming and going like waves on a roiling ocean. Light spilled from doorways, shadows moved in door frames, inside hot parlors and kitchens, disheveled bedrooms and common areas. A small town turned, by whisper and shout and worry, to a living, breathing scale model of cities distant and frightening.

A one-armed shadow detached itself from beside a yard post whose paint was flaking and silver in the moonlight, adjusted its trouser front, and saluted Jonath with a gesture full of mockery.

"Grendl," Jonath said. "Surprised you aren't pissing behind your own business rather than on someone else's."

The dwarf fell in beside Jonath. "Needed some air," he grunted. Then he indicated the candle-lit windows, the shadows, and the rutted street with a broad sweep of his hand, scars flashing dull red in the stray light from an oil lantern on a nearby porch. "Reminds me of Dung Tide, in Drilithae, just past the docks and the warehouse district. Seen it?"

"Yes," Jonath said, frowning, uncertain if Grendl was baiting him for being born in the swamp. "How's Sek?"

"She's fine. Tough gal. Refused to see Idsiyushti, which I can respect. Took that blade like a fighter."

"You train your girls well, then."

"I didn't train her to do that. Swamp did, I imagine."

"Her grandfather was a moonshiner out in the deep dark. So was her great-grandfather. Said to sell not only liquor but potions and curses to the folk too far wrapped up in the swamp religion to even bother with the witch. Used to piss Miq right off."

"What about her father?"

"Lit out when her mother gave birth. Too many children, so the story goes. Lit out and joined the army. Got himself gut-stabbed right before the Chaos."

"Lucky him. Lots more folk got gut-stabbed *during* the Chaos. Gut-stabbed, head-stabbed, heart-stabbed. Fucking mess."

Jonath looked down an alley and saw shadows moving around one of the fires burning in the town square. An out-of-tune lute was playing out there in the flame-lit night. He heard children playing a game that involved laughter and screaming. He found himself almost missing the hot nights when the men would sit on Grendl's porch, the women would shop and gossip, and the children would play seemingly quieter games of hoops and sticks and ball.

"Did you fight in the Chaos?"

"Yes," Grendl said after a moment. "Was in charge of a dwarven ax, a squad. We'd been sent to Desade because it was getting difficult for my clan to bring goods down from the mountains without running into trolls or gobs or much worse—all driven mad and violent by the wars of men and elves."

"Peacekeepers," Jonath said. "That's what Drilithae called 'em after our glorious emperor took the throne from the elves. What you and your dwarven ax were, I suppose. What I was."

"That when you were knighted?"

"Yes. Towards the end, when the emperor was consolidating his power. I had just been a soldier before that, a fresh-faced officer."

"An officer? I hadn't realized there were that many noble families here in the swamp."

Once again, Jonath was uncertain whether or not Grendl was trying to get a rise out of him. "My great-great-grandfather made his money at sea. My great-grandfather invested that money on a tiny horse farm which my grandfather inherited, built up, and passed to my father. What money my father made from it, he eventually used to buy me a commission."

"Why?"

Laughter echoed out of the shadows, unrelated but still poignant. "My father and I didn't agree on much of anything. He thought the army would make me more reasonable, more mature—and figured a commission would give me a leg up in the army, being from the swamp and all. He died before I was knighted. My mother moved to Esgen afterward. She's a seamstress."

Grendl seemed to think about this. "Fathers and sons never agree, doesn't matter man, dwarf, elf, or gob, I imagine."

Grendl stopped. Jonath continued on until he realized the dwarf was no longer beside him. He turned and met Grendl's eyes, bright despite the swath of shadow that wrapped them both.

"Why did the soldiers come here?" Grendl asked.

Jonath blinked. "What?"

Grendl turned a slow circle, the swath of shadow cutting across him like a blade. The thumb of his lone hand was hooked into his belt. "Why did the soldiers come here? *Here*? They didn't come to my bar, they didn't go out to Jak's, they didn't go into Ned's store, or Drag's or even visit Mackasl and his swamp temple."

"They had wounded and needed Idsiyushti."

"Sure. And why? Why were they here to begin with?"

"They skirmished with the goblins out in the cane fields—"

"And lied about it!" Grendl held up his hand, fist balled. "But why were they in the cane fields? Why in the swamp to begin with?"

"Hunting for—"

Grendl spat. "There are no trolls here, Jonath! None. Haven't been for decades if not a century. Now I may be an outsider in this pissant town, but I fucking know trolls. I hunted them when...."

After a time, Jonath asked, "When what?"

"When I was constable back east, near Angol."

"Angol?" For a moment, the laughter and shouting, the lute music, the strange fact that the town had suddenly become more of a city, dimmed and vanished, retreated like a tide running back out to sea, leaving rotting things behind, slick things gasping as if unable to breathe. "They say there was a troll uprising in Angol. Attacked a city—a walled city. Came up through tunnels, old catacombs that hadn't been used for more than a century. Killed hundreds, just to steal children."

"They had help," Grendl said. He was now completely covered by the swath of shadow. Only his scuffed boots reflected any light. "A mage cracked the city walls and tore the place apart while the trolls came up from the bottom."

Jonath was silent.

"My ax and I tracked them, along with some undead hunters and another mage, a silver-haired elf. Queerest elf you ever met." Half to himself, he added, "He would've been drinking every damned night out at Jak's place if he could."

"Sphinx," Jonath breathed. Beneath the background noise from the square, his own voice sounded heavy and absurd.

"Aye." Grendl stopped. "You know him?"

"I know him," Jonath said. "He campaigned with us. In Desade and after. He was on the field when I was knighted."

Jonath could tell that Grendl stiffened at that, despite the cloak of shadows. After a moment, Grendl cleared his throat. "My point is that I bloody fucking know trolls. There ain't any trolls here! And Sphinx—abyss take his queer, wizardy ass!"

Jonath, weighed down by memory and confusion, started to defend his old companion but a drunk staggered from the narrow alley between two houses. Jonath caught the drunk by the arm and turned away at the smell of whiskey, puke, and urine.

Ashakarahad returned to the clearing in the cane fields just after dawn, when the sun was climbing and the air was still humid and motionless. Tendrils of low fog, more like fingers of steam, crawled up from the ground. Someone from the town had knocked the remains of the burned-out huts to the ground and trampled the charred fragments, just visible now through the crawling fingers of fog. Ashakarahad stopped at the edge of the clearing. She sat and watched the fog tendrils grasp their way along, searching for something that they never seemed to find, eventually vanishing as the sun rose higher.

She stood and began to search the clearing, kicking aside the trampled remains of the huts, the trampled cookfires, the trampled tools and broken cookware, ragged skins, and rotting leather cords and straps, all covered in soot and dirt and goblin blood. Approaching the smoldering corpse pile, Ashakarahad stopped and leaned on her staff. Blackened bones were all that was left of the corpses, and even those were no longer recognizable as having once belonged to any sort of goblin. When the last of the fog was gone and the sun had cut the shadows creeping through the clearing into jagged stumps, Ashakarahad kicked through the goblin bones and ash, her metal-covered boots sending a few lonely sparks crawling for the sky.

Nothing.

The sun climbed overhead in a wash of wet heat. A breeze finally began, the sugarcane dancing and whispering. Ashakarahad looked up at the sun and unstrapped the leather from her shoulders, unbuttoned her jacket, loosed her collar. She took a long drink of tepid water from her canteen, momentarily thinking of Idsiyushti and her whiskey gourd, of brown skin covered in a sheen as the young witch climbed naked from the swamp after washing herself.

Ashakarahad turned a slow circle, a dusting of ash on her boots. It took her nearly fifteen minutes to find the tiny, mostly-clogged trickle of a stream that gouged a small crease between cane stalks. The stream looked more like the remains of seasonal run-off, but she could now see a narrow trail that led from the stream back to the clearing. Goblin prints were buried beneath the trampled stalks.

She refilled her canteen once she'd cleared debris from the stream. She added neutralizing powder and then looked back over her shoulder, could barely make out the clearing through the cane. There were more goblin tracks following the stream. Lots of tracks, although easily lost under the trampling debris that had covered the stream in the first place. Ashakarahad followed the tracks, straddling the stream and pushing through the cane. Birds were calling to each other overhead and behind her, over the clearing. The tops of the cane were still whispering in the breeze, although Ashakarahad could barely feel its touch.

The stream widened slightly. The cane surrounding it fell back, forming another clearing. Ashakarahad stopped abruptly. In the center of the clearing was a short, stocky standing stone, another remnant of the mage-lords. Before the stone was a crude altar of what looked like chipped basalt. Feathers and dolls made from sugarcane leaves decorated the altar, dancing, whispering with menace in the breeze. Reaching out a hand towards the altar and the standing stone, she felt it, felt the power waiting there, hiding, impatient. Her heart leaped into her throat. The staff vibrated in her hand. She almost sobbed.

The power of the mage-lords.

The invisible shackles hummed deep down in her bones, in her teeth, the base of her skull, her vagina dentata. She rocked back on her heels and let the hum wash through her, its pain a welcome, needed relief to the heavy silence that had proceeded it during her decades-long search. Behind the hum, the faces of the Eld, her clan mates, her father, her lovers and enemies, all faded into unrecognizable shapes and features under the weight of the shackles, suddenly swam forth, beckoning.

At last.

Jonath of the Battlefield was helping the Jebs family lift a part of their collapsed tent frame — the result of a drunk who'd stumbled too far — when the word *constable* was shouted across the square. Jonath ignored the shouts and ordered Jebs senior and the two Jebs juniors to keep pushing and holding despite the heat and sun. The Jebs girls finally tied the structure back into place with linen strips.

Jonath rolled his shoulders and wiped his brow with the brim of his hat. One of the Jebs girls — Della? — pointed over his shoulder from atop a rickety crate. "Constable," she said. Jonath turned and saw Grig, dirty militia tabard tight over his even dirtier clothes, pike in hand like a walking stick, leading Ashakarahad through the square. The demoness wasn't wearing her customary leather armor. Her blouse was open at the collar and her cleavage was making several heads turn.

Ashakarahad ignored the stares. She had her armor wrapped up and slung over her back like a pack, and she carried her staff across her shoulders like a pole for carrying buckets. She also looked tired, which Jonath found disturbing.

Inside Jonath's office, where the air was hot and sticky, the remains of his spoiling lunch not helping, Jonath and Ashakarahad shared tumblers of gin while she told him of her search through the deep dark, along the soldiers' trails, back to the goblin clearing, to the altar hidden in the cane. Marin entered, sweating, poured himself a triple measure of gin and sat while Ashakarahad told the story all over again.

"You're saying these goblins worshipped some sort of risen dead?" Marin spluttered after a time. He poured himself another heavy shot of gin and drank it down in a single gulp. He poured yet another but ignored it as he stared at Ashakarahad in anticipation.

"No," Ashakarahad said. Their three bodies increased the temperature in the office, as did the candles that Jonath had to burn because Marin's eyesight was weak even with the wire-rimmed spectacles he wore to read. But the demoness didn't appear to be sweating. Neither had she closed her collar and nor donned her armor.

"But that's what you seem to be implying," Marin said eventually.

"No. I'm saying that I found a place where the goblins worshipped something presumably goblin-related. But the site where they worshipped was a place a power, a ruin of the ancient mage-lords. The kind of thing that brought me here, to the swamp, in the first place." She sipped gin and took a deep breath. ?My research suggests that places of power like that, places left over from when the mages ruled this continent, have influence over the undead. I'm not sure how or in what way yet, but there it is."

"But we haven't actually seen the dead here, near town," Jonath said. "The dead are way out in the deep dark where no one goes."

"Yes," Ashakarahad said. "I'm aware. Still, it's the tales of the undead out in the deep dark that brought me here. Along with the ruins and stones associated with these places of power. But there wasn't any actual power or magic or, obliviously, undead until now."

"So you're saying that the soldiers did get attacked by the dead?" Marin asked.

"No. I think they attacked these goblins, who happened to worship at a place of power that, in other cases, has been associated in some way with undead and the ancient rulers of this land. And then afterward the soldiers *said* they were attacked by undead, possibly as a way to cover up the fact that they massacred the goblins."

"But the goblins didn't worship the dead."

"I don't actually know what goblins worship," Ashakarahad said. Her teeth were showing more and more and Jonath suspected she was growing impatient. "But I doubt they worshipped anything other than their own gods. They just found that place of power and borrowed it, if you will."

Jonath sat back and pinched the bridge of his nose. He looked into his empty tumbler but decided against pouring another drink. The candles he'd lit for Marin burned in thick stubs at the edge of his desk, the flames unwavering in the heavy air, like solid spears of fire making the air even hotter and overripe. "I'm confused as to what you're trying to tell us. You've been looking for a place of power in the swamp for some time. Now you've found one. But why the urgency? The soldiers are gone."

"Because I don't think it was any sort of coincidence the soldiers attacked the goblins, massacred them, spilled so much goblin blood only to have the place of power the goblins worshipped suddenly become active! A place of power all the old texts say is somehow connected with the dead!" She leaned forward. "And I think it's obvious their story of troll-hunting was horseshit too!"

Jonath nodded slowly, his eyes still on one of the seemingly motionless flames. It was pretty much exactly what Grendl had said the night before. The dead, trolls, and horseshit. If this were Desade, during the Chaos, then this would somehow all make sense—soldiers massacring folks they weren't meant to and lying about it with absurd, outrageous tales. Of course, during the Chaos, absurd, outrageous tales weren't actually that absurd and outrageous.

Jonath looked over at Marin. The old knight hadn't been in the Chaos. Instead, he'd served in older, more mundane campaigns for the glory and honor of the empire, back when the emperor, well, empress, had been an elf. But not the Chaos. Jonath looked at the demoness sitting across from him, his eyes unconsciously falling to her open collar and cleavage. A shiver threatened to shake his shoulders. Once again, memories of the Chaos rose faster than he could fight them back down. He grabbed the dusty bottle of gin and drank the remaining contents down without offering any more to his guests.

Grendl was sitting at a corner table, counting coins and making notations in a ledger with a pen, when Jonath came through the tavern doors, marched to the table and said, "We need to take a ride."

"What?"

"Ash found something out at that goblin site. I'd like you to come take a look with me."

"I have a business to run, constable."

"I'm not asking you because you're a tavern owner and a whoremonger. I'm asking because, as you mentioned last night, you have some experience with these kinds of things."

"What kinds of things?" The pen went back into the inkwell as if Grendl were absently sheathing a dagger. "I'm not a constable anymore. You are. I actually am just a tavern owner and whoremonger." Across the tavern, silence had fallen, drinks and utensils poised half-way to mouths, eyes and ears turned. Upstairs, someone was fucking one of Grendl's girls, the only sound in the universe of the tavern now.

Jonath looked around at the staring faces, the frozen movements. "You tell me what kinds of things," he said. Then he left as abruptly as he entered, the only sound in his wake the moans of the whore upstairs.

On the road, Grendl said, "I didn't take you for the melodramatic type." He wore a broad-brimmed hat with a series of feathers fanning out the back. Jonath eyed the short-hafted war ax strapped to the saddle of Grendl's mule. Grendl followed his gaze. "Melodrama makes me nervous. Shouldn't the demon and the witch be here with us?"

"They'll meet us there. Don't really want to think how she and Idsi will get there ahead of us."

"More cyclones," Grendl said.

Jonath grunted. "Flashy magic tricks make folks nervous."

"Exactly what Sphinx used to say," Grendl said. "Right before doing some flashy magic tricks."

In spite of himself, Jonath laughed. The barrage of memories from the Chaos were tempered by memories of Sphinx, beautiful and severe, saying and doing just that.

The goblin clearing was hot and desolate, but there were gathering clouds in the sky and a taste on the breeze that suggested an unseasonal storm was coming. A hot storm that just might make things boil even more, maybe with a wind that ripped things from the ground and tossed them about if you weren't careful. Tempers were already too tight—they needed to end this soon and assure the families they could return home. As it was, people were going out to their farms and homesteads to fetch more belongings and livestock and bring them back to town. There was almost no room left and a hard storm—or a storm of any kind—would only make matters worse.

Ashakarahad stepped through a break in the cane when Jonath and Grendl climbed from their saddles. The demoness led them back through the whispering, weaving stalks to the thin stream and up along to the clearing with the standing stone and the crude altar. Idsiyushti was seated cross-legged on the altar, her dirty dress whipping lightly in the hot breeze. She held her chin in her hands, elbows on her knees, staring at the standing stone. Rot and decay, both sweet and cloying, made Jonath wrinkle his nose, and the heat seemed to cling to him like a blanket wrapped tight with spiked leather straps.

"It's hard to breathe in here," Grendl said.

"Got it!" Idsiyushti shouted, unfolding and jumping up like a drop of oil popping in a frying pan.

"Got what?" Jonath asked.

The air snapped and cracked and a nimbus of light smeared itself around Idsiyushti. Her dress whipped about her body and she raised her arms.

"Wait! What?" Grendl shouted. The ax was suddenly in his hand. Jonath's crossbow was off his back and cocked. Ashakarahad had her staff held in front of her, a grimace on her face that showed her sharp teeth.

Then the demoness was shouting, "I said just *find* the power not touch it—"

But the nimbus surrounding Idsiyushti was suddenly all around them and, with a twist of sound and a fracture of light, deafening, blinding, Jonath was falling backward through the air.

Tears and blood ran down Idsiyushti's cheeks. She smeared both uselessly with the back of her free hand,

83

felt her head spin. She squeezed her eyes shut and called on a shard of her dwindling magic to push back the pain of her headache and wounds. The rest of her magic she sent into Jonath, willing him to live, to stop bleeding, willing flesh to knit.

Jonath moaned. Idsiyushti opened her eyes and laughed out loud with relief. The constable, bloody and cut, his clothes turned to rags, lay on his back. Idsiyushti removed her hand from Jonath's forehead and uselessly smeared the blood and tears on her other cheek.

"Told you he'd come around," Grendl said. The dwarf was sitting on the ground near the trickling stream, washing blood and dirt from his face and beard with his lone, scarred hand. His jerkin was in a shredded heap nearby and his tunic was tattered, dirty, and bloody. His arm was corded and thick, covered with fresh cuts and old scars over broad-stroked tattoos done in ink blacker than night. Grendl normally kept himself covered, so the tattoos had surprised Idsiyushti, as had the nub of his left arm, pale gray flesh puckered just below the shoulder.

The sugarcane stalks surrounding the small clearing had been shredded and bent, like toy soldiers swatted by a child-god during a tantrum. Only the jagged stone altar seemed untouched by the destruction. Ashakarahad was nowhere to be found. Idsiyushti had screamed herself raw shouting for the demoness, but then, after collapsing once more into the dirt, naked and bloody, her dress in tatters and blown off, Idsiyushti had turned to tend to Jonath and Grendl.

Jonath moaned again and started to sit up. Idsiyushti tried to push him back down, but the constable batted her hands away before rolling over and vomiting into the shredded remains of the cane. Idsiyushti, exhausted, hurt, breathless, watched Grendl slowly, painfully rise and bring a leather canteen over to Jonath. The constable drank and spat, drank and spat, and then steadied himself with Grendl's hand, standing, wobbly.

"What the fuck happened?" Jonath asked.

"The stone exploded," Idsiyushti breathed. Jonath looked at her and frowned. She was too tired and sore to cover her dirty, bloody nakedness.

"You're bleeding all over the place," Jonath said. He stepped forward but Grendl held him back.

"She healed herself, and us," Grendl said. "She's not bleeding anymore, not really. Not badly. Neither are we."

Idsiyushti nodded at this, her vision blurring, black around the edges with exhaustion. "Although I think there are still tiny pieces of rock in me. I was right in front of the stone when it exploded."

Jonath continued to stare at her. Then he finally pulled himself taller. "How are you still alive?"

"I raised a sort of magical shield at the very last instant, without thinking. I guess that did it."

Jonath took a deep breath. Then, "Where is Ash?"

"She's gone," Idsiyushti replied. "I don't know where. I looked a little but I needed to tend to our wounds, so I came back."

Jonath blanched even more, his lined olive face now almost as white as Caeri's. He looked past the altar to the shattered remains of the standing stone. "Did that thing tear her apart?"

"It didn't tear us apart," she said, "so I can't imagine it would tear her into pieces too tiny to find."

Jonath seemed to think about this, nodded. "We need to find her."

"We need to get back to town," Grendl said. He stepped away from Jonath and bent to pick up his ax with a stiffness that spoke of pain and age and exhaustion. "I'll go get the horse and mule."

"No, we need to find Ash," Jonath said. He grabbed his head and held it with both hands, swaying on his feet. He kept his balance, however, eventually pulling his hands away, his face a mask of pain and anger.

"We need to take care of ourselves," Idsiyushti said. "And I need something to cover up with."

Grendl turned and started to follow the stream away from the destruction. "I'll bring a saddle blanket too."

Ashakarahad screamed. Using a two-handed swing, she crushed the helmet-covered head of an armored, bipedal creature with a crude ax-like weapon she'd wrested from the creature's own clawed hands. Blue-black gore leaked from the crushed helm and the creature collapsed, joining four others of its kind, each armored in crude, heavy, black metal. Ashakarahad dropped to her knees, lowered the ax. There was no other movement on the jade beach except the to-and-fro of the violet-foamed, crimson waves that steamed as they broke.

She didn't remember losing her staff or her pack and the leather armor tied to it. Her blouse was ripped, dirty, and bloody. Her trousers were torn and stained. Only her metal-encased boots seemed untouched save for the gore of the things that had attacked her as she'd staggered onto the beach.

Her head hurt. Her memory was jumbled, odd, disjointed. She remembered massive dizziness and the sudden, painful pull of the ancient shackles that bound her, followed by blinding sun overhead and a cool, jasmine-scented breeze. Then the crush of jade sand and the gentle billow of grey-green foliage that looked more like lichen than shrubs or weeds. Out of nowhere, the black-armored creatures began to howl, charging her, weapons raised. Her confusion grew along with the dizziness but then she was fighting, punching, clawing, kicking. She'd grabbed the ax-like weapon in a moment of desperate recklessness and wrested it free. Now the creatures were dead.

The invisible shackles throbbed and hummed like metal drums charged with lightning.

Ashakarahad sat back and dropped the weapon. She held her head in her hands for a moment, ran her fingers along the ridges of her horns. She reached around on her belt and found her canteen, took a long drink. The tepid water smelled of the swamp, strangely reminded her once again of Idsiyushti climbing naked from the brackish water, pulling duckweed from her long, dark, shimmering hair. Ashakarahad closed her eyes and used that memory to try to dampen the dizziness, the throb of the invisible shackles. She could hear distant cries in the air now, like far away birds, and the breaking of the crimson, steaming waves was soothing and gentle.

The standing stone in the goblin clearing had exploded.

Ashakarahad opened her eyes. The dizziness was almost gone, replaced with images of Idsiyushti, Jonath, and Grendl frozen against a bright flash that seemed to turn them to shadow and mist. She groaned. What had happened to them? Had they survived? Her own people were capable of shifting through realities, planes of existence, universes, narratives, like water through a sieve at times, especially when compelled by ancient forces beyond their control. The standing stone, a relic of the swamp's ancient past, with its surprising hum of long-buried power. Idsiyushti, impetuous, a tempest wrapped in a thin, dirty dress, had touched the stone with her brand of fey-touched magic. The exploding stone must have had enough power to send Ashakarahad through the ether, away from the swamp, to wherever she was now. Her heart raced. The explosion had not freed her from her captivity, the pain of the shackles was proof enough of that. Instead, it seemed the explosion had merely shifted her to another place, another time, still captive to the ancient mage-lord summoning and binding.

Perhaps being worshipped by the goblins had awakened the stone even more than she had realized. Perhaps it was something Idsiyushti had done—Ash searched her aching head for anything she'd read or heard about interactions between the fey and the mage-lords, but there was nothing. She sighed. Idsiyushti was young but the roots of magic were deeply seated in her, no matter how showy she tended to be—or perhaps because of that. Ashakarahad tried to imagine learning to control magic at the human age of four or five, learning at the feet of a nameless elf. She thought about Idsiyushti's impetuous, stubborn use of fey magic to convert whiskey to water and nourishment. Then she thought of Idsiyushti sitting on the altar before the stone, reaching out, brashly disregarding what Ashakarahad had told her.

There were some, she knew, among her own kind— powerful sorcerers in their own demonic right—who would champion Idsiyushti's temerity. But there were others who would curse Idsiyushti for the same. Ashakarahad was neither but she still felt a wash of anger beneath the dwindling dizziness.

In time, Ash struggled to stand, her back and legs aching. She had a few cuts and scrapes, several bruises, but she was otherwise unhurt as near as she could tell. The dizziness was finally fading. She searched the sand for a short time, looking for her staff or her pack and armor, but found nothing. Then she searched the corpses of the black-armored things. They were canoids, with sharp teeth and short muzzles and silver eyes. Their armor was crude to the point of being nearly genius, the work of a barbaric artisan with a twisted mind and a feverishly skilled hand. The metal was an alloy she could not name, nor could she make sense of the etch-work that gave the armor the appearance of the carapace of a terrifying insect.

The cries of the things that sounded like seabirds were growing closer. Ashakarahad looked to the chartreuse sky and decided not to stick around in case the seabirds weren't seabirds after all. There was a cliff, a bluff overlooking the crimson, steaming waves, and she saw a path climbing towards it, leading off through the gray-green moss-scrub. She took the ax-like weapon and a couple of knife-edged implements from the corpses. She also took some ornaments and jewelry whose value and meaning she had no idea of, along with a length of hemp-like rope. She left filthy blankets and objects of whose use she had no idea and began to follow the trail. The bright sun was high but not hot. The air still smelled of jasmine, although she could see no sign of the plant anywhere.

It hurt when Idsiyushti breathed in the hot smoke from the pipe but eventually the gatflower dulled the pain in her chest, the pain in her head, in her limbs and neck. The cuts, scrapes, and punctures merely itched after a time, and the cloying salves she covered herself with felt cool and refreshing. She forced herself to sleep, although sleep was a strange haze, a vortex of magical energy that dropped her into successive pits of nothingness and then tossed her back up unexpectedly like a stone rolling down an incline, bouncing to different heights, chips and pieces of itself flying off and vanishing into the scree.

She sipped broth and tea when she finally awoke, climbing from her sleeping pallet stiff and slow. The gatflower made her head spin slightly and she stubbornly refused to use magic to make it stop. Instead, she hobbled about and prepared more broth, ate it outside, seated on the ground beside the rock borders of the cook fire in her garden.

She was wrapped in a blanket and bandages, in the lingering haze of the gatflower and the peppery warmth of the broth when Jak stepped through the garden gate and cleared his throat. Idsiyushti looked at him long and hard until he held a liquor jug up and smiled. She tossed her tea into the dirt and motioned him forward. The whiskey was good, probably imported, like the bottles Marrah said Grendl had hidden away. It burned away the haze of the gatflower and warmed her in a way the broth did not. She blinked and drank again. The warmth was soothing, calming. She smiled and thought of using her over-taxed magic to convert the whiskey, dismissed the thought after another sip.

"You doped the whiskey," she said, her voice thick. "Crystals of Errund."

Jak took a seat on a log near the fire and nodded. "A shipment came through from Esgen a while ago. This was the last of it. Figured you could use it more than anybody else." Blond and green-eyed and clearly from foreign parts, he was dressed as he ever was, like how she thought a court dandy probably dressed. His collar was unbuttoned because of the heat, shirt open to reveal his chest. He's pretty, Idsiyushti thought. Maybe too pretty for the swamp.

At some point, he'd told her of his years growing up in Drilithae, of his mother who ran both a well-to-do brothel and some sort of necromantic coven. He'd talked of his time with his mother's whores, how they never really satisfied him. Of his time with the boys and men in bathhouses and taverns and dormitories at the university. But he'd confessed that he was only truly, deeply satisfied by watching other people fuck, by devising intricate scenes for them to act out while he watched. Men, women, any combination thereof, it didn't matter.

He'd been educated well, at his mother's expense. Showered with culture and luxury and, in return, she'd had him trained to become what amounted to an assassin. His mother was paid kingly sums to have people killed then raised from the dead by her coven, most with the memories of being dead and dying still lingering upon waking. Her clients were the rich nobles of the empire, Jak's targets were people those clients felt needed to be taught some sort of expensive, perverse lesson.

Quite often Jak had been partnered with another debonair killer, a handsome, stylish man with cruel blue eyes. They had eventually become lovers and for the first time, Jak had finally felt satisfied. A few years of happiness passed and then something had gone horribly, horribly wrong. Jak hadn't elaborated—couldn't elaborate around the obvious pain the memories caused—but he'd wound up with the title to a little farm outside a nameless town in a swamp a thousand miles away, and his mother had sent him there, all but banishing him from the heart of the empire.

Of course, Jak made a living selling liquor, furnishing entertainment, and telling outrageous lies. Maybe he had just been trying to impress her with well-told stories of magic, queer sex, and murder-for-hire. On the other hand, she was an abandoned foundling who had learned magic from the fey and had first learned love in the arms of a dryad whose name was fourteen syllables long. The truth always seemed outrageous.

"Thank you," she managed. Truth or lie, the memory of Jak's confession always gave Idsiyushti pause, especially when he gave her a gift. But she couldn't imagine anyone in town wanting to pay him to murder her so she always let his beauty and his smile relax her into accepting without further thought.

The crystal-laced whiskey numbed her and fired her at the same time. She felt her pains sluicing off and sinking into the soil beneath her.

"How are you?"

"I'm healing," she said. "But I need rest in order to use more magic. I have to find Ashakarahad and make sure Jonath and Grendl heal up fine."

Jak waved his hand in dismissal. "The constable is up and about, too hard to keep down. I brought him some whiskey too—without the crystals—and he thanked me but sent me on my way. Which is too bad. He didn't look like he needed any more nursing, but I wouldn't have minded if he had." Jak's beautiful smile widened mockingly and he winked with melodramatic lasciviousness.

Idsiyushti laughed, feeling miles and miles away. "The elf who taught me how to be a witch eventually sent me away because he thought I was too impulsive, that I'd picked up too many bad habits from the faerie folk that he couldn't undo. Said I was too reckless." Idsiyushti felt liquid and slow, like she was melting. "Marrah says the same thing sometimes, although I'm not sure she's one to judge. Even Ash kinda said it. And then I blew us up."

Jak looked at the whiskey jug. "Okay, well this shit makes you maudlin. That's good to know."

Idsiyushti continued, "Marin said that he doesn't want me attracting undue attention." She began giggling then, the giggles taking over. She felt herself start to fall sideways but Jak reached out and supported her, pulled the blanket back up over her bare shoulders.

"Don't listen to them," Jak said. "You're hurting, feeling guilty, and no one can blame you for that. But don't let it change you any more than it needs to."

"You mean don't let them tell me to grow up?" She sat back against the wall of the hut and closed her eyes. The warmth from the scratchy blanket, the fire, the hot, wet air, the crystal-infused whiskey, the remnants of the gatflower—it was almost too much. She felt herself sweating, felt the sweat sting her wounds.

"How is Grendl doing? I should check on him too."

She heard Jak shift. "He's Grendl. I think he was the least hurt out of the three of you. But he's more stubborn than Jonath—"

"He's a dwarf."

"And an embodiment of the stereotype," Jak continued, laughing. "I brought him whiskey too, with crystal. He looked at me askance, sniffed the jug, spat on the ground, said that if it weren't for the infusion, he'd use it to fry up some biscuits because that was all it was good for. Asshole. Still, he did thank me once he made sure no one could hear him—"

Idsiyushti fell into a dreamless sleep.

Unsurprisingly, the explosion of a standing stone out in the deep dark, among the sugar cane and the remains of massacred goblins, did nothing to ease the tension in the air. The few families who had left the town square after the threat of the soldiers appeared to have passed, returned. So did new families, panicked and anxious, hauling their few belongings atop carts and wagons pulled by tired mules and sickly horses. Even some of the loners who fished and farmed out at the edge of the deep dark, unwashed, unkempt, crawled into town and found a patch of earth to squat over. The once quiet square continued to grow to look like a raucous bazaar in some foreign port rather than the sullen stretch around which a swamp town had been built. The shouting of men and women, drunk or sober, the screams and laughter of children, and the barking of more dogs than recent memory could account for greeted Jonath each time he made his stiff, aching way out to the porch fronting his over-hot office. The square was brightly lit at almost all hours, like a harvest festival gone mad and drooling. Across the square, the windows of Grendl's were always brightly lit.

Violence and petty theft were on the rise and Jonath fully expected at any moment to open the door of his office to find an army of angry townsfolk waving torches and makeshift weapons, demanding that he put a stop to all the nonsense. But the mob never formed, not in so many words. The tension continued to mount, tempers flared. It wouldn't be long before another one of Grendl's girls was stabbed — or worse. It wouldn't be long before someone's daughter or son was taken to one of the dirt alleys beyond the square and fucked into a bloody mess, perhaps left with a cut throat or a smashed-in head.

What was even more horrifying, in his own mind at least, was that Jonath had no idea why the townsfolk had succumbed to the fear and moved their families, pulling cattle and pigs and barefoot children behind overloaded carts, to the square *now*. Sure, he'd urged them to come, but that was when the threat of the soldiers had been plain. Now the soldiers, by all accounts, were gone. Did the explosion of the stone really terrify the folk that much? Or was it the massacre of the goblins?

Jonath could count on one hand the number of folk in town who had anything to do with goblins. Most folk ignored the goblins—and the goblins generally stayed clear of most folk. Miq was known for trading moonshine to them and probably others traded with them as well, but mostly, there was just mass, agreed-upon avoidance. The Winall House still had the burned-out foundations at the edge of its property of the cabins the old goblin slaves had lived in back when the empire still allowed that sort of thing. Even after the Slavery Proclamations were signed into law, making slavery illegal and protecting the rights of everyone who wasn't either rich or an elf, most of the so-called slave races stayed on as servants or cheap labor. Dwarves, goblins, certain human clans, some trolls, other monstrosities that the old elves who had established the empire long ago, on the blackened ruins of the nearly mythological mage-lords, had decided were nothing more than cheap fuel for the fire of conquest, all found it hard to throw off the yoke. But in the swamp, away from the cities and the rest of the empire—now laboring under the burden of the first human dynasty in history—the folk had let go of their slaves and, eventually, even their servants. The goblins had faded into the swamp and seemed more than content to stay there, just out of reach.

So why had the imperial patrol seen fit to wipe them out? The empire was not at war—not anywhere near the swamplands at least. And there had been no edict that Jonath—or Marin—knew about. And even if there were, the sergeant would surely have mentioned it. Because otherwise, the wholesale slaughter of goblins—or any of the former slave races—was strictly forbidden, carrying heavy fines and punishment. Jonath had seen soldiers tear the land apart, but that had been in an actual war, under the attrition of the Chaos, not in a field of sugarcane less than a day's ride from a small backwater town that rarely appeared on any imperial map.

Then again, maybe that's why the soldiers attacked the goblins. Maybe they figured since most people had no clue that the swampland was even inhabited in the first place, no one would miss the goblins at all.

Jonath went out the narrow back door of his office, onto a street that was lit by windows and porch lanterns, with even more people milling about, moving, shrouded in anxiety. He waved to a few who noticed him and made his way to the edge of town. Once there, it was almost a straight shot—except for the Billik house and their small apple orchard, through which he trespassed—to the dark, fence-wrapped graveyard beside the hulking basalt slabs of the chapel to the swamp gods. The narrow, glassless windows of the chapel were alight now, had been for several nights on end. Some of the concerned townsfolk had found new resurgence to their centuries-old faith.

The graveyard was lit by a series of lanterns spaced unevenly between the raised mausoleums and urns, hanging from crooks stuck into the ground. The flickering flames in the lanterns were like fireflies, and Jonath wondered who was lighting them. The graveyard was kept up by the chapel and the town coffers, the work done by Yun and Rell, the town's two-man undertakers' union. But the graveyard was only lit when the town gathered to bury one of their own and no one had died recently, not to Jonath's knowledge.

Voices raised themselves in chant from the chapel. The evening had turned to deeper night, the moon crawling along through a haze of shimmering swamp heat. The air smelled of flowers and muck and the strange spice that hung about graves.

Jonath stared at the bas-reliefs decorating the chapel walls, crude things of insanity and monstrosity. Jonath's family had settled the horse farm three generations back, his great-grandfather starting the ranch with stock brought in from Esgen, possibly even farther north. But for the most part, they'd never been ones to visit the chapel and learn the tenets of the swamp faith. Jonath's aunt had been a believer and she'd dragged him and his cousins to the chapel when they were younger, but Jonath's father had put a stop to Jonath's attendance after Jonath had started spouting verses from the texts in a sing-song voice, chanting a language that was not meant for human speech.

The flickering torches in the graveyard painted the bas-reliefs with movement, tentacles and creeping violence coming to life. Jonath shivered. Perhaps old Mackasl and his swamp priests could feel the tension in the air too. Perhaps they could read something in the swamp. Maybe they even knew about exploding standing stones—it was unlikely but the swamp religion had grown up out of the deep dark, where the ruins of the mage-lords still poked like teeth and finger bones. Maybe, just maybe, Mackasl—and Yun and Rell—were waiting for some sort of rapidly-approaching inevitability.

Ashakarahad saw the city on the horizon from the top of the weathered cliff. Tall spires, twisted and bent while still reaching upwards like desperate, broken fingers. Spans of bridges joining the spires. Domes, squat structures nestled among the spires like fat bullfrogs waiting for a meal while half-buried in the muck and reeds. The setting sun, bright but still not overly hot, glistened and reflected off of glass, dark metal, and stray chrome. Blue and green lights, others white hot, began to appear, some moving, some fixed.

Ashakarahad shuddered under the teasing touch of a fleeting memory. Despite the details, it was clear the city was a long way off, splayed out against the horizon as if a mechanical sky had lost its footing and come crashing down out of the clouds. She turned back to the beach far below but the beach had become obscured by a low fog the color of washed-out charcoal.

She decided against trying to find enough scrub for a fire and simply sat in the dirt, levering herself down with the haft of the ax-like weapon. She ate a little of the unidentifiable jerky she'd packed back in her camp in the swamp. How far away was the town, the swamp, the empire now? She thought of Idsiyushti, felt stabs of regret and anger, both tinged by a whisper of a desire that was surprising and feral.

Desire was so ingrained in her kind as to be ubiquitous, but since waking on the cold floor of the ruined tower, Ashakarahad had been less driven by her demonic nature and more driven by a desire to find a way home. She closed her eyes and measured her breathing, forced her mind to clear so that even the ever-present hum of the invisible shackles was as far away as the chrome-and-glass city.

Her kind, the Eld, were multifarious, many twisted beyond all evil, others compassionate beyond the upper bounds of humanity, exaggerated reflections of the many worlds and peoples around them. Ashakarahad had always considered herself to be an even-tempered sort. Not feeding on hatred and maliciousness, not thriving on excess, on over-filled hearts filled with misery, poetry, and song. If she had one weakness, it was that she thrived on sensate experience and empirical knowledge—that weakness she suspected was at the root of the call that shackled her mindlessly to the will of the long dead mage-lords, leaving her mind lost and empty for centuries, leaving her starving and terrified once awakened in a world that only knew her captors by legend and myth and scattered ruin.

Her memories had returned with a stupefying crash. Returned, that is, save for her initial call and capture and her time imprisoned. The shackles had appeared the moment she had left that ruined tower, a constant reminder that while her captors had long since vanished into legend, her captivity had not truly ended, had merely changed form. But she had scrambled up and away and fed her mind as quickly as she could, feasting on songs and tales from travelers—at first by force when she, ravished by need, captured all manner of folk, of all races, with her bare hands and interrogated them for their stories. The ravishing need slowly lessened and she once again began to master herself, master patience and civility. She no longer kidnapped travelers and terrorized them. She approached them with caution and humility and talked to them. Most were still terrified of her, but many would talk with her around campfires and tavern hearths, especially if she paid them with the coin she had taken from her prisoners back when the ravishing need had consumed her.

Eventually, she discovered libraries and the university at Drilithae and decades passed as the vellum pages, some unread for centuries, turned with careful touch in flickering candlelight until the Desadian Chaos changed the face of the empire once again.

She opened her eyes, still sitting at the edge of a cliff overlooking an unknown, alien beach hidden by dense fog, the distant tendrils of the city rising behind her like jagged, jumbled shadows. She sat without her pack, her armor, her bladed staff, most of her supplies, her journals, her navigation tools. She shivered.

She felt the sun go down, felt the air on the cliff grow cooler. She heard the buzz of insects and ignored them. She felt the touch of the jasmine-scented breeze, breathed it in, released it.

Despite the exhilaration of being on another alien world, despite the anger at still being shackled, despite the longing and loss, as the sun set and the temperature began to drop, a single thought slipped in and made her sit straight up, back tight.

She had no way of making tea.

The chuckle began low, in her chest. It became full-throated laughter that shook her shoulders, brought tears to her eyes, and caused her wounds to ache. Finally, she turned and looked over her shoulder at the distant lights of the city. She knew answers would be found there, although quite possibly not the answers she wanted. She sighed. The lights of the city danced and blinked, but their beckoning was more like the come-along of a pretty, painted whore, promising respite but not resolution.

Ashakarahad stood and began to look for a better camping spot under the pale, pink light of the three fat moons, all strangely full and seemingly flying in formation, that had begun to crawl through the night sky.

Idsiyushti was digging in her garden, the aches and pains from her wounds ebbing and flowing like the ministrations of a tender, yet determined lover. Like Marrah, which made Idsiyushti smile. The sun was hot, the air wet and thick, her body sweating beneath her thin dress, moisture pooling at the small of her back. She welcomed the warmth with an abandon that bordered on manic. She pushed against the waves of pain, which turned to pleasure and back again with a suggestive whisper that, at times, made her clamp her thighs together.

Exactly like Marrah.

Her magic was steadily returning—she'd lit all of her candles last night with a single snap of her fingers. She'd infused a poultice for Sek. She'd only felt the slightest hint of dizziness during the infusion, and she'd welcomed that dizziness as she did the pain now. She would not be defeated.

Marrah had finally come to visit and stayed the night—taking the poultice back to the Grendl's when she left in the late morning. Marrah had looked guilty and burdened and tended to Idsiyushti with the dedication of someone trying desperately to overcompensate. Idsiyushti hadn't minded. She'd missed Marrah's touch, her smell, her laugh.

They'd shared gatflower and the crystal-infused whiskey and touched each other with a caution that dissolved into frenzied abandon. In the morning, Marrah had sheepishly promised to not stay away too long. Then she shoved two fingers into Idsiyushti's still-wet cunt and pumped up and down, her arm a piston, like she was working a pump handle, like her guilt and anger had distilled into a single, harsh moment that made muscles ache and tendons stiffen and Idsiyushti scream and gush. Marrah had laughed, risen, and left all in a single motion as Idsiyushti drifted back to sleep.

Does Idsiyushti know about you and me?" Jonath asked. Marrah wiped his spent, slick cock with a rough rag. She looked up at him with dark, shadowed eyes.

"We don't usually talk about my work." She was still dressed. Jonath preferred her that way—her dress lifted high, her tits spilling from a loosened bodice. He liked to make her lie back, legs spread, and fuck her, make her drip onto the underside of her own dress, which was stained with patterns that always made his blood race. He knew he couldn't be the only man in town who wanted his whores to stay dressed, but it reminded him of times not nearly far enough away, of violent back alleys and the edges of the military camps, close to the steaming latrine pits.

He pulled away and walked, half-naked, over to the tiny room's single shelf. He drank whiskey from the jug he'd put there, the liquor burning his throat. In the room next door, a low, male voice was grunting as the sound of a lash cracked. From the sound of the curses and insults hurled before and after each crack, each grunt, Caeri was wielding the lash. For many reasons, Caeri was considered the house favorite, but Jonath always wanted Marrah. Caeri was flame-haired and pale-skinned and too foreign, where Marrah was pretty and dark, with the blood of the swamp in her veins.

Marrah was watching him. He put down the bottle and pulled his trousers on. "What?"

"I was with her last night," Marrah said. "She's healing but she's weak. The rock, when it exploded, should have killed her. And probably you too. But—" Her voice broke. She looked away. Then she wiped her eyes and tucked her tits back into her bodice. Jonath was almost sorry to see them go, but the sense of dread and tension that he had hoped to fuck away, at least for time, seemed to be wafting in from the window overlooking the square. He buckled on his belt and pulled on his boots.

Marrah turned back. "She shouldn't have been out there."

"Of course she should," Jonath said. "She's a witch. Our witch. I needed her out there."

"That's not—I know. She's just—I worry about her, that's all. Maybe too much. I think it's why I don't visit her enough." This last was almost a whisper and Jonath wondered if she realized he was still in the room.

He cleared his throat. "She's a little brash, sure, but she can take care of herself."

"She caused the stone to explode!" Marrah hissed.

Jonath rubbed his forehead. He grabbed his battered hat off the floor. "I don't think she did it on purpose." He winced at the pains he still felt. He frowned at the thought that they still hadn't found Ashakarahad, at the fact that Marrah was probably right. He didn't, however, know what else to say, so he put coins on the shelf, grabbed the whiskey jug and left.

****

There's been no sign of Ashakarahad," Jonath said. "We have no idea what happened to her after the explosion."

The night was hot, hotter than previous nights, and tempers in town were close to flaring. So Jonath had called a meeting of the closest thing the town had to a council. Grendl was still angry that he'd let himself be convinced to let them meet in the coolness of the tavern's basement rather than in the too-hot courthouse. Oil lanterns were lit and kegs were overturned for chairs. Shadows were chased into corners that smelled of dampness and lingering chill. Idsiyushti, upon descending the stairs from the kitchen above, had wondered out loud why they didn't all live underground.

"Water seepage," Grendl had explained. It had taken him nearly half a year to shore up the walls of the basement and make them as watertight as possible using dwarven stonework. Even then, the swamp water that crawled along through the soil like a slithering snake still found a way in.

Now Grendl, lone thumb hooked into his belt, leaned against one of the basement's upright supports, watching Jonath and Marin and Jak with suspicion and guilt. The town had become a powder keg almost overnight and here he was, worried about the local law and the competition getting a good look at his stock. It, all of it, made him want to laugh.

Drag, the blacksmith, sat with his dirty hands wrapped around a heavy pewter mug of ale he'd brought down from the common room above. Grendl had refused to tap a keg then and there in the basement, feeling guilty again but not wanting to start a trend. In the past, the square had served as a sort of town hall until Marin had convinced them to build the courthouse a few years back. People, anyone who wanted in on the conversation, or just wanted to listen, would sit on the courthouse benches, or out front on the courthouse porch with the doors wide open, or lean against the wall, beneath a window, smoking, drinking, nodding their heads. But now the courthouse was too hot and the square looked like the insane love-child of a traveling circus and a drunken merchant bazaar.

"What're we gonna do then?" Drag asked. "So the demon's gone, good riddance if you ask me, but now what? The soldiers're gone. The gobs are dead — didn't even know they were alive to begin with, livin' out in the cane. So you got a magic stone explodin' out there in the cane too. My business is boomin' but I can't get my boys out from under the skirts of Grendl's whores, and I damned well know when troubles aimin' to smack us good. You can smell it, feel it out there, like when Mackasl gets to drinkin' and then preachin' the old ways right up in your face."

"The soldiers lied about killing the goblins," Jak said. The atmosphere in the basement had tensed considerably when Jak had entered. He wasn't usually considered part of their rudimentary council, but Jonath had asked him to join them just the same. Drag wouldn't sit near Jak, and Ned, Ten, and Zrik, the owners of the mercantile, muttered that they'd punch Jak if he so much as looked at them funny, although Grendl was certain that Ten was no stranger to Jak's late-night entertainment, if the stories were true. Marin harrumphed at them and Jonath told them to sit down and be quiet. Jak merely smiled politely, blowing a kiss at Ned and winking at Drag. Idsiyushti glared and let tiny flames dance along her fingertips, which cut the muttering and posturing faster than anything. Meanwhile, the others gathered in the cellar—Set, Relint the cobbler, Wil the cooper, Orin the head of the four-man carpenter union—looked as if they were trying to fade into the stonework itself.

"The soldiers are gone," Zrik said. "Who cares if they lied. Killin' gobs may be a crime but who're you going to arrest, constable? They're *soldiers* and they're *gone*."

Jonath cleared his throat. "Well, it's true. The soldiers are gone and the goblins are dead and the strange obelisk—"

"The what?"

"Standing stone, Wil," Marin said.

"The strange standing stone exploded," Jonath continued. "We took apart the altar the goblins had built near the stone and burned what we could of anything we found in that clearing the goblins were living in. There was no sign of either undead or trolls—which the soldiers said they had originally been hunting."

"You certain?" Ten asked.

Grendl cleared his throat. "I know trolls and I know undead. No sign. Trust me." Ten and his brothers looked thoughtfully at Grendl and, as one, scowled.

"So, why does it feel like my town is getting ready to tear itself apart?" Jonath asked. "We should be getting ready for the harvest festival. Folks should be out working their farms or fishing—"

"Making whiskey," someone said.

"My point is that the entire town has become like an old boil waiting to erupt!"

Pointedly, and for no obvious reason, heads turned towards Jak. "Now wait a minute," he said. "Why in the abyss would this be my fault?"

Idsiyushti was on her bare feet then, shadows cast by the lanterns dancing on her face. "If you actually think this is Jak's fault, you're all fools!" The dancing shadows seemed alive and angry. Heads quickly turned away, shoulders flinched.

"She's right," Marin said. Idsiyushti glared but took a deep breath and stepped back. "Before the soldiers came, the nights in town were peaceful. Folk came in to shop, share stories, tobacco, liquor, a joke, a handshake. Kids played together on the street until their mamas called them home."

"Then the constable scared everyone half to death," Set said. "Runnin' around tellin' folk to come into town because the big, bad soldiers and their monsters were out there in the deep dark. Meanin' no offense, constable, but it seems to me this is all your doin'."

The accusation hung heavily in the air.

"You ever been to war, Set?" Jonath asked. "You ever see soldiers who have been wounded, or who are dragging their wounded companions around on horseback? You ever seen what a desperate soldier can do? Will do?"

The candlemaker paled and shook his head. "You know I've never done anything other than militia work, constable."

"Around here," Grendl said, "militia work doesn't compare to soldiering. I don't care how many drunken fistfights you get into."

"Grendl and Jonath are right," Drag said. "The militia hasn't seen any real action since before Skex became constable. I was there for that. Back when the Winalls were still holdin' parties up at their place and had gobs workin' their fields."

"Out at Kree's farm," Marin said. "That was a terrible business."

113

"Terrible and bloody," Drag said. "Amazin' what a big family'd do to protect one of their kin."

"Protecting a known rapist and child-killer," Marin said.

Drag frowned and nodded. He took another sip of his ale, eyes distant and clouded.

"All right," Zrik said. "We get the picture. But get this picture! Folks're stealing right in front of us, tryin' to walk right out the store, plain as day! We stay up at night to watch the place in case someone breaks in!"

"I told folks to come stay in town," Jonath said. "I don't deny that. But this, this is something I wasn't expecting. So I want to expand the militia. Have folks form into scouting parties, go out, out of town into the swamp, see what's out there. Put 'em to work, get their minds thinking about something other than sitting around and causing trouble."

"Why not just tell 'em to go home?" Orin asked.

Jonath looked at Grendl, who shrugged. "Because I'm not sure I'm convinced there isn't any actual danger out there."

"How's sending folks out there supposed to put their minds at ease then?" Ten asked.

"It isn't." The voice was Jak's. He was sitting, legs crossed, studying Jonath, fingering the hilt of a slim knife sheathed in one of his boots. "It's to get folks ready. Am I right, constable?"

Jonath cleared his throat. "Yeah. Jak's right."

****

Idsiyushti returned to the clearing in the sugarcane when the moon was high and the swamp was alive with night sounds. The wind was hot, blowing the trees beyond the cane into a waving dance high above their thick, tangled, exposed roots. The burned remains of the goblins and the clearing stank. She ignored the stench as she made her still-aching way under the glow of a summoned puff of light that clung to her left shoulder with claws that were cold and piercing. The stained basalt altar was no longer there—broken apart by order of Jonath of the Battlefield—but she wasn't interested in the altar. It was the standing stone that had given the goblins whatever it is that they thought they'd found in that doomed clearing.

Idsiyushti stood barefoot where the altar had been, shards of rock and splintered bits of cane digging into the soles of her feet. The wind whipped the cane into a frenzy, a slithering whisper surrounding her. The hem of her thin dress joined the dance, as did her hair, dark tendrils reaching out for a hold on something that she could not see.

No one knew she'd come to the clearing. She'd left the meeting in Grendl's basement and started on her way back to her hut. But at the edge of town, despite her fading aches and pains, she'd changed her mind. The night was thick, and the light and noise from the square were like a strange, haunting melody that seemed so incredibly out of place. She glanced back but all she could see of the square beyond the small houses and shacks was a bright, flickering glow. Marrah was supposed to be working at Grendl's. Idsiyushti had thought about staying when the meeting was over. Even thought about trying to pay for a tumble with Marrah upstairs on one of the shapeless straw mattresses. But she hadn't. Instead, at the edge of town, Idsiyushti had decided to go to the goblin clearing.

Now, the whispering of the cane was so loud that she couldn't hear the swamp. She closed her eyes and let the whispering take her, let it wrap around her like a blanket, building from a rapid, deep whisper to a roaring shout, a demonic wail that made her think of Ashakarahad.

She curled her toes around sharp stone shards and gasped. Power built around her, crawled up through the shards, her thighs, her cunt, her stomach, tits, shot out of her mouth with a roar that she couldn't hear but tore her throat. She balled her fists. She grasped for the power, felt pieces of shattered cane whip past and around her, cutting her anew, felt her hair twisted and pulled, felt her dress rip in a mockery of the explosion that had left her torn and naked.

The roar was white-hot and building, a rage threatening to burst from her heart, through her ribs, a tumult that threatened to uproot the cane completely and fling it into the dark sky, showering the distant town. Her throat was raw with the scream, yet she was lost in its grip, lost in the tearing and rending of the roaring wind. Her nails cut into her palms. The shards beneath her feet cut as well. Her mind reeled. Colors swirled beneath her closed eyelids. Magic poured through her, twisted all the aches and pains from the explosion and rearranged them into something new, something alien, desperate, hungry, forgotten.

She tried to shape words of power out of the scream, tried to shape the roar and wild magic of the wind. Slowly, with a pain that was far deeper than even the pain of the shattering stone, a pain deep and hidden and rising, clawing its way from the soles of her feet up to her lungs, she wrested control. Aware of the blood from the holes her nails had dug in her palms and from where the stone shards had scored her bare feet, Idsiyushti called on that blood, ignoring the distant memories that shouted warnings in the voices of the long-gone fey and the silver-haired elf.

Overflowing, Idsiyushti shattered, just as the standing stone had, shattered and broke and left nothing but a blasted hole surrounded by broken cane and jagged remnants of herself.

The voices that remained, whispering in her head, were fluid and guttural and utterly alien. The presence that remained was ancient. And for a moment, she was somewhere else, in some other time. She was standing in a dark, dank room that was musty and cold and not unlike Grendl's basement. But the stones around her were worn and ruined. There was no light but she could see her breath cloud before her face. Her feet hurt with the cold. There was something out there in the darkness. Something on the floor. She stepped closer. In the light of her breath, she saw intricate lines and runes etched into the stone. But the thing beyond the etchings remained dark, brooding, sinister. Idsiyushti blinked. The alien voices faded and she stepped forward, eyes on the inky blackness beyond the etched stones. She reached out, fingers shaking, and touched something solid and shimmering, felt it break.

Then she was back. The hot wind had ceased, the cane no longer dancing, roaring. The scream tearing from her throat tumbled to nothing, leaving her sore and thirsty. Idsiyushti opened her eyes and blinked away tears. The summoned puffball that had gripped her shoulder with cold claws was gone, the darkness around her thick and black. Gasping for air, she forced her aching fingers to straighten. The pain in her palms was almost soothing. Idsiyushti sobbed twice and then let herself laugh out loud. Her head spun, but the dizziness passed. Somehow, her thin dress still clung to her body.

Power still seeped through her, snapping, feverish. She used it to summon another light puff and sent it floating ahead, singing to itself in a way the previous puffball had not. The cane field was torn and broken, looking like a monsoon had passed through, only without the rain and the mud. Idsiyushti could see the goblin clearing through the remains of the cane, see a bright glow hanging over it. As she carefully stepped through the debris on bleeding feet, Idsiyushti watched the glow descend and land in the clearing. Her breath, through her torn throat, was short, reluctant. She was greeted with a barrage of voices shouting questions and orders. In a rush, the dim glow went out and it was then that she remembered that she'd made it past the shimmering barrier in that cold room but hadn't been able to see into the blackness beyond.

The falkr descended on the town square with a screeching fanfare, riding glowing nimbuses of light that scattered the townsfolk and tents like a broom scattering motes of dust. Panic ensued and more than one cookfire was trampled and kicked, setting alight dry wood and cloth. Whiskey casks split and exploded. Screams shot through the night air, chased by the dancing lights of the spreading fires, which cast hellish shadows on the buildings nearby.

The falkr were fury-born, dressed only in steel-shod boots and gauntlets, heads hidden beneath ornate helms, tits ritually scarred, pubic hair shaved into stylized sigils that denoted rank. They wielded two-handed swords, blue flame licking along the blades, never quenching as long as the swords were drawn. They were the shock troops of the Imperial Army — mercenary hold-overs from the vanquished elven emperors. Terror was their ally. One of them, the tallest, fiercest, had her sword sheathed across her back and cradled Idsiyushti, unconscious and tiny by comparison, easily in her arms.

The townsfolk scattered, screaming, into alleys and side streets. Two of the falkr used their enchanted blades to call down the breath of the elements to douse the fires that were starting to rage. They let the whiskey casks burn.

Jonath of the Battlefield ran out of his too-hot office, raised his crossbow and nearly put a bolt through the left breast of the falkr leader, stopping only when he saw she was carrying Idsiyushti. He stood gaping at the unconscious witch, at the falkr, at the fact that he'd nearly shot a military officer.

The falkr stopped screeching and the square descended into ragged wheeze punctuated by the barking of scattered dogs and the cries and wails of the townsfolk hiding in the shadows and alleys.

Grendl kicked open the door of his tavern, ax in hand, and shouted, "What the fuck is going on?" He saw the falkr and stopped. He stared for a moment and then spat into the churned dirt beyond tavern porch. Wide-eyed militia members, harried and dirty, pikes held in shaking hands, rushed out of the alleys. They too stopped and stared and several threw down their pikes and cowered.

The fires flickered one final time and then died as the falkr magic touched the square again and then fled into the night in a susurration that ran chills up and down Jonath's spine. He lowered the crossbow, eyes still on Idsiyushti. The falkr leader saw him, saw his sash and tarnished chain of office. Lightly, with an air of leadership that would not allow questions, would not allow defeat, she walked to the base of Jonath's porch.

"I am Sigiswinth," the falkr said, her voice terrible and glorious behind the faceplate of her helm. "I command these sisters. I have your witch."

"I can see that," Jonath said. "And you nearly burned my town to the ground."

The falkr leader stood up straighter at that, scarred breasts highlighted by the glow of one of the whiskey fires that had been left to burn. Idsiyushti shifted in her arms, murmured something, but did not wake. She looked almost childlike and innocent despite her dirty, torn dress and her bloody hands and feet. There was an intricate manacle attached to her left wrist. Jonath's heart sank.

"We have attended to the threat, as you can plainly see," Sigiswinth said.

Jonath forced himself to look around at the debris of the town square. Faces, scared and angry, were peering from the shadows of the alleys and the windows overlooking the entire scene. Jonath removed the bolt from the crossbow, set the crossbow to lean against his office doorframe. "What is this about? What have you done with Idsiyushti?"

"Your witch is under arrest," Sigiswinth said. The other falkr, swords still drawn, blades still crawling with blue fire, moved into formation behind their leader. "But first she needs a surgeon."

"She is our surgeon!" Grendl shouted from across the square. The falkr turned to regard him.

Sigiswinth turned back to Jonath and said, "Then my sisters will tend to her." With no further command, two of the falkr stepped forward, sheathing their swords, flames extinguishing, and took Idsiyushti from their leader's arms. Jonath started to step down from the porch, eyes on Idsiyushti, but the falkr leader held up her now-empty hands. "We shall speak, constable. Now."

Jonath stopped short, fought the urge to reach for the dagger sheathed at his hip. "Fine. But first I need to make sure Idsi is properly tended to."

"No, we talk now," Sigiswinth said. She crossed her gauntleted arms across her breasts.

Jonath heard his teeth grinding. "It can wait."

"No, it can't."

Jonath balled his fists. Why the fuck had they arrested Idsiyushti? "Why can't it? The goblins are dead and the soldiers who massacred them are long gone! And Idsiyushti had nothing to do with either!"

For a moment, the falkr said nothing. Then, "We've been hunting the soldiers you speak of for some time. It is a shame that they stopped to murder more goblins. But it isn't a surprise since they have been murdering goblins for several months now, always slipping out of reach after each attack."

Jonath blinked.

Sigiswinth continued, "But your witch confessed to us, confessed that she and her demonic servant not only accessed the obelisk but drew enough power to destroy it!"

Jonath's teeth stopped grinding and his blood ran cold.

Sigiswinth took the steps to the top of the porch two at a time. She jabbed a metal-sheathed finger into Jonath's sternum. "Where is the witch's demon?"

The town square looked like a mad, violent, strangely bloodless battle had swept through it. Townsfolk moved through the debris of torn-down tents, scattered belongings, fire-touched cloth and wood, and the still-glowing embers of burned-up whiskey casks. They moved like sleepwalkers moments before waking, or, more accurately, like sleepers just awakened to discover their entire world had been stripped clean, bones scattered and lost. In the main room of the tavern, only a few lost souls sat and drank, Chrona tending the bar, listless and exhausted. Upstairs, one of the girls sobbed but Grendl knew it wasn't at the hands of a customer. There were no customers upstairs, not anymore.

Across the square, in the hot, pink light of the callous dawn, Jonath stood on his porch, angry, barely holding himself together as far as Grendl could tell. Marin sat in a wooden chair nearby, looking older than Grendl remembered, older than even on the worst nights, when the judge needed help up the stairs to fall asleep in one of the girl's arms, dick snuggled limp and warm, otherwise unused, in her hand. Five falkr stood in a tight semicircle, bare asses to the stale, hot breeze of the early morning. Their swords were sheathed now, but they kept their helmets on, even their leader, who stood in the center of the semicircle. Jonath had waved Grendl over some time ago, but the barkeep had merely shaken his head.

Grendl had no love for falkr. Sure, they were pleasant to look at, mostly-naked females in random, revealing pieces of armor that Grendl had never been able to figure the value of when it came to protection in combat. Their swords were enchanted, well-made, rumored to be ancient dwarf-forged blades, given to ancestral falkr by some long-vanished elf warlord. But the falkr were haughty and arrogant—it was even said that they raped dying men on the field of battle, but Grendl, despite his dislike, his hatred even, figured that rumor to be nothing but bullshit and twisted fantasy. They were ill-clad warrior queens who loved bloodshed and violence, but Grendl's dislike stemmed from none of that. In fact, he grudgingly respected them for their prowess and arrogance and their flaunting of their vital parts in the midst of battle. No, Grendl hated them because where they went the falkr brought with them misfortune and a fanatic love of outdated yet whimsically-shifting Imperial law, a love that was blinded by their own lack of actual humanity, their lack of natural mortality.

When Grendl had been appointed constable back east, he'd been the first dwarf to be granted the honor in the now-human empire, a result of actions deemed heroic during the white-noise of the Desadian Chaos, reparations for nobly losing an arm while fighting for what turned out to be the winning side. His ward had been small, mostly barbaric human tribes who had never left the eastern forests and barely knew that the rest of their race had advanced out of barbarism centuries earlier, that one of their own now sat on and threw tantrums from a throne that was becoming increasingly irrelevant. But there were a couple of small, walled cities in his ward as well, relatively modern, the inhabitants viewing their barbaric brethren as nothing more than ill-mannered, ill-clad cattle. To make matters worse, trolls and the dead called the ward home too. The trolls, strangely intelligent, were hunted by imperial decree because Malthius the First, newly minted emperor, thought they were ugly and terrifying and in possession of valuable land. So the trolls formed guerilla groups, organized resistances that plagued the human tribes and the human cities.

The dead were vastly less intelligent things that the emperor decreed protected because, when he was a boy practicing with wooden swords instead of going to sleep, a pretty ghost had walked through the wall of his bedchamber, smiled at him, and touched his penis with a cold, deft hand.

So, Grendl hunted trolls and protected the dead from poaching by humans, barbaric or otherwise. And when one of the barbaric tribal leaders in his ward lost a daughter to a pack of ravenous ghouls, that tribe went to war, unsanctioned, against the nearest dead. The world came crashing down on Grendl's head and in the white-hot middle of the conflagration, the falkr had descended and laid waste to the human tribe—and to several members of Grendl's ax who had tried to stand in the way of the falkr and protect a group of children. In the end, imperial law had been upheld, without restraint, without question, in broad, bloody strokes. Even the suicide of the human tribal leader didn't stop the massacre. The tribe was all but wiped out, the survivors forcibly relocated and ordered by distant magistrates to make reparations to any undead that had the intelligence to understand what was happening. Grendl had nearly come to blows with the leader of the falkr after the massacre, but she had simply flown out of his reach, riding a glowing nimbus, sword alight, laughing. And then the falkr were gone and the human dead remained, some joining the undead, who took over the tribal lands and twisted them to their bidding.

Grendl had traveled to the relevant magistrates, fifty leagues distant, but he was given a cursory audience and his words fell on deaf ears. Despite his much-talked-about victory with Sphinx a year earlier against the trolls who had sacked one of the human cities in his ward, the magistrates were not only angry at Grendl's inability to contain the human tribesmen, which had caused the imperial army to send the falkr to clean up the mess — flying, almost literally, over their magisterially-wigged heads — they were furious that a one-armed dwarf had been given the job of constable in the first place, trolls and legendary elf notwithstanding.

Grendl, himself angry and shaking, had stormed from the magistrates' office. In the hall beyond, by some not-quite-coincidence, Grendl met the falkr leader who had ordered the massacre of the human tribe. She laughed again. Smirked. Only this time she didn't fly away when Grendl punched her in the mouth. Bleeding, she attacked, sword drawn and alight with blue flame. The magistrates' hall rang with the blows of her sword on Grendl's ax. Other falkr pulled them apart and the magistrates stepped from their chambers, black robes twisted tight, wigs askew, and ordered Grendl arrested. The emperor, disappointed and confused, had ordered Grendl released from prison but had stripped him of his rank and office. Not long after, some minister somewhere had convinced Malthius the First that the pretty ghost who'd touched his cock had most likely been a bad custard eaten at dinner and that the dead should not be protected from slaughter after all.

The days and nights beneath the orange sun and the trio of pink moons seemed longer than days and nights in the swamp. Ashakarahad quickly lost the sense of how long she'd been walking, hunting, camping along the rim of the jagged cliff that overlooked the crimson ocean. The spires and lights of the city haunted the horizon, never closer, never farther away, never-ending, regardless of how far or long she walked. She ate the rest of her jerky and began setting small snares, catching what looked like furred reptiles whose thin meat tasted of juniper and salt no matter how she cooked it. She drank from trickles of water that ran clear and cold, despite running down towards the crimson-colored waves below.

She found heavy-shod tracks but saw no other sign of the black-armored canoids who had attacked her on the beach. She also found gullies that ran down to the sand and she'd climbed down to scout, but each time the beach looked vastly, terrifyingly different than it had above, as if the gullies were portals to beaches on completely different worlds. Once or twice she camped on those beaches, weapons close at hand, but other than the whisper of sand in the wind and the sounds of small animals that she never saw, there was nothing.

It was on the fourth or fifth or, perhaps, even tenth night beneath the trio of pink moons who followed the exact same course regardless of the day, week, or maybe even year, that Ashakarahad began to hear voices in the darkness. She had been camping on the ridge of the cliff and when she'd first heard the voices, she sat silently, alert, watching the night, seeing nothing. The voices simply stopped a couple of hours later—they didn't fade away to the left or to the right or towards the city, they simply ceased.

In the morning, she found no new tracks. She eyed the next cold trickle of water she came across with suspicion, and she did not trap, cook, and eat the furry reptiles the next day for fear that either the water, the furry reptiles, or both, might contain some agent that was affecting her mind or, at the very least, her hearing. But that night, the voices came again, simply starting out of the darkness, not approaching from any particular direction. Hours later, they ceased as they had the night before. Ashakarahad sat silently, motionless, hands gripping the ax-like weapon. She'd listened to the voices but could not understand what they were saying. The words and tones seemed hauntingly, frustratingly familiar, precise, delivered with purpose, but she seemed incapable of putting the words and tones together into any sort of meaningful exchange.

The next day she again went without water and food. She was weaker for it, slower, but the voices didn't seem to have any intention of approaching her camp—assuming they even knew about it or her—so she decided to take a chance that they wouldn't attack, that they weren't planning on preying on her weakness.

She followed a runnel down to a beach that was golden and lavender-streaked in the minutes between the setting of the orange sun behind the spires of the city and the steady, unchanging rise of the pink moons. Ashakarahad made her camp on the beach, head spinning slightly from hunger and thirst, but she sat and breathed and focused, letting the dizziness, the hunger, and thirst slip away as best she could. The voices started again, echoing off the cliff walls, bolstered by the waves crashing out past a narrow shoal she'd seen just as she'd begun her climb down to the beach, when the strangely-no-longer-orange sun still offered a little light. Ashakarahad stood, trying not to shake, ax-like weapon at the ready. But the voices continued indifferently, never approaching, never receding, uttering things that were half-familiar and frustrating. Slowly, she sat back down. The voices continued for the usual span of time and then, once again, stopped.

Maybe it was the hunger and thirst, maybe her mind was finally beginning to break, but for the first time since she fought the canoid things on that first alien beach, the invisible shackles began to pulse and ache and weigh her down.

She climbed back to the top of the cliff and set some snares and caught breakfast. She made a fire and cooked the trio of furry reptiles and ate them with relish. Then she found a clear stream not far away and laid on her belly, stained shirt soaking up nearly as much water as she could get into her mouth. She rolled over and lay on her back, stared at the climbing nimbus of the orange-again sun. She fell into a fitful sleep and awoke sometime around what she guessed was late afternoon, soaked again from having rolled partially back into the stream.

She set more snares and cooked more furry reptiles. She now had a collection of pelts that she dried over the fire, thinking of sewing together the rudiments of a blanket. When the sun set once more and the trio of pink moons rose like they were locked to each other, she stood, tucked the furs into her belt, grabbed the ax-like weapon and waited. When the voices started, coming out of the darkness as if she'd suddenly emerged from a suffocating deafness in the midst of a bustling marketplace, Ashakarahad stepped forward and called out. The voices ceased. Then they started again, changing cadence and tone, more rapid now. For once, they receded into the night. Ashakarahad followed and the invisible shackles throbbed, painful and urgent.

Idsiyushti woke with a piercing headache. She'd been in and out of consciousness for hours, days, weeks? She couldn't tell. Each time she crawled into seeming wakefulness, the headache slapped her back down. Her bedding seemed distant, confining, her magic gone, a dim spark that flickered in and out but would not ignite. She could smell herself, unwashed, covered in some sort of reeking herbal tincture. Her body ached, the pain dim, confusing, nauseating—at least until the distant, confining blankets and the cloying herbs joined the headache to sink her back into tormented nothingness.

This time, however, under the hammering of the headache, Idsiyushti stayed awake. She felt the oppression of the twisted bedding and exhausted herself even further trying to kick free. She could still smell herself and whatever herbal concoction had been rubbed on her skin. Her body was stiff, ungainly. The low ceiling hung above her but the cottage was dark, the only light trickling in through the heavy drapes she'd made from bolts of cloth she'd picked up at the mercantile, trading for a selection of hangover cures and powders to be applied to whiskey-flaccid cocks during visits to Grendl's girls.

Her left wrist felt heavy and she touched it with her free hand, felt metal and leather and was confused. She held her wrist up before her eyes, squinting against the pain. She could barely make out the thing, but it looked like an intricate gauntlet of ancient design.

"The falkr put that on you when they brought you here after tending to your wounds."

Idsiyushti flinched and tried to sit up, the headache's icy talons raking her spine, burning coldly all the way down to her toes. She gasped, only managed to roll over.

Marrah sat in the darkness, on a low stool beside the table Idsiyushti used to cut herbs and grind powders. She was framed by wreaths of hanging, drying fronds, leaves, flowers, cloves of garlic, a single, decaying rabbit that had been rubbed down with an oil that kept it from stinking up the cottage while its maggoty flesh melted off its bones. Marrah was dressed in a loose blouse and skirt—not what she would normally wear at Grendl's, not a barmaid-whore getup meant to be removed in whatever manner by whichever asshole was paying to use her body and time. Nor was she dressed the way she did when she went out to Jak's place and danced and laughed and kissed Idsiyushti under the hot, wet moon, while the rest of the queerfolk drank and sang and carried on until the monsoons hit and they were forced to stay hidden in town, the hot rains battering shutters and roofs, churning the streets into sucking mud.

Idsiyushti couldn't remember when she last saw Marrah. She tried to think…. After the stone exploded. That was it. Beneath the vice of the headache, her heart skipped a beat. She tried to smile. Her blood often raced when she was with Marrah, their kisses electric. Sometimes they'd share crystal, liquor, gatflower then orgasm so hard together they swore they could hear Jak cheering them on from behind his bar nearly two miles away.

Idsiyushti blushed. Passion, embarrassment, and guilt sent goosebumps along her pain-wracked, dirty skin.

"Hi," she said.

"Hi," Marrah said, a smile touching her dark eyes, dim in the shadows. Marrah kept her brown hair short—not man-short because some customers liked to pull it when they were fucking her and others thought hair that was too short was too queer. Now her hair framed her round face in such a way that she looked like a shadowy ghost peeking through the even more-shadowed wall.

The headache, like a massive wave that had receded in hideous mockery, came crashing back. Idsiyushti moaned and brought both hands to her head. Marrah was at her side then, hands touching, trying to soothe.

Idsiyushti looked inside herself, tried to see past the pain, could barely make out the dim spark of her magic. There was no way she could use sorcery to force the headache away.

As if reading her thoughts, Marrah whispered, "It's the bracelet. That's what Grendl said. He said it's the bracelet that the falkr put on you."

"It hurts," Idsiyushti managed. "My head."

"I know. Grendl said he thought you would be in pain. Because of the bracelet."

"And my magic is gone. I can't reach it!" Idsiyushti felt herself starting to panic. Marrah was a sudden weight that was holding her down—Idsiyushti groped for the comfort and safety there, the familiarity.

"That's the bracelet too!"

It took several moments for Marrah's words to sink in but when they did, all she could manage was a weak, "What?"

Marrah stretched herself out and sank down onto the sleeping pallet, wrapped Idsiyushti in her arms. Despite the pain, Idsiyushti felt the spark of arousal. Marrah's rough blouse scratched, caused sweet pains beneath the wail of the headache. Frustration and loss suddenly welled up and Idsiyushti began to sob.

Marrah kissed her cheeks, shushed her with gentle whispers. Marrah's legs, beneath her skirt, wrapped themselves around Idsiyushti. Marrah's breath smelled

135

of beer and onions but the scent made Idsiyushti happy despite the pain, the panic, and the tears.

"Why am I wearing this?"

"The falkr put it on you. Jonath protested, grew really angry when he saw it, but he couldn't get to you—the falkr had you. They looked so fierce, their swords glow with fire and they don't wear any clothes!"

"Ow!"

Marrah lowered her excited voice to a whisper, "Sorry. But the falkr brought you here when Marin told them where you lived. They were going to put a guard on you too, but, I don't know, Jonath convinced them not to somehow. I don't know much, just what Grendl told me. He was out on the porch, watching. I was upstairs but Sek was crying so bad, Caeri and I couldn't get her to stop. So I went and stood behind the bar with Chrona, but it was hard to see out the windows."

"Why am I wearing this thing?" Idsiyushti's own voice was rising, sending painful echoes through her own head.

"I don't know!" Marrah hugged her tighter. "Grendl said it was something to keep you from doing magic. The falkr rescued you, that's what it looked like. They brought you back to town—you were bleeding! But I don't know why they put the bracelet on you."

Idsiyushti blinked. Then she remembered and tried to look at her hands in the dim light, could see only puckered scars that added more aches when she balled her fists.

"The falkr tended to you," Marrah said. "I don't know what they did, don't know if it was magic or what. But they had that bracelet on you and they brought you back home."

"Thank you for coming," Idsiyushti finally said. She closed her eyes and tried to stop crying.

"Of course—I was really worried about you. Grendl gave me some time off. He knows about you and me. I'm not sure he likes it, but what I do in my free time...well, anyway, he saw what happened, saw what the falkr did to you and came back inside. He saw me and walked right up and explained about the bracelet. Then he said that I had the night off and that I was to come and watch over you. He said that you would be really confused and in pain when you woke up. Because of the bracelet."

"How did he know?" Idsiyushti turned her head and wiped her tears on Marrah's scratchy blouse. Marrah leaned forward and kissed her again.

"I don't know. Grendl just knows things. He's been places. I think he was in the Chaos—how he lost his arm. He seems to know a lot about the falkr."

"But why would they do this?" Idsiyushti heard herself wail.

Marrah pulled back as if slapped. Then she drew close and held Idsiyushti tight once more. "I don't know," she said, sniffing. Idsiyushti felt Marrah's tears join her own.

The voices seemed to veer towards the distant city, then away, never moving directly to or from, always at some angle or curve. But the city covered the horizon, so there was no way to tell how the voices truly moved. Ashakarahad merely followed. The voices grew fainter and louder at irregular intervals, as if fleeing and then returning to make certain she was still there. The pink, triple-moon-lit night deepened, grew hotter than it had been closer to the edge of the cliff and the crimson sea. Other sounds joined the rising and falling voices, night sounds, animal sounds, what Ashakarahad thought might be mechanical sounds.

Then the voices swirled around her, like dust whipped up in a circling wind. She stumbled, dropped the ax-like weapon. She spun in place. The voices buffeted her, wrapped her in invisible tethers, dragged her down. The dark ground grew darker, blacker, vanished completely by the time she should have reached it.

There was nothing, just jets of a hot, charnel wind that whipped around her from different directions.

Abruptly, the darkness became anything but. Ashakarahad heard herself scream as she covered her eyes. She met the ground and she was on her knees, the shock traveling up her thighs, her spine, across her shoulders. She slammed forward and rolled, stopping against a dead stump that vibrated with the collision. She blinked away tears. Slowly, like a pot of water set to gently boil on a low fire, the tears gave way to bright, dancing stars, then to a blurred landscape. Finally, she could see. A river, wide and slow, its waters thick and purple, like a vein cut through the earth, separated her from a vast plain that was covered in tufts of bluish scrub grass. Black mountains framed the plain. She felt panic rising again and she fought it back. The air was thick and hot. The sound of the purple water was like a sucking hiss. A wind blew from across the river, from across the plain, down from the black mountains—the same charnel wind that had blasted her when she had fallen through darkness. She looked around. The orange sun was high. The city was behind her, farther away, but still stretched across the horizon.

In the middle distance, a single standing stone reached for the sky. Ashakarahad squinted, could see that the stone showed no sign of age or ruin. Its surface was covered in bas-relief inscriptions that mirrored what she'd seen on the ruins in the swamp, in the cracked and flaking pages of ancient texts and scrolls forgotten in vast libraries.

She turned back to the river. The charnel wind, like the breath of a slaughterhouse that had fallen to ill use, hit her full on once again. Behind the distant, black mountains, the orange sky was filled with reaching, grasping hands on long, pale arms. Ashakarahad blinked yet again. Slowly, as if relinquishing an unseen grasp on an unseen reality, the arms and hands withdrew behind the mountains. The charnel wind died with a hot sigh.

Chrona slipped as quietly as she could through the brambles and deadfall of the ruined hedge maze, stepping over statuary that was little more than lumps of shadow in the dim light of the rising sun and the heat shimmers of the fading night. She had never visited Idsiyushti's hut beneath the leering remains of the tumbledown Winall mansion and her breath caught under the gaze of the blank, black windows. Despite her resolve, despite the weight of the *thing* hidden in the folds of her skirt, despite Grendl's furtive directions given in the dim tavern basement amidst liquor that no one was drinking since everyone who would drink it had been conscripted by the falkr, Chrona felt rising panic. She stopped and calmed herself, eyes squeezed shut, cheeks puffed out, free hand resting on a broken, tentacled monstrosity whose marble face was nowhere to be found.

The hut was squat and dim, built from planks clearly taken from the mansion, the roof a mix of sod and cracked shingles. The herb garden was an ordered break from the overgrown ruin of the maze, but the cook fire beside the hut was cold and lifeless. Garden tools were left untouched. A snaggletoothed cat, blue-black, meowed once before scrambling along the roof of the hut and vanishing on the far side. The cat surprised Chrona and she spent several moments trying to calm herself once more.

The falkr are not here, she told herself. They hadn't followed her. They didn't know she'd left town, couldn't possibly care. Unless they knew what Grendl had given her.... She shuddered, her stomach twisting into tighter knots.

Marrah opened the door at Chrona's knock, peaking out like a timid mouse. Her coal-black eyes widened. "Grendl gave me time off to take care of Idsi," she said in a rush.

Chrona looked upwards as if Marrah's whispered words might somehow call down a flight of the falkr, swords ablaze, breasts bare in the most fearsome, unsexual way. "I'm not here to drag you back to work. I have something. For Idsiyushti. Grendl gave it to me. Said to come here." Her words were equally whispered, equally rushed. Chrona straightened her shoulders and took a deep breath, tried to smile, failed. "I'm here to help."

Marrah hesitated, staring, then nodded and opened the door wide. Inside, the hut was dark, lit only by a tiny flame burning in a wide bowl on a low table that was otherwise covered with herbs and trimmings and whatnot, things that Chrona tried not to stare at. The air in the hut was heavy with gatflower, hot and wet, but not stale, perhaps due to all the herbs. Or Idsiyushti's strange magic that everyone said was learned from the fey.

The young witch was on a dirty pallet, sleeping fitfully, her dark, pretty face screwed up in unconscious pain. Chrona looked back at Marrah. The tavern girl was dressed in a cloak which was gripped tight at the throat by a brown-skinned hand gone pale. Beneath the cloak, Marrah appeared to be wearing only a stained shift. Chrona turned back to the pallet and stepped closer, slowly, not wanting to wake Idsiyushti. The witch smelled like she needed a bath or, rather, had bathed in something other than water and soap, something pungent and herbal that tried to hide Idsiyushti's natural scent. Chrona had heard that some sailors out beyond the swamp liked to oil themselves to cover their lack of bathing, that it wasn't a bad combination, natural smell and the oil, although Chrona couldn't imagine the smell to be anything other than nauseating.

Idsiyushti shifted, the blankets slipping. She was naked and covered in small scabs and a residue that seemed to be the source of the cloying smell, her dusky skin turned to a coppery-red.

"What have you bathed her in?" Chrona asked.

"Nothing," Marrah whispered. "The falkr did that. To treat her wounds."

"Gah."

"Yeah." Marrah stepped past Chrona and knelt beside the pallet. She let the cloak fall to the ground and reached out to touch Idsiyushti's forehead, to move a lock of dark hair aside. Chrona watched Marrah, frowning. So Grendl had been right. There was talk out in the swamp of all the queers in town, but Chrona had done her best to ignore that talk once she decided to move from Baker's Beans and rent a small room from Ned, out behind the mercantile.

Chrona cleared her throat. "How is she?"

"She's hurting. The gauntlet-thing the falkr put on her keeps her from using magic. And it gives her a terrible headache. She's exhausted, despite constantly sleeping. When she wakes, she's confused and doesn't seem to understand why she can't use her magic to make the pain go away."

Chrona's frown deepened. The air in the hut was making it difficult to breathe. She pulled the *thing* from her skirt. "Here. Grendl gave me this."

"What is it?"

"A key, I think."

Marrah took it and looked at it in the dim, dancing light. It was a long, twisted thing that looked at once ancient and new. "A key for what?"

Chrona sighed. "The falkr bracelet, of course."

Marrah's jaw dropped. "How did Grendl get this? Did he steal it from—" She broke off and looked around, at the door and the covered windows.

"No, he had it in a trunk in the basement," Chrona said. She felt the flutter of panic too—what if the falkr broke into the hut right then? What would happen to them? Would the falkr drag them out and execute them in the herb garden with flaming swords?

"Why would Grendl have it?"

Exasperated, scared, Chrona said, "I don't know! He just did!" On the pallet, Idsiyushti moaned and rolled over. Chrona lowered her voice. "He said he used to be a constable. He didn't tell me how he got the key, but I guess maybe he got it because he was a constable and kept it."

Marrah's eyes were wide with fear and indecision. "But the falkr!"

"Grendl said to free Idsiyushti, then run. Run far away. Maybe try to find the demoness if she's still alive. That's who the falkr are after, I guess."

"Ash? Why?"

"Just take the bracelet off her!"

Marrah looked from the key to Chrona and back several times. Then her round face set and she moved fast, her shift a white streak in the shadows. She picked up Idsiyushti's wrist and studied the bracelet. She took so long that Chrona started to step forward to help her find the keyhole. Instead, Marrah touched the key to the bracelet and the bracelet fell to the pallet with a loud *crack*.

Idsiyushti screamed.

Jonath sat in his too-hot office, in the near darkness of a single candle. He was unwashed, unshaved, his tunic unbuttoned, chain of office piled on the corner of his desk. A gourd of gut-rot gin was on the desk, open. A filled tumbler was next to the gourd, the murky contents reflecting the flame of the candle. But Jonath was too exhausted to drink, too angry and frustrated to pour the gin back into the gourd and store it away.

The falkr had conscripted the frightened townsfolk to work on cleaning the wreckage of the square, the wreckage caused by the arrival of the falkr in the first place. Jonath had argued, many of the townsfolk had argued, but the falkr had been fierce and angry. Their hands twitched towards the hilts of their swords and their lack of clothing made them all the more terrifying. Grumbling, the townsfolk set to work, clearing the debris of the burned whiskey casks, the knocked down, torn tents and tarps, the kicked-over pots, the scattered belongings. They looked alternatively like looters and military engineers, picking up lost trinkets and panic-tossed valuables while mending, shoring up, and rebuilding after a pitched battle.

Despite the grudging headway the conscripts had been making on the ruin of the square, more and more folk were simply gathering up their belongings and limping off into the darkness, towards their homes out in the swamp. They were scared and tired, but the presence of the falkr had broken the strange tension that had been festering, had burst the bubble that had driven the simple, usually congenial townsfolk to increasing levels of bizarre behavior. Then again, the temple was packed now, worshipers spilling out under an old, mildew-stained tent that had once been used by a traveling minister, erected now in the cemetery and lined with ewers and candles and townsfolk avoiding the falkr and avoiding going home. The falkr left the worshippers alone, just as they generally allowed the conscripts to pack their belongings and leave town. Slowly, the square became less squalid, less chaotic. Sometimes the only voices heard were those folk who felt it their duty to remind the rest of the town not already attending the constant services at the temple that only law and order and the will of the gods would save them.

It was as if the falkr had answered Jonath's anxious concern for the town by invading and spreading a return to old-time religion and traditional values—even though none of the falkr followed the swamp religion or had any idea what it was about. The pall that had been gripping the town was partially swept away with a sweep of a falkr's fiery sword, by a falkr's war screech. But it had been replaced with something else, a new kind of fear, a new shadow that caused the townsfolk to shuffle off with heads bowed or embrace the moss-covered stones of the temple and breathe desperate life back into it. The priests, Yun, Melt, Crick, and ancient Mackasl, in their wrinkled robes that smelled of sweat, mud, and decay, used to just wander into town on market day, purchase one drink apiece from Grendl's place and then sit together by the standing stone in the square, generally being ignored save for the few devout. Now, the swamp priests were wandering the square, supervising the reconstruction and clean-up, glaring at the families and folk who opted to stay behind.

Jonath rubbed his eyes. He needed a bath, he needed sleep. He probably needed food. This was what he wanted, wasn't it? The town back to a semblance of order? The fear that he had accidentally instilled by calling the outlying farmers and homesteaders into town for their own safety eased? Though many were leaving, returning to the deep dark, nothing had really changed out there, not in Jonath's view. The townsfolk would just rather risk the lurking unknown than the wrath of the falkr. Jonath realized after a time that he couldn't blame them. Perhaps the falkr would even protect the farmers and fishers beyond the bounds of the town — even the queers out at Jak's place-from whatever Jonath was afraid of, from whatever he was certain was still bubbling out there. Jonath let himself, for the first time, wonder what his predecessor would have done. Somehow, he doubted Skex would have brought the townsfolk in for protection. If the tales were true, Skex would have raised a posse and chased the soldiers into the swamp. But Jonath knew that the tales were only just threadbare yarns told around bottles of gin and whiskey by old men on Grendl's porch. Skex had been an old drunkard and bully with a chain of office. The militia under Skex may have handled local thugs, violent and twisted as those thugs may have been, but trained imperial soldiers? Jonath wondered if Skex had ever seen war, or if he had, if it had been lost in his youth and drinking.

Maybe Sphinx had been right, years ago, when he'd told Jonath, straight to his face, that Jonath felt too much sympathy for the common folk to be a man in his position. Jonath had laughed it off at the time. Sphinx helped the desperate and the poor, tried to raise up the underdog, often at great expense and pain to himself. But the silver-haired elf had refused knighthood, had refused to serve as a constable, had refused anything other than what amounted to mercenary work. He was far wiser, it seemed, than Jonath would ever be. Even

Grendl had walked away from a constable post, eventually settling for a whorehouse in a backwater far away from his constabulary.

Jonath didn't remember when his eyes had finally slipped closed and his head had come to rest on his arms on the desk. But when Sigiswinth kicked open the door, Jonath's head shot up. He blinked away darkness and confusion, feeling lost and empty.

The falkr leader crossed the office in quick strides. Jonath blinked at her sweat-covered tits before dragging his gaze up to the eyeholes in her helm.

"Sigiswinth," he said with a thick tongue.

"Your witch has slipped her chains and fled the village."

Jonath shook his head. "What?"

The falkr grabbed the still-full tumbler and splashed the gin into Jonath's face. He spluttered and blinked, his eyes burning. He reached for a dagger but she pinned his hand beneath her gauntlet.

"Jonath of the Battlefield," she said as he tried to wipe the gin from his eyes with his free hand, panic and anger rising. "I've heard the tales about you coming out of Desade, but they surprise me—the reality is such a disappointment!" She grabbed him by his open tunic and dragged him across the desk.

"Captain!" Another falkr shouted from just beyond the office door. Jonath grabbed at Sigiswinth but she was slick with sweat. He shouted but the voice of the

149

falkr by the door drowned him out. "Captain! Let him go!"

Sigiswinth dropped Jonath to the hard, painful floor. Jonath bit his tongue and rolled away, looking up bleary-eyed at her near-naked, muscled body to see her pointing to the falkr by the door. "Watch yourself, Maeve!"

The falkr by the door stood her ground. There was a new tension in the air, heavy and strange. "We need him, Captain, if we are to follow the witch into the swamp. Those were your exact words before you marched in here."

Sigiswinth said something in a language Jonath did not understand. Then she walked towards the other falkr and said, "Fine. Bring him."

Chrona had been gone since before dawn. For several hours after her departure, Grendl sat at a table in a corner of the dark tavern with a bottle of expensive whiskey and his short-hafted ax. He'd waited as the hot night turned to hot dawn. He'd finished the whiskey, never keeping his eyes far from the front door. Two hours after sunrise, Caeri came downstairs, groggy, barefoot, her shoulders barely covered by her shift. The girl looked at Grendl, the bottle and the ax, the front door. Then she turned and walked into the kitchen, returning after a while with a platter of fried eggs, bacon, beans, and a hunk of yesterdays' bread. She served Grendl who grunted his thanks. Caeri looked at him then at the front door again. She went back to the bar and poured herself a shot of something Grendl couldn't see. Caeri downed the shot with a gasp and went back upstairs without a single word. Grendl ate, eyes on the door. He finished the meal and pushed the plate away, pulled the ax close.

One of the falkr walked through the door an hour later. She wore a helmet and was all tits and menace, but her sword was still sheathed, which didn't make Grendl feel any better. She looked around the room. Grendl knew how to tell her apart from the other falkr, knew how to read the insignia and sigils on her faceplate, the runes on her gauntlets, her tattoos, the shaved pattern of strawberry pubic hair, but he didn't bother. She walked over to the table. She folded her arms across her tits and Grendl knew she didn't give a single shit about his ax. He sat back and waited for the accusation, the announcement of discovery. Did they really think one falkr would be enough to arrest him? Probably. They might be right, but that one falkr would pay dearly. He suddenly wished he'd donned his armor, but it was tucked behind the bar with his sword.

They stared at each other. Through the holes in her faceplate, her eyes were gold, flecked with crimson. He felt his cock stir, but he kept his face as empty as possible. In a dark tavern on an even darker wharf, over mugs of ale that Grendl knew had been cut with horse piss, Sphinx, the seemingly immortal, queer elf, had looked at him and said, "Your problem, dwarf, is that you only get it up for women you can't have, who don't want you and could kick your ass in a fair fight. Dykes and falkr are the only things that turn your head and make you hard."

He tightened his grip on the ax.

The gold eyes flecked with crimson flicked down and back up. The falkr sighed. Then she said, "I'm called Aeldreth. My captain wants a word with you."

"About what?"

"Your village witch has escaped our custody. Sigiswinth has temporarily relieved your constable of his duties. Reports say that you once served as a constable too. You are to take his place. For now."

Grendl was taken completely by surprise, not the least of which was due to the number of words the falkr had spoken in a row. Grendl sat back, relaxed his grip on the ax. So they didn't suspect him? Didn't know that he'd given Chrona that old manacle key he'd had tucked away in his chest in the basement? And Jonath relieved? Grendl didn't really see eye-to-eye with the knight, but they'd both traveled with Sphinx at some point, and Grendl had come to realize that the elf was pretty discerning about traveling companions. Jonath was also famous in his own way—tales were told of him across the empire. Granted, tales were told of Grendl too, but, still, Jonath? Looking up into the falkr's gold-crimson eyes, it suddenly occurred to Grendl that he'd never bothered to ask how Jonath had come to be constable in this back-water town. He knew Jonath had grown up in the swamp, but that was no real explanation. He had a sudden, yet deep, earth-grinding feeling that there was very little coincidence here.

"Well?" The falkr, Aeldreth, asked. "Coming?"

Grendl's eyes slipped to her tits of their own volition. He dragged them back up and cleared his throat. He slid the ax into his belt and rose from the table.

Ashakarahad felt as if she were definitely losing her mind. She could see the long-reaching plain around her, the standing stone under whose shadow she now sheltered. She could see the distant city as it spanned the horizon. She could see the purple water of the river churning silently. She could see the black mountains beyond the river, still smell their charnel reek.

She could also see the table and chair, both intricately worked from wood that she could not identify, wood as hard as metal, yet warm as if with life, that had been brought to her from nowhere. She could see—and smell and taste—the fruit and meat, both unidentifiable yet quite good, laid out on the table on platters of rune-worked silver. She could see the water and what she assumed was a type of wine in their crystal decanters that, no matter the time of day or the temperature of the air, were beaded with moisture. Both wine and water were cool and refreshing. But she did not see who had brought the table and chair, did not see who replenished the food and drink. She could not see the people or creatures who talked to her in urgent voices, with words she did not understand but found increasingly familiar.

She felt oddly rested despite her confusion and the fact that her invisible hosts only saw fit to give her the table and chair, forcing her to sleep on the ground with only her arm as a pillow and her dirty, ragged clothing as a blanket. During one of the long periods of silence, when she could not be sure if she was indeed alone or if her invisible hosts were silently watching her, she overcame her misgivings and stripped naked. She felt the cool breeze of whatever mild season touched the unknown plain as she washed herself from one of the pitchers of cool water. Then when the sun was high and the sheltering shadow of the standing stone was shortest, she washed her tattered clothes as best she could from the pitcher as well. When the pitcher was empty, she would replace it on the table and look away. When she looked back, no matter how quickly, the pitcher would be full again.

She meditated in the sun, letting it warm her and dry her since her hosts had provided no towel or cloth that she could use for that purpose. She'd laid her clothes on the table, leaving the chair empty so she wouldn't have to sit naked in the short grass beneath the standing stone. Her clothes steamed under the sun and she watched the steam rise and dance for several moments before closing her eyes and turning her thoughts inward.

Confusion and panic lurked just beneath the surface. She had no idea where she truly was, no idea how the standing stone connected her to the empire and the swamp, no idea who lived in the distant, gleaming city, no idea who spoke to her out of thin air. Only the weight of her invisible shackles convinced her that at least some of her mind remained. She had always had little real memory of her time serving the mage-lords, of the time after her summoning, her shackling. The weight of the invisible shackles were just a constant pressure, a constant lash in the hands of a long-vanished master. Yet when she focused on that weight now, that thrum running through her wrists and arms, the panic and confusion subsided.

She opened her eyes and stared at the spires of the city, blinding under the alien sun. From one end of the horizon to the other, an endless stretch of chrome and glass. The shackles became warm, oddly inviting, as she continued to stare. Shadows and light began to play and dance among the distant spires. Teasing, drawing her attention, beckoning. Her breathing became measured, following the pattern of the rhythm of the shackles, the beckoning of the city. Then the panic returned without warning, with an overwhelming crash.

Ashakarahad awoke with a gasp, her breathing labored as if she'd been nearly smothered. Before her, the city beyond the plain lurked, watched. She pushed back from the table and stood, forced her breathing to calm, forced herself to stretch and perform a slow, conditioning dance that was both martial and artistic, its origins forgotten, its patterns embedded in her memory and muscle like haunting instinct.

She finished to find her clothes dry and her skin turning a subtle, healthy crimson-orange. She dressed and felt no surprise when, after she'd finished, the urgent voices, the invisible clamor, started once again.

By the end of the first day after fleeing into the swamp, Idsiyushti's body had started to grow numb to the aches and pains that had plagued her. Now her head only throbbed when she coughed or laughed or, once, when she'd slipped in the mud and come crashing down on her hands and knees, Marrah and Chrona rushing to help her back up. Her magic had returned like a violent wave when Marrah had removed the falkr manacle, but that power was so electric and fiery that it sparked dangerously behind her eyes, racing up and down her spine as if waiting to explode outwards in a ball of destruction, whenever she even thought about using it. So she let Marrah and Chrona take care of her instead of using her magic, let them stop every hour to wash her down with a rag dipped in tepid, stinking swamp water, let them touch salve to her wounded hands and feet. Marrah was affectionate and gentle. Chrona was precise and efficient. When asked why she had run away with them, Chrona, with a sharp look in her eyes that dared them to take the issue further, simply informed them that Grendl had ordered it. She didn't know why and Idsiyushti, studying the severe, older girl, figured that Chrona was afraid she'd offended or angered the dwarf somehow, was being punished without knowing why.

The three of them, along with a mule named Herch that Grendl had loaned Chrona for the journey, stayed away from the trails and roads leading through the swamp. Instead, they crossed thick mud and water and navigated around the dense root labyrinths at the base of trees too covered in moss and kudzu to even name, pulled themselves up onto small tufts of dry land when they could to check each other for leeches and bites. Chrona and Marrah had tried to get Idsiyushti to ride Herch, especially through the water, but the witch refused and Herch seemed all the happier for it, his large brown eyes looking at her as if with relieved amusement.

Near nightfall, the air still hot and moist, the swamp cloying and dark, when they sat around a meal of jerky and dried fruit, sipping lukewarm water from gourds, Idsiyushti had had enough.

"Did you bring whiskey?"

"No," Chrona said, eyes narrowing.

"Gin? Port? Any sort of wine? What about beer?"

Chrona sighed and sat back, exasperated. "No, no, no, and no! You barely say two words this entire time and when you finally do decide to talk, it's to ask about booze! Just because I work in a damned tavern—"

"Chrona!" Marrah glared.

Idsiyushti sat back against a large tree root and closed her eyes—the salt of the jerky still on her tongue. "Then in the morning, we'll go over to Miq's place."

"What? No!" Marrah reached out and grabbed Idsiyushti's hand. "We can't! We have to stay hidden!" Idsiyushti opened her eyes and looked into Marrah's wide, astonished gaze.

"And we can't just go wandering off anywhere—" Chrona scolded. Her dress was dirty and stained. Her hair was pulled back, but Idsiyushti could see that mud plastered the lower strands of her ponytail.

"We could get lost!" Marrah finished.

Idsiyushti laughed, making her head throb. "You don't know where we are now. Neither of you does. Miq's place is just past that copse of trees to the right." Both girls turned to look where Idsiyushti pointed. Marrah turned back, embarrassment showing in the dim light. Chrona turned back, looking angry.

Chrona opened her mouth, but Idsiyushti cut her off. "You've both been crawling through the swamp, dragging poor Herch behind. I'm done looking for leeches on a donkey's dick. We take the roads tomorrow—"

"We'll be found!" Marrah and Chrona, one in bewilderment, one in anger, shouted in unison.

"I have my magic back! I still hurt, but in the morning, I'll cover us in a spell. No one will be able to find us if we're careful."

"Walking the roads isn't careful," Chrona said.

"If we come across someone, we'll hide off to the side," Idsiyushti said, closing her eyes again and sitting back. She gave Marrah's hand a squeeze, but she could still feel the girl's wide-eyed stare.

"Whiskey certainly won't help—"

"Can you really hide us?" Marrah asked, cutting Chrona's protests off.

Idsiyushti opened her eyes again. She smiled and pulled Marrah off balance and into a kiss. She felt Chrona look sharply away. Idsiyushti held the kiss until she felt Marrah's body quiver. Then she licked Marrah's lips and let her go. Marrah sat back and wiped her mouth with the back of her hand.

"Okay," Marrah said. "We'll try."

Chrona turned back, but in the fading light, her face was unreadable.

****

Somehow, in subtle, increasingly disconcerting ways, the scene was changing. Ashakarahad never saw it change, not at first, but she felt something different, something visceral and haunting, each time she looked at the sun, or the vast plain, or the table and its setting, the one lone chair her invisible hosts had given her. Doubts and concerns plagued her as she looked about, at things, at nothing. But there was nothing definite, not at first, and she would shake her head as if to clear it, to wave away the doubts like gnats buzzing in her ears, lift her wrists to feel the weight of the shackles, a familiar attachment to the semblance of an unchanging reality.

Eventually, she found that the texture of the wood table had changed. It was softer, smoother, lines of striation visible beneath varnish where, before, there had been a thick coat of dark paint. A different table? Maybe. But then, one warm mid-day, she looked up and saw that the sun had a purple hue that had nothing to do with its usual rising and setting. The grass on the plain changed altogether, becoming moss-like rather than blade-like.

When the taste of the water in the carafe with its constant beads of chilled moisture changed to something metallic, Ashakarahad said to the otherwise empty plain, "I'm losing my mind."

"We wouldn't know," the voices said, nearly in unison.

"This place is changing. There are little differences."

"Perhaps your memory is no longer what it is."

Ashakarahad laughed. "I think I remember just fine—" And then she stopped. She stopped because these voices she understood.

She stood up from the table and looked at the purple-hued sun—the sun, she realized now, of a world far away and partially covered in glass forests that she'd visited—when? Sometime before her service to the mage-lords. But the memory started slipping away. The voices rose again to a clamor, no longer speaking in unison, speaking in overlapping waves of words and sound like when she'd first followed the voices into the night, away from the edge of the cliff overlooking the crimson sea. And as if the moments before had not happened, these voices were once again voices she could not understand.

Overhead, the purple sun was warm, growing warmer. She undid the top buttons of her tunic and, in exasperation, wiped sweat from her brow with the back of her hand. She spun and the voices seemed to retreat, taking with them the remnants of her memory of the world she now saw. She cried out, but the voices did not seem to respond, continued babbling frantically. She shouted, cursed, picked up a goblet and tossed it out onto the plain.

She spun again, still shouting, and the standing stone was before her, towering, suffocating. The table was gone, so was the chair, but she could see grooves in the dirt where they had been, could see her boot prints around where the table had been standing. But there were no prints that led to where she was standing now.

The river, now black and green, still slowly churning, wider than she remembered, was right beside her, below her, beneath her, inside her.

Ashakarahad looked out across the plain. The purple sun was high and the shadow cast by the now-gigantic standing stone was a narrow slip of black. Dizziness gripped her and she shouted again, her lips and tongue framing words she had not spoken aloud in decades, centuries, the language of her clan, the language of the abyss, remembered now as if by instinct. The plain, the river, the stone wove in and out, circled around, made her sick and weak until she screamed out once more in her native tongue and the world stopped.

Mage-lords.

Hatred, longing, relief poured through her. It made a strange, absurd, perfect sense. Her voice was now cracked and strained when she said, "You! You are the mage-lords!"

"We are."

Ashakarahad dropped to her knees, the narrow shadow of the standing stone swallowing her, the sound of the river churning past, nearly hiding the one lone, crystal-clear voice that spoke to her out of the din.

"This place isn't real," she whispered.

"Yet here we are," the voice replied.

Ashakarahad sat back on her heels, defeated. "So I *am* losing my mind. I've caught some illness. Or I was badly wounded in the swamp when the standing stone exploded and this is a fever dream."

The scene shifted again, blatantly, visibly. The standing stone was gone. The sun was orange. And the vast city that spanned the horizon was gleaming, closer, almost within reach. She blinked and stood. She could once again see shapes and shadows moving against the chrome and glass, distant memories of things, places, people fractured out of time. She could hear dissonant music and laughter and words that she knew were curses.

She spun again at a sound behind her. The standing stone, towering, terrifying, looming like something leaking poisonous resin. She stepped back, her chest tight, her breath hot. There was a sudden flash of light that folded outwards from nothing and then a figure appeared, streaked with silver. The figure strode forward and struck the standing stone with a column of red fire that it held in both hands.

The standing stone shattered.

Ashakarahad was thrown backward. Her lungs burned and her face felt like it had been splashed with

163

acid. Then she was on her knees, dizzy, nauseous. The wet heat of the swamp, the smell of rotting vegetation and stagnant water wrapped her tight, pulling her close. She vomited into the underbrush and when the convulsions stopped, she wiped sulfurous tears from her eyes and looked around. A ruined standing stone, one she didn't recognize, stood nearby. She took deep breaths and studied the trees, fighting down panic. Her invisible shackles cracked and popped, alive with hungry electricity. She was in a clearing she'd never seen before, but it was definitely, breathtakingly, a clearing in the swamp, in the forgotten backwater of the distant empire. She spat bitterness from her mouth and laughed.

Grendl had just finished giving Ned an order for provisions when the merchant's eyes shot up over Grendl's head and narrowed. Grendl glanced back and saw Jak climbing the stairs to the mercantile's porch.

"Yes, well, we'll see about getting this to you right away," Ned said. He scratched at the list with a charcoal pencil, then quickly disappeared inside.

"Grendl."

"Jak. You've scared off the help."

"I make my orders with Ten," Jak said. "He always seems less skittish. As long as his brothers aren't around."

Grendl stared, waiting. Jak returned the stare for a moment then looked crestfallen, the wind leaving his body in a silent semi-rush. He shook his golden-haired head and blinked, straightened his shoulders and the moment passed. He smiled.

"Word is you're the new constable while Jonath is out in the deep dark."

"Temporary constable, aye," Grendl said.

Jak nodded. "I just wanted to inform someone official that I'm closing down for a few days. Probably at least until—"

"The falkr are gone for good."

"Yes, to put it bluntly."

"The falkr don't care who you fuck," Grendl said. He stepped past Jak and descended the stairs. Jak followed so Grendl continued, "They'd probably offer you more protection, if you're worried about it, than Jonath could. To be fair."

"That's not fair at all and you know it."

"To be honest, then." They crossed the tent-filled square, which, under the falkr, had become organized and uncluttered, a strange nod to a time of semi-organized fairs and harvest festivals, a time before the soldiers showed up and Jonath panicked, before the stone exploded. Grendl stopped at the base of the tavern stairs. "What do you want, Jak?"

"Like I said, just letting you know that I'm closing my bar down for a few days. Figured you'd be happy about that."

Grendl had turned to go up the stairs. He stopped, slowly turned back. "You're doing this because of me?"

"No, the falkr. Like you said, they don't care who anyone fucks, but they *will* conscript whoever they get their claws into, it seems. I just figured you'd approve of that one choice, since you don't approve of many of my other choices."

"You aren't scared of what's lurking out there in the swamp?"

"Never was," Jak said. "Jonath was. He wanted me to move into town. He didn't want folks just traipsing about in the dark, drunk, love-lost, maybe walking a little bow-legged, out to my place and back."

"Jonath said he would give you incentives to move."

"He did. But Jonath isn't here."

"And you don't think he's coming back."

Jak hesitated.

Grendl stepped close, glared up into Jak's pale eyes. "I don't want this constable job. At all. But I've got it, and I can't convince Marin to give it to anyone else. But I won't hear talk of Jonath not coming back, because I do not want to keep this miserable job! So keep your trap shut and your 'concerns' to yourself."

Jak spluttered. "Of course. You miss my point."

"Keep your damned bar open," Grendl said. "Because if folks get wind that you *aren't* open, even if it really is because of the falkr, they'll think you're afraid Jonath ain't coming back, that maybe there's something out in the deep dark after all. And then we have more panic. I don't want any more panic. We just cleaned up the fucking square!"

"But—"

"No! You get your queer ass back out there, sell some liquor and dance and sing and suck cock, do whatever it is that you do! And then Jonath will be back and we can pretend we never had this conversation."

Grendl spun, but stopped when Jak whispered, "And if he doesn't come back?"

Grendl shook his head. He climbed the steps to the tavern porch and went inside without looking back and without saying a word.

After visiting Miq's, both Mara and Chrona stopped questioning Idsiyushti. Marrah looked worried, reaching for Idsiyushti's hand more often than not, although never sharing her worry aloud. Chrona glared and fretted at her stained dress, her dirty hair, at random sticks and twigs. She even took to abusing poor Herch, slapping him on the flank, flicking his long, tired ears, cursing at him. But neither girl confronted Idsiyushti all that day.

They'd left Herch on the tiny hillock in the morning and crawled towards the rise of trees beyond which smoke from a cook fire could be seen. Idsiyushti stopped them and motioned for them to hunker down behind tree roots while she stood, eyes closed, arms outward, dress suddenly whipping about her, dancing up above her knees to her thighs in an unfelt wind. She opened her eyes with a snap and both girls cowered backward, stifling gasps. Idsiyushti's hair whipped about her head and then the unfelt wind seemed to stop, hair and dress ceasing their frantic movements.

"What...?" Chrona started to ask but Idsiyushti shushed her. Then the witch bid them stand and the three of them walked through the trees, through the root maze and, to Marrah's horror and Chrona's annoyance, walked right onto Miq's property, right out of the shadows into the light of morning. Miq was nowhere to be seen, but they could hear harsh whistling broken by a wheezing cough coming from the far side of a ramshackle cabin on the other side of the cracked yard with its smattering of chickens. The birds ignored them and Idsiyushti led the way toward the shed that housed the stills. Minutes later, the whistling and coughing still coming from the far side of the cabin, the girls carried a small barrel of whiskey, several gourds of water, and a large sack of dried provisions back into the trees. The chickens never once looked up at them and the lone, bony cow munching on brown grass at the back of the shed behind the stills merely glanced in their direction and looked away.

They returned to the tiny hillock and ate a short breakfast of jerky and bread, washed down with whiskey. Then they tied the rest to Herch's saddle and left the hillock to crawl through the brackish water once more. The found the road beyond Miq's and stopped to pick leaches off each other one last time. Then Idsiyushti led them further into the deep dark along the fading road.

They camped that night in the ruin of a house whose stone and mortar foundation rose above the wild grass, and whose chimney canted at an impossible angle. Idsiyushti explained that the ruin was the remains of the Kree plantation. Chrona gasped and looked around quickly before composing herself and frowning.

"I've heard of the Krees. Disgusting," she said.

"What's disgusting?" Marrah asked, gathering sticks for a fire.

"They say that one of the Krees was a child killer and rapist," Idsiyushti said, clearing space in the grass for the fire.

"We are *not* talking about this!" Chrona said.

Marrah glanced at her then turned to Idsiyushti. "What happened?" she whispered.

Chrona uttered something that sounded like a growl and stormed away, stepping past Herch with a swat to his flank—which he pointedly ignored—and then over to a gnarled oak that overshadowed a tumbledown well house.

"The old constable, Skex, led the militia out here and there was a big fight," Idsiyushti said.

Marrah looked around at the foundation. "Did they burn the place?"

"Must have."

"Wow. A child killer. Really?"

Idsiyushti finished pulling the grass. She stood and kicked at the soil with her bare, dirty feet. "That's what they say."

Marrah brought the sticks over. "Who did he kill? And who did he rape?"

"I don't know," Idsiyushti shrugged.

"Hey!" Chrona shouted. "Stop being disgusting and come look at this!" She was standing near the well house, peering past the leaning walls and half-collapsed roof. Marrah put the sticks down and followed Idsiyushti across the cracked earth. Leaning close, they tried to see what Chrona was trying to point out, but the shadows had grown even longer in the short time it took to cross from the ruined foundation. Idsiyushti sighed and snapped her fingers. A glowing, blue puff appeared and floated lazily past the fallen, wood wall to illuminate the cracked stone and mortar of the well. The blue light glinted on moisture and algae.

"There's still water in the well," Chrona said.

"Maybe it's poisoned," Marrah said.

"I don't think Skex and his men were that desperate," Idsiyushti said.

"We can clear some of this away," Chrona said. "The wood looks rotted."

"And filled with spiders and snakes," Marrah said. She shivered to emphasize her words.

Chrona rolled her eyes. "We clear it away and we can have fresh water. Refill the gourds. That way we won't need to sneak back into Miq's or anyone else's for a while."

Idsiyushti smiled. "And we use the wood to build a lean-to over by the old hearth and we stay here for a few days. The falkr won't find us."

"How do you know they won't?" Marrah asked, wide-eyed and suspicious.

"Miq had no idea we just walked in and took what we needed. The chickens didn't raise the alarm. Neither did the cow."

"Chickens and cows are stupid," Chrona said.

"And because the only person to ever see me when I used my magic to hide was Ash," Idsiyushti said. "I don't know how she did it—"

"She's a fucking demon," Chrona said, scowling. "You don't know that the falkr can't see you too. They have their own magic."

"We won't stay long," Idsiyushti said. "But we need to rest and wash and get our breath back. The falkr don't even know about this place and I doubt anyone would think to look out here right away."

"But Miq will miss his stuff, and he'll raise the alarm," Marrah said.

"Damn it," Chrona said. If she were anyone else, Idsiyushti was certain the barmaid would've spat into the dirt. Instead, she shook her head. "No, he won't. Miq only talks to folk if he can sell 'em something. He won't report a theft like that because he'd rather come look for us himself."

"And he can't see us if I hide us," Idsiyushti said.

Chrona closed her eyes and frowned. "I can't believe I'm saying this but—yes."

Hunched over a large mug of sour ale, coins and receipts laid out before him on a table in a corner of the tavern's backroom, Grendl rubbed his eyes. He smelled Caeri's heavy, bitter-sweet perfume as she approached.

"Boss? Y'okay?"

Grendl nodded and reached for the ale mug, grimaced as he swallowed. "Just wishing I hadn't sent

Chrona off. She liked doing the books more than she liked working the bar."

"You shoulda sent one of us," Caeri said. She was short and a little round, with deep cleavage and sparkling blue eyes often hidden behind a curtain of strawberry blonde hair.

Grendl shook his head. "I'm more business than sentiment, you know that. Two of my whores gone off? No. Besides, the town just avoided one riot. Don't need to start another by sending *you* away."

"Uh-huh," Caeri said, offering a mock curtsy. "Marin of Etrusq wants to see you. He gave one of Macon's kids a piece of candy to come over and fetch you."

"Shit. Wait—Marin *of Etrusq*? Why so formal?"

Caeri shrugged and smiled. "He's sweet, even if he does smell of port and onions. He pays well to fall asleep with his head between my tits and that's his *title*!"

"All right, fair." He scowled at the coins and receipts. "I told you this constabling shit would be nothing but trouble, didn't I?"

"You did. And still do—every chance you get." She cocked her hip at him with a wink and then went to the breadbasket to take out three loaves before returning to the main room.

"Shit. Shit. Shit." Grendl thought about making the old judge wait, but he was in no mood to work the books now anyway. He collected the coins and put them back in the strong box and gathered up the receipts, tucking them into a thick ledger.

Marin's office was on the ground floor of his two-story cottage, a wood-roofed, brick dollop sitting behind a small garden which, in turn, sat behind a squat, white-painted picket fence. He chose to work from home rather than in the larger courthouse that usually sat empty, looming over Jonath's cramped constable's office. Grendl couldn't blame him, though, what with Grendl's own quarters located behind a locked door in the basement of his own tavern.

Marin was sitting behind a large oak desk that was possibly older than the old knight himself. He was sipping whiskey from a crystal glass, the murky, amber liquor shimmering in a crystal decanter near at hand. Marin cleared his throat when Grendl entered, poured whiskey into a second glass and pushed the glass across the desk. Grendl hesitated, scowling, then crossed to the desk, picked up the glass, and downed the drink. It tasted of smoke and the swamp and it burned, washing the sour ale and the bitterness of the last couple of days from Grendl's throat.

"Miq's swill," Grendl said. "Normally I don't go for it, but sometimes, well, just sometimes it's what you need."

"Couldn't agree more," Marin said, pouring out another measure for both of them. Grendl sat in an overstuffed, leather-covered chair across from Marin.

"So. You couldn't come over to talk to me because I don't keep Miq's shit on hand?" Grendl asked.

"Something like that. You're acting constable. You technically work for me now."

Grendl sighed. "I already told you, Jonath is coming back, damn it. I'm not keeping this job. I'm a one-armed dwarf with my own business to run, so don't get too full of yourself or too used to the idea."

Marin sat back. "Is that any way to talk to a judge?"

"Yes."

Marin chuckled. "It's interesting what sort of fellows become constable. In this town, at least. Rather, maybe it's just interesting how two former adventurers, strangers to each other, both wanting nothing more than to retire away from fame, glory, and blood, can be so completely different."

"Marin."

"Fine! Fine. We need to prepare. The 'peace' the falkr scared the townsfolk into won't last. They're still scared, they're still frustrated."

"Jonath will be back."

"Will he? The falkr aren't known for taking what they view as incompetence and insubordination lightly."

"Trust me, I know. I don't agree with Jonath's decision to sequester the swamp folk in the town square. I mean, it did raise profits, but, as a constable, I wouldn't have done it. Still, as you said, it's interesting how two people with common backgrounds can be completely different."

"I think there are several of Jonath's decisions you don't agree with, but that's not why I called you here. Do you know why the falkr came here?"

"Rumor is they're after the demon. Some say they're after those soldiers too."

Marin shrugged. "Maybe." Grendl frowned, but Marin didn't appear to be accusing him. Instead, the old man continued, "I can believe they were after the soldiers—they are a sort of military police force, after all. And to an extent, I can imagine they could be after Ashakarahad. Lots of…people come to the swamp to hide away from the empire. We really know nothing of our demoness from before she set her camp at the edge of town. Perhaps, in the past and out in the world, she was more…demonic, shall we say?"

"Maybe. But she vanished into thin air. Or blew into so many tiny pieces that we couldn't recognize them for pieces of a horn-headed she-demon."

"Yet the falkr left here with Jonath to find Idsiyushti instead. Her escape really angered them."

"Pissing off falkr isn't actually hard to do."

Marin cleared his throat. "Indeed. But what I find troubling is the timing. First the soldiers—if the falkr were on their trail, sure, I can buy the falkr showing up now. But then there is the goblin massacre. And then the exploding menhir next to the goblin altar. And *then* the falkr appear, saying they are looking for Ashakarahad."

"Maybe they got wind of the soldiers—maybe the soldiers have been leaving a trail of dead goblins throughout the land—but when the falkr got here, they decided to look into Ash—she isn't, obviously, an imperial citizen and, you know, she's a demon."

"It still doesn't add up. Too many coincidences in the shape of events prior to the falkr lighting up the sky and cleaning up the town. Certainly if they were hard on the trail of the soldiers—perhaps because the soldiers, as you say, were leaving a trail of goblin corpses throughout the land—then I might be able to believe that things spiraled out of control between the soldiers leaving and the falkr arriving. But the first thing they did was put Idsiyushti in a manacle and demand to know the whereabouts of Ashakarahad. And they found Idsi out at the goblin clearing, which just happened to also be the site of the explosion—the most recent in the chain of events. But why put Idsiyushti in a manacle? Being a witch is not against imperial law. But being a witch living near a demon, standing among the remains of a bunch of dead goblins, next to an ancient menhir left over from a time of rampant sorcery and power, a menhir that *exploded* in the presence of said witch and the demon? Not exactly what happened but is it enough to strip Idsi of her power?"

"For the falkr? Sure—they like being in control, like to make sure they hold all the cards, all the surprises, all the ends of the chains hooked to all the shackles. I think it's the only thing that gets them wet."

Marin poured more whiskey into their now-empty glasses. "You clearly don't like them."

"What gave it away?"

"My point is that the soldiers lied about being here. What if the falkr did too?"

"The falkr are pretty much the emperor's right arm, militarily-speaking. Why would they lie to the likes of us, nameless people in a nameless town in the middle of a good-for-nothing swamp?"

"The soldiers *are* the right arm of the emperor, militarily-speaking. And *they* lied to us."

Grendl sat back, grimacing. "Fuck, I hate this."

"If two branches of the emperor's military—one low and one high—lied to us, what does that imply to you?"

Grendl stared into his whiskey glass. "Fuck if I know. I just said I hate this."

"Try to play along. What does it imply?"

"For fuck's sake. The falkr have their own magic. Maybe they were looking for the demon and somehow sensed the explosion at the goblin clearing. When they get there, they find Idsiyushti. Maybe it's just that simple."

"And if it isn't? Again, if they all lied to us?"

Grendl sighed and said, "Then we're fucked."

****

Strangely, Ashakarahad felt more lost in that unfamiliar part of the swamp than she did on the beach of the crimson sea, fighting black-armored canoids, than she did chasing voices in the mocking shadow of the distant, unending city, on a world with an orange sun and three pink moons that moved in unison, between a sluggish, purple river and a timeless obelisk. Lost in the heat and smell of the swamp, the moisture in the air that made breathing heavy. Lost in the cloying taste of stagnant water and thick moss. The cries of unseen animals and birds. The lumbering movement of things hidden in the trees, followed by splashes of water that left only ripples in the murk. No matter how far she ranged from the ruined standing stone, equally as unfamiliar and yet so similar to the timeless standing stone on the plain wracked by charnel house winds, nowhere in the surrounding area was any place she'd visited before.

The trees were tall and thick and danced on hot breezes that were barely felt. Root mazes were dense and unnavigable, forcing her to climb from limb to limb in the trees above in order to pass. She made rope snares from thin vines that she pulled from trees. She caught a rabbit and a snake, cooked them both over small fires that were more smoky than hot because the only tinder she could find was green and wet.

Her equipment was all but gone. She had with her only what she'd had in that other place, on the plain from which the shadow of the standing stone and the city reached. Her pack had been lost in the explosion at the goblin clearing—how long ago?—and, oddly, she had no memory of having the ax-like weapon and the black-iron short swords with her on the plain with the table and the voices. Her armor was gone, and her clothes were dirty and ripped—although where she had mended them in the shadows of the obelisk and the unending city, the mends still held, suggesting that her time, at least in part, in that other place had been real. She had her belt, flint and steel, two long knives, odds and ends that lived in her belt-pouch. A candle stub. A whetstone. Salt and pepper in tiny horn containers. Charcoal pencils, but nothing to write on. A fishing hook and some line, but both proved useless in the murky water when she tried. She'd watched fisherfolk in the swamp catching gigantic specimens of various fish, but she'd never gotten the hang of it.

She was in the deep dark, out past any region of the swamp surrounding the town she'd known, past any region of the swamp she'd explored. Or at least not close to any of the deep dark regions she'd ventured into. Another ponderous thing moved its invisible bulk through trees in the distance, and she thought of the tales the townsfolk told of monsters in the deep dark, trolls and scaled leviathans that walked on land and swam in the black water. Night Hags. The undead. Ashakarahad shook her head and laughed at the trees. Before the explosion, she'd hunted the swamp for signs of the undead because, according to legend and the ancient tomes in the archives of Drilithae, undead were known to haunt the lands where the ruins of the mage-lords were found. But she'd seen nothing of the undead—or trolls or hags—in her time near the town. Only the remains of the massacred goblins.

Ashakarahad ranged outwards from the small clearing, moving roughly in a spiral that she could follow backward if needed. But she came across no roads, no tracks. By early evening of the second day of exploration, she came upon another standing stone, this one surrounded by the tumbledown ruins of what might have once been a tower. The stones of the tower were dark and cracked, covered in kudzu and honeysuckle. She disturbed a nest of brightly colored birds the size of her fist when she started exploring. The birds screamed at her and flew off into the trees, their haunting echo followed by the sound of something large and ungainly once again moving through the undergrowth and into water.

She made camp among the ruins, building a small fire that cracked and popped and sucked at the dried vines and small, broken branches she found in the ruin's cracks and crevices. She found several birds' nests, some filled with speckled eggs, but she left the eggs in favor of trapping something more substantial at the edge of the trees. She used honeysuckle vines to build several snares. She found a trickle of sweet, cool water running in a rivulet through the cracks of something that might once have been a sculpture—not a standing stone, something else entirely—and she drank deeply. She climbed atop several hewn blocks and surveyed the clearing and trees and watched the hot sun slowly start to descend as she waited on the snares.

Grendl should have known there was going to be trouble when no one showed up for the usual dinner rush.

Sek sat on the stairs leading up to the second floor, head in one hand, other hand absently playing with the hem of her dress, waiting in vain for the first of the night's paying fucks. She and Caeri had argued about which of them was going to help Grendl behind the bar during dinner and which was going to get the first of the evening's upstairs clients. Grendl had slammed his fist down on the bar, bringing both women to wide-eyed silence. He'd cleared his voice and, as calmly as possible, flipped a silver coin before announcing that Sek was whoring and Caeri was bartending.

Sek had squealed in glee, tiny tits bouncing up and down beneath her thin blouse as she clapped her hands.

Caeri glared at Grendl, said, "I thought you said I was the better whore. That I made more money!"

"What?" Sek had asked, her face falling, her bouncing slowing to a confused stop.

"Oh for fuck's sake!" Grendl roared. "Sek! Upstairs and on your damned back! Caeri! Behind the damned bar!"

But it had been for naught because no one came through the doors. Not for a drink, not for a bowl of the stew Grendl had simmering in the back, nor the potatoes he'd cut up, ready to fry, not for the bread he'd bought from Breth, the baker, or the fritters or pancakes bought from the same. Not for a tumble with either Sek or Caeri. Grendl polished the bar until his arm grew tired and Caeri sulked until he made her go back and tend to the stew and potatoes. Sek lost her excitement and took her seat on the stairs. Grendl eventually tossed his rag down and looked up to see Sek with her head against the banister, asleep.

Voices outside the tavern were suddenly raised in anger. Someone began pounding on the closed tavern door. Sek jerked awake and scooted away from the banister, back against the wall, eyes wide. Caeri ran from the back room, apron on, hair tied back, pale hands dusted even paler with flour. Grendl stared at the door, listening to the voices and the next wave of pounding. He grabbed his ax and stormed across the tavern.

"No!" Sek shouted, followed by Caeri's "Wait!"

"Quiet!" Grendl growled. He threw open the door and the crowd beyond, led by Macon, the blacksmith's eldest, stepped back as if recoiling from a punch to the jaw. A few folk tumbled down the stairs, picked up by the folk that were crowding the tavern-side of the square.

"What the fuck is going on?" Grendl demanded. He held the ax at his side but Macon and several others, each carrying torches despite the still-light hour, stepped further back until they met the folk behind them. The air in the square was hot and wet, and the presence of the torches, pitch popping and cracking, added a dull flicker of acrid smoke that made the air feel even hotter. Drag and Marin pushed their way to the front of the crowd. Drag grabbed Macon by the collar and shook him.

"What is this?" the blacksmith asked while his eldest son quailed.

"What's going on?" Marin asked. But their voices were lost in the subsequent round of shouting. Grendl shouted for quiet. Marin shouted for quiet. Drag shouted for quiet, then raised his voice even louder and shouted again. This time folk around him shrank and cowered, the ripple passing through the crowd, a wave of stunned silence following.

"What the fuck is going on?" Grendl asked again. He stopped close to the cowering Macon. Drag let his son go and stepped back. Macon looked down at Grendl and his face paled even further.

"We—" Macon started. "We—"

"We don't want Jonath anymore!" someone from the back of the crowd shouted. Voices raised in agreement continued to shout as Grendl tucked the ax into his belt and went back into the tavern. He returned carrying a wooden crate, placed it on the porch, and stepped up onto it. The voices dropped to silence as Grendl glared out across the crowd.

Macon, still cowering, cleared his voice, looked at his father then up at Grendl. "We want a new constable," he said. "We want you, Grendl."

"Listen, you lousy swamp shits," Grendl said. "I've been acting constable for three days! And I haven't done anything but knock Lestr there about because he fucked Sek and didn't have the coin to pay for it! What makes you think I'm any good as constable? What makes you think I damned well *want* to be constable?"

"You would've fought the falkr," someone shouted.

Macon said, "They say you fought a falkr when you were constable back east."

"I didn't fight a falkr, I punched her in the face. And that cost me my job, dumbass! Why the fuck would I have fought the falkr this time?"

"They just came in and took over and Jonath did nothing," Macon said.

Drag grabbed his son again and said, "That's enough talking, boy. You're giving me a headache. You're all giving me a headache!"

"You don't fight the falkr," Marin said. "They serve the emperor directly."

"Grendl did!" a voice reiterated.

"One punch is not a fight!" Grendl shouted.

"They say you fought with weapons until you were pulled apart!"

Drag cleared his throat, frowned. "It's true. They do say that," he said without releasing Macon.

Grendl looked about for a patch of the porch that wasn't being used to stand on and spat. He tried to spot Jak, wondering if the queer had been talking to the others, spreading concerns about Jonath's return. But there was no sign of Jak. With the exception of Ten, there was none of Jak's Queer Legion in the crowd at all. "All of you shitheads just go home! Or back to your damned tents!"

"Tents we live in because of Jonath," Macon said despite his father's grip.

"You don't live in a tent, boy!" Drag said. Macon looked away.

"None of you were under any obligation to come live in the fucking town square," Grendl said. "I heard what Jonath told the militia to tell you. I heard what Idsiyushti and the demon told you. They said that you *should* come into town, but you didn't have to. Miq didn't. Jak didn't—"

"Both of whom are abominations in their own right!" a voice shouted, the crowd parting. Mackasl, the old, bent high priest of the swamp gods, dressed in heavy robes, carved cane in dusky, wizened hand, fire still burning in his rheumy eyes, stepped forward on the arm of one of Ned's daughters, who was dressed as a novice.

Grendl said, "That still doesn't change the fact that none of you swamp folk were forced to leave your homes! You came here and filled my coffers with gold, fucked my girls, and filled your bellies with my liquor! Then you swelled Mackasl's pews, so much so that he had to put a damned tent up in the graveyard!"

"My people and your people are not the same," Mackasl said. "My people came right to the temple, prayed and worshipped. Your people drank your ale and whiskey and lay with your whores."

"Bullshit," Grendl said. "They did both. Your people are my people when the sun goes down and my girls' skirts go up." Mackasl shook with anger and Ned's daughter tried to console him.

"What about Jonath?" Ten asked. "Jonath did nothing! What would you have done, Grendl?"

A chorus of questions, essentially all the same as Ten's, followed. Grendl eyed the crowd then looked down at Drag and Marin. Marin shrugged, but there was a smile in his dark eyes. The old fucker was enjoying this. Torches crackled and a dog barked on the other side of the square, joining the raised voices. Grendl could see that women and children were beginning to the fill the back ranks of the mob. Mackasl glared up at him.

Eyes fixed on the priest, Grendl said, "I wouldn't have done anything differently. Now get out of my sight, all of you!"

Dusk was red, vibrant, and hot. The air was wet and thick, filled with languid insects. In the shadow of the ruined tower, lulled to a light sleep by the sound of water trickling through the cracks in the vine- and moss-covered stones, Ashakarahad awoke at the first sound of a cracking twig, a surreptitious footfall. She reached for weapons she didn't have, the realization knocking her fully awake. Grinding her teeth against her own panic, she drew a dagger and rolled to her knees. She had built a little fire in a natural hollow between several stones that formed a sort of roofless cave, but the fire had begun to smoke heavily in the short time she slept. She pivoted on one knee and kicked the remains out now, eying the remnants of greasy smoke that danced up past the stones into the thick air. She gripped the dagger and waited.

There were more footfalls but nothing showed through the opening to the ruins beyond. Rubbing aches and pains and slowness from her joints, Ashakarahad moved into a low crouch, dagger ready. She drew her other dagger, held it in her off-hand, blade down. She was not the best knife fighter but there was little choice now if it came to any sort of combat. Overhead, the sky was so red, purple, and orange that she wondered, briefly, if the world was on fire.

The stones, slick with moisture and swamp growth, were slightly taller than she was. There was no way for her to see into the rest of the ruin or the surrounding trees and brush without leaving the little shelter. And if whoever was out there decided to scale the stones and stand over her, she would be nearly helpless if they had spears or bows or worse. She spat into the remains of the kicked-out fire. She took a deep breath, stood, and, turning slightly sideways, stepped from between the rocks.

The stench greeted her first, a heavy musk that permeated the ruins yet hadn't reached into the shelter. Goblins. Twenty, twenty-five, half-dressed in leather scraps and cloth rags tied as shirts and trousers. Male and female and several smaller ones that Ashakarahad guessed were goblin children, hiding behind their parent's legs, peeking out wide-eyed. Older children stood beside the adults and, like the adults, held spears, stone knives, rusty hatchets, what looked like fishing poles. Some carried heavily mended nets, others spades and rakes and, in one case, a pitchfork, broken-handled but still overly-tall for the goblin holding it. The broken pitchfork was like a banner held above assembled troops.

The goblins looked weary-eyed. Many rested on their tools and make-shift weapons like the very earth was trying to pull them into it and the tools were their only means of support. They looked up at her, bleary eyes stopping, almost as one, at the daggers she held in a readied guard, before climbing upwards to her face and horns. No one moved except for one child who squeaked and hid further behind another.

Slowly, as smoothly as her still-stiff body would allow, Ashakarahad sheathed the daggers. There was no collective sigh of relief. There was no sudden, aggressive drive forward. There was no change in the thick air, no sudden spike in tension, nor a sudden cessation. There was nothing. The goblins simply continued to stare up at her.

Uncertain of what else to do, Ashakarahad tried to talk to the goblins. They continued to stare up at her. She tried different languages, none of which elicited a response other than the curious, collective stare. Slowly, achingly, she sat down, crossed her legs, and started again. The more mature goblins were now at head height with her, but that didn't seem to help. There was nothing other than the stare and the odd shuffle from one dirty foot to another.

Ashakarahad closed her eyes and leaned back against the ancient stone. Her horns scraped and she rolled her shoulders, the stone's coolness almost foreign in the hot, wet, deepening night. Time crawled. She opened her eyes, surveyed the goblins. A strange intuition was creeping into her brain, like a lost memory worming its way up her spine, into the base of her skull. Something she should have known or realized, taunting her from the edge of her awareness. She worked her mouth for a moment, felt her sharp, jagged teeth with the tip of her tongue. Then she spoke what she came to think of as a ritualized greeting in the long-dead tongue of the mage-lords—the language she suspected she had been speaking without effort in that other place, on the plain between the river and the standing stone, in the shadow of the alien chrome and glass city.

The goblins, eyes wide, stepped back as if slapped. They turned to each other and began muttering in a guttural whisper that was harsh and incomprehensible. Ashakarahad sat up and tried more phrases that she'd gleaned from ancient, crumbling texts in the libraries at the universities in Drilithae, Desade, and far-off Volteq. The goblins, almost as one, stopped muttering and turned to stare at her anew. They cocked their heads, as if trying to hear every word she said—or, she presumed, missaid. She tried every phrase she could think of. Then she tried stringing sentences together from whole cloth, uncertain but unwilling to give up.

A susurration, a subtle movement from the back of the goblin gathering. The trees whipped in a sudden, cold wind that was brief and poignant. Once more, a far-off thing crashed, unseen, through the undergrowth and splashed into water.

A creature, like a broad-shouldered goblin that was nearly twice as tall as the others—nearly as tall as a man or a woman, yet still heads shorter than Ashakarahad at her full height—stepped through the crowd. The goblins parted, stepping aside without looking at the newcomer, as if sensing its presence by the very vibrations in the air that its passage made before it. The creature was dressed in human clothes, patch-worked, stitched, surprisingly color-coordinated. It wore what looked like a chain of office made of green copper. Another chain of bones and feathers joined the first. It carried a tall staff of black wood that was etched with runes that were both forgotten and familiar—the runic system of the mage-lords and the standing stones. Ashakarahad gaped.

The creature spoke with a harsh voice in truncated syllables that Ashakarahad realized, with heart-stopping awe, were the words, pronounced far more accurately, of the mage-lords. A sibilance bit the night air, an echo of the words and conversations from that other place. The creature continued to speak in words so familiar that Ashakarahad ached, but despite the sibilant underscore and the memories of the plain, she could understand nothing of what the creature said. She had glimpses of possible meaning and tone but there was nothing else.

The creature rolled its yellow eyes—a gesture that made it look even more human—and said in the common Imperial tongue, "They cannot understand you, giant goat-fiend, because you are not speaking in a dialect that makes any sense to them. You are speaking as if you were a child who learned their letters but never learned how to pronounce them."

Ashakarahad blinked. "Giant goat-fiend?"

The creature sighed. "You are much larger than any humans or elves, therefore giant. And you have horns—although they are more the horns of a ram than a goat, but, surely, semantics. Finally, you have the look and smell of a fiend from beyond the Abyss, freed from the summoning circle, although I can still sense the long chains that bind you."

Ashakarahad had to work to close her mouth after she realized that her jaw had dropped. The weight of the invisible shackles increased as if by their mere mentioning, trying to drag her down into the earth. Yet when she tried to speak, all she could say was, "Semantics?"

"Yes, semantics." The creature thumped the end of its staff on the ground. "Only moments ago you were rattling off a barrage of languages and were attempting to massacre the tongue of the Ancients. And yet 'semantics' confuses you?"

"What? No! I'm just—" Ashakarahad shook her head and slowly levered herself up to stand over the creature and the goblins. "Forgive me. I made the mistake of presuming that you—one of your—well—"

"You presumed that a hobgoblin such as myself can't possibly be learned."

Ashakarahad sighed and nodded. "Yes."

"And that, my dear goat-ram-demoness, is why so many of my people lie in a pile of ashes and bone chips in a clearing miles from here."

"I am one of the Eld," Ashakarahad said, aware that she was rambling, trying to apologize, trying to regain some kind of footing, trying to resist the sudden pull of the invisible chains. "I'm not just a goat-ram-demoness. My people are ancient and far-reaching—"

"And conjured into the thrall of those who have the magic and knowledge to do so. Conjured for good although, more often than not, for ill. I don't recall asking and I don't recall saying that I cared." The creature looked down at the assembled goblins, who were, by now, gazing at it fondly. "You stink of that place, the place where my people were massacred. You stink of the menhirs, and you reek, positively reek, of the Plain, not to mention the Abyss."

"The menhirs are the standing stones—"

"Yes, try to keep up." The creature stepped forward, reached up to poke Ashakarahad between her breasts with a bony, clawed finger adorned with ornate rings of human and elvish design. "You have released things into this swamp that we have tried to keep out. But your kind—fiends and humans and elves and dwarves—have no love for us and you do not know what it is that we do. And now you have caused us to fail."

"I am the only one of my kind here in the swamp." Her head was reeling, like she was trying in vain to wake from a confusing dream.

"Wonderful," the creature said. "I'm sure the humans in their town will thank you just the same when the dead are feasting on their flesh."

Idsiyushti and Marrah had a hard time keeping their hands, mouths, whispered words, stifled giggles, and quiet moans to themselves as they lay on their makeshift pallet in one corner of the ruined Kree house. Above them, the cracked and leaning hearth leered, not unironically, in Chrona's opinion. So Chrona made her pallet on the other side of the ruin, beneath her own lean-to made from vines and boughs and the siding of the fallen-down well shed.

They shared a common cook fire and Idsiyushti used magic to forge candles from beeswax and herbs gathered from among the trees. Ignoring the strange lack of flicker despite any hot breeze that crept through the ruin at night, Chrona would use one of the candles to read the only book she'd brought with her—a secret tale of lust and adventure that she kept hidden even from her two companions. But, even though she'd read it several times before, reading the book while Idsiyushti and Marrah quietly fucked each other in the shadow of their own candles on the other side of the ruin made Chrona uncomfortable. She masturbated slowly, carefully, after the other two seemed to fall asleep, when her own candle was out and the book was tucked away, because she didn't want either Idsiyushti or Marrah to think that she was fingering herself to the sounds of their own, queer lovemaking. Instead, Chrona fantasized about strong men, burly, big-dicked, darkly handsome, with locks of black hair curling in the wind. Fantasized about Prince Erebert, the protagonist of the novel, or Crumwell the Singular, a bard of no equal measure, in either poetry or love, best friend of Erebert. Or even Hildred, bent and crooked, with broad shoulders and a massive prick, leering eyes and tangled beard, a dwarf who favored young girls and old maids alike—nothing like Grendl and his seemingly calculated disinterest in even the charms of his own whores.

From the darkness, Idsiyushti watched the older girl touch herself. The witch felt a mixed thrill that conflicted with pity, but there was no other choice. She crept closer and whispered Chrona's name. She repeated the whisper but she wasn't close enough and she didn't want to get closer in case she scared Chrona or made the older girl feel even more uncomfortable. But there was an urgency. Idsiyushti focused her power and whispered Chrona's name one last time, letting a subtle wave of sorcery and fey glamour carrying the sound to Chrona's ears alone. Chrona gasped and stopped moving.

Idsiyushti then allowed herself to continue her approach. She got close enough to smell Chrona, body odor and swamp and heat, the same as both herself and Marrah, although Chrona refused to wipe herself down with the herb sachet that Idsiyushti had put together in lieu of soap and being able to wash completely. The well-water was plentiful but they had nothing to collect enough for a bath and both of the other girls were not fond of bathing in the swamp water beyond the trees because they didn't have Idsiyushti's callous disregard for leeches and snakes.

Forcing herself not to wrinkle her nose at what amounted to Chrona's stinky prudishness, Idsiyushti leaned close and whispered, "Miq is over there, just beyond the tree line."

Chrona sat up. "What?" Despite the implication of Idsiyushti's words, Chrona straightened the front of her dirty dress and ran a hand through her tangled hair.

"He's not looking for a roll in the grass," Idsiyushti whispered, chiding. "Be quiet and sit still. I've covered us with an invisibility spell but it's a lot of work to keep us all covered with you all the way over here and Herch tied by the well."

"I knew he would find us!" Chrona whispered.

"Yeah, well, he probably just followed the smell of his own whiskey. It's Miq. He's his own kind of freak."

Chrona looked up at the stars, shimmering above the heat of the night. "Why's he waiting?"

"Hopefully because he can't see us. And I doubt he can really smell the whiskey. Maybe he's noticed the work we did taking the wood from the shed to make our lean-tos."

"How would he know the difference?"

"I don't know! Maybe he comes out here on his own. Maybe he's got a strange sense of nostalgia."

Chrona stared. "Nostalgia. You surprise me, Idsiyushti."

"Why? Because I'm some backwoods witch? I'm not illiterate!"

"Sure. Well, just a surprise, that's all."

"Jonath, Grendl, and Marin are well-educated. Mackasl's too, although you couldn't tell beneath his robes and swamp gods talk."

"All of them men. Men of the world, for what that's worth. Not many women are educated around here."

Idsiyushti shook her head. "Damn it! Miq's out there. Watching from the shadows. Only you would try to start an argument about being smarter than everyone else at a time like this."

Chrona drew herself up and glared. "Thank you."

"That wasn't—fuck it. Just stay here and don't light your candle." Idsiyushti didn't wait for a response. She slipped back into the shadows and was over the stonework of the foundation before Chrona could react.

The grass slipped and slithered in the breeze, waving in front of Idsiyushti as she kept low to the ground. She paused just long enough to strengthen the illusion covering both her and the interior of the ruined house. She looked back but could see neither Chrona nor Marrah. She'd left Marrah wide-eyed, trying to grasp at Idsiyushti as she moved off towards the edge of the foundation to watch Miq while he tried to watch them, or the ruin, or whatever he was watching. She'd gone back to give Marrah a quick, hopefully comforting kiss on the lips, squeezing the girl's hand, before slipping off to talk to Chrona.

An image of Ashakarahad danced unbidden before her eyes and Idsiyushti shook her head. Sometimes, when she was lying with Marrah, Idsiyushti would think of Ash, which caused tingles of desire mixed with layers of guilt, guilt at the explosion of the standing stone, guilt at her own desire, both of which she tried to hide. Marrah was sweet and beautiful, although nothing like Ash. She really cared for Idsiyushti, and Idsiyushti cared for her. Idsi looked back at the crumbling foundations and its deep shadows. What kind of demon had Ash been anyway? She hadn't seemed like the kind of sex demon the legends and trashy stories always talked about. Idsiyushti smiled at that bittersweet image. On the other hand, having a whore for a lover, even a relatively young one, meant there was never a lack for stories or laughs or a thrill at the way Marrah could move and submit, demand and crave.

Still smiling, Idsiyushti looked back at the tree line. She focused her sight, both physical and sorcerous, and there, in the shadows between the gnarled roots, was a figure wrapped in darkness, motionless. Miq. Idsiyushti watched him for some time. He never moved. If it weren't for the fact that she was convinced that a man like Miq must snore like a dragon on a rampage, Idsiyushti might be tempted to think that he'd fallen asleep. She frowned. Maybe Miq was more than just a swamp-dwelling whiskey maker. Maybe he had a wild history, like Jonath and Grendl. Maybe he was an expert tracker and woodsman. Maybe he'd been a member of the Imperial Hunt, a yeoman of exceptional skill, a minor legend hiding in the swamp like a semi-famous dwarf masquerading as a tavern keeper. Her frown turned to a mischievous grin. Staying low, she crept forward once more.

****

Marrah took a deep breath and sat up. She exhaled as quietly as she could, looked around, tried to see the illusion that Idsiyushti said covered them. But she could only see the shadows that embraced the ruined foundation and the hearth with its leaning chimney. She could see the stars above, twinkling as if obscured by a cloud of steam that rose from the heat of the swamp. She could barely make out Chrona over in her corner. She had no idea if Chrona could see her, but she felt the other girl's contempt nonetheless. Chrona had always been too good to be a whore and Marrah—and Sek and Caeri—knew Chrona looked down on them, looked down on the whole town. Marrah often wondered aloud to Caeri and Sek why Chrona worked for Grendl, why she stayed in town, why she didn't pack up and leave and go live in Esgen or far off Drilithae or somewhere that had culture, history, money.

"Because she's nothing but a dressed-up bumpkin," Caeri would answer. "Too good for us, but not good enough to be anything other than some country cunt over in Esgen or anywhere else that didn't stink of the swamp, or animals, or piss and rotting meat."

"I asked her why she didn't go to one of the universities," Sek said. "She said she was surprised I knew what a university was and then walked away."

Marrah had thought about that. "I bet she's afraid that she won't actually be smart enough at a university so she stays here and pretends to be the smartest in town."

"Maybe," Caeri said. "I think she's just too romantic to leave. She pretends to be all high and mighty and smart, but deep down, I think she wants to live here because she thinks that some knight—I mean other than Jonath or Marin—will ride in and sweep her away on his big, white horse. If she goes to Esgen or to university, I think she's afraid she'll see the real world, see that no knight is going to sweep her off her feet unless it's to fuck her and run." Marrah had marveled at Caeri's wisdom, bringing herself to wonder why *Caeri* worked for Grendl, had come to the swamp from so far north. But Marrah never asked because she liked Caeri—who sometimes covered for her so she could go out to Jak's or Idsi's on nights she wouldn't normally be able to— and she didn't want to chance making Caeri angry.

Beyond the ruined foundation, past the well, lightning split the night. A crack and sizzle followed and the stars faded momentarily as the interior of the ruin was lit up in stark contrast. Marrah jumped and saw Chrona sit up, surprised. Heart leaping out of her chest, eyes watering and dancing with spots as the contrast change faded and the shadows returned, Marrah scrambled up and crawled over to the edge of the foundation. She carefully peeked over the stones and blinked her eyes at the dancing spots that colored the darkness out beyond the overgrown yard. A figure moved against the dark tree roots, running towards the well and then veering towards the ruined foundation. Herch shifted and snorted, pulled against his lead. Then the spots faded and Marrah could see that it was Idsiyushti running across the yard, the hem of her dress flapping around her knees. Idsiyushti's dark hair streamed around her like it was caught in its own storm and the witch began waving her arms in the air as she ran.

"Get up! Get up! Get up and run!" Idsiyushti shouted.

Marrah, heart still racing, stood. She glanced back at Chrona and saw the older girl already standing, straightening her dirty dress. Idsiyushti reached the foundation and leaped over it, not bothering to find one of the breaks that had once been a door.

"Gather everything up," Idsiyushti said. Her eyes were wide and bright, filled with the light of sorcery. Marrah stared. Idsiyushti was beautiful. "Chrona, go fetch Herch and try not to be too mean to him. We have to leave!" Idsi turned to Marrah. She offered a weak smile and stepped forward to touch Marrah's cheek. Electricity danced in the air and Marrah's heart nearly raced out of her chest. "Hey, come on! We have to go," Idsiyushti said.

"What happened? What's going on? Where's Miq?" Chrona sounded angry.

Idsiyushti turned. "Dead. We need to move!"

Marrah felt her heart suddenly stop, the shift from excitement to horror so sudden her knees nearly went weak. "You killed him?"

"What did you do?" Chrona asked at the same time.

Idsiyushti balled her fists. "I didn't kill him! He was already dead, but I couldn't get close enough because something was trying to hide him."

"Hide?" Chrona asked.

"Something else killed him and covered it up with magic so we couldn't tell. Like how I hid us."

"Why?" Marrah gasped. Her heart was suddenly racing again and she forced herself not to look away from Idsiyushti, not to look out at the dark trees.

"To trick us," Idsiyushti said. "Maybe. To better trap us, maybe. Make us sit tight thinking that Miq was out there watching."

"Who would do that?" Chrona crossed her arms over her chest and stomped to the foundation stones and glared into the night.

"Damn it," Idsiyushti said. "Not who. What. And we need to go! Now!"

"Idsi, why?" Marrah whispered, panic rising fast now.

"Because Miq was killed by something that was already dead!"

****

Despite Grendl's order to keep serving liquor, business was slow. Jak sat on his front porch, in a cane rocker, honeyed whiskey in a stemmed goblet on the table beside him. The night was heavy and hot, the darkness having encroached on his property fast and hard, leaching colors and hiding the outbuildings. Inside, Peler tended to the bar—which, by the sound of it, meant strumming his mandolin and exchanging jokes with the few regulars who avoided the whole town square-falkr fiasco by never actually going home.

Thome had even made it out last night, for the first time in nearly a month. He'd been sick with a high fever, and Idsiyushti's ministrations had finally cleared it, but he hadn't been able to tear himself away from the sawmill and the town square until the previous evening. And he hadn't gone home or back to work this morning either. When Jak had passed by the bar half an hour ago on his way out to the porch, Thome had given Jak a wink and Jak had commented on how his coloring seemed to be returning. Thome had laughed and said he was certain it was the company and the booze.

Not all the regulars showed up, of course. They hadn't seen Ten, for example, in a couple of days. Ned's nervous younger brother refused to be counted among Jak's so-called Legion of Queers, but he still made it out most nights to sip bourbon and suck cock. He'd offered to get Jak off on several occasions, but Jak had politely refused, mostly due to the vehement looks Ten and his older brothers would dole out whenever Jak or any of the other regulars were seen in town.

The yard was dark and empty. Laughter permeated the wall behind him and a smile touched his lips although he knew the laughter was the product of alcohol and nervousness, maybe even exhaustion. There were three or four others inside with Thome and Peler — Kel and Seran, both in drag, pristine despite the heat and the tension in town, Valen, an old dyke who everyone thought would have taken over the brothel before Grendl rode in with more gold than most could count, and Scrum One-eye, an old codger who had once been a swamp priest and who now spent his time sipping whiskey and port and crafting dirty limericks that mocked the alien verses of the swamp gods. Somewhere around the place, probably upstairs or out in the kitchen, were a few others: Yun, Reg, Thrace, perhaps even Mira and Letty, a pretty pair of femmes who reminded Jak of much older versions of Idsiyushti and Marrah. Still, on such a hot night, Jak had expected a much higher turnout, maybe ten or fifteen more. More laughter, more songs and limericks, more fucking upstairs in one of the bedrooms Jak had set aside just for such. Tonight, though, it seemed unlikely that any of the beds would get used. Seran and Kel had fucked everybody there already, with the likely exception of Valen, but on any other occasion, Jak would have bet money that by the end of the night, Seran and Kel would be upstairs with Thome and Peler, Scrum One-eye sipping a drink and watching from the shadows. But not tonight. Jak could feel it in the air. With Idsiyushti's arrest and escape, apparently with Marrah in tow, and the terror of the falkr…. It would have been better if Grendl had let him close up shop for a few days.

Another round of laughter passed through the wall. Jak sighed. Then again, where would these last few holdouts go? Grendl's? He doubted it.

Jak stood and stretched. He stepped to the edge of the porch and watched the darkness. Damned if he wasn't feeling melancholy. No, Grendl had been right. Staying open was the best thing. Only now Jak'd need to go into town tomorrow and see if he couldn't convince more regulars to come back out. Maybe he could lower prices for a while. There had to be something he could do.

Behind him, the laughter stopped and Peler's random chord progressions ceased. Heavy footsteps sounded on the wood floor and the front door opened. Jak turned to see Valen lit by the oil lantern above the doorframe.

"You should come see this," she said. She sounded strangely urgent. Jak followed her inside. Someone had built a small fire in the stone hearth, but no one had really bothered to care for it since the night was so hot. Wide-eyed Seran and Kel, doused in sweet perfumes that clung to every surface in the room, urgently fanned themselves with wood-panel fans. Peler looked pale and shaken. Scrum One-eye pointed to something behind the dark-stained bar.

Jak smiled at them all but followed Scrum's finger. On a shelf behind the bar, Jak displayed his so-called relics, objects collected from his travels. Less-than-exotic trinkets that he wove intricate lies about. To one side of the shelf was a wooden totem he'd actually picked up at the bazaar in Esgen but told people he'd bartered from a far-off hill tribe that favored queer sex over straight as a means of cultural exchange and trade. Around the neck of the totem was the chain that held the amulet that was his mother's parting gift.

The amulet, a horned and ridged thing, rune-encrusted and truly exotic, was vibrating and humming, the sound tickling the air. Jak blinked. He looked around at his patrons, but they all stared at him. Seran and Kel stopped fanning themselves, gathered their skirts, and backed away from the bar. Jak looked back at the amulet. Thoughts of his mother's coven flashed before his eyes and then he was around the bar and holding the amulet. Voices raised in question behind him, but he ignored them. He held the amulet in both hands and felt its reverberations ride up his arms, through his shoulders and down his spine.

****

Crashing through the undergrowth, splashing through shallow, murky water, it was difficult for Idsiyushti to tell which was louder, Marrah and her panicked footfalls and stifled squeaks or Chrona and her angry cursing. Herch, for his part, trotted along almost silently.

"We have to go back to town," Chrona repeated. "If something killed Miq, we have to tell Jonath! We have to warn people!"

"What kind of undead was it?" Marrah squeaked, ignoring Chrona. Idsiyushti knew she was trying to hide her panic with questions—while Chrona was trying to hide hers with exasperation. "A drowned corpse? A wight? What if it's a vampire? What will we do if it's vampires?"

Idsiyushti spun, dropped Herch's reins, found each girls' hand and pulled them down into a crouch, their dresses and knees covered in dark, warm water. The splash of the sudden movement underscored Idsiyushti when she said, "Both of you, shut up!" Marrah sobbed, reached down with her free hand into the shadows of the water as if she was trying to grab the muck beneath. Chrona, like she'd been burned, pulled her hand away from Idsiyushti and glared about at the hot night. Herch quietly snorted his derision.

"I don't know what killed Miq," Idsiyushti said. "It was undead—that's all I know."

"We have to get back to town," Chrona said, ignoring Idsiyushti.

Marrah pulled her free hand from the water and wiped it on her dress. "But the falkr will be after Idsi!"

"Miq is dead!" Chrona said. She stood, dripping water, hands on her hips, dark eyes hot and fierce in the darkness.

Idsiyushti felt her teeth grinding in her own head. "Chrona—"

"The falkr can help! Jonath can help! The militia! We have to let them know!" Chrona's voice rose to a bitter, piercing shout with each syllable.

"Chrona!"

The air around them grew suddenly cold and thick. Idsiyushti saw her breath frost before her face, even in the dim light of the stars. Chrona, suddenly wide-eyed, spun in place, her dress and legs splashing. Something large crashed through the trees and water off to the left. Chrona squeaked. Marrah began crying louder. Idsiyushti reached out and grabbed one of Chrona's legs, reaching up under the hem of her drenched skirt to grasp her calf. Chrona screeched, but Idsiyushti held firm. She closed her eyes and shouted words of power, felt fire shoot up her spine, felt it lance from the top of her head out into the night.

The air grew warm again. The swamp and the trees grew still and silent. Idsiyushti squeezed Marrah's hand when it became obvious that the girl was trying to stifle her tears.

"Good girl," Idsiyushti whispered. Chrona still stood, fierce, angry, and scared, trying to look in every direction at once. Marrah had her eyes closed, face screwed up, lips pursed. "They can't see us," Idsiyushti said.

Shadows gathered and slipped through the trees, barely disturbing the hanging vines, branches, murky water. Forms squat and gangly, wreathed in torment, radiating hunger, anger, hatred. A tall thing, white skin against black clothing, impossibly tall, impossibly thin, impossibly white, impossibly black, limbs fluid and boneless. Dead eyes stared at the three girls and the mule, through them, above them. Idsiyushti closed her own eyes and concentrated on her spell, the energy flowing through her, around her. The stench of the dead was a sudden, stomach-churning wave that threatened to overpower her.

"Where are you, witch?" The tall, thin thing asked in a voice that might not have been real. "We know you are here, but we cannot see you. Come out, witch. Show yourself and we won't stand here all night and wait you out. You cannot hide from us forever—"

Idsiyushti shaped the spell of invisibility surrounding them, bolstered it, carved it with need and pain and desire. Then, with a shout that shocked the other two girls into screams of their own, Idsiyushti let the spell go.

They were no longer invisible but shards of magic blasted out in all directions, piercing the forms and the shadows surrounding them. Dead voices howled. The tall, thin thing splintered and flew apart. Idsiyushti grabbed Herch's reins and Marrah's hand and ran, shouting for Chrona to follow.

Jak had always thought it a tavern-keeper's cliché to keep a weapon behind the bar, but he kept a long sword there nonetheless and it slid easily into his hand. Kel squeaked, Seran swooned, and Thome asked, "What the shit, Jac?"

"Valen, head out back. Peller, get upstairs. Find everyone else and bring them in here," Jak said. His mother's amulet was in his off-hand now, vibrating, humming, and he stared at it as the others stared at him. He turned and shouted, "Go!" Both queens squeaked and Scrum One-Eye spat into the only copper spittoon Jak allowed anywhere near his property. But people moved and Jak stood in the center of the room, sword catching the light of the dying fire.

Within minutes, Yun and Reg came in from the kitchen, Valen close behind. Both men were trying to pull on pants and tunics. Valen had armed herself with a large cleaver from the kitchen, offset with the long knife she'd pulled from her belt.

"What the fuck, Jak?" Yun asked.

"They were out back, by the shithouse," Valen volunteered.

"Screw you, dyke," Reg said. "Is it the falkr?"

"No," Jak said. "Just be quiet for a moment."

"Gotta say, Jak," Yun continued. "You need to clean the outhouse. Smells like something died in there. Smells up the whole yard."

Jak's breath caught. The amulet's vibration was the only thing he heard for several moments. When he could breathe again, he realized that he'd broken out in a cold sweat. "Valen, go find Peler and the others, get them in here."

"What's going on?"

"Just go!" Jak went to the front door, which was still open. He peered out into the night but could see nothing but darkness, the yard and the outbuildings hidden beyond the edge of the light from the oil lamp next to the door. He slipped the amulet around his neck. Could he smell the dead smell Yun had complained about? There, maybe. A whiff.

"No. Jonath couldn't be right," he muttered. "He couldn't."

Voices raised behind him indicated that the others had joined them in the common room. Jak turned. Valen, Peler, Letty and Mira, all looking confused. Not Thrace, though. Jak's grip on the longsword tightened. Where was Thrace?

"I'm going to punch Jonath if he thinks he can start coming in here after all this time—" Letty started in, anger twisting her rouged face. The amulet was vibrating even more. The hum was setting Jak's teeth on edge. He didn't know whether to thank his mother or curse her.

Jak said, "It's not Jonath. I want everyone to arm themselves." A chorus of questions and squeals followed. A large crash coming from the doorway to the kitchen cut everyone off. Silence fell almost instantly, broken only by the sounds of their confused breathing, Kel's quiet sobs, the humming of the amulet, and the distinct crackle of flames.

"Out!" Jak shouted. "Everyone out!" If there was a fire and it reached the liquor stores, the whole house would go up. But outside...the smell of the dead, the vibration of the amulet, the darkness barely lit by the only oil lamp on the porch.

Grendl had just laid his head on a hard, silk-covered pillow when Caeri began pounding on the door.

"Grendl!"

"For fuck's sake, what?" He kept the door locked, even when he was inside. The room was his sanctuary, the coolness of the basement seeping in, the darkness, no matter the time of day, a reassuring weight.

"Fire! Jak's place is on fire!"

It took a moment before Grendl said, "Fuck, shit, and damn," and rolled from the bed. He opened the door and Caeri barreled into the room. In the light of the lantern she held, his nakedness, muscular, scarred, tattooed, aged, was like a flash of lightning. Caeri averted her eyes, which Grendl found both annoying and amusing.

"You can see it from upstairs," Caeri spluttered. "Flames touching the sky!"

Grendl grabbed trousers and a tunic with his heavy fist. "Help me get dressed!" He pulled both on followed by a belt and a studded leather doublet as Caeri huffed and grunted, forcing boots on Grendl's feet. Then they were both racing toward the door. Grendl stopped and grabbed his ax. The weapon was probably useless for a fire but some old instinct grabbed at him and wouldn't let go. If it was Jak's place that was burning, then someone who had a grudge against Jak and his Legion of Queers might have set the fire, and that someone might not be too friendly at the moment.

Upstairs, the town square was once again in an uproar. People were pointing and shouting, some even crying, at the glow that lit the night, visible beyond the rooftops lining the western side of the square. Old Marin limped up to the tavern porch and wheezed out that folk had already started running out to Jak's,

215

carrying buckets and rakes and whatever they could find.

"Rakes?" Grendl asked, but he didn't wait for an answer. He ran, followed by Caeri and, at a distance, Marin. The town was alive, nearly every window alight, folk peering out, leaning into the night and shouting questions, directions, curses. Others, many half-dressed, cocks and tits hastily covered while on the run, joined the race towards the flames.

Grendl smelled the fire moments before he heard the screams. Ax in hand, he raced ahead, leaping barely-seen fallen logs, underbrush, a startled, barking dog, all lining the narrow path that ran between Jak's property and town. Legs and lungs pumping, like a barrel running and shouting, forcing townsfolk to leap aside, Grendl roared and cursed. He burst onto Jak's property to see both the main house and the barn alight, flames reaching for the hot night sky. Townsfolk raced about, shouting, screaming, but none were fighting the fire. Instead, they were wrestling with dark shadows that kicked and bit, ripped or tore. Blood flowed freely, steaming on the ground. Grendl stumbled to a halt and stared. Dark shadows flitted from figure to figure with a fluid grace that was terrifying and beautiful.

Then one shadow appeared in front of Grendl. Pale eyes, tendrils of shadow pouring from flared nostrils, teeth as sharp as—Grendl slammed his ax into the things face, kicked the thing in the chest, pulled the ax back, spun, slicing the thing's shattered head from its neck. The thing melted into glowing ash.

"Son of a bitch!" Grendl spat as he leaped aside and cut and slashed, another shadow melting into ash. "Fuck you, Jonath! Fuck you!"

The boneless, twisting shadows, the pale, reeking, scabrous dead, the whispering *things* that ripped and fed were gone. Several of the creatures had turned to glowing ash at the cut and hew of Grendl's ax and when Grendl finally found time to catch his breath, dropping to one knee, leaning on the ax's short haft, the battle was over.

Screams and cries cut the night, vying for attention beneath the hungry roar of the flames and billowing smoke as the growing conflagration engulfed Jak's house, barn, one of the sheds, the outhouses. Sweating, covered in ichor, with several cuts that tore his leather doublet, tunic, trousers, and the flesh beneath, Grendl forced himself back to his feet. He buried the head of the ax in the churned earth and wiped his eyes—eyes that were stinging from the smoke and heat, from sweat and blood, stinging from angry tears.

Jak limped from the liquid darkness between the shifting lights of the flames, a bucket in one hand, a blood-smeared long sword in the other, used as a cane.

Short of breath, Jak handed the bucket to Grendl and said, "Here. Water. Drink."

"You should save this for the fire," Grendl croaked.

"If you think this bucket of water will do anything against that fire, by all means…."

Grendl drank. The water was cool and crisp, only slightly oily. He handed the bucket back. Townsfolk were appearing out of the shifting, feeble darkness, hesitating over the few corpses that had not turned to ash—some burned and blacked, some hacked and cut— to stand and stare at the flames. Townsfolk who had run to help with the fire, who had followed Grendl's bellowing shouts as he ran. And several members of Jak's so-called Legion of Queers. But there were many missing, straights and queers, and that worried him.

"Who was in the house?"

"No one," Jak said. "Thrace, maybe. There were about ten of us who made it out here when the house went up."

Grendl looked at the conflagration-lit yard, the burning structures, the hacked corpses, the piles of ash. "What the fuck is going on out here?"

"The dead," Jak said as if that explained it all. Tears streaked his face. His clothes were blackened and ripped and bloody in places. He pulled an amulet out of the ruins of his tunic. "My mother gave this to me when I left Drilithae for the swamp. It's a ward against the dead—dances around on its own, vibrates when they're near. I thought she gave it to me as a joke, a kind of insult to injury. But it was no joke."

"How did she get it?" Grendl asked almost absently as he started moving towards the gathered townsfolk, thinking of shooing them away back to town. He'd seen plenty of magic amulets in his time.

Jak hesitated, wiped tears and sweat on his tattered sleeve. "She's a necromancer. Has an influential little coven and a successful whorehouse in the Garter District. Know it?"

Grendl stopped. "Yeah. The district and the whorehouse. It's a small-ass empire for something so fucking big."

Jak merely nodded as Drag shouldered his way through the crowd.

"We need to get these people out of here, back to town," Grendl said to no one, to everyone.

Drag hefted a hammer that was black with soot and blood. "We should all stick together. A few folk were running with me from town and something grabbed them from behind."

Grendl spat. "Shit." He looked at the crowd. "Where's Caeri?"

"She was one of the ones grabbed. I turned back for her but—"

"She was with me!"

"Was," Drag said, shaking his head. "You ran ahead, passed right by me. I shouted out to you, but, well. Caeri caught up and stayed nearby until…."

"Shit!" Grendl shouted. He closed his eyes and ground his teeth. Then he turned to Jak. "How many of yours survived again?"

"Six or so, I guess. I saw Thome and Reg go down. And I haven't seen Letty and Mira since we made it out into the yard. Thrace was somewhere about too, like I said, but I haven't seen him either, not since before the fire started." As he spoke, Jak appeared to grow older, wearier, every word, every name a burden that was going to weigh him down into the grave.

Grendl nodded, anger and heartache raging in his own chest. The heat from the raging flames was becoming oppressive. Overhead, the trees surrounding the property were already starting to catch, moss and kudzu smoking and sparking. But the swamp was too wet for the fire to spread quickly or far. Or at least Grendl hoped so.

"Let's get moving," Grendl said finally. He glanced past the flames, towards the smoking trees. Caeri was out there. Others were out there. Other outlying properties—it amazed him that Jonath had been so right. Grendl wondered if it was worth trying to reach the farmsteads, trying to find those who'd been grabbed in the night. He thought of Caeri then, her red hair and pale, freckled tits. He wondered if, once he found her, he'd just have to hack her to pieces like the rest of the undead.

At some point during their flight, when all sense of time had been lost and they were little more than wet and muddy and exhausted, Chrona had asked, "But don't you fly around on a whirlwind? They say you fly around on a whirlwind! Why are we running?"

Out of breath, trying to focus on invisibility, no longer hurling defensive spells randomly at night-shrouded trees and roots because the undead no longer surrounded them, merely followed at a dogged pace with terrifying tenacity, Idsiyushti muttered, "I can't. I barely have enough strength for myself. There's no way I could carry all of us." Idsiyushti didn't hear Chrona's reply.

The hot, horrifying night unfurled around them, a tunnel that led through shallow bogs, around thick root mazes, across fallen trees. They were stumbling, moving slower and slower with each step. Marrah had long ceased to hold onto Idsiyushti's hand and now the girl lagged behind, limping, crying silently. Clouds of insects bit at them. Chrona swore continuously. Then she stumbled and went down, splashing into black, stinking mud. Marrah, still limping and crying, caught up to Chrona and helped the older girl stand. Idsiyushti, looking back, her own features twisted by pain and exhaustion, witnessed the little scene. She stumbled to a halt, watched Marrah approach, watched Chrona, mud-covered, finally give in to tears. Herch, reins in Idsiyushti's tired hand, stopped and snorted at the mud beneath his hooves.

Idsiyushti's shoulders sagged. She looked around. They had entered a sort of muddy hollow, the trees dancing overhead, barely visible in the hot darkness. She closed her eyes and extended herself. The undead were a long way back, still coming, still tracking them blindly, but none were close by. Marrah reached Idsiyushti's side and stopped, stared. She was less covered in mud than Chrona, but her dress was torn, hanging off of one shoulder, revealing the swell of her left breast. At some point, Marrah had lost her boots. She was barefoot now, her feet covered with mud, possibly cut and bruised. Idsiyushti guessed that was why she was limping.

Chrona sobbed loudly once and then sat back down in the mud, head in her hands. She made no further sound, but she seethed anger and terror in equal measure. Something large and loud crawled through the trees beyond the hollow. Chrona's head snapped up and followed the sound.

"We have to keep moving," Idsiyushti said.

Marrah simply sniffed, tears crawling down her dirty face.

Chrona turned back and shook her head. "We can't. Where are we going to go? Where are we even now? This doesn't look like it leads back to town."

Idsiyushti touched the weakening spell of invisibility, felt it tremble. "We are further into the deep dark. The undead…. They herded us away from town."

Chrona's head dropped again. Into her hands, she said, "I thought they couldn't see us."

"They can't. But they still sense roughly where we are. And they can follow our tracks when we are out of water and the invisibility spell has moved on after us." Idsiyushti reached out and tugged the torn shoulder of Marrah's dress back up over the girl's shoulder. Marrah, still crying silently, smiled weakly, but did nothing to keep the fabric from falling back down when Idsiyushti let go. Idsiyushti reached down and grabbed Marrah's hand, squeezed it.

Turning and surveying the hollow, Idsiyushti found a cave of sorts, made from the twisted roots of two trees. She let go of Marrah's hand and Herch's reins and stepped carefully through the mud. They could all squeeze inside the cave, even Herch. She grabbed some dead vines, walked back and smeared their muddy tracks. Satisfied, shoulders still sagging, she motioned for Marrah and Chrona. Marrah approached, still silent, leading Herch. Chrona shook her head and stayed sitting in the mud. Idsiyushti walked over and looked down at her.

"Come on," she said. "We'll hide and rest."

"They'll find us," Chrona sobbed.

"They'll find you for sure sitting here like a half-buried toad."

Chrona looked up, teary-eyed, and opened her mouth to argue. But then she closed her mouth and nodded. Idsiyushti helped her stand and used the vines to smear their tracks to the cave. She used more of her waning strength to cast illusions on the mud of the hollow to help hide their location, and then she crawled into the cave after the others.

Jak walked carefully, painfully, still using the long sword as a cane. He'd taken a wound to his thigh when the dead things swarmed the yard as the buildings on his property had started to burn. He'd bandaged the wound with cloth from his ripped shirt, but there had been no time to find a proper cane or walking stick. Around him, weary and scared townsfolk huddled together as they walked, eying the night-wrapped trees and the twisting path. Valen walked beside him, the leather jerkin she usually wore scratched and torn, one arm held close, wounded in some way. In her free hand, she held the meat cleaver she'd taken from the kitchen. In front of them, Kel and Seran, dresses ripped and muddy, wigs slightly skewed, walked arm-in-arm, radiating an almost primal dignity despite the night's miasma of fear. Scrum One-eye walked in front of the two queens, muttering to himself. He'd picked up a cudgel of some sort and his clothes seemed somehow to be the least abused out of all of them.

The light of the fire from his place was behind them, brightening up the sky. Jak's heart had sunk so low that each time he glanced behind he found that he was actually glad to see the glow and not the figures of the dead crawling along behind them, haloed by the fire that was destroying his home, his livelihood. The dead were nowhere to be seen now—not the walking dead at any rate. They found townsfolk beside the path, some torn apart, some drained of blood, others dead without any sign of struggle or violence. Grendl and Drag, eyes raw with smoke and tears of frustration and anger, lagged behind the group. Jak and Valen eventually joined them mostly due to Jak's limp and helped them behead each of the corpses they passed. Drag half-heartedly stumbled over the inhuman words the swamp gods wanted recited over corpses while Grendl—and eventually Jak and Valen—worked to make sure each corpse could not rise again.

There was no sign of Caeri, but each corpse that was found caused a sharp intake of break from Grendl, which was slowly let out when it became clear the corpse was not the redheaded whore. Fear and tension filled the night. Grendl and Drag were clearly so on edge that it was dangerous. Jak was hurting physically and emotionally, the tip of his longsword now covered in so much mud from supporting his weight that he figured it would be more useful as a club than a blade. The townsfolk ahead were at the breaking point, crying, moaning, holding onto each other, jumping at even the simplest of the most innocuous sounds of the swamp. Eventually, the huddled townsfolk ceased their forward progress and whispers began to reach the ears of those following behind.

Grendl reached the crowd. "Damn it, people! Keep moving!"

Eyes turned, wide and white, staring at Grendl.

"I know you're scared, but we have to keep moving," Drag said.

Ned, shaking and pale, stepped from the crowd and asked, "What if they've already attacked the town, and they're waiting for us?"

"Then we're probably fucked," Grendl said. "But if we stay here, we're *definitely* fucked. Keep moving, Ned. Think of your kids!"

Ned started shaking more. "That was Zriq you hacked to pieces back there, Grendl! Two corpses back! Before you did Lirek! She was my third cousin! She was to start training at the temple next season!"

"I said the words over her," Drag said, reaching out. Ned shrugged him off.

"You don't even care!" Ned shouted at Grendl.

"Fuck this," Grendl said. He shouldered past Ned and began to walk through the crowd, which reluctantly parted, wide-eyed and staring.

"Jonath was right," Jak said over the whispers and talk. Valen was watching him. "Jonath was right. We were attacked tonight—my place destroyed—people lost and hurt because we—I—didn't listen. If I had.... Look, there's still so many folk in the town square, in the town itself, that the dead wouldn't attack them like they did my place. I'm sure of it. It's the outlying farms and homesteads that are in the most danger."

Grendl stopped and turned back. Jak, who felt like collapsing into the mud, straightened himself up instead, met Grendl's sharp gaze.

Grendl finally nodded. "Jak's right." Eyes turned from Jak and the whispers and talk ceased. Ned sniffed and wiped the snot from his nose, the tears from his eyes.

"But you don't actually know that the town is safe, that they haven't already been attacked," Ned said.

"I lost everything tonight," Jak said, his heart aching, his head spinning, his voice forcibly not cracking, his hands forcibly not trembling. Valen reached out and touched his shoulder, a strong grip. There were tears in her eyes. "I have to hope that there is something left for me, for us. Or fuck it, I might as well sit down and let those undead bastards just take me. We have to keep moving." Jak felt the weight of all of the stares. Ned eventually nodded.

The first outbuildings they came across as they approached the town were dark and quiet. A tremor ran through the small crowd, and Grendl, Drag, Jak, Valen, and even Scrum One-eye stepped forward to lead the way. But the glow of the town became apparent soon after, lights in windows, the cook fires in the town square. Voices and unhurried shouts followed. The sound of a mandolin reached them from somewhere. The crowd breathed a sigh of relief and then someone spotted them, and townsfolk rushed out, surrounding, hugging, holding, scolding, questioning. Grendl, waving his ax, led the way into town.

It quickly became obvious that some sort of rudimentary resistance was being mounted by the clergy of the temple, although whether it was in response to the destruction wrought by the fire, the undead, or just the hot night itself was unclear. Old Mackasl, supported by Yun, stood on the porch of Grendl's tavern, ancient eyes shining despite being nearly blind. Power seemed to snap and pop through the air of the square. But this was no mob, unlike the last time Grendl had seen Mackasl standing before the tavern. Instead, the swamp priest was leading a vigil and the townsfolk of the square were watching and waiting, patient, terrified.

Or perhaps it was Marin, dark-skinned, white-haired, finely-dressed, leaning against one of the tavern porch supports, mahogany pipe in his mouth, smoke wreathing his head, that forced the folk into solemn silence. Marin detached himself from the porch and went down to meet Grendl, Jak, Drag, Valen, and Scrum One-eye, the folk in the square parting in wide-eyed silence.

Marin stepped up to Jak. "Your place?"

"Lost," Jak said. A low wail began at the edge of the crowd, a susurration of pain and confusion that grew as folk left behind began to realize that some of those who had gone to fight the fire had not returned. The sound framed Jak's reply like a tightening fist.

Marin nodded, face grim. "Wasn't just a fire, was it?"

"It was the fucking dead," Grendl spat. "They really *do* lurk in this shithole of a swamp!"

"We all knew that, Grendl," someone said from those gathered in the square. "Out in the deep dark. You outsiders just don't listen—"

"Not now!" Marin shouted. He took a deep, rough breath. His pipe had been tucked away yet smoke still seemed to wreath his head. "We've heard that other properties were attacked. Further away from town. We don't know how many. Word only just started to come in right after you went to Jak's."

"Shit," Grendl said. "Where the fuck are Jonath and the falkr? How can they not see the fire at Jak's? It's lighting up the whole damned sky!"

"Maybe they can," Jak said. His face was thin and drawn, his voice strained. "But if other places have been attacked tonight, then maybe Jonath and the falkr are also under attack. Or helping out someplace else, someplace much worse off."

"Exactly," Marin said.

The words of the swamp gods tumbled to a halt. Grendl looked up at the tavern porch and met Mackasl's shining eyes. "Talk to me, old man."

Mackasl—and Yun and Ned's daughter who Grendl finally noticed—bristled. "We felt the rise of the dead and their march on the town several hours ago—"

"And you said nothing?" Jak asked, taking a limping step forward, muddy sword gripped tight. Scrum One-eye and Marin grabbed Jak's shoulders. Jak shrugged them off but went no further.

"We were uncertain of what we felt until it was too late," Mackasl said. "I have not felt the presence of the walking dead for many, many years. Decades. That they have now chosen to mount attacks this far from the deep dark and this close to town is…unexpected."

"Those soldiers said they were attacked by the dead," Drag said.

"They lied," Grendl said. "They were 'attacked' by those damned cane field gobs. Burned every last one of

230

'em for their effort." He turned. "I'm promoting you, Drag. Head of the militia—what's left of it. Take your boys and whoever else you can and arm yourselves properly. Get out there and build bonfires around the edge of town. Get folk living in the houses on the edge to either help you or move closer to the square." Grendl paused to take a deep breath. Through the dull pain of a headache he had barely noticed until now, he forced himself to say, "Jak, I'm conscripting you too. Take your queers and some of these folk here and start building barricades in case we need to close off the square."

"Most straight folk aren't likely to listen to me, Grendl," Jak said. Grendl watched people step from the crowd, step up to stand with Jak. His Legion.

Grendl climbed the steps to the top of the tavern porch and turned around. "Listen up! You do what Jak tells you! Any questions?" He held up his ax. There were, of course, no questions, nor moans of protestation. Only the same wide, solemn stares.

Grendl turned to Mackasl, wrinkling his nose at the musky smell of peat and decay that shrouded the old man, Yun, and Ned's girl. "The shattering of that standing stone that the gobs seemed to be worshipping—could that be connected to the dead attacking now?"

Mackasl stared down at Grendl, face tight, eyes narrow. Finally, "Yes. Maybe. The swamp speaks little of the ancients and their stones, but who knows what twisted power the ancients harnessed for their evil purposes."

"Do your swamp texts mention anything about the stones and the dead?"

"The swamp keeps no texts," Mackasl said. His near-blind eyes flashed in the murky light from the tavern's oil lamps. Beside him, Yun straightened and glared, as if to add weight to the old man's statement. Ned's daughter simply nodded.

Grendl spat. "Of course not. Just old men and their words. Fine. Call on the power of your swamp and help protect this town."

"Only devotion to the swamp can protect this town," Mackasl said. "Not you. Not Jonath. Not those naked sluts who do the emperor's bidding. Devotion!"

"Good to know," Grendl said. "Make all the sermons and devotions you want. Just get your people out of that temple and help protect this fucking town."

"How dare you—" Yun began.

"Mackasl," Marin said from the bottom of the stairs.

"And if it is time for the town to finally be swallowed by the swamp?" Mackasl asked the old knight.

Marin sighed. Smoke still wreathed his head. "Do your prophecies mention anything about the swamp rising up and claiming its own with the help of the dead?"

"The walking dead are abominations!" Yun spat.

"You know it doesn't," Mackasl said, ignoring Yun. "But if the dead are just another of the abominations in this town, if they are a sign that the swamp will rise and claim its own, then there is nothing we can do." Marin stepped aside as the old man all but dragged Yun and Ned's girl down the stairs and into the crowd.

Idsiyushti dozed, her body aching, drained, yearning for a soft sleeping pallet, whiskey, wine, anything other than heat, mud, and fear. She pulled Marrah close as they both faded in and out of restless sleep. They were dirty and smelled of the swamp, but there was little they could do about that. Idsiyushti felt Marrah's warmth and she thought about reaching out and slipping a hand past the edge of Marrah's ripped blouse to cup smooth skin.

Marrah murmured as if she could sense Idsiyushti's thoughts in her sleep. Idsiyushti smiled weakly, thought of biting Marrah's neck, of teasing her until she was wet and pleading, thought of feeding off of their shared energy and passion, sopping up the girl's orgasm like bread in gravy. She could nourish herself on Marrah's desire, converting moans and convulsions, gasps and kisses into a form of sustenance that could help replenish her fatigue-drained magic, not unlike the fey trick of surviving on liquor alone for days on end. But they'd left Miq's whiskey behind when they had fled, along with their water gourds, blankets, nearly everything, and although it would be an easy, delightful way to replenish a small amount of much-needed magical energy, Idsiyushti could sense that Marrah was also too exhausted. Instead, she kissed Marrah's dirty hair and held her close. The older girl murmured and let out a quiet snore.

The night was hot, wet, cloying. Only twice did Idsiyushti feel a probing touch against her spells. Each time the probe woke her from a frenetic, jumbled dream that had more shadows and darkness in its jagged images than were actually out in the hollow beyond the root cave. Both times the touch brushed against the spells, Idsiyushti sat up, wide-eyed, gasping, trying to concentrate in order to keep the spells from reacting in any tell-tale way. The first time, Marrah moaned in her sleep. The second, Marrah jumped and squeaked quietly. Her hand had been caught beneath Idsiyushti's dress, hot against Idsiyushti's hip. Marrah muttered an apology, but Idsiyushti, after making certain the probing touch had done nothing more than flicker against the spells, pulled Marrah close and kissed her. Marrah's hand slowly crept back up under Idsiyushti's dress, running in tingles along sweaty skin. Idsiyushti thought again of drawing energy from Marrah, but sleep took them both almost immediately. Neither Herch nor Chrona seemed to notice.

The spells shattered an hour before dawn. Idsiyushti all but screamed, biting her tongue to keep herself quiet as she woke, confused. Marrah fell away from her. Chrona was already awake and staring into the darkness of the hollow beyond the roots sheltering them. She turned, startled, when Idsiyushti sat up so abruptly. Herch shifted his weight, black eyes watching Idsiyushti intently.

Idsiyushti felt sick to her stomach. Moaning, she fought the urge to vomit and shook her head, trying to clear her vision.

"What is it?" Marrah whispered, her voice full of fear and confusion.

"Something broke the spells," Idsiyushti said. Her head was spinning. "They can find us now."

"What?" Chrona asked. She rolled to her knees and crawled towards Marrah and Idsiyushti, angling around Herch. "Cast them again! Cast them again!" Herch brayed as if in agreement.

"Be quiet!" Idsiyushti said. She held her head in both hands. "I just need a moment. I need to be able to think!"

Marrah reached out, touched Idsiyushti's leg. In the darkness, it was clear she was crying again. "Just try to focus. Take your time. It's okay."

"Please be quiet," Idsiyushti whispered. She was rocking back and forth now. The backlash of the shattered spells caused chaos to swirl in her head, jumbling up things that might have been dreams, might have been memories. For the hundredth time, she cursed herself for leaving the whiskey behind, the one thing she could have used to replenish her power quickly without, for instance, draining Marrah dry. Her body ached, her neck was cricked. Her shoulders were tight and sore. Her breathing was ragged and she felt overly hot, as if in the grips of a dangerous fever. "I just—I need—"

"Quiet!" Chrona hissed. Herch pranced nervously. The cave suddenly smelled overwhelmingly of fear and donkey. Then there were footfalls, heavy, measured. Other sounds followed, a burst of movement and breathing that was strange and fluid and terrifying. Marrah slapped both hands over her mouth, eyes wide. Idsiyushti tried to stand, wobbled, fell back to her knees. Hot tears were stinging her eyes and burning down her cheeks.

A gnarled grey head, wreathed in stringy ashen hair, a strange hat of mottled leather atop the tufts of hair, looked into the cave. Chrona shrieked and lashed out. The head vanished and the sound of rushing feet broke the desperate stillness that followed. Idsiyushti sobbed and raised her hands, tried shouting a spell, the words of which came crawling unbidden up her spine.

Then a monstrous abomination was before them, blocking the opening of the cave. Idsiyushti gestured but her spell drained away, a mind of its own, and she cried out in rage. She balled her fist, ready to strike. The abomination reached out and covered her fist, its mouth open, words that Idsiyushti couldn't understand issuing forth. Idsiyushti's vision blurred, darkened, and then she was in the abomination's arms. She kicked and screamed and fought, but the thing held her tight, whispering words that were alien and terrifying.

The abomination knew her name, repeated it over and over.

Screaming, Idsiyushti tumbled to the ground, somehow loose from the creature's grip. Behind her, Chrona and Marrah were screaming too. Herch was stamping his hooves. She tried to roll over, to see her friends, her lover, to reach out to them, protect them. But the thing was in the way, towering over her. Idsiyushti scooted backward in the mud, her dress wet and heavy. Another creature stepped into her line of sight. It was another abomination, gray-skinned, thin, much shorter than the first. It carried a cruel staff which it raised and brought down, the butt thudding deep into the mud. It spoke one word, which echoed, shaking the earth of the entire hollow, shaking the trees and the root mazes.

Idsiyushti's vision went black at the sound of that single word. And then, as if washed away by cool, clean water, her vision cleared. She stared. The hobgoblin stepped back. Ashakarahad tried to smile, tried to look reassuring despite her sharp, jagged teeth. Chrona and

Marrah were calling out to Idsiyushti, calling out for her to stop, to listen, to calm down. Slowly, carefully, Ashakarahad bent down. Sobbing, Idsiyushti rushed into her arms and held on for dear life.

The hobgoblin gave Idsiyushti a wooden cup that contained something dark, bitter, and vile. She gagged it down under watchful eyes and fought the urge to throw the empty cup across the hollow. The hobgoblin, some sort of matriarch for the small band of goblins, took the cup and tucked it into a pouch at her tattered belt.

A moment later, the drink hit Idsiyushti. She fought down a fresh wave of nausea, took several deep, terrifying breaths, and then the nausea slipped away. As did her headache, most of her body aches. She felt a warm glow coursing through her body, felt the well of her magic begin to bubble once again, distant, weak, but definitely there, definitely rising. The power she'd exhausted against the undead and in maintaining concealment during the night was recharging faster than she'd have managed with sleep and food, or fucking Marrah, or channeling the power of whiskey.

"Bane root," Idsiyushti said, blinking. "Thistle and..."

"Miter powder, ground miter powder," the hobgoblin said.

"Yes, of course. Thank you."

"You came out here and didn't bring proper supplies. What sort of witch are you?" The hobgoblin sat back, clutching her staff, yellow eyes sharp and piercing.

Idsiyushti tried to muster the strength to be offended, but she knew the hobgoblin was right. She could have stopped to gather herbs, roots, and spices, but instead, she'd opted for trying to survive on Miq's whiskey until it was too late. She knew it had been pure defiance, but now, after the nightmarish chase and exhausting night, she wasn't sure who or what she'd been defying. Idsiyushti closed her eyes and let herself bask in the warm glow of the drink before saying, "I didn't leave town of my own free will. And I—we—left our last camp in a hurry. I had been bound by the falkr—"

"The what?"

"The falkr. They serve the human emperor. And the elf emperors before that. Tall females who wear little armor and not much else and carry big, flaming swords. And they fly."

"Ah," the hobgoblin said. "The dead are harrying them a long way from here."

Idsiyushti hesitated. If the hobgoblin knew about the falkr, perhaps she knew about Jonath and Grendl, about what was going on in town. On the other side of the hollow, Ashakarahad helped Marrah tend to Herch.

Ash, so tall, broad-shouldered, elegant in her own way even in her ripped blouse and stained clothes. Marrah, her torn dress partially mended with thread and a needle that Ash had carried in her belt pouch, looked tired yet relieved. They made a pair that touched Idsiyushti's heart and made it swell in a way that, strangely, took her off guard. Chrona's voice, not far beyond, was harsh and irritating as she scolded the goblins and fended off their attempts at helping her build a cook fire.

"The falkr had me captive," Idsiyushti said, turning back. "They had me bound such that my magic was unreachable and didn't recover while I rested. Marrah and Chrona freed me and we fled into the swamp. I didn't have time to gather the proper supplies. I didn't have time to really rest and recover either. I thought I did, while we traveled, but when the dead found us, I exhausted myself and we left nearly everything we had behind. All I have left are some medicinal herbs but they wouldn't help me, not like this."

The hobgoblin grunted. "The dead were also using their own magic against you, chipping away at your will." Idsiyushti stared at her. The hobgoblin sighed. "You learned your ways at the feet of the fey, witch. Why is it so surprising that a hobgoblin would know anything at all about the ways of magic?" The hobgoblin sniffed in what Idsiyushti took to be derision.

Idsiyushti blinked and looked away. "Forgive me. I—Mistress, I don't know what to call you."

"You never bothered to ask. Gobs and hobgobs are just another form of scampering swamp animal to—no, that doesn't do anyone any good." The hobgoblin shook her head. Then, alarmingly human-like, she sighed and straightened her shoulders. "You may call me Ceàrain."

Idsiyushti blinked. "That sounds elven," she said.

"It is." Ceàrain levered herself up with her staff and walked towards the collection of goblins surrounding Chrona. She shooed them away and snapped her long fingers in the direction of the fire Chrona was trying to build. Flames jumped almost instantly. Idsiyushti smiled. She was transported back to her time with the fey, when she'd been so young, so small. The trees and leaves and grass had smelled sharply all year round, regardless of the temperature, rain or sun. Colors had been vibrant and alive. Sounds had been beyond musical. Laughter had been a language all its own. Idsiyushti wiped a tear. The problem with memories, she knew, was that there was no way to be sure that what she remembered was what had really happened. Time colors all things, sometimes with shades of gray, sometimes as vibrant as the dawn. And the fey were nothing if not masters of vibrant colors and illusion.

Marrah, followed by Ashakarahad, walked over to Idsiyushti. Marrah sat down and put her arm around Idsiyushti's shoulders, kissed her cheek.

"You look better."

"I'm starting to feel better," Idsiyushti said. "You look better too."

Marrah winced. "I will only after a hot bath. And a new dress."

Idsiyushti looked up at Ashakarahad. The demoness slowly lowered herself to the ground as if stiff and aching, her head still towering above them despite being seated. "It is good to see you, Idsi."

"You too, Ash," Idsiyushti said. She reached out and touched Ashakarahad's hand, squeezed it. "Thank you for finding us. And I'm really sorry I tried to attack you."

The demoness laughed long and loud. "I didn't find you. Ceàrain and her clan did."

"What happened to you? After the explosion?" Idsiyushti reached out with her other hand and touched Marrah's muddy dress-covered thigh, completing a sort of chain, a connection between all three of them.

"That's hard to explain," Ashakarahad said. "I went to another place, another world."

"How is that possible?" Marrah asked.

Ashakarahad laughed again. "That's what my people do. We travel to different worlds. Sometimes we get summoned, sometimes we get caught." Her orange eyes flared. "This time, I don't know what happened, but I suspect it was the power of the mage-lords trapped within that standing stone. I was sent away but I wasn't released so, somehow, I wound up back here in the swamp."

"Wait. Released?" Marrah looked at Idsiyushti.

"It's why I'm in the swamp in the first place. I was summoned to this world long ago, trapped here. My memory is vague and scattered, full of holes, and I don't remember much of my time as a prisoner. Or a slave. But the empire of the mage-lords fell, and with them, my captivity faded over the millennia. But I was still trapped here. I've been searching for a way to free myself ever since. I figured the ruins in the swamp were my best lead, my best chance."

"That's why you wanted me to try to activate that standing stone," Idsiyushti said. "I'm so sorry." Ashakarahad smiled, revealing her jagged teeth. Idsiyushti pressed on, "What did you do in this other world?"

"Fought, once. Wandered mostly. Followed some voices, looked at a city that never seemed to end and never drew any closer no matter how far I marched. Found a river and stood in the shadow of mountains that were black as night and smelled of death."

"That sounds terrifying," Marrah said. Ashakarahad simply smiled again, wider this time.

"How did you get back?" Idsiyushti asked.

"I'm not sure about that either. I found another standing stone and it shattered. Well, someone shattered it—I don't know who. Then I wound up back in the swamp."

"A standing stone like the one in the goblin clearing? Like the one in town?"

"Yes, basically. But there were voices too. I couldn't see who was speaking, shouting all around me, like they were trying to stop me. At first, I thought they wanted to help me, but, no. The voices belonged to people who just wanted to trap me again, like I'd been trapped here. It took a long time to figure that out, but I'm certain it's true. So I tried to resist and after a time, I succeeded. Then a figure appeared, someone cloaked, their face hidden, and they broke the standing stone."

"Who were they?" Marrah asked, eyes wide.

Ashakarahad glanced across the hollow at Ceàrain and the goblins. "I don't know. But the voices, the people seeking to trap me—they were the mage-lords. I'm sure of it now. Or their descendants. You see, I'm still bound to this world, so when I left it, I went someplace where they still have power."

"But the mage-lords have been gone for thousands of years."

"Exactly," Ashakarahad said. "History tells us the mage-lords just vanished, leaving a fallen civilization. But I think they actually just left this world for another and when the stone exploded in the goblin clearing, I was sent where they went, or where their kin went." She shrugged her broad shoulders. "Anyway, when the stranger broke the stone there, I ended up back here, in the deep dark, near a different standing stone. I was lost—still lost, I guess. Eventually, I was found by Ceàrain and her clan."

"You're lucky the dead didn't find your first," Marrah said, shuddering. Idsiyushti squeezed her thigh.

Ashakarahad laughed again. "Ceàrain said the same thing. Several times."

Scrum One-eye fetched Jak a walking stick to use instead of the longsword. Townsfolk watched Jak with glassy eyes as he hobbled about, longsword over his shoulder, but they did as they were told—working together with Jak's so-called Legion to find furniture, crates, and debris that could be used to barricade the square. The night was hot and the dawn was approaching. Some folk muttered that they thought the dead wouldn't bother them during the day, but others shushed them and asked if they were certain of that. They weren't.

At the edge of town, Drag and his helpers were erecting and lighting great bonfires. The smoke drifted back across the square, filling the air with a haze that underscored the heat of the approaching morning.

"What we need is a storm," Jak said, looking up. Unseasonal clouds drifted high up in the sky, above the smoke, blotting the stars. But the rainy season was a long way off. There was little the weather would do to thwart the dead now. Instead, the wet, sapping heat would try to break the townsfolk as they scrambled and worked at a fevered pace.

Word of the undead and those lost responding to the fire spread through the town quickly. More folk were out of their homes and in the square, adding to the number of people who had been living in the tents and lean-tos, adding to those who had gathered to hear Mackasl preach from atop Grendl's porch. People dragged large pieces of furniture to the square, offering them up as material for the barricades. Jak saw battered and faded tables and chairs, a broken bed frame, and not a few rickety bookshelves. But there were also family treasures—a richly-painted chest, a large dining table that looked heavy and ancient and freshly polished, the pieces from a fine four-poster bed that still had delicate lace hanging from them. Jak's heart sank further as he directed people to move their heirlooms into place beside the battered and bruised, cast-off pieces. He would never have imagined that folk would give up their treasures so easily. But then, all of his treasures, his pride and joy, his collections and memories, were gone, lost in flame and smoke and the shadow of the ravenous dead.

Fear hung heavy in the hot, wet air, but the shouts between the barricade builders and the folk working with Drag to build the bonfires were growing, containing hints of humor and competition. The bonfires were causing the pre-dawn sky to begin to glow and Jak's heart wrenched again as he forced himself not to look at the firelight far out over where his property had stood.

Jak's leg was also giving him trouble. He found a chair that wasn't currently being used for the barricades or the bonfires or anything else and sat down. Some folk glared at him, others looked at his pale face, the streaks of ash and blood on his torn, silk tunic, and quickly looked away. He rested the long sword across his lap and sat with his wounded leg extended. A girl he didn't know, pretty and polite, brought him a mug of whiskey that was surprisingly cool going down. He turned to thank the girl but she was already gone, dress whipping around her as she joined several people pulling down a tent that was in the way of the barricades. Children stood nearby, wide-eyed and crying, members of the family who owned the tent. The rest of the family stood beside their few belongings, forlorn, silent. Finally, the father and the eldest children joined the barricade construction and the mother gathered the youngest into her skirts and whispered to them.

Jak watched the children and their mother for a moment then forced himself to stand with help from the walking stick and limped, heavy-hearted, to another barricade to inspect its progress, longsword over his shoulder.

The bonfires lit the layer of smoke that obscured the stars, creating a red-orange false dawn. Grendl looked out the window of one of the small rooms the girls used to entertain clients and sipped from a tumbler of smoky bourbon. Behind him, the small bed, stripped of its dirty sheets, straw-filled mattress laid bare, joined the small sideboard shelf with its ceramic wash basin and water pitcher to furnish the room. Three fat candles were in three ornate sconces on three different walls, but the candles were unlit so that Grendl could see down into the square and out across the rooftops to the glow of the bonfires. Even without the candles, the room was hot and musty. The bourbon was slowly starting to taste like piss.

Down in the square, the townsfolk seemed desperate and harried. The tumult of the small tent city had turned to yet another form of chaos—this one more like a slightly organized version of the destruction wrought by panic when the falkr had first appeared, descending from the sky. Tents and lean-tos were being hastily dismantled and people's property was being lined up and stacked. Furniture, crates, casks, blankets, trash, even a painting that looked garish in the light of the fires, were all hoisted up and put into place on the barricades, ready to close off the few narrow alleys and two broad lanes the led into and out of the square. The bed and shelf behind him should be taken down and added to the piles, he knew, with the tables and chairs from downstairs in the common room. The heavy, scarred bar itself would also make a valuable contribution. But Grendl ignored that thought and continued to stare.

The tension that had gripped the town had found another avenue, another outlet. He had no idea what Jonath would make of what had happened since the constable and the falkr had gone off in search of Idsiyushti and Ashakarahad. He didn't know what the falkr would make of it either, but he didn't care about the falkr. He barely cared about Jonath's reaction and admitted that his caring was tainted by concern about the future of his own business and his connections in the town. But Jonath was, like it or not, a kindred spirit of sorts, one of the few people in that little backwater that had any real connection to the life Grendl had left behind, to the memories which lurked just beneath the surface, staring out into the world from behind Grendl's eyes.

He left the room and went downstairs. At the bar, Sek was lining jugs of water and small beer next to baskets of bread and potatoes. She looked tired and scared and Grendl gave her a weak smile and tried not to think about Caeri out there in the swamp, somewhere between the town and Jak's place. He was down to one whore. He had no idea what Jonath and, more importantly, the falkr would do to Marrah and Chrona if they were caught with Idsiyushti. He sincerely hoped that Jonath would prevail and show cool reason, bring the girls back to town to be judged by Marin over at the courthouse, maybe under the eyes of a tribunal of sympathetic townsfolk. But the falkr…. Convincing the falkr to show mercy and reason might not be easy. His only real hope lay with the fact that Idsiyushti should be able to take care of both girls, and herself, out there in the swamp. She had fey magic, and if the fey didn't want to be seen or heard or found, there's no way they would be.

Grendl went outside and found Marin standing near a small campfire, holding a hastily sketched map of the town. There were marks for the barricades and the locations of the fires Drag's conscripts were building. Jak stood nearby, glancing from the map to the surrounding buildings as if judging distances and locations, leaning on a walking stick, sword over his shoulder. Both men looked like explorers trying to find their way, trying to map a deep ruin or an expanse of jungle that had never known the touch of anything other than birds and snakes and big cats. Behind Jak, that old dyke, Valen, stood like a caravan guard or hired muscle. She'd found a long-handled ax and had it slung over her shoulders. Grendl eyed her and sighed, Sphinx's words about desire echoing across the back of his skull. All three looked up at Grendl as he approached. Valen was unreadable. Fair-skinned Jak looked even more pale and pained, although, for a moment, there was something hard behind his green eyes, something that flashed like a thin-bladed dagger in some distant, sunless alley. Marin looked old and thin, but a fire burned in his dark eyes that belied his age, almost a counter-point to the edge Grendl now saw in Jak. The old knight was clearly enjoying himself while the rakish queer looked less like someone who had lost everything and more like some who wanted cold vengeance for that loss, which caught Grendl strangely off-guard.

"Five families just made it into town from their farms and homesteads," Marin said. "They ran and came empty-handed. Some of them lost folk on the way."

"The dead chase them out?" Grendl asked, trying to regain his composure.

"Yes."

"Others might have tried to do the same," Jak said, his old mask slipping back into place with a smoothness that was equally surprising. "Hold-outs from when Jonath put out the word. But who knows if they'll make it."

Marin changed the subject, "Drag says that there are things moving out in the swamp, in the trees, just beyond the reach of the bonfires."

Grendl took a deep breath. "Have folk from the edge of town been moving to the square?" He looked at the map. There were scattered homes radiating outwards from the center of town that were beyond the radius of the fires.

"Yes, although some are staying, ready to put up a fight," Marin said.

Grendl frowned. It wasn't likely to be much of a fight. "Jak, make sure everyone who can fight has a weapon of some kind. Anything at this point—although with the dead, who knows what will work the best."

Jak nodded. "We could really use Idsiyushti right about now."

Marin chuckled and said, "We could also use the falkr right about now."

Jak laughed as he limped off. Over his shoulder, he said, "The dead attacked right after the falkr arrested Idsiyushti and tried to take away her magic, right after the falkr and Idsiyushti—and Jonath—disappeared into the swamp. Call me paranoid, but…." His words trailed off as he moved away, followed by Valen. Grendl watched them both, looked at the longsword across Jak's shoulder, wondering. What had Jak said about his mother? A sorceress who ran one of the big brothels in Drilithae? Grendl knew the place although he'd never met Jak's mother. But that flash in Jak's eyes…. There was no doubt that Grendl had seen it before, but it was in the eyes of professional killers. Perhaps Jak too was running from something, something other than a rich, disgraced, queer life in the capital.

"Could he be right?" Marin asked, interrupting Grendl's musings.

"About being paranoid about the falkr? Who knows? I think it's just as likely those soldiers stirred up the dead when they attacked the gobs."

"Why? How? And what about that exploding standing stone?"

"Don't know," Grendl said, shaking his head. "Has Mackasl moved his people into the square?"

"No," Marin said. "It looks like they want to fortify the temple and take a stand there."

"Son of a bitch," Grendl said. Grinding his teeth, he forced Jak from his mind and went back into the tavern to don his armor and gear. Then he took a long drink of a rare, aged brandy from the private stock he'd stashed behind the bar. He took several long, deep breaths and then went back out, all while Sek watched him with wide, dark eyes.

The temple to the swamp gods was awash in the lurid glow of nearby bonfires and torchlight. The tent that had been erected for worship and temporary habitation had been pulled down, and the graveyard was now spotted with smaller bonfires tended by members of the temple flock armed with picks, shovels, and hammers. The temple grounds, while still within the town proper, were at the very edge, always had been, abutting a deep lagoon of black, moss-covered water whose surface was only broken by the skeletons of decaying plank gangways and docks, none of which had been used for decades. Several skiffs had been launched, however, each carrying bright, smoking torches and oil lanterns, lighting up the surface of the lagoon and the faces of the frightened faithful acting as crew.

Grendl found Mackasl in the graveyard, being tended to by Ned's daughter, whose name Grendl still could not recall. The two were looking out at the collection of small fires, Mackasl nodding sagely, the girl clearly miserable. Smoke from the graveyard fires and the bonfires built by Drag's conscripts made a cloying fog that all but obscured the temple itself from the graveyard and burned tears into the eyes of the faithful. Grendl pulled a rag from his pouch, soaked it in a bucket sitting on the wall of the temple well, and covered his mouth.

Mackasl cast his rheumy eyes at Grendl and frowned. His gray-white, kinked hair peeked out from under a heavy, dirty cowl. "You'll not make us leave this place, whore master. We will await the judgment of the swamp gods right here, right now."

"Just gonna give up like that?"

"We're not giving up!" Ned's daughter said. Her olive complexion looked sallow in the firelight and smoke.

"Hush, girl," Mackasl said. "We will await judgment. If that judgment is that we shall die at the hands of the forsaken dead, then so be it. But we will not die without a fight."

Grendl said, "Ah."

The girl spat. "You're an unbeliever, you one-armed whore master." Despite the insult, her voice lacked conviction.

Grendl shook his head. "We aren't likely to be able to help you out here. We've barricaded the square. Bring your…flock and join us. You'll be able to await the swamp gods' judgment among your family members and we could use the help."

"No," Mackasl said. "We know the truth, dwarf. You and the rest will see for yourselves. We will only aide those who chose to aide themselves."

"By what? Staying out here in the open, in a fucking *graveyard* while the dead attack?" Ned's daughter blinked and shook visibly at Grendl's words. He looked at her, but she drew herself up and turned to stare into a nearby fire.

"You are not welcome here," the girl said without turning back.

"Your family is already in mourning, girl," Grendl said. "Don't force them to needlessly mourn you as well."

"She is with her family now," Mackasl said. "Leave us, whore master. We have preparations to make."

"Are you really this stubborn?" Grendl asked. "You'll risk the death of your followers just to prove that you are somehow more faithful than the rest of the town?"

Mackasl sniffed. The girl turned back, her eyes wide and rimmed with tears.

Grendl turned in a circle and shouted, "Listen to me! The square is barricaded. We have food and arms. Your families are there!"

"Grendl!" Mackasl hissed. He reached out but Grendl shook his hand off.

"You can stay here and be foolish and dead! Or you can 'help yourselves' and come with me back to the barricades!"

Voices shouted back, a cacophony of dismissal and frustration. Grendl said, "Shit."

"Go, whore-master," Mackasl said. There was anger and fear in the air, almost as thick as the smoke from the fires. Folk in the graveyard and in the temple proper were coughing and spitting.

Grendl looked at the girl again. Something seemed to change in her face.

"My uncle," she said.

"Lost on the path between town and Jak's place."

"That den of vile faggotry," Mackasl spat.

"I'm sorry," Grendl said to the girl. He turned and walked away. Eyes followed him through the smoke. The fires crackled and popped, but all else was silence. A lone voice broke into prayer inside the temple. In the light of the fires, beneath the smoke, the bas-reliefs on the temple walls danced and writhed. Grendl looked quickly away.

Shouting rang out behind Grendl but he ignored it until a hand touched his shoulder. He spun and Ned's daughter quailed.

"I've changed my mind," she said after a time. "I want to go back to the barricade." Other forms appeared out of the smoke, ragged, teary-eyed folk who looked scared and defeated. Mackasl's shouts followed them.

"You will pay for giving up on the trust of the gods!" Mackasl waved his staff in the air but Grendl turned and led the way back to the square. As they approached the nearest of Drag's bonfires, the smoke thinning in favor of rising to hide the sky rather than obscure the world around them, a crack of thunder rang out and a pulse of air nearly knocked them all the to ground. Grendl staggered and spun. A glowing nimbus, a wall of wavering light, cut the graveyard and the temple off from the rest of the swamp and the town. The faithful picked themselves up and stared.

"Oh no," someone said. Ned's daughter was looking from the barrier to an alley that led to the square, tears freely running down her cheeks.

The pre-dawn sky was almost completely hidden by smoke. The light from the encircling bonfires burned orange and red and painted the newly abandoned homes and buildings beyond the barricades with colors that were at once garish and terrifying. In the direction of the temple and the graveyard, the strange shield that had been raised began to glow a dull grey, as if the dancing fires were somehow drawing the life and energy from it. None could see past the shield so none knew what was happening at the temple, in the graveyard, or out on the lagoon. None knew whom the shield was meant to keep from the temple—the dead or the faithless townsfolk.

Tears of sweat and fear and dirty anger stained the faces in the square. Children wailed in brief spurts that were quieted by the atmosphere itself. Waiting became an insidious game of blind panic coupled with maddening inaction, especially after Drag and his bonfire builders returned to the square and the last of the swamp's refugees were safely behind the ramshackle barricades. Wine and whiskey were passed around freely, empty casks being fitted onto the barricades, as if drinking was necessary for the survival of the town. Perhaps it was.

It was the crawling fingers of long, jagged shadows growing at angles along the fronts of the homes and buildings, wavering and dancing with a rhythm that had nothing to do with the bonfires, that signaled the attack. Seeping into and out of gaping windows and open doors. Twisting around solemn, oil-lantern-lit porches and wooden stoops. A cold breeze briefly announced the arrival of the crawling shadows, but the breeze died almost instantly and left the town suffocating and molten. A dog barked somewhere beyond the square and was silenced shortly after, a single, high-pitched yelp echoing across the square.

Some said the graying shield that surrounded the temple and the graveyard pulsed and shimmered minutes before the crawling shadows began reaching down the alleys and dirt lanes. Because of this, most folk concluded that the dead were able to bypass the bonfires by coming from the lagoon, first assaulting the temple, somehow bypassing at least one part of the shield. Angry voices would eventually be raised at this, directed at the memories of Mackasl, Yun, the swamp gods, the temple itself. Other voices were raised at Drag and Grendl for not foreseeing that the path from the lagoon through the graveyard was a weakness, allowing the bonfires to be ignored. But this was much, much later.

Grendl saw the creeping fingers of shadow, bent and grasping, from the second floor of the tavern. The tavern's gabled rooftop was now within the layer of smoke that blanketed the sky and threatened to sink down and fill the rooms beneath. Grendl had closed nearly all the second-floor windows as best as possible, wet rags shoved under the sills, but the smoke was like a creeping fog. It reminded Grendl of his nights onboard a ship that crawled, slowly, nervously, through poisonous fogs along the distant Adril Coast while screaming, nearly invisible bird-things clung to jagged rocks and hurled insults at the sailors.

Grendl turned at the sight of the shadows and ran downstairs, ax in hand, the buckles of his leather armor jangling like a folk minstrel dancing a harvest jig. The tavern's common room was empty and quiet. Sek was waiting by the door to hand out jugs of water and help attend to any wounded that were dragged into the common room—Grendl had grudgingly volunteered it since it was the largest ground-floor space fronting the square. Sek's face was drawn and ashen and she gripped a short sword in both hands.

Outside, bells, chimes, even pots and pans were already ringing. Shouts were echoing through the smoky air. Confusion swept through the square like a wave, chased by a torrent of panic and fear, which in turn was chased by a surge of anger and raised weapons. Picks, hoes, mallets, shovels, swords, axes, pikes, a billhook or two—Grendl saw Drag waving a massive hammer at a group of townsfolk before one barricade. At another, Jak, longsword raised, was hobbling with the help of his walking stick, shouting, surrounded by dykes and fags and drag queens, each armed and each shouting in turn. Townsfolk followed. Ned's daughter stood near her father, their grief plain on their faces as they shouted and joined another rush to a third barricade.

Marin was beside Grendl then. The old knight was dressed in oiled leather and chain, a broad, curved sword in one hand, a dagger in the other. Screams sounded and both Grendl and Marin were running. The dead crashed against the barricades. On the rooftops, men, women, and children fired burning arrows and crossbow bolts. A cold that was unreal and terrifying and black as pitch began to crawl along the ground, trying to slow the defenders, trying to drag them down into despair and loss. The dead tried to climb the barricades and were met at the top with spears and pikes and poles. More arrows rained down. Some of the dead were alight, trying to catch the barricades on fire as they thrashed and wailed. But Jak had ordered folk to coat the barricades with as much water as possible so the wood failed to catch, simply smoked in places while the burning dead fell back and writhed into nothingness.

Some dead found their way through the buildings and homes surrounding the square. They were met on the porches and in the square itself, hacked apart and set afire. Others made it to the rooftops, either by climbing the walls or climbing up through the buildings. They were met by desperate folk who shot them and stabbed them and hurled them back down to the ground. Others made it to the top of the barricades and passed the polearms and pitchforks, making it down the other side. They were met by Grendl and Marin and Drag and Jak and the Legion of Queers, who had started singing ribald tavern songs as they fought, the lyrics of which Grendl knew but tried to ignore.

Townsfolk fell as well, dragged from the rooftops, dragged back up and over the barricades, dragged into houses and homes and out into the hot, fire-painted night. Torn and ripped, mauled, drained, violated by dead hands, teeth, claws, rotting cocks, and even writhing tentacles. Most of the folk, however, men, women, young and old, held their own, screaming, kicking, hacking, stabbing. Children ran around with torches, at once delighted and terrified, lighting the hacked-apart dead and turning them into melting ash. Blood, tears, and sweat flowed. Laughter joined the screams, though no one could say who it was that was laughing—the townsfolk or the attacking dead or both. More voices picked up the songs of Jak's legion. The flames from the bonfires sparked into the air and caught some of the outlying homes, quickly, brightly eating into them. Dawn, high above the smoke and fighting, was beaten to the mark by the hot, too-bright glow of flame and battle, a wilting, sweltering battle that was equal parts standstill and payback, fought long and hard.

By midmorning, the dead still came, only slightly slower in the thin, smoke-hazed daylight. The townsfolk fought and bled and stood their ground, holding the square while the town, the swamp, the world around them seem to burn.

Idsiyushti woke to Chrona shouting, "Damn it! Get your gob hands off me!"

"Chrona, shut up," Idsiyushti muttered. She tried to roll over, but someone was shaking her.

"Idsi, you have to wake up." Idsiyushti opened her eyes and blinked. Marrah was leaning over her, face full of concern.

"What is it?" It was nearly dawn by the look of the pale sky, dotted now with dark clouds. The air was hot and thick, but she could tell, deep down, that an unseasonal rain was coming, not too far off. She turned to see Chrona attempting to shoo away a goblin that was making motions indicating that the older girl needed to get up.

"The sky above your town burns," Ceàrain said, attracting Idsiyushti's attention.

Idsiyushti's heart sank. "What do you mean it burns?" She rose quickly, steadying herself against Marrah. The girl held onto her until Idsiyushti found her balance and gently pulled away. She took a deep breath, smelled the decay of the swamp, the mud of the clearing, the remains of their campfire, the bitter odor of the goblins, the musky smell of Marrah and, no doubt, herself.

"The sky is alight, as if by many fires," Ceàrain said. Idsiyushti looked up at the surrounding trees, but she could see nothing except the streaks of the rapidly approaching dawn. Ceàrain sighed. "My scouts have seen it. I have seen it. But you cannot see it from here."

Ashakarahad led Herch over to Idsiyushti and Marrah. Chrona, angry and glaring, joined them. A goblin stepped passed Ceàrain and held out a stained skin filled with liquid. Chrona quailed. Ash took the skin and thanked the goblin, although Idsiyushti doubted the goblin understood the words.

"A drink to help wakefulness," Ceàrain said. Ashakarahad took a drink and grimaced.

"Bitter and hot and thick," she said, handing the skin to Marrah. The girl glanced at Idsiyushti then drank, nearly gagging. Gasping for breath, she handed the skin to Idsiyushti. The witch sniffed at the spout, smelled an acrid blend of things she wasn't sure she could recognize and took a drink. The liquid was hot, thick, and bitter, just as Ashakarahad had said. But it went down smooth and numbed her mouth after a moment. She took another drink and felt a subtle fire spread along her limbs, not unlike a softer touch of the crystal-laced whiskey Jak had given her right after the explosion in the goblin clearing.

She shook her head, her tongue suddenly thick. She handed the skin to Chrona who spat and refused to touch it. "I'm not drinking that gob piss'n'shit!"

"Chrona!" Idsiyushti scolded.

"They saved us!" Marrah said. "Don't be so rude!"

"We didn't need saving!" Chrona said. Her face was twisted with hatred, smeared with old mud. Her hair was slicked to her head, a pair of flies flitting about the tangled ends. She looked like something that had come crawling from the deep dark itself, a hag or a drowned corpse too fresh to start to bloat.

Idsiyushti and Marrah stared.

Ashakarahad shook her horned head.

They left the clearing surrounded by the goblin clan, most of which vanished into the twisted undergrowth with barely a sound. Marrah led Herch while also holding Idsiyushti's hand. Ashakarahad walked beside them, purposefully slowing her gait. Behind the mule, Chrona walked, muttering, kicking at mud puddles, loose sticks, and roots. The goblins who were visible turned to watch her, fascinated. Goblin children trailed behind her, wide-eyed and gaping. Some would come close, try to touch her, but Chrona would turn and lash out, muttering louder.

"What is wrong with her?" Marrah asked.

"She's scared," Idsiyushti said.

"I've never seen her act like this. I didn't think she could," Marrah said.

Idsiyushti squeezed her hand. She looked up at the dawn sky and the distant clouds. There was still no sign of the fires Ceàrain spoke of.

"The town is burning," she said anyway.

Marah sighed. "How far away are we? I don't recognize this place."

"I don't think we're heading back to town," Idsiyushti said after a moment, suddenly confused.

"What?"

Ashakarahad spoke before Idsiyushti could continue. "Ceàrain is leading us someplace else."

"Why?" Idsiyushti and Marrah asked in unison.

"We seek your constable," Ceàrain said from up ahead, over her shoulder.

"We should be returning to town, helping out!" Idsiyushti said.

"There is little you can do to help your town now, witch," the hobgoblin said, again over her shoulder. "You must gather your strength first."

"But the falkr want to arrest Idsiyushti!" Marrah protested.

"Then they are foolish," Ceàrain replied.

"More like single-minded," Idsiyushti said, confusion turning to anger. "The falkr and Jonath have no real magic! How can they help us save the town?"

"They can't," Ceàrain said. "Not from where they are."

Behind them, Chrona kicked at another goblin child, who giggled with a harsh warble and danced away. Taunting Chrona had become a game for the goblin children and no one made a move to stop it.

It wasn't long, however, until the number of goblins began to increase. They faded in from the surrounding trees and root mazes and even the stagnant water, eyes ever outward, watching. Chrona eventually fell into a sullen, brooding silence and the goblin children grew tired of teasing her. The children fell back and watched the surrounding deep dark with the other goblins.

The day was hot and muggy and nearly silent. An occasional slight, teasing breeze would bring with it hints of wood smoke and it became apparent they were not actually that far from the town, making Ceàrain's talk of the fire that much more poignant. But there was something else on the breeze, something thick and heavy, sweet, sick, decaying. Idsiyushti found herself watching the trees and the stands of wild cane and the glimpses of dark water as intently as the goblins.

Marrah slipped her hand from Idsiyushti's and placed it on Herch's neck, perhaps to comfort the mule or herself or both. Ashakarahad seemed to alternate watching the trees and watching Ceàrain, who plodded ahead, charting a course that kept them mostly out of the water.

Then the goblins were gone. All of them, slipping silently into the trees, water, undergrowth. Idsiyushti froze. Marrah gasped, pulling Herch to a lurching stop. Chrona stumbled and uttered a quiet sob. Ashakarahad slid a dagger from a belt sheath. Ahead, Ceàrain held her staff high in the air, slowly turning in a circle, eyes tight and scanning.

"They have found us," Ceàrain said. "We must go. Quickly." Her gnarled staff began to glow with a dull, throbbing blue light that was both faint and sharp, like a small candle glimpsed through sagging shutters.

Idsiyushti's renewed magic snapped along her spine, rising from its coil just below her navel. Her heart raced and her face and hands were suddenly flushed and hot. Energy crackled in the air. A low fog began to creep from between the trees and after a few moments, Idsiyushti realized the fog had been summoned by Ceàrain, as if made up of the recent memories of the goblin clan that had just vanished into the swamp.

Chrona sobbed again. Ashakarahad sheathed the dagger and spun, moving around Herch in a quick motion, her boots squelching through the mud.

Chrona squeaked when Ashakarahad picked her up and put her on Herch's back, astride their nearly empty saddlebags. Eyes screwed tight, curses flowing from her mouth in tiny, sharp whispers, Chrona clung to Herch's neck like a muddy urchin afraid of falling off the world. Herch snorted and then they were all moving again. Ceàrain was a fleeting shadow ahead, staff raised, blue light a spectral beacon. The fog grew dense and cold, its touch at first welcoming in the morning heat. But the cold began to seep into their bones, making their muscles ache.

"It's too cold," Marrah whispered, splashing through water and mud.

"I think the fog is mimicking the shroud of the undead," Idsiyushti said. "I think it should make it more difficult for them to find us. Like what I did last night. Only more effective. I hope."

"Can we trust Ceàrain?" Marrah asked, walking quickly, eyes locked on the flitting form of the hobgoblin.

"If she wanted to give us to the dead," Idsiyushti said. "I imagine she could've done that at any time and with less effort." But Marrah's concerns had crossed Idsiyushti's mind too. What did they actually know about Ceàrain and her goblin clan? Next to nothing aside from the fact that humans—other humans—had massacred other goblins nearby. Still, despite the clinging cold of the wet fog and the questions it raised, the coolness eventually seemed to energize them where the heat of the swamp would normally have worked to sap their strength.

They reached a wide stretch of bottomland, muddy, with small pools of water clouded with insects. The trees thinned out, their leaves whispering in a breeze that none of them could feel. Suddenly, the goblin clan was around them again. The fog thinned and vanished. Ceàrain spun in place again. Then she shouted, "Run!"

They ran, stumbling, their breathing and muddy footfalls the only thing ringing out across the bottomland. Herch trotted and Chrona clung tight, muddy face screwed up in misery. Ashakarahad had daggers in either hand and was jogging along behind Herch, head turning, eyes scanning. Idsiyushti ran beside Marrah. They helped each other when they stumbled, touching hands briefly, locking eyes for tense moments. Idsiyushti kept energy in a closed fist, ready to form it into a spell and release it. But there was nothing to release it at. Not at first.

The edge of the bottomland hove into view. Out past the bobbing goblin heads to either side, shadows began moving. Then the shadows became solid forms. The dead were keeping pace with them, laughing, jeering, or so it seemed—the bottomland was still silent save for gasping breath and panicked footfall. Idsiyushti tightened her fist, the energy it held popping, clawing at her, wanting to be let loose. But she held the fist closed—

the dead were running, flowing, crawling, keeping pace with them but not attacking. She looked ahead to the line of trees above a small rise—a natural embankment—that marked the edge of the bottomland. Wild cane was waving along the embankment in the unfelt breeze. Beyond the cane, more shadows moved.

Ceàrain raised her staff. The goblins squawked almost as one. Idsiyushti, in some instinct-driven moment of synchronicity, lashed out with her fist. Energy flew, from Idsiyushti, from Ceàrain's staff. The energy met, twisted, melded together, lashed at the cane and the shadows beyond. The cane exploded in a shearing wall of heat and flame. Pieces of rotten, burning meat blasted into the air. The smell of instantly roasting flesh was like a wave that washed over the bottomland, making Idsiyushti and Marrah gasp and stumble.

But Ceàrain charged up the slope of the embankment. Herch followed, was up faster than the rest, Chrona screaming from atop his back. The goblins scrambled up and were gone. Out on the bottomland, the dead broke their silence and began to howl, jeer, scream. They charged at the embankment, dead eyes alight, mouths gaping, shadowy tendrils that might have been limbs, cocks, tits, reaching and grasping. Marrah screamed and tried to climb the rise. Idsiyushti shouted curses that tore at her throat in rage and desperation. Blue-green flames ripped from her fingertips, incinerating the first ranks of the charging dead, causing wet undergrowth to smoke, honeysuckle-covered bark to smolder. Halfway up the slope, Marrah slipped in the mud and slid back down. Idsiyushti, flames still pouring from her hands, chasing themselves through her veins, tearing at her mind and soul, tumbled to the ground with a gasp as Marrah, trying to stand, knocked Idsiyushti's muddy, bare feet out from under her. The blue-green flames shot wildly through the air and dispersed.

Ashakarahad sheathed her daggers and grabbed both girls, tossed them bodily up the rise and onto the hot scorched earth of the exploded cane. They landed in a confused, panicked tumble of disarrayed dresses and bare, muddy legs. The demoness took a last look at the charging undead. Then she took three long strides up the slope of the embankment. She bent down and picked both girls up, arms around their waists, slung them over her broad shoulders like muddy sacks of grain, and ran.

Jonath was running as well. He was covered in sweat and gore, his boots thick with mud, his leather jerkin scratched and cut. His body ached and his vision would blur if he didn't force himself to concentrate. He crossed the top of a low berm, the remains of what might have once been the boundary of a small rice field or the ancient remains of a forgotten earthwork. Beyond, the ground was wet but blissfully free of mud. Overhead, the sky was crawling with clouds, but the heat pouring off the ground, from the trees and the swamp, was heavy, unrelenting. Still, he could taste the unseasonal rain hanging in the hot air, even though he was sure it would be a several days before it fell. He risked a look over his shoulder but could see nothing of his pursuers past the berm or anywhere in the stand of trees and wild cane beyond.

He ran on. His breathing was heavy, labored, measured as best he could. His sheathed broadsword slapped his back and shoulders. In his tired arms, the crossbow was heavy. He'd fired off the last of his bolts quite some time ago, but he doggedly hung onto the crossbow as if it had some esoteric connection to the world prior to the sudden appearance of the attacking dead.

Sigiswinth and two others, both wounded, one near death, were somehow all that were left of the squad of fierce, legendary falkr. The attacking dead, drowned ones and ghouls of some sort, along with a pair of what Jonath was pretty sure were vampires, one male, one female, both agonizingly beautiful despite leering mouths and prehensile body parts that shouldn't be prehensile—they had all appeared while the falkr and Jonath had camped in a small hollow half a day's ride from the goblin clearing. Sigiswinth had finally been convinced that Idsiyushti wasn't fleeing back to the clearing. So the falkr captain had grudgingly led the way further into the deep dark, to the more remote homesteads—most of which had been abandoned, either recently due to Jonath's call to come into town, or sometime in the distant past, decay and kudzu laying claim now. They had searched fifteen homesteads by the time they found the hollow and set camp.

The attack had come just after sunset. The dead had eventually been beaten back, the two vampires laughing, fondling each other, taunting Jonath and the falkr from the tops of the trees. But during each subsequent attack, flitting shadows rushed in and danced away, claiming blood and victims with each strike despite the best efforts of the defenders. By midnight, the laughter of the vampires had faded away and the rest of the attacking dead had vanished into the trees. Jonath, crossbow virtually useless, bolts spent, longsword nicked, tumbled to his knees and listened to Maeve, one of the two wounded, surviving falkr, argue with Sigiswinth over whether or not they had time to burn their dead. Sigiswinth, sounding like she was in tears of anger and frustration beneath her heavy helm and faceplate, finally prevailed. Maeve grudgingly deferred to her captain's rank and the bodies of their comrades vanished in blue flame, sparked by Sigiswinth's sword, while Jonath stood nearby, watching the shadow-wrapped trees, crossbow raised like a talisman, willing the falkr to hurry, his hopes sinking—if the dead could defeat that many falkr, then how did the rest of them hope to survive?

Their flight through the swamp had been slow, hindered by darkness and the wounded, Maeve and Aeldreth, who had to be dragged along, feverish, bleeding. The flight had also been hounded by hit-and-run strikes from the dead. They'd eventually found themselves crossing a series of berms in a barren bottomland, finally coming to rest in a ruined structure whose three crumbling stone walls covered in honeysuckle gave them a sense of fleeting protection. Sigiswinth and Jonath lit several small fires around the ruin and repelled a series of quick assaults, the dead attacking and withdrawing almost at random, until the sun broke the sky once more. In the silence that followed the last attack, as the early morning sun began to climb, Jonath had stood in the space that should have been a fourth wall and looked out across the treetops to see the glowing sky, the traces of thick, hot smoke. It was then that he knew his town was aflame. His heart had raced and he'd fought a wave of nausea. Memories of the Desadian Chaos had flooded him with a nightmarish intensity. Dragon attacks on villages, children put to the sword while their unarmed parents burned. Magic twisting through the air, ripping civilians apart, crushing lives and whole regions of space into nothingness. Tears stung his eyes. His nice town, his quiet town—his tired shoulders tensed in anger and his mind lurched in a spiraling sense of helplessness.

Now he found Sigiswinth standing in the exact same spot, in the place of the missing fourth wall, flaming sword in hand, as he ran back to the ruin. He felt her eyes burrow into him from beneath her helm and he shrugged, trying to catch his breath.

"They're still out there, beyond the trees. Obviously, they seem to be holding back," he said. He held up a brace of rabbits. "This is all I could get. I hope it will be enough. We need to move again soon. We have to get back to town."

Sigiswinth looked at the rabbits. Her arms were corded, shoulders tight. Mud, scratches, and one deep-looking cut marked her pale torso, bare breasts, and thighs. Sweat, dirt, and blood had solidified on her skin in obscure patterns, like a new set of ashen-brown rank tattoos, earned at the hands of the dead.

She took the rabbits. "It will have to do." Smoke from one of the small fires drifted between them. "Thank you, constable."

Jonath blinked. Sigiswinth's gratitude seemed so out of place that he thought he might have imagined it.

He turned and looked behind him, at what he assumed Sigiswinth had been watching as he returned — despite her thanks, he doubted she'd been watching for him. Out across the bottomland, across the berms and tall grass, there was no sign of the dead. He breathed a heavy sigh of relief, a sigh that turned sour and doleful when he raised his eyes once again and saw the thick layer of smoke above the trees, the smoke from the burning town.

"What were you looking at?" he asked, tearing his eyes away from his sense of failure and lacking anything else to say other than offer to prepare the rabbits.

"That," Sigiswinth said, pointing. Near the middle of the crisscrossing series of berms, a lone standing stone rose, no more than six or seven feet high. Runes and glyphs in the usual patterns of the ancients covered it. But there was no sign of honeysuckle or kudzu or moss or anything growing on it. Except for its weathered cracks, the stone almost appeared new in the late morning light. A chill gripped Jonath.

A lone crow, black and sleek, landed on the top of the stone. The crow squawked three times and then took flight once more. Far out past the edge of the berms and tall grass, figures once again began to move among the trees, the wild cane, and the pools of green-black water.

Ashakarahad glanced to the side every ten steps or so as she ran. Trees darted past, large rocks, stands of dark water. The land was sloping upward, dropping back down a moment later, as if that part of the swamp consisted of gentle, rolling hillocks.

The goblins had vanished once again but other figures darted through the trees—gangly shapes, loping, grasping, crawling, flowing like boneless shadows. Terror followed, drifting tendrils of despair and wretchedness that crawled along the ground, through the treetops, over the brackish water, like twisted memories chasing after glimpses of decay and hunger.

Ashakarahad winced. Idsiyushti and Marrah rode her shoulders, her great arms curled around their waists. The girls bounced and cried, cursed, shouted, but Ashakarahad could still hear the hiss and snap of the spells Idsiyushti cast at the dead. Ashakarahad saw flame and white-hot fingers of lightning touch trees and water and shambling, reaching things to either side. The air, hot and heavy, was laden with the smells of the two girls—unwashed and covered in the cloying touches of the swamp—as well as the charred reek of the dead. Ashakarahad wondered how long Idsiyushti could keep casting, especially since, by her grunts and curses, she wasn't in any sort of comfortable position.

But Ashakarahad remained silent. When she wasn't glancing to either side, she kept her eyes on the path and the ground ahead, looking for pitfalls, for deep mud, rocks, roots, stagnant pools and drops into water. She looked for rapidly approaching dead, watched to make sure that none were able to make it past Idsiyushti's spells. Ashakarahad had no idea what she would do if any of the dead did reach them—she certainly couldn't use either of the girls as a weapon and dropping one or both just to draw her daggers seemed futile, cruel, and suicidal. So she ran, measured her breathing, ignored the sweat that was covering her body, ignored her thirst, the aches and pains in her legs, arms, and shoulders. She had grown too accustomed to this world in the centuries of her captivity—she chided herself for being more human now than one of her own kind.

Ahead of them, Ceàrain would appear and then disappear, moving in and out of the landscape, staff raised to deliver a sweeping deluge of flame that scorched trees, steamed water, cleared underbrush, created a path for Ashakarahad to follow. Presumably, the hobgoblin was also destroying the dead, as burning corpses could be seen along the path, but Ashakarahad ignored the smoldering husks and simply ran.

A cruel, echoing laugh started to crawl and bounce through the trees and the underbrush. Ashakarahad cursed once more. Her shoulders ached. A deep pain was beginning to send shooting spasms down her back. She could hear Marrah gasping with each heavy step. She could hear Idsiyushti shouting the words to spells, but could tell the poor witch was growing exhausted. Idsiyushti was no combat sorceress like those found in the imperial army, or prowling the streets and alleys of Drilithae and Desade or the ports of far-off Serene. Nor did she have the stamina and skill of one of the Eld's battle priests, who fetishized war and suffering, striding

279

across the Abyss to devour worlds and souls. No, she had been trained by the fey and the fey did not stand and fight—or even run and fight. The fey preferred to hide and twist reality with illusions and subtle shifts of perception. They weren't likely to constantly hurl fireballs and forked lightning spikes at moving targets. But Idsiyushti seemed to twist the magic of the fey with the machinations of her humanity. She could do amazing things despite her training, maybe even because of it. She was youthful and precocious, but perhaps that youthfulness and precociousness allowed her to blur the lines of fey training and pull forth something far more destructive and powerful. Either way, Ashakarahad hoped it would be enough.

The laugh sounded again, an eerie, twisted corkscrew of sound that washed against the trunks of the trees. Ashakarahad risked another look to either side and saw that the loping figures of the dead were closer, keeping tighter pace. They were now successfully dodging the flames and lightning strikes. Ashakarahad had been running for what felt like hours and Idsiyushti had been casting spells nearly the whole time. The witch certainly couldn't keep it up for much longer and it seemed as if the undead knew it. Ashakarahad wanted to say something, anything, to keep Idsiyushti focused, to keep both girls from panicking, but she could do nothing other than breathe in and breathe out, as if her throat and lungs were locked in a trance, focused solely on the effort of escaping the dead.

Once more the laughter peeled through the trees, echoed across an expanse of duckweed-covered water that suddenly opened up to Ashakarahad's left. The duckweed surged and things leaped from the water, reaching, gasping, spitting drops of gore that smoked and hissed when they hit the ground. Both girls shouted in warning and Ashakarahad lunged forward. Muscles in her back clenched in pain, but she dove deep and pushed harder. Her measured breathing became ragged.

But then the expanse of water and its charging dead were behind them. Ahead, Ceàrain appeared again, standing next to a mud- and sweat-covered Herch, Chrona still clinging to the donkey's neck like a tattered rag that had been found in a puddle and then tied to his mane. The dead were running faster through the trees around them, converging in leaps and flowing strides. The goblins suddenly appeared from nowhere, surrounding Ashakarahad, running with her. Several looked like they'd seen combat, sporting wounds and crude bandages, carrying weapons tipped in gore. Their eyes were fierce, their faces twisted, but they ran in silence, never once looking up at the demoness or the girls on her shoulders. Instead, the goblins formed a vanguard, an escort. The dead reached the edge of the running goblins and those goblins lashed out with daggers, rusty swords, hatchets, pikes, tools and crude implements.

Ceàrain shouted, staff held high, but her words were muffled, nearly silenced by the mocking, jeering laughter that echoed around them, shrill, high-pitched, fevered.   Ceàrain's words fought back, however, booming like thunder that refused to die and fade away. Lightning and fire rained from the sky, burning the undead. Talons of thorns and undergrowth erupted from the muddy ground, gripping, tearing, grappling. The dead lurched and staggered. The laughter faltered.

Ashakarahad ran on, watching Ceàrain.   The hobgoblin's combat magic was spectacular in its destruction. Distant memories of her people's terrible Abyss-striding battle priests danced once again through Ashakarahad's exhausted mind.   Then she reached Herch, Chrona, and Ceàrain, the goblins fanning around and encircling them, weapons held at the ready. The dead swarmed around them, leaping from the trees and the water. Dead faces leered. Dead mouths, filled with black ichor, howled and jeered in whispers that spoke of a vast emptiness, of horrifying silence.

Ashakarahad stumbled to a halt, gasping.   She dropped to her knees and the girls scrambled off with movements that told how equally tired and sore they were. Marrah was sobbing and Idsiyushti crawled in the mud, shaking her head, trying to rise, eyes fixed on something beyond Herch. Ashakarahad, gasping for breath, closed her eyes, but snapped them open again when a wave of cold washed over her. The donkey and his hapless rider shifted and Ashakarahad saw the stump of a standing stone behind them. The stone's surface looked nearly fresh, the runes hot and glowing, the stones itself steaming in the hot air. Ashakarahad blinked and stared. Marrah and Idsiyushti helped each other stand and Idsiyushti hobbled towards the stone, staring.

"Idsi—no!" Ashakarahad tried to shout but, beyond the ring of goblins, the undead began, as one, to howl. Ashakarahad drew her daggers and stumbled to her feet.

Ceàrain stood beside the stone. She reached out and touched her staff to the stone's surface, chanting something that Ashakarahad recognized, with effort, as the language of the mage-lords. Lights flared, heat and cold washed over them. The air popped.

Ceàrain stood back, looked at Idsiyushti, then looked at Ashakarahad. "Go! All of you! There is no more time!"

"Go where?" Marrah asked.

Idsiyushti said, "There."

The gate appeared like a spiral out of nothing, unfolding, tugging, drawing them in. Ashakarahad gaped and then turned to stare at Ceàrain, realization rising almost languidly from the depths of her exhausted mind. The hobgoblin merely nodded and indicated the gate. Ashakarahad looked back out at the howling dead. Then she was moving, grabbing Herch's reins. She followed Idsiyushti and Marrah, who were stumbling forward, hand in hand. The girls vanished into the gate. Ashakarahad followed, sulfurous tears ringing her eyes.

Jak lost track of time in the ebb and flow of the battle for the town. His leg ached, his sword arm was tired and sore, his mother's amulet was a constant reminder of the presence of the enemy—its incessant hum a background murmur that Jak was certain was part of his very being, had always been there, would never go away.

The flowing, twisting ranks of the dead broke against the barricades, tried to wash over them, were pushed back or pulled down and set aflame by exhausted, blank-eyed townsfolk. The sky overhead was gray and orange, the hot sun rising up above the layers of smoke and gathering clouds, its warmth bolstered by the many fires and the seemingly constant flow from one barricade to the next, of rising and falling axes, mattocks, hammers, dulling swords. The wounded townsfolk were becoming a hazard. Some folks were merely slowed by their wounds, others had to be carried from the barricades or the houses to the tavern's main room where Sek and others tried to bandage them, comfort them, save them. But no one was moving quickly or sure-footed anymore. Jak had even seen Grendl stumble once or twice, the dwarf recovering with a grunt and a curse, ax flying, a hacked-apart walking corpse falling in his place.

Jak swung his longsword, edge nearly gone, and hammered the head from a dead woman whose face was twisted and running with rot and black ichor, whose tongue had become a maddening bundle of dancing tendrils. Her bare tits were swollen and bleeding gore and she reached for him even as he battered her headless body down to the ground. Jak stabbed the point of the sword through the dead women's gore-spewing, tentacle-tongued mouth and pinned her skull to the muddy earth. Staggering back, he grabbed a torch from a nearby child who watched the fight with tired, lost eyes. Jak lit the dead woman's still-thrashing body and used the sword to hurl her head into the resulting explosion of flames and oily vapor.

Jak handed the torch back to the child, who took it and simply wandered away. Jak looked back at the barricade but, for the moment, there were no undead to be seen. He spun and found no undead trying to reach him, trying to reach anyone else nearby. Across the square, Grendl and Drag bought down another attacking corpse. Elsewhere, townsfolk were shambling about like corpses themselves, tired, exhausted, their faces soot- and mud-smeared and otherwise blank. Seran and Kel, dresses ripped and bloody, stood back-to-back in a ring of oily ash and hacked corpses. Valen was rising from a crouch over what looked like the corpse of a boneless child with claws for hands and feet. Beyond them, the rest of the Legion, now silent, ribald songs lost to the almost decadent cacophony of battle, fought and danced slower and slower. Yet, around them, the ranks of the dead were thinning away into ash and smoke and fleshy sludge.

Jak hobbled to the low, rock boundary wall that surrounded the square's rune-encrusted standing stone. He sat on the wall and leaned forward, resting his head on his forearms, which in turn were resting on the cross guard of the sword, whose gore-covered tip was slowly sinking into the dirt. Sweat stung his eyes and his ears were ringing. His mother's amulet was humming to itself, dancing in the air as it hung down from his neck.

"Here, Mister Jak," a little girl of nine or ten said, holding out a battered waterskin. Jak took the skin and drank the tepid water, head tilted back, muscles in his shoulders threatening to spasm. When he finished and looked back, the girl was walking away, handing another skin to Scrum One-eye, who looked pale and old, but who gripped his borrowed hammer and scarred wooden shield like a war-weary veteran. Jak grunted at the sight.

Then the amulet around his neck vibrated violently, its hum rising in intensity to a ringing chime, a high-pitched bell that rang out across the square. The air on his sore back became suddenly cold. A shiver ran along his limbs and he saw steam rise off his forearms. He blinked. Then he turned. The runes across the surface of the standing stone were glowing a dull blue. The runes flared and his mother's amulet went deathly silent, stopped ringing, stopped dancing, hanging around his neck like a sudden weight that had appeared from nowhere.

Jak gaped at the standing stone, gaped at the fact that he could see his own breath, and then he threw himself backward. Energy pulsed outwards from the stone, pushing him even further through the dirt and mud, his back scraping, hands and legs painfully crab-walking, sword dropped and forgotten. The stone pulsed three times. Then it stopped. The cold dissipated. The glow in the runes faded.

Jak stared. Slowly, as if recovering from a bout of temporary deafness, he became aware of commotion in the square. A ragged cheer rent the air and Jak blinked, thinking at first that the cheer was because of the strange behavior of the standing stone. But the stone was silent and dark, just as it always had been. Jak sat up and looked around. Folk near the barricades and the few left up on the rooftops were cheering, weapons and fists raised in the air. They looked tired and ragged and wounded but there was an expression of delight and relief on their faces rather than blank, lost determination.

Across the square, Grendl tossed his ax down and took a long drink from a liquor jug he seemingly grabbed from thin air. The one-armed dwarf's armor was covered in blood and dirt, gouges and cuts. His face was black with soot and he splashed liquor on his face, drops beading up on his beard. He dropped the empty jug and wiped his face with a dirty rag from his belt.

Jak shook his head, turned, and hobbled over to his fallen sword, eyes on the standing stone. He picked up the sword and touched his mother's amulet with his other hand. The amulet continued to be silent and motionless. Jak wanted to laugh. The thought of the inactive amulet sent shivers of delight through his aching shoulders. The dead were gone, at least for the moment. Jak sobered, staring at the stone. He rolled his shoulders and tried to pull his tattered and ripped jerkin back together. He turned and made his way, slowly, sword once again a rudimentary cane, past Scrum One-eye and Valen towards Grendl and Drag and Marin, who looked ancient and grizzled, black skin and chain armor somehow shining despite the gore that covered him. None of them, apparently, had seen the standing stone's strange behavior and they laughed and drank in quick, exhausted celebration until Jak arrived.

****

The swirls of crimson and purple gave way to the brightness of the orange sun and the bleakness of the vast plane. The smell greeted Ashakarahad first—the distant charnel wind from beyond the black mountains mixed with something new, something that reminded her of a disused perfumery she'd once found off a maze of alleys in Desade before the Chaos, windows darkened with soot, courtyard filled with dead leaves. She hit the ground hard, as if she'd tripped over the threshold of the gate while running at full speed. She slid forward on hands and knees. The skin on her palms was scraped, but her knees were protected by the steel kneecaps of her boots. She sat back and shook the dust and blood from her hands. The city lined the horizon, chrome and glass shining in the orange light. The sound of the slow-churning river behind her was the only sound except for her breathing.

The standing stone, whole, unmarred, was on her left. She looked up at the orange sun and a cool breeze—rotting meat and thick perfume—cooled the tears that were still running down her cheeks. The whisper of voices began as a susurration above the churn of the river.

Ashakarahad closed her eyes and let out a long, frustrated scream that ended in silent sobs.

A boot scraped the ground. Ashakarahad turned to see Ceàrain standing on her right, opposite the stone.

The hobgoblin was leaning on her staff, watching Ash with eyes dark, reptilian, and piercing. The weight of the invisible shackles was sudden and exhausting. Ashakarahad wiped her tears and looked down at her wrists, at the blood of her scraped palms. Her heart was hammering in her chest.

Ceàrain thumped the butt of her staff once on the ground. The tide of voices ceased, leaving only the churn of the river.

"You were the one I saw when the stone broke," Ashakarahad said. "Right before I went back to the swamp."

The look on Ceàrain's face was not entirely goblinoid.

Ash sat back. "Who are you? Who are you really?"

Ceàrain walked over to stand before Ash. Slowly, levering herself with her staff as if she'd aged decades in the time since opening the gate in the swamp, Ceàrain sat. The top of her head with its scraggly ashen, fur-like hair came up to Ashakarahad's breastbone.

"My people are descendants," Ceàrain said.

"Of the mage-lords."

"No." That single word was followed by a sudden flurry of the voices from the invisible speakers. Ceàrain looked annoyed. She tapped the haft of her staff, laid across her crossed legs, three times with half-gloved fingers. The voices ceased once again. "Goblins are descendants of the *servants* of what you call the mage-lords. We keep the secrets of the Masters. We've done so since the time of transition, when our Masters left the world to come here, to the city."

"And your magic?"

"Is nothing compared to what our Masters could do," Ceàrain said. Ashakarahad nodded, reminded once again of the world-eating powers of some of her own kind. "You were left trapped in that other place, in the swamp. Partially. Your chains draw you here, to the Masters, just as surely as whatever ritual bound you in the first place."

Ashakarahad took a deep breath, chewing on the taste of rot and perfume. "I've guessed as much. Why don't you and your clan come here? Why don't you follow your Masters? Obviously, you can—"

"Oh, I visit from time to time. But right now I am only here because of you," Ceàrain said. "The Masters left traces, so many traces, so many pieces of themselves across their old world. We are the custodians, the caretakers of what they've left behind. We make sure the dead, for example, still feel the repulsion of the very ruins that draw them in the first place. We make sure very few discover the way of the Masters and we try to keep them from causing too much trouble once they do. The human emperor knows a little of the truth. As did the elven emperors before the Desadian Chaos. And that helps us. Sometimes."

"None of that makes any sense."

"The Masters rarely made sense." Voices raised again, silenced with a glare from Ceàrain. "They still don't."

"Are the Masters the ones speaking?"

"Some. The curious. Like school children, really. They are probably sitting somewhere watching us rather than attending to their studies." She glared out at the plane, but there was no response other than the slow churn of the distant river. Ashakarahad rubbed her scraped hands together. The sting of her fall bit deep. The weight of the shackles was like a bottomless ache in her skull. She didn't recall the pull of the shackles being so strong during her time on the plane before.

"How do I get free?" Ashakarahad asked. "How do I go home?"

Ceàrain smiled, only there was no humor there. Behind her, the city scored the sky all along the endless horizon. Ashakarahad raised her eyes and watched the patterns of light play off the structures of the city. Slowly, the city began to fade. The weight of the shackles pulled her as if trying to drag her into the ground.

"You got here before because blood had been spilled when my clan's stone shattered. You got here now because you passed through one of the master's portals and are still bound to the Masters, to this place. But there was no blood. The Masters do love a sense of irony."

Ceàrain reached out and touched Ashakarahad's knee, the hobgoblin's hand nebulous and fading.

Then the purple and crimson light returned along with the weight of Herch's reins and the sound of Chrona's terrified scream.

It was a strange reunion that followed the nauseating pulse of crimson and purple light that dumped Idsiyushti, Marrah, Ashakarahad, and Herch, with Chrona screaming and clinging to his neck, at the base of a standing stone in a wide, flat series of berm-marked paddies and grass fields. The dead moved among the trees not far away while, on the other side of the fields, standing between tumbledown stones in a broken wall of a ruin, Jonath of the Battlefield gaped. Beside the constable, the falkr captain stood, blue-flamed sword raised.

The dead began to charge from the trees, their whispered moans and laughter a susurration that sent chills through the hot, wet air. Aching and stiff from being carried by Ashakarahad for what had felt like endless miles of blurred swampland, Idsiyushti turned and raised her hands. Her power was diminishing again, fading fast. She was hungry and thirsty, dirty and confused by travel through the portal, but the lightning she called, and the fire she commanded, splayed out across the berms and fields and bit into the dead as if they were matchsticks waiting to be struck.

The fight and retreat to the ruin were quick, yet painful. Marrah took a cut to her shoulder that ripped her dress even further. She staggered and cried out and Ashakarahad grabbed her once again and carried her forward. Idsiyushti, heart hammering in her chest at the sight of Marrah's wound and near fall, lashed out at the dead, screams and laughter tearing at her own throat as the fire and lightning lanced and danced. Smoke began to blind her but she followed Ashakarahad, Marrah, and Herch, the donkey having had the good sense to immediately begin running towards the ruin with the still-screaming Chrona on his back.

But the rush of the dead from the trees was brief and unsustained. Almost like the afterthought of some absent-minded god, the standing stone pulsed with a blinding light. A wave of energy emanated, sliding across the fields. The wave was like the single toll of a cathedral bell that buffeted the dead and drove them back. The dead vanished back into the tree line nearly as quickly as they'd appeared and Idsiyushti staggered into the ruin, her bleary eyes seeking out Marrah and her wounded shoulder. Inside the ruin, near a low cook fire, two other falkr lay on crude pallets of dried leaves and vines. They were both wounded, one appearing unconscious, barely breathing. Sigiswinth ranted and shouted, but Idsiyushti ignored her, first tending to

Marrah with the few remaining herbs and tinctures that had survived the journey and flight in Herch's saddlebags and her own belt pouches. Then, without much thought, Idsiyushti moved to the fallen falkr and tended to them. Sigiswinth continued shouting, but the falkr captain's voice was weak and distant, as if she were putting up a fight simply for appearances. Ashakarahad stood over Idsiyushti as she worked, and the falkr captain never came near.

Idsiyushti woke to encroaching darkness and the flicker of the cook fire on the kudzu-covered walls of the ruin. She felt Marrah's arm around her, holding one of her breasts through the scratchy material of her dirty dress. Idsiyushti squirmed back against Marrah and was tempted to go back to sleep when she heard Marrah murmur. But she looked up and saw Sigiswinth sitting cross-legged nearby, stitching a wound on her own upper arm. The falkr's torso and breasts were dirty and gore-smeared, but the wound she was self-tending looked cleaned, the stitches tight. Sigiswinth had removed her helm to reveal close-cropped, snow-white hair, violet eyes, and ears that were more elf than human. Her face was lean and drawn, a scar slashing across her right cheek, bisecting her pale lips. She looked old and beautiful, radiant and terrifying. Idsiyushti stared until Sigiswinth looked up from tying the stitch off one-handed—Idsiyushti realized then that the falkr had removed her heavy gauntlets as well, revealing pink hands with long fingers, scarred and callused.

"You saved Aeldreth's life, witch," Sigiswinth said. "I had all but given her up for dead. Like her sisters."

Idsiyushti blinked. She only vaguely remembered tending the mortal-seeming wounds of the unconscious falkr, finishing off her supply of medicines and using the last of her dwindling magic, draining herself once again. The thin, whispered voice of the elf Idsiyushti had called teacher came back unbidden, an oft-repeated warning that, while some humans could harness great amounts of magic, using so much magic, all at once, could age that human prematurely. Idsiyushti, staring at Sigiswinth's face, suddenly realized that she was dreading looking into a mirror.

"And Maeve," Sigiswinth continued, "will hold a sword once again, it seems. You have my thanks." The falkr captain looked away. Idsiyushti tried to raise her arm, tried to focus on the patch of skin that had been covered by the magic-quenching manacle Sigiswinth had order placed on her back in the goblin field. But she couldn't find the strength to focus anymore and when she tried to look back up at the falkr captain, at her scarred face, Idsiyushti fell back into a black, heavy sleep.

****

The night descended hot and heavy. The smoke from the bonfires and the burning homes beyond the square had finally thinned, revealing scattered glimpses of stars and night-wrapped clouds.

"Gonna rain soon," Drag said. "Out of season. Don't know what that means."

"Means we're gonna get wet," Grendl said. "Means that keeping the bonfires lit will be a chore. Means that, maybe, the dead will get the hint and slog back off into the deep dark permanently and forget about us."

There had been no sign of the dead since the attack on the square had abruptly ended in the late morning. Amidst the momentary jubilation that had turned into weary celebration followed by wary reconstruction of the barricades, Jak had hobbled forward to explain what he'd seen the standing stone do. Marin had tried to dismiss Jak with a laugh, but Drag had, with a dark look, told the old judge to be quiet.

"There's things about this swamp that shouldn't be laughed at. Not now," the blacksmith had said. Grendl had walked over to stare at the standing stone. It was dark and solid and silent. Jak had hobbled to stand nearby.

"You're sure?" Grendl asked.

"Yes," Jak replied.

Hours later, the bonfires had been rekindled and the burning houses had been tended to, generally left to smolder since the house fires had raged too long to be put out. But the smoke and the heat and the loss affected the townsfolk after the elation of the end of the attack had faded to aches and pains and exhausted collapse. The wounded were gathered and tended to in the main room of the tavern, although by some miracle quite a few were able to be bandaged and stitched, given a shot or two of strong whiskey, and allowed to walk back out into the square. Children were generally silent, exhaustion and fear blending to drain cheerfulness or tears away, leaving behind only wide eyes in dirty faces.

Folk ate and sat around the fires that were scattered around the square. A few tents were raised once more, but most folk were too tired and sore, too amazed to be alive, too stunned by what had actually happened, to do anything other than find someplace to curl up and sleep or sit and stare or hold tight to loved ones. A few folk started praying and two self-appointed swamp preachers positioned themselves at opposite ends of the square to shout out their sudden realization of the truth behind the inhuman majesty of the swamp gods.

Grendl led a small group of folk to the temple grounds. The wall of energy that had been raised around the temple and the graveyard snapped and popped and showed no signs of coming down. Grendl had shouted at the barrier but there had been no response from beyond it. Folk in Grendl's party began to mutter about how the dead had circumnavigated the bonfires by way of the temple's magical shield, but the real damage had yet to be realized. Twenty minutes later, Grendl led the party back to the square and the members broke off to numbly help rebuild the barricades or bring wood to the rekindled bonfires. More furniture was dragged from homes, most with the owner's blank-eyed approval, to be piled up and shoved into place, or broken up and burned.

A warm breeze began to blow, dragging the smoke that still obscured parts of the sky into the square like a thin fog. The dark clouds way up above the smoke were still there, growing, their menace unspoken but, at the moment, nothing more than an empty threat.

Someone began singing a low, slow, dirge-like song. Eventually, others began to pick up the threads of the song, and soon the square was filled with pockets of singers. Others found drums or lutes and began to play ragged, out-of-time accompaniment. With weary feet and tired smiles, Seran and Kel, still in tattered drag, led the Legion of Queers in a dance that slowly drew cheers and applause from the beleaguered townsfolk. Grendl stood on the porch of the tavern, mostly to escape the heat and smell of the make-shift hospital his common room had become, and watched the dance. Across the square, sitting on an upturned whiskey cask and flanked by Valen and Scrum One-eye, Jak was singing in a cool, clear voice to the accompaniment of Peler's lute, which had somehow survived the fires and the dead. Grendl watched and listened while sipping whiskey from his private stock. The liquor burned, smoky, cloying, but it soothed him, as did the song that was carrying out across the square. Grendl went back inside, through the common room to the stairs leading to the basement. He descended in darkness and felt the cool basement air rise up and greet him and he refused to think of it as descending into a dark, forgotten tomb.

Ashakarahad had agreed to stand watch while the others sat around the cookfire primarily because she was tired of the constant questioning put to her by Jonath and Sigiswinth. What had happened to her? Where had she gone? How had she gotten there? Was she sure that she hadn't been hallucinating, that she hadn't been blown clear of the explosion and knocked unconscious? Maybe she'd suffered such a blow to the head that she'd wandered off—which is why no one could find her body in the goblin clearing—and merely day-dreamed her journey?

"Yes, and in that confused state," Ashakarahad had said, "I hallucinated traveling through several ancient portals, at least once with three young women and a mule in tow." But this sarcasm had only garnered even more, albeit not altogether irrelevant, questions and Ashakarahad had announced that she'd stand watch and gone to do just that. She'd heard the falkr captain protest but the others made some sort of rebuke and Sigiswinth fell into a brooding silence.

Ashakarahad stood in the break in the wall of the ruin, staring out at the heat shimmers rising from the abandoned paddies and fields. The day was nearly gone, the heat shimmers soon lost among the long shadows that crisscrossed the tall grass and berms. Overhead, thick clouds were gathering, but Idsiyushti had assured them that rain was still a little while off.

So the demoness stared at the standing stone. The thing was squat and broken and touched by age. The encroaching night took the stone in its embrace and it vanished into the darkness, a stone figure fading from view as if receding into the distance while not actually moving at all. For a fleeting moment, Ashakarahad found herself almost longing for the orange sun and the unbroken standing stone on the plane before the city. She closed her eyes and saw distant chrome and glass, saw Ceàrain reaching out to her, heard the voices of the old Masters tittering like schoolchildren, heard the slow churn of the swollen river. She smelled perfume and decay and opened her eyes. Staring out into the darkness, Ashakarahad loosened her daggers in their belt sheaths, rolled her still-aching shoulders, and pricked her ears up against the crackle of the fire and the voices at her back.

Texts she'd encountered in the library at Drilithae had suggested theories regarding the mage-lords' use of the standing stones as sorcerous waypoints and gates, rather than just markers and monuments. She was glad that at least some of those theories—or parts of them at any rate—were correct, although most of the authors of those theories were long dead and would never share in her discovery.

But the activation of the stones, that was something else entirely. Somehow, some way Ceàrain had activated the stones. Ashakarahad had heard the hobgoblin shout words that contained echoes of the language of the mage-lords, guttural and dissonant. Then Ceàrain had touched the stone with her staff and the gate had opened. And on the plane before the city, Ceàrain had sat and reached out to touch Ashakarahad, had shattered the standing stone on the previous occasion, sending Ash back to the swamp both times. No theory she'd ever encountered suggested that the goblin clans were the descendants of the servants of the mage-lords. That hobgoblins like Ceàrain knew history and lore—and obviously powerful magic—that no other elf, dwarf, human, falkr, or whatever knew.

Where was the goblin clan now? Had the undead attacked them? Had they survived? Ceàrain seemed more than capable of fending off an attack, but were the rest of her clan capable enough? Where had Ceàrain been when the soldiers had descended on the goblins in the cane field? Why had the goblins, like the ones who had escorted them through the swamp while fleeing the dead, not just vanished into the cane like silent shadows? Why had Ceàrain let the goblins die? Too many questions. Of course, the obvious partial answer was that Ceàrain and the rest of the clan had been away from the goblins in the sugar cane field when the soldiers attacked, somehow taking the goblins by surprise. Or perhaps goblins hadn't fled because they were protecting something, like the stone that eventually exploded.

Ashakarahad stared into the hot darkness. The standing stone across the fields seemed to have caused the dead to flee a few moments after she and her companions had come tumbling out of the portal. One or two theories in the library's musty tomes had suggested that the stones had once acted as protection fetishes of some sort. And while it was reported that the activity of the dead was heightened near sites where the standing stones were found, some scholars suggested that this was because the stones were no longer acting as protection. The dead weren't necessarily drawn to the stones, as was commonly thought, but simply responding to the fact that they were no longer being pushed away, like water crashing into a lock that had previously been closed.

Ashakarahad frowned. Ceàrain had known how to activate the stone. And she'd known how to make sure that the portal she'd opened had led to the stone nearest to Jonath and the falkr. The matriarch of a clan of goblins thought to be no more than walking, talking grubs by most inhabitants of the empire. Ashakarahad looked back at the fire. Sigiswinth was sitting in the corner of the ruin, near her wounded companions. Her piercing eyes shifted from the flames to Ashakarahad and stared.

According to Idsiyushti and Marrah, Sigiswinth had told the folks in town that the falkr had originally been chasing the soldiers because the soldiers were attacking goblin clans without provocation and without imperial license—hatred and ignorance and a bloodlust run to the near-barbaric, a stain of the Desadian Chaos left over on the souls of once-good men. But then her story changed when she found Idsiyushti out at the ruins of the standing stone and the goblin clearing. After they'd arrested Idsiyushti, Sigiswinth showed a sudden interest in Ashakarahad herself. Ash had met several falkr in her time at the capital, but she'd never met Sigiswinth nor any of her sisters. Nor had she left the heart of the empire for the desolate swamp and the nameless town because she'd encountered any trouble with imperial law. Although viewed with suspicion, she'd been afforded most courtesies, even for one of the demonic Eld. Even in Drilithae, even among contemporary wizards and necromancers, Ashakarahad's tale of being summoned and held captive for centuries by the ancient mage-lords seemed no cause for alarm. In a world suffused by magic and myth, her tale and her presence was just another bit of fantastical reality, accepted almost without question.

Sigiswinth continued to stare. Ashakarahad turned back to gaze deep into the darkness beyond the ruin. Why wasn't Sigiswinth arresting Ashakarahad now? Why wasn't she questioning Ashakarahad even further, more harshly? A long moment passed before realization finally dawned. Sigiswinth knew. The falkr knew. Somehow, the soldiers might have even known. Presumably, the emperor and countless others know, have known and have labored to keep that knowledge secret. Knowledge about the goblins and the standing stones and the connection to the mage-lords. Ashakarahad's head spun and then she fought back laughter. It all made a strange, nearly-perfect, miserably hilarious kind of sense.

I'm warning you—" Sigiswinth said. She stood, arms crossed over her dirty, bloody tits. Jonath said something that Idsiyushti couldn't pick up but was echoed by Ashakarahad, who towered over both man and falkr.

"What are they arguing about?" Marrah asked. She sat beside Idsiyushti, helping make a stew of wild greens and left-over rabbit meat they'd found bundled in a corner of the ruin. They used a pot that they'd convinced Chrona to scour. Now the older girl sat huddled on the other side of the fire, watching Idsiyushti and Marrah work, eyes narrowed and heavy, looking all the more like a lost, muddy beggar huddled in a dark alley in some distant, unforgiving city.

"I don't know, but I suspect that it has to do with us," Idsiyushti said.

"Wonderful," Marrah whispered. Idsiyushti knew that she was worried about being arrested by the falkr for setting their captive witch free. But there was nothing either one of them could do about that now — well, Idsiyushti could use magic to attack Sigiswinth and the wounded falkr but that just seemed obvious and boring and best left for the dead things still wandering, unseen, in the woods beyond the fields.

But the argument just beyond the opening in the ruin's walls was becoming heated, the whispers more focused and deep, harsh, ringing out against the ancient stones. Idsiyushti looked over to see that one of the wounded falkr, she couldn't remember her name, was shifting her attention between Idsiyushti, Marrah, Chrona, and the argument just at the edge of the firelight. The falkr wasn't wearing her helmet, like her captain, which Idsiyushti now attributed to the fact that the wounded falkr had had their helmets removed for treatment and rest. This falkr appeared much younger than Sigiswinth, although Idsiyushti knew she had no real basis of comparison because the falkr were neither human nor elf nor fey. Still, this falkr had bright eyes, a narrow face that lacked scars, and full lips that were actually attractive and inviting. Her hair was pale—although not as pale as Sigiswinth's—and was long, braided intricately in rings that could be piled atop her head, beneath her helmet.

The falkr said, "You truly have a gift for magic."

Idsiyushti blinked. Marrah looked up from stirring the pot and Chrona flinched. Idsiyushti said, "I'm a witch, remember? You shackled me to keep me from using my magic."

The falkr shook her head. "No, that was her." She pointed to Sigiswinth with her chin. "Her idea. Her orders. She distrusts human magic."

"A lot of people do," Marrah said.

"This is true," the falkr said. Out beyond the opening in the ruined walls, whispered voices were raised again. Marrah and Chrona turned to look but Idsiyushti watched the falkr, who kept her bright eyes on Sigiswinth. Idsiyushti saw something there, something dissonant.

"Thank you for your ministrations," the falkr finally said. "You have certainly helped me and my sisters."

"Sigiswinth wouldn't let me bind her wounds," Idsiyushti said.

"No," replied the falkr. "She wouldn't. It's not her way." The falkr sighed and finally looked away from the argument, turning back to Idsiyushti.

"Do *you* know what they are arguing about?" Marrah asked.

The falkr shrugged. She was sitting with her knees drawn up, her boots off, her calves and feet pale in the firelight. Her arms rested on her knees and her shrug made her look less like a warrior and more like someone, anyone, who just wanted to be somewhere else. She'd been wounded across her back. Idsiyushti figured the shrug caused pain, but the falkr's face didn't show it.

"I think I know, but I could be wrong," the falkr said.

"Is it about us?" Chrona asked, her voice a rusty squeak that surprised Idsiyushti and Marrah. If it surprised the falkr, the falkr didn't show it.

"After a manner of speaking," the falkr said. Her eyes shifted to the stew pot as it started to steam. The rich scent of the greens, rabbit, and the few spices left over from Herch's saddlebags, was inundating the interior of the ruin. "I think it's about how you got here. Through that standing stone."

"That makes sense," Marrah said. "But it was pure magic and Idsiyushti had nothing to do with it. Didn't you?"

Idsiyushti shook her head.

"No," the falkr said. "No, she didn't. And that's part of what I think they're arguing about."

Idsiyushti studied the falkr for a time, her pale skin, her half-hidden tits partially covered by her arms and knees, the bandage wrapped around her lower torso, just barely visible. "Do you know about the stones?"

The falkr, who had once again shifted her gaze to the argument, looked back at Idsiyushti. She returned Idsiyushti's stare for several moments. "Yes," she said. "In a way, it's why we came all the way down to this forsaken swamp from Drilithae."

"I thought you were after those soldiers," Chrona said, voice still a rusty squeak.

"Yes," the falkr said. She looked back in Sigiswinth's direction, eyes narrowing. She shifted her shoulders and this time didn't hide the pain she felt, didn't bother keeping it from twisting her features for a fraction of a second.

"Did the soldiers know about the stones?" Idsiyushti asked.

"We think so, but we aren't sure. Mostly they were just interested in killing goblins," the falkr said. "And that's the problem."

"You mean to say that the goblins are connected to the standing stones?" Marrah asked, stirring the stew. The falkr turned her head to look at Marrah so quickly that her braided rings snapped around to hit her in the face. Idsiyushti smiled.

"Don't answer that, Maeve!" Sigiswinth shouted, returning to the fire, her face twisted in anger. The dirt and dried blood on her pale arms and tits were terrifying in the firelight.

"Yes, Marrah, they are," Ashakarahad said, arms folded across her chest, still standing in the opening in the wall. Sigiswinth spun, fist raised. She reached for her sword.

Ashakarahad stood her ground. The young falkr beyond the fire, Maeve, said, "Captain!" in a voice that had more calm authority in it than it probably had any right to have.

Marrah, still stirring the stew, said, "Oh." Then she turned to Idsiyushti and asked, "Do you think arguing about it will keep the dead away?" Heads turned to glare and Idsiyushti laughed.

By dawn, the bonfires were burning low and the smoke they produced was no longer obscuring the brightening sky. The thick, dark clouds, bringing the promise of unseasonal rain, were still gathering, roiling at times, but no rain fell. The dawn was hot and the air was wet. The town square smelled of smoke and sweat and whiskey and the makeshift latrine pits that folk had been forced to dig, where shit and piss were dumped and then set alight with pitch and oil. The greasy, disgusting smoke reached up to join the thinning blanket of bonfire smoke. But there had been no further sign of the dead other than furtive glimpses of forms moving way out in the trees or at the water line among tied up fishing boats and barges, most of which the dead had left untouched.

Grendl caught a strong whiff of a burning latrine pit from the top of the courthouse, whose sparse contents had all been gutted to reinforce the barricades, and whose windows had all been shattered and destroyed in the attack the previous day. The remains of several of the attacking dead had been dragged out of the courthouse, leaving greasy, smeared trails through the double doors, down wide, wooden steps to the still-smoldering remains of a fire where the burning corpses had added to the stench in the square.

Still, despite a cough that rattled his chest at the sickening whiff of smoke, Grendl was relieved. If the dead continued to stay away, the townsfolk might be able to clean up the square and not worry so much that the burning latrine pits and corpse fires would let disease complete the job that the attacking dead had started.

"Where the fuck is Jonath?" Grendl asked no one in particular. Beside him, Marin stared out past the smoky remains of buildings and the bonfires, towards the rising sun as it colored the cloudy sky and peeked through the dense treetops like a flashing stab from a bullseye lantern.

"I'm having a hard time thinking that he—and the falkr—were caught out there in the open and were just left alone," Marin said. "That they even survived any of this."

"You're no help," Grendl said. He leaned over and spat into the mud two stories below the sloping roof. He glanced back up and behind, towards the courthouse bell tower where he'd posted someone to keep a watch in all directions as the day dawned. The bell tower didn't actually have a bell because the town council had been afraid the bell would cause no end of disturbance about the town. So when Marin had finally convinced them to build the courthouse in the first place — tearing down the old one-room justice-of-the-peace building to do so, he'd agreed that there would not actually be a bell in the tower. Of course had there been a bell, it might have been used to warn folks of the attacking dead. It might also have been used to rally more folk to rush out to Jak's place and be picked off as they tried to fight the fire.

"Chrona and Marrah are out there," Grendl said. "With Idsiyushti."

"If Idsiyushti got her magic back, they might still be all right," Marin said. "She's a smart girl. Willful. A little scandalous, maybe. But she's smart and she has power."

"Which the falkr took from her," Grendl said.

Marin nodded. "Like I said, let's hope she got it back. Besides, you're assuming the dead are attacking elsewhere. For all we know, the folks in Baker's Beans are loafing about like nothing's happened. The swampland is vast, the deep dark not a place that many maps have filled out in detail. Still, that's a lot of dead folks to come back to haunt us out of nowhere. I'm not sure the swamp would have claimed that many lives."

"Yeah, I've been thinking about that," Grendl said. "But this swamp is ancient. And those standing stones—they have some magic in 'em, even if you don't bother believing what Jak saw. Ashakarahad seemed convinced that the standing stones were related to the mage-lords and that the mage-lords had something to do with raising the dead."

"True," Marin said. "And there are a lot of standing stones and ruins here about. More than I've seen all in one place elsewhere in the empire. So maybe there are so many undead around here because there are so many stones and ruins."

"Grendl!" They turned to see arms waving up in the bell tower, other arms pointing back into the square. They rushed across the roof, their footsteps weary and heavy, the wood and shingles creaking and groaning. Down in the square, folk were starting to rush about and point. The standing stone, a single stab of darkness rising out of the center of the square, was vibrating enough that the air around it was shimmering. The bas-relief runes and glyphs on its surface were glowing a deep violet.

Standing off to the side of the stone, Jak leaned on his cane, sword gripped in his free hand. He'd donned a clean shirt and somehow found the time and energy to wash his face and comb out his blond hair. He looked up at the courthouse roof, looked back at the glowing stone, looked back at Grendl and bowed in a sardonic flourish that Grendl could only interpret as *See? I told you so.*

Sigiswinth was livid. She shook, her entire body a tight wire that was barely under control. Her fists, tucked back into heavy gauntlets, were balled. Her shoulders, dirty and dark with dried blood, were tense. She hadn't donned her helmet and her usual taut, pale face was even tauter and paler. Beside her, Maeve, also without a helmet, her torso bandaged, stood gripping Sigiswinth's arm, her hands scarred, and bare.

But neither falkr had her weapons drawn. Maeve looked from Sigiswinth to Ashakarahad, her face unreadable. Sigiswinth jerked her arm away and spat into the tall grass at the base of the short, stumpy standing stone.

"You're sure this will work?" Idsiyushti asked. The witch was standing near the stone, around the other side from Ashakarahad. Marrah stood further back, her face filled with worry and emotion. Further back still,

Chrona stood beside Herch, the donkey far cleaner than the tavern girl. The unconscious falkr, Aeldreth, was strapped to a makeshift stretcher formed from dry limbs and woven grass and material from Idsiyushti's and Marrah's dirty dresses, which were both now much, much shorter. Jonath stood back behind Sigiswinth and Maeve.

Ashakarahad nodded.

"I mean," she amended. "I think it will work. I've only studied the language and magic of the ancients through old books, and I barely had a grasp of how the language should actually sound, but yes, I think it will."

"Just try to sound like a goblin," Jonath said across the distance. "Should work."

Ashakarahad shrugged. "I didn't think I could do this until I saw Ceàrain do it. But Ceàrain has far more training than I—"

"And can actually speak goblin," Jonath said.

"Yes. Still, the language of the mage-lords isn't goblin. Or the other way around. Not technically." Ashakarahad glanced back at the falkr. Maeve remained silent and stoic, while Sigiswinth's faced had screwed itself up in a vicious snarl.

"You can't do this!" the falkr captain hissed.

"No, I think I can," Ashakarahad said. "But, if you mean I shouldn't, well, that's probably true." She'd meditated on what she remembered of the old library tomes, on her time in that other place in the shadow of the city, on the words Ceàrain had said, both in that place and as the hobgoblin had opened the gate.

Already, the demoness had said words that she hoped matched some of the glyphs that could be made out as bas-relief on the standing stone. Already, Idsiyushti had channeled magical energy into the stone, directing as best she could, following Ashakarahad's directions, which were slipshod at best. Still, the bas-relief runes began to glow a dull purple, and the hot, wet air around the stone began to vibrate.

"I cannot let you do this," Sigiswinth said, stepping forward, hand reaching once again for her sword.

Maeve followed and grabbed her captain once again by the sword arm. "We need to do this. We can't survive another attack. And Aeldreth will die if we don't. We have to get her out of here!"

Turning, Sigiswinth shouted, "You do not command here!" But the other, younger falkr, face twisted suddenly in pain as she tightened her grip, stood her ground. She met Sigiswinth's gaze, solid and volcanic.

"We can't go on like this," Maeve said.

Ashakarahad turned back to the stone and Idsiyushti, ignoring the falkr. Sigiswinth would not be able to reach her or the witch without either Jonath or Maeve giving warning. "Okay," Ashakarahad said. "Let's keep going." Suddenly, the language runes of the mage-lords scrolled out before her mind's eye as if someone were writing them down on a tablet that was endless and constantly moving past the writer. Ashakarahad spoke the runes, as best she could. She'd spent time listening to Ceàrain talk to the goblin clan. She'd also spent a little time listening to the goblins quietly talk amongst themselves, chattering to each other when no one else had been near, standing around Herch and petting the donkey gently like children petting an old, tired, patient dog.

"Okay," she heard Idsiyushti say. Magical energy snapped through the air, smelling of ozone and reminding Ashakarahad of the mad flight through the swamp, the girls on her shoulders, Idsiyushti hurling lightning and fire left and right. The air around the stone began to hum louder. "I'm thinking of home, of town," the witch said. "What else?"

"Just keep it up," Ashakarahad said, eyes now closed, the glyphs of the mage-lords scrolling faster. "And don't over-power it. I don't know if we'll survive another explosion." Idsiyushti didn't respond. Ashakarahad continued, trying to force her tongue and lips to conform to a language that was long dead on that world and, she hoped, vaguely related to the derivation that had become the goblin tongue.

"The dead!" Ashakarahad ignored Jonath's shout. "In the trees!"

"We can't let this happen!" Sigiswinth shouted.

"Captain!" Maeve said.

Ashakarahad refused to open her eyes. The language of the mage-lords rolled faster, faster, and she wondered if this was how actual sorcerers felt after they had memorized their spells and incantations and had to call them to mind. Of course, actual sorcerers had direct power, not the borrowed power of a young hedgewitch from the depths of the swampland. Ashakarahad tried to focus. The scrolling glyphs were moving faster and she was having a hard time reining them in, as if her memory was running away ahead of her.

"Whatever you're going to do," Maeve said, "do it quickly!" The sound of swords scraping from scabbards rang out. The glyphs of the mage-lords were a whirlwind now, and Ashakarahad fought desperately to keep up, imagined that the wheels in her head that were doing the scrolling would soon start smoking and wobbling. Her own voice sounded harsh and foreign, something lost and distant. Then her voice was joined by other voices and she thought that Ceàrain and the goblins had returned. But the voices were the disembodied voices that had kept her company, questioned her, debated with her, while she had been in that other place. The watchers from the city of chrome and glass.

Idsiyushti's energy snapped loudly. The witch cried out, but the energy continued to flow and crack and Ashakarahad still refused to open her eyes. She heard Marrah shout, but the scrolling glyphs, nearly a blur, were demanding too much attention. The chorus of voices ringing in Ashakarahad's ears was a discordant distraction until she realized that they were trying to help her. She altered her tone and phrasing and, suddenly, her voice rang out loud and clear and in a tongue that she should never have been able to master. The words echoed across the berms and wild rice, jarred into the stands of wild cane, silenced the growing mewing of the approaching dead that Ashakarahad at that moment became aware of.

Ashakarahad, head back, throat roaring, shouted. Idsiyushti's magic cracked loudly. There was a sudden, roaring rush and Ashakarahad snapped open her eyes to see a purple gate cycled open. On the other side of the glowing standing stone, the donkey, Herch, whinnied as if in approval.

The portal cycled open with a snap, purple and writhing. Jonath said, "Fuck it," and threw the useless crossbow to the ground. The dead had been slipping through the trees and cane at the edge of the wild rice paddies, shuffling a few steps forward as Ashakarahad and Idsiyushti began doing whatever it was they were doing to the standing stone. But when the hum of the stone reached Jonath's ears and Sigiswinth was all but being bodily restrained by Maeve, the air around the stone began to shimmer as if inundated with waves of rolling heat and the dead had mewled and howled and charged.

It was no easy feat to race across the berms — and mud and water and wild rice — but the dead were making a show of it. Long strides, dead arms pumping, flowing, mouths agape as if to catch the maximum amount of breath. The types of dead were numerous and Jonath didn't stop to catalog them as he tossed the crossbow aside and ran.

Herch, with Aeldreth's pallet in tow, bouncing and heaving behind his hooves, and with Chrona dragged along beside, galloped through the portal as if the mule had figured the portal had been opened for his purposes alone. Marrah seemed to hesitate, eyes going from Idsiyushti to the portal and back. Maeve screamed something at Sigiswinth and, swords drawn, both falkr raced after Herch and Aeldreth. Sigiswinth stopped short of entering the portal and turned back, sword raised, as if on guard. Maeve spun in response, glaring at her captain. Jonath shouted at the top of his lungs, waving them both on. Ashakarahad shook her horned head as if clearing it. Then the demoness looked out across the lowland at the charging dead and shouted something to Idsiyushti.

Marrah finally tore her gaze from Idsiyushti and raced around the standing stone, bare, muddy legs dark in the early morning light. She reached the falkr but stumbled to a halt as Sigiswinth raised her sword. Jonath's heart sank and he forced himself to run faster. Ashakarahad was moving by then, taking great strides towards Sigiswinth as the falkr captain's sword, now blazing bright blue, stabbed itself towards Marrah's gut. The blade was met and forced into the mud, blue flame flaring, by Maeve's sword. Then both falkr were grappling. Ashakarahad reached Marrah and grabbed the shaken girl, pushing her past the falkr and into the portal where she vanished. Sigiswinth spun on Ashakarahad, flaming sword raised, but Maeve struck once more, clubbing the falkr captain on the back of the head with a heavy helmet that neither falkr had donned. Sigiswinth crumbled into Ashakarahad's arms and then time seemed to speed back up in a way that made Jonath almost hesitate and lose his footing—he hadn't realized that time had seemed to slow in the first place. The portal flared and Ashakarahad pushed Sigiswinth into Maeve's arms. Then both the demoness and the falkr were gone. Idsiyushti turned and raced for the portal, mud flying out behind her bare feet. Jonath reached her and watched the portal slowly beginning to cycle closed. Idsiyushti's magic must have been keeping the portal open and now that she was moving and not concentrating on it, the portal was closing.

The howls of the dead were alarmingly close. Jonath swore he felt the hot ichor running from the mouths of some of the dead splattering on his back. He could sense the cold, life-sucking hands reaching for him and Idsiyushti. He could hear the writhing of appendages that the dead shouldn't have. The portal was open only to half its original height. Both he and Idsiyushti ducked and threw themselves forward headfirst into the collapsing opening and the world went blindingly purple and twisted. Jonath fought an instant wave of nausea and tried desperately to recall the instructions given to him years ago by Sphinx for calming the mind and body during the sudden shift through a magical portal.

The howls of the dead snapped to a silence that was heavy with a turbulence that Jonath could not place, could not describe. Then he and Idsiyushti, side by side, stumbled into hot, early morning daylight, falling to the ground, the hard-packed earth of the town square. Jonath came up short against the old stone retaining wall that had been built around the town's standing stone years before his birth. His head was spinning and he was fighting back the need to vomit.

Rough hands lifted him up and over the wall. He opened his eyes. The town square was organized chaos. Folk were running about, others standing and staring. Smoke was heavy in the air, wood smoke and the acrid smoke from burning corpses and burning waste. His mind reeled and he once again fought back the memories of the dragon attacks during the Chaos. Barricades of broken furniture and odds and ends that defied definition in that moment choked off alleyways. Greasy stains of blood and mud pockmarked the ground. Jak stood staring at him, leaning on a cane, sword over his shoulder. Grendl strode forward, looming large despite his height. He punched Jonath hard on the jaw with a fist made of dwarven stone.

Grendl stood over Jonath, fists balled. Ashakarahad stepped forward with one great stride. The horned demoness cast a long shadow on the dirt of the square, even under the thin, hot, early-morning sun that was hidden behind smoke and clouds. She said nothing, but Grendl, grimacing, backed away while Jonath moaned on the ground and tried to sit up. The constable's face was swollen, growing purple and red. He rubbed his jaw and blinked around the square. Jak put a hand on Grendl's broad shoulder, but the dwarf shook it off.

Jak was exhausted and his leg was hurting again, but he had a sinking feeling that he was certain was connected to the standing stone, the purple portal, and the appearance of Jonath, Ash, Idsiyushti, Marrah and the falkr. And Grendl's mule, who had led the charge from the portal as if an army of ancient gods from some lost afterworld were hard on his tail. Chrona had been clinging to the mule in ragged, filthy desperation and a wounded falkr had been strapped to a makeshift stretcher dragged behind the wild-eyed mule.

Behind them stumbled Marrah. She looked frightened, dirty, her short, black hair a tangled mess. Her dress had been ripped off just above her knees, her legs scratched and bruised. One of her shoulders was bare, the front of her dress torn and haphazardly repaired, barely covering her ample breasts.

The falkr captain and another falkr, both without their customary helms covering their heads and faces, appeared next, Sigiswinth stumbling and shaking her head, supported by the younger falkr. This caused a new round of gasps to run through the panicky folk. Unhelmeted falkr covered in blood and dirt and bandages. Jak had seen falkr without their armor before—well, one falkr called, appropriately, Pale. She had been disgraced somehow, a fallen warrior who had been banished from the emperor's service for some arcane crime that she never talked about, not even drunk. Pale had found her way to the Alley, Drilithae's immense brothel district that was almost a city-state unto itself. Eventually, she had found herself under Jak's mother's sway, and she became a top earner until the day she drank two bottles of gin, snorted a fistful of Crystals of Errund and walked to the harbor at dusk, never to be seen again. So Sigiswinth's features were no real surprise to Jak, but the younger falkr's were. He blinked at her pretty, stern face.

Ashakarahad loomed through the portal and into the square so close behind the falkr that Jak had been surprised that the demoness hadn't run them down. The appearance of Ash, alive and well, was, of course, a surprise all on its own, and Jak spent a moment trying to close his gaping mouth. The demoness was not wearing her armor—other than her steel-covered boots—and the only weapons she had were a brace of long daggers that were more like short swords. Her orange-tinted features were fixed firm, lips tight. Her tunic and trousers were dirty, but she looked far more presentable than everyone else who had come hurtling through the portal so far. With the possible exception of Grendl's mule.

Jak had been hobbling forward when the purple portal had begun to shrink. He felt like he was moving through thick, stale air, or some sort of sticky liquor that was simultaneously restraining and intoxicating. The stench of burning wood, burning flesh, and burning shit almost smelled sweet under the hypnotic pull of the twisting portal, whose shrinking and inevitable closure felt like some elemental pull was dragging the whole square into its depths. The amulet on the chain around his throat began to buzz once more.

Jonath and Idsiyushti had burst from the collapsing portal, both of them almost diving into the earth before the standing stone. Idsiyushti rolled like a professional acrobat and came to her feet, her ripped and dirty dress settling around her thighs after flashing the square her legs and muddy, bare feet. She came up in a crouch, her dark eyes wild, undeniably touched by sparks of magic that reminded Jak of the eyes of some of his mother's apprentices after they'd broken from contact with something beyond the boundaries of reality. Jak took an involuntary step backward.

Jonath was dressed in his ragged and battered leather and chain armor. He had fetched up hard against the low retaining wall that someone had built around the standing stone ages ago, somehow holding onto his sword, chain of office flashing in the pale light, his olive face almost pale. Grendl had been on him like a heavy ax felling a tree with a single stroke.

Shouts and cries echoed through the square as the portal collapsed on itself with an audible snap. Idsiyushti gasped and fell forward onto her hands. She shook her head and when she looked up, the sparks of magic in her eyes were fading. While Ashakarahad was helping Jonath to his feet, Marrah was doing the same with Idsiyushti, and Jak hobbled away from Grendl. He put his cane and sword in the same hand and reached out to offer Idsiyushti another hand up. The witch took his hand with a smile that seemed more relief than thanks, and he helped Marrah pull her to her feet. Idsiyushti clung to Marrah and tightened her grip on Jak's hand for several long moments. Valen was there suddenly, as was a squeal from Seran, and more arms wrapped around Idsiyushti and Marrah, sharing relieved laughter and tears. Then Idsiyushti pulled away and straightened her ripped, shortened dress, squared her thin shoulders and looked around the square.

Shouts, questions, and rapid explanations filled the air. A hot, sharp wind picked up. It tumbled over the courthouse, across the barricades, through the square, kicking up dust and debris, trailing away smoke and fumes, kissing cheeks with a heavy touch. Then it trickled into a short, singular breeze that trailed into stale nothingness.

The medallion continued to vibrate, even as the glyphs on the standing stone faded once again into bas-reliefs. The hum of the stone and portal also vanished with the closure, but Jak could hear the medallion vibrating louder now, feel it through his leather jerkin, through his chest. Pain shot through his leg as he shifted his weight and glanced at the standing stone. It was, indeed, once again cold and lifeless. Fitting, Jak mused. He turned to look at the roof of the courthouse, at the bell-less bell tower.

Beside him, Idsiyushti touched his arm and said, "Your leg."

"It's nothing," Jak said, not thinking. "There are plenty worse laid up in the tavern." Not far away, the falkr captain, who looked pained and disoriented, was in some sort of argument with Grendl, Jonath,

327

Ashakarahad, and the younger falkr. Jak ignored them, watching the bell tower.

"The dead did this?" Idsiyushti asked, looking around.

"Yes," Jak answered.

"Mercy," Marrah breathed. Jak turned back to them, saw them holding hands, looking all the world like two urchins staring for the first time into the wide mouth of the lane that led into Drilithae's vast bazaar. Jak looked over at Chrona, who had sat down hard in the dirt and was looking up at Grendl's tavern with tears streaking her dirty, brown cheeks. The once-stoic girl, so calculating, so forthright, looked like someone had dragged a tattered, patchwork ragdoll through mud and soot and washed it afterward with a spray of dirty swamp water.

Jak opened his mouth to tell Idsiyushti to take herself, Marrah, and Chrona to Grendl's and throw themselves into a big bath before seeing to the wounded. He wanted to say it, desperately wanted to say it. But movement caught his eye and he looked back at the bell tower, heart hammering, knowing what he would see. His mother's medallion was vibrating almost painfully and the lookout in the tower was waving a swatch of red cloth frantically, trying to tell the folk in the square that the dead were attacking again.

****

Idsiyushti felt shrunken and drained once again, as if the dead had already gotten a hold of her and drawn the life from her very core, drying her out, shrinking her to the size of a rotten apple. She'd expended so much energy in their flight through the deep dark, fighting the dead, healing the falkr. And then opening the portal of the mage-lords, linking herself to the words that had echoed from Ashakarahad's mouth and roared themselves in discordant syllables from voices too many to count through her cobweb-laden head.

Marrah's hand in her own was warm and comforting, but she could feel the girl trembling deep down, knew that Marrah was just as exhausted.

Idsiyushti looked up at whoever was waving a red tablecloth in the bell tower. Jak started shouting and waving his sword. Heads turned away from the argument going on between the falkr, Jonath, Grendl, and Ash and started pointing. Then they started shouting and screaming as well.

The dead, it seemed, were attacking the town once again.

Idsiyushti's stomach churned. She looked at Marrah and she knew that the anguish in her own eyes was really a mirror of the horror in Marrah's. She squeezed Marrah's hand, trying to reassure her.

People were running now. The square was nearly in as much motion as it had seemed when they'd first tumbled through the narrowing portal. A sudden waft of burning shit crawled up Idsiyushti's nose and she gagged.

Then Valen was once again at her side. Valen's dark, lined features were focused and drawn, and Idsiyushti could read pain there, pain and anger. She was dressed in battered leathers and carried a sword. In her off hand was a jug whose cork had been pulled. Idsiyushti took the jug and drank, expecting water. Whiskey burned her mouth and lips and she gagged again. Then she was drinking long and deep, as if her life depended on it. And maybe it did. Maybe all their lives did. She hummed the Hymn of Conversion and the whiskey churned inside her, coursed through her, lit her on fire and flared the dying embers in her core. She drank deep, the jug tilted up, whiskey running down her chin. Nearby, Jak protested, as did Marrah, and Idsiyushti held up a hand to silence them as she finished the rest of the jug. Valen chuckled, took the empty jug and grabbed Seran, who was gaping at the bell tower, by the arm and walked away.

Idsiyushti's core, her essence, her existence was glowing and vibrant again, like a lever had been pulled, a trap door opened to the well of her power. She no longer felt like a shrunken, rotten apple. The edges of her vision waved and shimmered, but she felt a focus she hadn't felt since the whiskey they'd stolen from old dead Miq's place had vanished during their manic flight from the dead, since the herb drink Ceàrain had given her. Her senses were heightened, popping, snapping for her attention.

"I've always wondered what the fey did to you," Jak said. "You look like you've slept for a week. No one should be that affected by whiskey, I don't care how good it is!"

But Idsiyushti turned to Marrah and drew the startled girl into a deep, soul-searing kiss. She ran her free hand up under Marrah's ripped, shortened dress, felt the skin of Marrah's thigh, the tiny hairs there, felt the curve of her ass, squeezed. Marrah squealed but held Idsiyushti tight, returning the kiss. Idsiyushti pulled back and said, "Get to the tavern and see to the wounded. I need to see what's happening, then I'll join you." Marrah, breathless, blinked and nodded. Without protest, she turned and ran towards the tavern's porch.

Idsiyushti turned and found Jak staring. "My mother would have burned down half of Drilithae to have you," he said, green eyes alight with wonder and mischief. Then he turned and hobbled quickly towards the barricades.

Idsiyushti found herself in the cramped bell tower with Grendl and Jonath, Sigiswinth and Maeve. Fires still smoldered in buildings throughout the town beyond the square, and she could see a shimmer of magic surrounding the temple of the swamp gods and the graveyard. Grendl explained, in terse, clipped sentences, what had happened with Mackasl and that no one had heard from the temple since before the first attack. At the edge of town, the bonfires still burned, although lower and weaker, according to Grendl, than the first attack. The fire-tenders, Drag leading the way, were running back to the barricades.

Out beyond the perimeter of the town, among the trees that hadn't been felled for the bonfires, among stands of cane, waving willows, and pools of green water, the shades of the dead moved.

Jonath looked at Idsiyushti. "You are positively glowing. What happened?"

"Whiskey," Idsiyishti said. Jonath blinked. "Valen gave me some whiskey. A jug's worth. I drank all of it."

Grendl asked, "Valen? A jug? Was this jug reddish with a blue stripe around the neck? Runes on the side?"

"Yes."

Grendl bristled, fists balled, and turned back to survey the gathering dead. "The entire jug? That whiskey was worth more than this entire fucking town. I don't know what's worse—the fact that you'll probably die from whiskey poisoning in an hour or that you'll be pissing out the entire jug if you don't."

Ashakarahad appeared below the bell tower, standing on the courthouse roof. "I don't understand," the demoness said. "The use of the standing stone should have warded this area from the dead. Like when we used it to reach you, Jonath."

"Ceàrain activated that stone," Idsìyushti said. She felt herself wobbling slightly, but the energy coursing through her veins and the heat in her gut and behind her eyes was exhilarating.

"Of course," the demoness said, half to herself. "We probably didn't do it correctly. Which has drawn the dead rather than repelled them." Idsiyushti laughed at Ashakarahad's tone, but Sigiswinth shouted for them to all be quiet. She and Maeve were studying the dead, the ranks of which were just reaching the bonfires. The dead things stopped their forward motion. Their ranks rippled and new figures stepped forward. Figures that were mottled and bluish, with torn, pocked flesh, wearing the wet, torn robes of the priesthood of the swamp gods. Idsiyushti, Grendl, and Jonath, almost as one, turned to look at the magical barrier surrounding the temple.

"That can't be," Grendl said.

"Something or someone is keeping that barrier raised," Jonath needlessly said.

"Either someone's still alive in there or the dead have found a way to keep the barrier up to fool us," Grendl said. He punched the low, wooden wall of the tower.

The dead priests and priestess raised their dead hands. Idsiyushti stared. She knew these dead, though she couldn't recognize individual features this far away. But she knew that she knew them. These dead were not the long-ancient dead from the deep dark, forgotten by time and preserved by the dark magic spilling into the world because of the mage-lords. How many other townsfolk swelled the dead's ranks now? The thought was a fist that punched her deep, just below her heart. But the whiskey glow fought back and she wiped a sudden tear and spat over the tower wall onto the courtyard roof. She squinted and pointed.

"I think that's your answer," she said. "I think that's Mackasl. Or was." The others stared but remained silent. All except Grendl, who let out a steady stream of whispered curses.

Energy swirled around the dead priests and, as one, as far Idsiyushti could see from the top of the courthouse, the bonfires went out as if doused by torrential gushes of water poured from monstrous buckets. Thick smoke was all that remained of the fires, rising up and writhing in the hot air like angry tentacles bent on revenge.

Ashakarahad looked in the direction of her old camp, out beyond the barricades and the now-dead bonfires and the edge of town, out among the surging, flowing ranks of the dead. She had taken most of her weapons and armor on her trek around the swampland and had lost most of them when the standing stone in the goblin clearing had exploded. Still, she had dim hope that there was something to salvage. But the camp was out of reach now and the dead, led by what was left of Mackasl and the black-robed priests and priestesses of the swamp gods, led by darker things that drank sunlight like wine-laced blood, were blocking the way. The chilling laughter that had sometimes dogged their footsteps on the flight through the deep dark began to peel between the dark houses beyond the square. An insane, twittering giggle that had no source and, for a moment, filled Ashakarahad with thoughts of invisible voices and a city that stretched across the horizon. If the invisible voices on that otherworld plane had belonged to young, immature mage-lords—as Ceàrain had intimated—then could this twittering be the same? Was an insane mage-lord watching the fight from the city of chrome and glass, directing the dead for some nefarious end that none of the folk in the town would ever know?

Ashakarahad descended to the square via a long, shaky ladder that creaked and groaned beneath her weight, rather than the narrow twist of stairs inside that barely allowed someone as nimble as Idsiyushti through. She still wore no armor as not even Drag had armor that would fit her, so she settled on hoping she was fast enough and strong enough that her already battle-scarred tunic and trousers would be enough protection. She took two antique-looking, long-hafted footman's hammers—spear-headed at either end, with wicked claws backing the hammerheads—from Marin's collection of old arms and swung them about, one in each massive hand. Idsiyushti, standing drunk yet clear-eyed and brimming with energy, whistled at the sight of the spinning, twirling. Seran and Kel applauded and Grendl shouted for all of them to cut it out and get ready. Ashakarahad looked about for Jonath and saw the constable standing on the wooden steps of the courthouse, once again arguing with Sigiswinth and Maeve.

Idsiyushti all but skipped across the square to the tavern to check on the wounded. Ashakarahad watched her go, watched the hem of her ripped dress bounce up and down threatening to reveal her ass, watched her brown, dirty, scratched legs, her bare feet. Fey magic. In a human. Fueled by whiskey. Ash was certain she could write several articles on Idsiyushti alone for the university at Drilithae. She couldn't even imagine how her people's battle priests would have reacted to the young witch.

Acrid smoke slid across the square, blocking Ashakarahad's view of the tavern entrance. She turned away. Jonath was still arguing with the falkr. Grendl was donning heavy chain and leather with the help of Jak and Scrum One-eye. Nothing like the imminent threat of *another* attack by the walking, crawling, flying dead to bring people together. Sigiswinth's voice carried across the square, cursing in the language of the falkr. Ashakarahad hefted the war hammers and walked over to stand with Jak and Grendl.

"You look tired," Jak said as Ash approached. "Magnificent but tired."

"And you look wounded."

"It's my leg—"

"Obviously."

"It's stiff, nothing more," Jak continued, scowling. "I can still fight."

Ash shrugged.

Grendl took up his ax and led them towards the center of the square. Scrum One-eye and several others of Jak's legion followed, armed, angry, and many in drag. Ashakarahad turned to survey the barricades, the folk running about, carrying supplies and makeshift weapons, delivering arrows to the defenders on the rooftops. Watched the children, tired and vacant-eyed, light torches with which to burn the dead with all the fervor of performing mind-numbing chores. The folk were tired and scared, the memory of their recent victory drifting away like the shreds of a dream. But folk were determined. Or so she hoped. Word of the dead swamp priests was just now filtering through the square.

"Where do you want us?" Jak asked.

"Here," Grendl said. "I'm not certain we can hold the barricades this time. Not with what I saw up there on the courthouse and not with the swamp priests. So be ready."

The medallion around Jak's neck was audibly vibrating. He seemed to be ignoring it. Beyond the barricades, beyond the square, the chilling laughter echoed louder. The shouts and mewls of the dead grew, creeping ahead of the horde. The smell of burning shit and wood still filled the air but now Ashakarahad could also smell the dead, as if a sudden gust had blown in from the pits beneath a charnel house, or from beyond a wall of distant, black mountains on the other side of a churning, otherworld river. Folk on the rooftops of the courthouse and the surrounding homes and shops, atop Jonath's office, atop the mercantile, began firing flaming arrows. More smoke and flame began to climb into the dense, cloud-layered sky. Ashakarahad took a deep breath, her hands tight on the long hafts of the war hammers.

One of the barricades to the left, between Jonath's office and the courthouse all but melted under tendrils of black mist that ate at the wood like acid. Then the dead were up and over and in the square and Grendl raised his ax and shouted some war cry or other, but Ashakarahad was already moving, great strides carrying her into the dead and the black mist and the screams of the townsfolk as they tried to flee.

****

The unseasonal clouds above the layers of smoke from burning wood, shit, and dead flesh, began to let loose. Rain fell, a few drops at first, and then in abrupt torrents that wiped the smoke from the thick air, put out most of the fires, and obscured vision as if the dead swamp priests had directed the black tendrils creeping over the barricades to reach up and become fog. The square became a slick of mud and panic in moments. But the dead failed to relent, even as the rain washed some of them away, sloughing off layers of dead skin, forcing the black tendrils to search and founder and become far less of a menace. Folk, soaked through, still fought. Bowstrings became useless so many rooftop defenders climbed down to the square. Some slipped and fell into newly-formed mud puddles, legs and backs twisted, joining the growing number of wounded.

Inside the tavern, the rain was a sudden, massive hammering on the steep, gabled roof that echoed through the tiny bedrooms upstairs and down into the common room. The smell of unwashed bodies and blood and infection pervaded the common room despite Idsiyushti's best efforts to diffuse it with burnings of herbs and incense and a number of small incantations that, being more fey than she'd like to admit, merely tried to mask the miasma with the smell of wildflowers and liquor. But the rain brought with it its own smell, heavy and thick, which seemed to finally chase the miasma out through the curtained tavern windows. Marrah, Sek, Ned's daughter in her swamp priest robes, and a couple of older children ran about the common room, tending the wounded as best they could. Outside, beyond the crash and hew of the rain, the screams and shouts and clashes on metal of the wet, muddy battle caused those inside, wounded and caretakers alike, to cringe and constantly glance at the main door.

Marrah watched Idsiyushti as well. The witch was the only one in the tavern who did not constantly turn to look at the door. Instead, she flitted around like one of the faerie teachers she often spoke of. She was dirty and tired, but the whiskey infusion was like a bright, burning fire that shone out of her eyes, poured through her pores, made healing sparks snap from her fingertips. But despite the not-so-subtle weave in her light step, Idsiyushti seemed more sober than any of them. Sek, by her own admission, had been taking a shot of rye for her constitution every half-hour and Marrah had only had small beer and a snort of someone's dwindling supply of crystal since she'd entered the tavern. She had no idea if the two children or Ned's swamp-sworn daughter had touched anything from behind the bar.

Still, Marrah's heart raced. The pounding of the unseasonal rain and the sounds of the muddy battle outside, combined with the stress of having been on the run from crawling death and leaping to safety through a strange, magical portal were getting to her. She jumped once again, as did all of them, even some of the wounded, except for, of course, Idsiyushti, when a mocking peal of laughter echoed in through the windows. Marrah froze at the sound. That laughter had dogged them on their mad run through the swamp, stopping only once they'd gone through the first portal to reach the ruin where they'd found Jonath and the falkr. Her heart skipped a beat and a cold sweat broke out on her forehead which she wiped away absently with the back of a dirty hand. Chrona—who was sitting at a table, Marrah now noticed, drinking from a gourd labeled potato mash liquor—began to shake visibly.

The laughter faded and was replaced by a sequence of rapid screams that made Sek scream as well and made the children start to cry. Idsiyushti swore. She stood from laying glowing hands across the belly of a wounded man whose face Marrah couldn't see and marched across the room. She grabbed Marrah by the shoulders and hit her with a hot, wet, tongue-probing kiss. Marrah felt her heart begin to race anew, felt her breathing quicken. Then Idsiyushti was gone, racing up the stairs, Marrah blinking at her ass beneath her fluttering, ripped-too-short dress as she ascended.

But the kiss had been like fire.

Marrah felt rage building, cutting through her fear and panic. Felt her muscles tense. She glance down at the moaning woman she'd been standing over, looked at the wound in the woman's shoulder, saw the dim life in

341

the woman's eyes, knew that the woman, if she died, would most likely join the dead out beyond the barricade—only she'd be inside the barricades, inside the tavern. Marrah spun and went behind the bar to the kitchen. She pulled down a heavy carving knife and went back to the main room. More screams blasted through the windows, whose thick curtains had been pulled closed long before Marrah and the others had returned through the portal. Sek looked at her, the older woman's eyes pleading. Marrah looked back at the door. Then she turned and ran up the stairs. Rage swelled in her heart, racing along her spine, nestled in her stomach. Her fingers hurt from how tight she was gripping the knife. But she was damned if she wasn't going to be by Idsiyushti's side.

Perhaps she'd known about it all along or had some inkling of what to look for—or perhaps she'd just gotten lucky—but Idsiyushti had found the small hatch that led from the narrow, packed attic to the peaked, gabled roof. Marrah followed after a quick search of the tiny rooms on the second floor. The attic was stacked with old furniture and twisted, dusty odds and ends that had been collected through the years, leftovers from the many whores who had graced the beds and floorboards of the place, long before Grendl rode into town on

Herch, bought the deed, and took over. The rain was a horrible, echoing pounding on the roof above and the light was dim, coming through two small, round windows that were more grime than not. She called out for Idsiyushti and stubbed her booted toe on a thick, heavy crate. In the gloom, Marrah saw that it was a crate of old whiskey amphorae, probably shipped into the swamp decades ago and forgotten about. A splash of rainwater hit her cheek and she looked up to see the roof hatch open above a short ladder made of thick, worn wood. She grabbed an amphora by its round ear-like handle, blew dust off of it, saw tiny cracks glistening with ancient crust. The amphora was heavy but the rage that was driving her found a way to shift the handle and the knife to one hand while she climbed the rain-slick rungs to the roof.

The day was dark with the rain, yet the air was hot, and the rainwater felt almost like drops of the hot bath water that she and her sister would splash each other with when they were little, out on the family farm a mile or so from town. Her heart suddenly ached at the memory. Her father had ridden away so long ago she could barely remember him. Her mother and sister had long since returned to the swamp, buried in the graveyard by the temple, her sister from some fever, her mother from just giving the fuck up on life. She almost gagged on the sudden thought that her mother and sister might have crawled from their common grave to join the ranks of the attacking dead.

The hot rain, thick and dense, drenched her instantly, her hair and dress clinging to her scalp and body like a second, glistening skin. Her overlarge boots, spares that she'd donned when she got into the tavern, were suddenly filled, the water strangely cold on her toes. The air was almost sucked from her lungs with the weight of the rain, and she nearly dropped the amphora and the knife before getting her bearings.

Idsiyushti stood between two gables, arms outstretched, looking thin and wet and small. Her dress was so soaked that she might as well have been naked. Her fingers were outspread and fire crackled between them. Marrah glanced at the dark sky, suddenly worried that lightning would strike down and obliterate them both.

Out past the roof, past the square, a pillar of fire crashed into the earth. Marrah blinked away from the flash of light. Then she made her way across the slick roof to stand behind Idsiyushti. The witch was surrounded by an aura that was hot and electric. Another pillar of fire crashed out of the sky. Marrah saw the pillar strike the earth beyond the square, on the other side of the courthouse. Then she looked down. The square was a muddy quagmire of writhing, fighting townsfolk and dark, cold shadows that were at once dead and horribly alive, rending, clawing, stealing the very life from their victims. The energy around Idsiyushti snapped and this time forks of fire lanced down throughout the square like lightning and smashed the shadows into smoking embers and wisps of dead flesh.

Without turning, Idsiyushti reached out and grabbed Marrah's free hand. Sorcery rushed through Marrah's blood, her body, her very being. The rain-hidden world spun as if blown about by a cyclone. She felt like she was going to vomit.

"Stay with me!" Idsiyushti shouted above the chaos. "I need you!"

The nausea vanished, leaving in its place a cold fist of ice that threatened to grip her heart. But her heart was fired by the rage that Idsiyushti had infected her with down below in the common room. The cold ice could only surround it, but it couldn't quench it. Marrah laughed.

Five pillars of fire punched into the ground, three in the square, inside the overrun barricades, two beyond, in the streets, the contents of which Marrah could see in her third eye—which until that moment, until Idsiyushti's touch, she hadn't been aware she had. Her mind was reeling. She laughed again.

More fire punched down. Five. Six. Eight. Twelve pillars of flame that scattered, withered, destroyed the attacking dead and their tendrils of shadow, claw, tooth, and bone. Marrah tried to call fire then, felt a sudden flicker, a sudden wave of heat. In her mind's eye, flame lanced down, thinner, weaker than the columns called by Idsiyushti. She laughed again, giddy. She had no idea what she was doing but the power flooding through her, power from Idsiyushti, was so intoxicating. Dizziness threatened to take her and she pushed it away. She reached out again and this time, among the heat and the waves of energy, she directed the thin fire at the ground. By her fourth try, she was directing the fire into ranks of the flowing dead. Beside her, Idsiyushti laughed and squeezed her hand. Marrah felt like her heart would burst out of her chest.

The rain could not hide the smell of magefire for long. It crawled up onto the rooftop and singed Marrah's nose hairs and made her face wrinkle. Beside her, as if the smell of the smoke were some sort of leach, Idsiyushti shrank in upon herself. Marrah reached out and wrapped an arm around her, holding her up. Small fingers of lightning jumped between them, but Marrah ignored the momentary pain. Thoughts of her own magefire were gone as well.

She shouted Idsiyushti's name but the witch just sagged further. Marrah leaned to the right and let the slick, sloped gable roof take some of their weight. In the hot darkness of the rain, Idsiyushti looked old and wizened, strands of her hair turning grey-blue like the old women who sat on the porches on the other side of the square from the old men, smoking and chewing tobacco, drinking gin to the old men's whiskey. She'd used too much magic all at once.

Tears burned Marrah's eyes, tears instantly washed away by the hot rain. She eased Idsiyushti to a sitting position on the roof, her back to the gable.

"Idsiyushti!"

The witch replied, her voice thin and distant, her words lost in the sound of the rain and the battle below. The amphora bumped against the shingles with a dull sound that snapped Marrah to attention. She let go of Idsiyushti, dropped the carving knife, and wrenched the wax from the cork in the neck of the amphora. She threw the cork over the side of the building and reached the amphora towards Idsiyushti. Perhaps it was the smell of the decades-old liquor, but Idsiyushti reached up and grabbed the amphora by the ear-handles and drank like it was milk from her long-lost mother's tit. Marrah laughed as she watched Idsiyushti's throat work the whiskey down.

Then Idsiyushti rolled to the side and vomited violently, the rain washing the sick away almost instantly. Marrah cried out, but there was nothing she could do except hold onto Idsiyushti's thin, shaking shoulders as the witch heaved so violently that Marrah's own guts hurt. A sudden weakness gripped Marrah, wrapped itself around her shoulders, caused her legs to ache. The magic she'd used, that she'd borrowed from Idsiyushti? Had it drained her too?

Idsiyushti wiped her mouth with the back of her rain-soaked hand and sat up. She looked at Marrah, eyes clear and bright. She looked young again, but the light was playing tricks, making the grey-blue streaks in her dark, wet hair remain.

"What the shit did you just give me?"

"I don't know. Whiskey? I found it in the attic in an old crate."

"Give me more."

"But—"

"More!"

And Idsiyushti drank long and deep. She gagged once but didn't vomit and when she finally let Marrah pull the near-empty amphora away her eyes were shining with a light that was so unnatural that Marrah nearly scuttled backward off the rooftop. Idsiyushti laughed and grabbed Marrah and pulled her back to wet, slick safety. Then she kissed Marrah again, her mouth tasting of vomit and whiskey and white-hot power. Marrah's back arched and she cried out as her blood tried to boil. When she opened her eyes, everything that she could see was wreathed in a blue-green hue. They kissed again, long and hard, tongues dancing, hands grasping and groping, skin wet and hot and connected.

Idsiyushti pulled back and smiled, her eyes glowing brighter than the full moon. Out beyond the roof, sheets of fire crashed down from the sky again, steaming in the torrential rain, blasting and obliterating, and Idsiyushti never, not once, looked anywhere other than into Marrah's eyes as the destruction blasted the dead away.

A single touch of the hot, torrential rain was enough for Ashakarahad to realize that it was more than an unseasonal swamp storm, that sorcery of some kind was driving it. Driving it to a strange, violent madness plummeting from the sky as if someone had lifted the crimson, boiling sea from that distant, other world and dropped it on the swamp and the town.

But the realization that the rain was, at least in part, artificial, was only a dim thought as she swung the long-hafted war hammers in rapid circles, long arcs, streaks of brains and gore, mists of dead flesh, bone, and shit. A few claws touched her, driving cold spikes into her flesh, but she shrugged them off. She found herself alone before one of the barricades. Townsfolk were either collapsed in the mud or gone, hidden by the rain. She stopped and caught her breath, saw sickening tendrils of black, dead air reach over, through, around the barricade, starting to melt the wood and metal and stone like it was butter tossed into boiling oil.

Jak appeared beside her at that moment, the same moment that the twisting apparitions of swamp priests and things that were no longer recognizable appeared.

She fought by Jak's side, hacking, hewing, slamming the heads of the war hammers into the spaces left untouched by Jak's flashing longsword, accompanied by the insane hum of his vibrating medallion.

Then fire had begun to rain down from the sky. Whole sheets of fire, columns, pillars, whirls of flame that ate at the dead in all of their hideous forms. Ashakarahad sensed Idsiyushti's presence in the flame and she stole a moment to glance about and up, seeing the tell-tale glow from the roof of the tavern. The descending flames were something that Ash had never dared imagine the young witch would be able to summon, much less control. But there was control, absolute precision in the flaming strikes. There was something else as well, another familiar touch. Marrah.

For a long moment, between side-stepping the twisted form of a creature—whose skin was pale and blue and whose face was locked in something resembling a leer, tongue lolling out, searching like the head of a snake—and slamming both hammers down hard, through the creature's head into its shoulders, Ash thought that the rain was somehow the work of Idsiyushti and Marrah too. But then, as the creature fell and turned to a muddy slick, Ash reached out with senses that, in that instant, she wished had more power than they actually had, and found something different, something more subtle driving the rain. Not Idsiyushti and Marrah. Not the dead swamp priests.

The combination of rain and fire was brutal and the dead horde slowly vanished, melting, washed away. Ashakarahad found herself once again with moments to spare, standing in an empty space alone. Jak was gone, a drowned rat driven further into the rain. Ash looked past the ruined barricade, beyond the mouth of the alley, saw shifting forms that were holding back, forms unrecognizable in the driving rain and the flashes of fire. She stared, blinked water from her eyes. There was a faint flicker of recognition.

She walked forward, boots sucking through the mud. The forms beyond the alley remained shadowed, unrecognizable. She raised the war hammers. Behind her, the entire square was obscured by rain, by the flash and steam of columns of fire. Three times the dead appeared, materialized out of rain, mud, and shadow, reaching for her, laughing maniacally, mewling, spitting. Three times she spun the war hammers and the dead melted away in explosions of sinew and bone and black ichor. Her body ached, her head hurt, water tried to blind her, stung her eyes.

The alley seemed suddenly very long, like a corridor between stone buildings with twisting foundations in a place ancient and forgotten. Wrapped in darkness and water, the alley suddenly smelled of roses and lilacs and the bitter leavings of alchemy. It seemed like the ground became slick as Ashakarahad walked, black cobbles rather than mud, cobbles that steamed and cracked in the heat of the day and the tongues of fire that Idsiyushti and Marrah sent down from the sky. Pale, ovoid faces peered from gaping windows in walls that should not have been there—walls made of chipped brick and ancient daub, not a trace of wood to be seen. Beyond the end of the alley, so far away now, receding faster than she could walk, the milling forms shifted position, almost as if uncertain. But they did not advance, did not attack.

The alley turned abruptly and Ashakarahad lost sight of the end, as if the passage was actually a flexible tube that someone had suddenly kinked. She found herself in a cobbled courtyard before an ancient, moss-covered fountain with water that was thick and black and covered with duckweed and kudzu. Ashakarahad spun, but the alley behind her was gone. The rain had ceased to fall. She walked over to the fountain. She could smell the brackish water, smell rust and mildew, flowers and spice. She was reminded once again of the long-disused perfumery lost in the twisted byways of Desade. The perfumery had been dark and bitter, full of iron pots and dead leaves that rustled in the breezes of the city.

A cold breeze touched her cheek now. The faint carrion smell now joined the smell from the fountain.

Ashakarahad looked at the cloudless, star-filled sky above her, a purple sky with black tendrils. Beyond the ring formed by the stone rooftops surrounding the courtyard, fingers of chrome and glass reached up to stir the tendrils in the sky. Ashakarahad spun in place, but the interplay in the sky between stars whose constellations she didn't recognize, the fingers of the city, and the black tendrils never changed. Her invisible shackles—nearly forgotten in the fight with the dead— were suddenly pulsing in time to the dizziness she felt. She looked down to see a silver-haired figure standing in the shadows beyond the fountain. The figure stepped forward and Ashakarahad blinked. The figure was Ceàrain, not silver-haired in the least.

Panic was racing through Ashakarahad's chest.

"What are you doing?" she asked, breathless.

"You are so close now," Ceàrain growled. "But we can't let you leave just yet. This must be finished. What you started."

"Out there, beyond the square, your clan—"

"We are helping in our own way."

"The rain—"

"There isn't much time left," Ceàrain continued. "We can only do so much, slow the dead for so long. But this place, this swamp. The masters left it to us to keep. Like a rancid cesspool left over after a tannery moves on, like the pits of chemicals running beneath the smoking chimneys of an alchemist. You were drawn here, like all the rest, like the dead have been since the time the masters left. But you, of all of them, can't remain."

"Then help me get out!" Sulphur tears blurred her eyes once again.

"We are. You are so close." Ceàrain walked around the fountain, the butt of her staff thumping against the cobbles. She looked up at Ashakarahad. "Just one more thing is needed. Something that will help free you from this place."

"Something—" Ashakarahad shook her head, drips of water flying from her horns. The weight of her shackles was growing more insidious, pulling, dragging.

"The blood of my clan inadvertently aided you last time," Ceàrain spat. "So now—"

"Enough blood has been spilled by the dead!" Ashakarahad said. The hafts of the hammers in her hands creaked as she gripped them painfully.

"Sadly, no," Ceàrain said. "Not enough. But the town will get something in return. They will not be left alone." Yet those words did not negate the look in her inhuman eyes. That look drove a fist of rage into Ashakarahad's gut. It was the look she'd seen in the eyes of the some of the Eld, demons of anger and hatred.

Something changed and Ashakarahad turned away. Behind her, a portion of the ancient stone fell away. She could see a glow lighting a gable atop a rooftop in some other place. "No," she said. "No!" She turned back. "NO!" But Ceàrain was gone.

The voluminous rain returned instantly, as did the heat of the swamp. As did the mud and the alley between the wood walls of the courthouse and Jonath's office. The smell of the swamp and the rain was so heavy that it drove the air from her lungs. She shook her head and a sheet of flame slammed into the ground in front of her, disintegrating four undead who were reaching for her with obsidian talons. She spun and ran back through the mud to the square.

Grendl watched Marin of Etrusq die, throat ripped out by dead claws shaped and colored like shards of obsidian. The old judge dropped his sword and collapsed, his body lost in the mud and rain and the sheet of fire that slammed down from the sky, turning Marin's killer to ash. The heat from the flame knocked Grendl backward and he struggled to keep his footing in the mud. More fire shot down from the sky, turning the rain into steam, searing the mud into cracked earth, turning more dead things into husks and outlines and greasy smears of ash.

The columns of fire seemed random but, despite the panic they instilled in the townsfolk fighting through the rain and mud, the fire only slammed down into the dead. It missed buildings and the living like some angry god was done with any dead things that walked, crawled, slithered, flew, deciding that blasts of fire from the sky were the only recourse. The thought of gods spun Grendl about. He and Marin had been trying to make their way to one of the barricades, following screams and shouts and the hideous laughter that just wouldn't quit, but the dead had appeared and Marin had died and more fire had struck. The barricade could barely be seen through the rain and steam, but Grendl could see more shapes that slithered and crawled and sucked the life from the living than he could panicked defenders.

He cursed and rushed forward. His ax rang in the air. His arm and legs ached and his armor was soaked through and in tatters, but somehow he'd remained victorious in each melee despite the bad footing and the low visibility. Grendl hacked and hewed and the dead things fell, destroyed or wounded enough to try to slink away to find easier prey. Then the townsfolk were gone and Grendl was alone. The dead things writhed, hollered in glee, displayed rotting, sharp teeth and leering, lolling tongues that moved like purple tentacles.

The dead parted and the swamp priests were there, the remains of the barricade melting away like wet paint in the hot rain. Bloated faces, the countenance of the drowned, the priests and priestess were recognizable by their robes alone. And their bearing, which was just as pompous and arrogant, in Grendl's angry opinion, as it had been in life. Grendl spat, wondered if Mackasl was in the group before him.

The bloated corpses of the swamp priests laughed, a strange, warbling mockery of the insane laughter that had been peeling through the square since the beginning of the attack, itself a mockery all on its own. Grendl's head spun. He raised his ax and wished that he hadn't dropped his whiskey flask sometime earlier, wished it hadn't been wrested from his belt by a wraith with sharp teeth for eyes and spurting cocks for tits, a wraith that had vanished beneath the abusive battering of Grendl's ax and frustrated cursing. But the flask had been gone and Grendl had had no chance to find it in the mud and rain and violence.

The dead swamp priests raised their bloated, palsied hands. Their runny eyes began to glow. Grendl set his feet in the thick mud, waiting. Sheets of fire slammed down into the swamp priests, turning the dead, air, rain, and mud into a hot, steamy, molten goop that succeeded in knocking Grendl from his feet, tossing him through the air to land hard on his ass. He rolled and blinked, his vision spotted and blurred. The dead priests were gone, as were the last vestiges of the barricade. He looked up at the roof of the tavern. A glow suffused a place between two gables but he could see nothing of Idsiyushti, who he knew must be up there hurling fire from the skies in feats of insane magic that he hadn't seen since his days traveling with Sphinx or fighting during the Desadian Chaos. He crawled to his feet and set himself before the opening where the barricade had been. Twisted, shifting shadows of nightmarish things were out there in the rain, milling beyond the square.

Behind and around him, the square was lost in the obscurity of the rain. He could see the shapes of corpses, either fallen townsfolk or fallen undead. He could see the remains of tents and camps and pieces of the barricades, broken and shattered furniture and refuse. The remains of a corpse-fire gleamed wetly in the near distance. A single child sat in the mud and cried silently. Grendl could see no one else, but the glow between the gables on the tavern continued to pulse. Behind the roar of the rain, he could hear columns of fire still slamming down, but other than a momentary glow in the curtain of water, he could not see where the fire struck, could not see what damage it wreaked.

Grendl looked back out at the milling, shifting forms before turning to the lone child. His feet, soaked through despite his heavy boots, were sucked by the mud with each step but the child saw him and held out its arms. Through the rain stumbled a pale falkr, the rain having washed away any blood and dirt and making her corded body shine. Her sword glowed with blue flame and she moved towards the child. She wore a heavy helm and Grendl couldn't be sure through the rain, but he thought the falkr was Sigiswinth. She hesitated, one hand to her helm as if in pain or confusion and Grendl was reminded of the younger falkr supporting Sigiswinth as they came barreling through the purple gate. He shouted a warning, but he was too late. The dead child, eyes now glowing white hot, leaped into the air past the flaming sword and latched itself onto Sigiswinth's exposed breast, stabbing deeply with claws that looked like long, rust-covered nails. The falkr screamed and wrestled with the dead child and Grendl cursed the rain and mud as he tried to run faster, harder, ax raised.

Then Jak was there, soaked through, hair plastered to his scalp, somehow keeping his footing with the cane in one hand and his longsword in the other. The sword rose and fell with expert grace and the dead child screamed and reeled. Its twisted face was slick with rain and blood and as Sigiswinth fell backward, the child reached for Jak. Jak spun and the longsword swept the dead child's head from its torso. Both head and body turned to rain-soaked ash and melted into the mud. Grendl reached Jak and Sigiswinth, who had collapsed, bleeding, chest torn open. Jak knelt awkwardly, slipped in the mud, caught himself, tried to keep Sigiswinth from rising. Beside them both, the flaming sword guttered as if in a sudden wind. The blue flames went out.

"Fuck this shit!" Jak said. He looked up at Grendl, in pain, exhausted. Then his eyes narrowed. Grendl turned, using the ax to support himself in the slick mud. The milling shapes on the other side of the destroyed barricade shifted and changed and slid forward, preceded by a cold, white mist that formed sucking mouths and bony fingers out of thin air.

Grendl levered himself up and raised the muddy ax. Seran and Kel, both wet and torn and sobbing silently, dresses sticking to their bodies like wet sheets, hobbled from the rain to stand beside Jak. There was no other sign of the Legion.

A massive ball of lightning shot through the amorphous ranks of the dead, like a scythe of pure energy that bounced and bounded chaotically from corpse to corpse, tentacle to claw to runny, luminous eye. Thunder shook the earth and knocked Grendl back down into the mud. His leg was twisted and there was wet grit in his teeth but he pushed himself back up and spat. Despite the pain, he rose, a hand reaching out to help him. He ignored the hand and readied his ax. Seran sniffed at Grendl's rebuff but turned, raising a battered short sword.

The dead were gone. In their place, standing with weapons that were more farm implements, lit only by the fading remnants of the destructive ball of lightning, goblins stood watching, staring. A silver-haired figure strode forward, a staff in its hands, and Grendl gasped, his heart racing at the improbability. After all this time, here, now. Grendl's weary, widening smile faltered, however. The figure continued forward, wavering slightly like a heat shimmer to reveal a hobgoblin. Its clothes were tattered and wet, yet somehow looked so damned regal that Grendl still wanted to backpedal and bow despite shaking his head at his mistake. The hobgoblin drew itself up and met Grendl's eyes and smiled a jagged smile. Two balls of lightning slammed down from the sky, behind the goblin ranks.

Idsiyushti sat back against the sloped roof, let the rain wash over her. In that moment, when the last of the fire had slammed down from the sky and the last of her will had finally slipped through the cracks in her existence, when the last of her whiskey-fueled power dissipated, lost in the absurd torrents of magic she'd called down, her body simply gave out. She felt like she was floating, like the roof of the tavern, the small part she occupied, was a raft in a sea of falling rain. She felt clean for the first time in days. She opened her mouth and drank, but her stomach roiled and she spat bile and water back out.

She felt Marrah take her hand, felt Marrah's fingers tighten around her own. Idsiyushti opened her eyes. Marrah, soaked through, hair plastered to her head, torn dress plastered to her skin, held Idsiyushti's hand up and kissed it. Idsiyushti tried to smile, guessed she succeeded because Marrah smiled in return. Such a pretty thing, Marrah. So gentle. And she had called down the fire too. That thought made Idsiyushti try to smile again.

"Just rest," Marrah said. "Take a minute and then we'll get you out of the rain." She looked exhausted too.

Calling fire from the sky would do that to you, it seemed. Especially untrained. Even trained by the fey and a lone elf, Idsiyushti realized she really had no idea how she'd commanded so much power, controlled so much fire.

Idsiyushti tried to nod in response to Marrah, but she couldn't. She was used up. The fire from the sky had all but consumed her. She wanted to say as much to Marrah, but her tongue was thick and she could barely work her jaw.

There was a small fire in her belly still, but she knew that that was about to go out. And when it did, she wondered if there would be pain. She wondered if she'd just slip away or if she'd scream, if she'd convulse, if she'd flop so hard that she'd roll off the roof to the square below, wondered if she'd take Marrah with her.

She wondered about the townsfolk. She knew that many were dead, she felt them die in the rush of contact that had expanded her being so much that she felt like a damned goddess, raining fire down on writhing, dead forms that she could see with some strange sight granted to her by her magic, a sight that let her be in all places at once, instantly. She had seen Marin die and her heart, far away on the roof of the tavern, had cried out. She had seen Ned fall, but didn't know if he was alive or dead—she felt she knew the answer but she just didn't want to think about it. She saw the dead child tear at Sigiswinth. She saw Jak, Kel, Seran, and Grendl rush to the falkr's side. She saw Maeve furiously battling the dead from the far side of the barricades, outside the square, where she and Jonath, with Drag and Valen, had led a charge once the barricades had melted away under the onslaught of the twisted magic of the dead swamp priests. She'd seen Drag take a blow to the head that felled him, unconscious. She'd seen Jonath stumble and nearly fall, his arm slashed open. She'd seen Maeve, sword aflame, standing over Drag, back-to-back with Valen, screaming, destroying the dead left and right, her body washed clean by the heavy rain, the bandages Idsiyushti had tied still holding. Idsiyushti had been proud of that. She'd directed columns of fire to dance around Maeve, Jonath, Valen, and Drag to obliterate their attackers.

She'd seen children run and fall, slipping in the mud, and taken up again by writhing dead. She'd seen people who had come to her for succor and support, for small magic and large, for council, for laughter, for mercy, die, sucked dry or ripped apart. But she'd avenged them all, raining fire from the sky with Marrah. She was exhausted. She was scared. But for everyone who died at the hands, tentacles, teeth, claws of the dead, so many more had survived, fleeing into the tavern or the courthouse, fighting on, gathering around each other as she directed the fire to stab down and protect them.

Marrah squeezed her hand again. "We need to get inside," she said.

Idsiyushti tried another smile, actually felt herself succeed this time. And then the pain started. Shooting pain that erupted every place at once, it seemed. She felt herself convulse. Marrah reached out and grabbed her, screamed her name. Idsiyushti vomited again, tasted blood and acid.

She fought the pain, fought it the way she always had. Searched deep down for the strength that had always been there, hidden, from the time she was three and left in the woods, her parents frightened of her, abandoning her. The strength she'd found to survive, to discover and be discovered by the fey, small flights of sprites and bumbling gnomes who had shown her how to live and love and convert liquor into raw power.

Marrah was shouting again, crying, cursing, begging, pleading, apologizing, but her voice was distant. Idsiyushti could only hear the fall of the rain. It was soothing, something she could focus on to drive back the pain. But it was a losing battle, she'd known that from the beginning. She wanted to tell Marrah, but she couldn't. How could she? The pain was suddenly back with such a force that her vision blurred. Her mouth was filled with more blood and she tried to swallow it back down, but it wouldn't go, so she forced her mouth open and tried to let the rain wash it away.

Marrah continued to scream. Idsiyushti opened her eyes. She wanted to tell Marrah she loved her, that she forgave her. There was no way for Marrah could've known. There was no blame. Marrah was doing what she'd seen Idsiyushti do so many times before. Marrah'd just provided the alcohol and it had been good and strong and had sent wave after wave of such great power through Idsiyushti's small body once it had been converted.

Her vision cleared momentarily. Marrah was no longer screaming, shouting. She was reaching for the whiskey amphora, sobbing. Idsiyushti dug deep one final time, lashed out with her bare foot and kicked the amphora over the edge of the roof. Marrah screamed and reached for it as it fell. Idsiyushti, mouth tasting of blood, sobbed, afraid Marrah would slide over the roof. But the girl held on, simply staring down, down, into nothing.

"Poisoned," was all Idsiyushti could say. The rain washed the blood from her chin. Marrah looked back, sat up. She stared and then her face broke into shards of horror and grief. Idsiyushti, sheered through, began sobbing too. Then Marrah was holding onto Idsiyushti with both hands, both arms, rocking gently. She was still crying but the rain washed away the tears. Idsiyushti tried to explain, tried to soothe, but her mouth was filling with more blood. Then the pain shot forth and blinded her once more.

Moments passed and then the pain was gone. The sound of the rain was starting to carry her away. Her vision cleared again and there was Marrah right in front of her. So close. So close it hurt.

There was no way for Marrah to have known that the whiskey in the amphora had been corrupted, had somehow become poisoned as it sat so long, undisturbed. Some ingredient gone sour, some disease leached into the liquor through tiny cracks and holes, maybe even some spell, like a curse, to keep the whiskey from falling into the wrong hands. But the whiskey had been so strong, even in its ruination, that Idsiyushti had been able to call forth such fire, such destruction, had been able to see her friends live and die, had been able to fight alongside them from the top of the tavern, been able to share all of those things with Marrah.

In so many ways, Marrah had helped Idsiyushti save the town. But in so doing, she had sealed Idsiyushti's fate. Idsiyushti was shaking now, and she couldn't see again, although the pain was gone.

At first, of course, she hadn't recognized the danger in the old whiskey. It had tasted odd, but it had an amazing kick. It was difficult to convert, had caused her to vomit, but the power she'd wielded afterward was so engrossing, so godlike. She didn't see the corruption, didn't feel the danger even with the nausea, until she'd used her magic sight near the end to look at herself and Marrah on the roof as if from afar. They stood hand in hand, glowing, filled with magic and power, filled with each other. But when Idsiyushti, laughing, high, ecstatic, had looked from Marrah to herself, she'd seen it. The poison had been like black and silver fingers crawling through her skin, her veins, her soul. She'd cried out but no one had heard.

Perhaps if she'd paid more attention, perhaps if she hadn't gotten caught up in the battle rage the corrupted whiskey had caused, been caught up in the swells of power and ability, the closeness of Marrah, the thrill of their shared magic, she might have caught the poison in time and converted it too. She knew how to do that, convert poison and disease to harmlessness. But she'd been so distracted, so hotheaded, angry, vengeful, powerful. She'd missed her chance. Words of warning echoed through the rain then, the words of the fey, of her elf teacher, of Ashakarahad, Grendl, Jonath. The words gripped her. The distant, fleeting memory of her teacher's yellow eyes filled with deep sadness shook her. She realized then, with a sudden finality, that her teacher had known, somehow, even way back then, about the rooftop, about the power she'd summon, about the poisoned whiskey. But the words of warning, the sadness in elven eyes, the sudden realization of what seemed like prophecy, faded as she looked again at Marrah.

Marrah pulled her close. She was rocking, screaming her heartache to the rain. Idsiyushti tried to hold her, kiss her, but she couldn't move.

367

Then slowly, gently, so sweetly that it seemed to cause new pain, the rain began to stop. Each lessening drop was like a gentle release, one after the other, until, when no more rain fell, Idsiyushti found a moment of new strength. She pulled back and touched Marrah's cheek. Then her hand dropped and she squeezed Marrah's hand for the last time.

The square before the alley was filled with mud, bodies, and the ruins of the barricades. Ashakarahad looked quickly for more attacking dead but all she could see was rain and sheets of fire glimmering further into the square. Driven by rage, she stomped through the mud and destruction towards Grendl's tavern. From nowhere, the dead reappeared, flowing from the rain, between columns of fire. She spun and danced, spitting angry curses. The dead turned to bone and slick ash. Mud covered her, refusing to be washed away by the blood and the rain.

Then a massive wall of fire, too many columns to count, lanced down, splitting, burning. Ashakarahad looked up and once again found the subtle glow on the roof of the travel through the black rain.

The glow flickered. Ashakarahad's breath caught.

The columns of fire stopped at almost the same instant. They were replaced by countless balls of snapping lightening, arcs that lanced out and bit through the remaining dead. And then the dead and the lightning were gone. A sudden, nearly palpable sensation filled the hot, wet air, a decreased pressure, like something had withdrawn from the world, leaving only a shimmering hole, leaving a pop, a sucking sound as it left. Ashakarahad staggered. She shook her head, tried to get her bearings. The rain was still falling, the square was still full of mud and bodies. But she knew, without a doubt, that the attacking dead had left that place.

The swamp seemed to sigh with relief.

The glow on the roof flickered once more and vanished. Ash stared for a moment, stared up at the roof through the rain. She blinked, her heart a painful stone sinking through cold water, rage fading to despair. She was running then, pounding through the mud and the ruin of the square. Mud flew like a mist. She ran up the slick stairs of the tavern porch, through the main doors into the common room. The wounded were everywhere and Sek was leaning against the bar, hunched over a bottle, looking for all the world like one of the recently banished dead. But she turned when Ash entered, eyes going wide, and Ash moved on, across the room and up the stairs.

She found the trap door in the attic after a brief search and when she finally climbed out on to the sloping roof, the rain was beginning to subside. Another hole seemed to be left in reality, a left-behind nothingness where the goblin clan's power had been, the initial power behind the tumultuous rain.

Marrah, soaked through, short hair plastered to her scalp, eyes closed, mouth open, lips moving. Through the last drops of rain, Ashakarahad heard Marrah singing a soft, gentle lullaby broken by heart-wrenching sobs. Ash stepped forward, her chest on fire. It took a long time before she could make her eyes work properly, before she could make them look down at the wet rag doll with nearly white hair that Marrah was cradling and rocking.

Idsiyushti.

"No," Ash breathed. "Dammit, no!" But she could come no closer. Marrah simply glanced at her, and Ash watched tears race down the girl's cheek as she continued to sing.

"Dammit, girl!" Ash glanced back to find Grendl, wet, tattered and torn, ax hanging limp. He shook his head. Marrah kept singing. Ash turned back and finally found the strength to walk the rest of the way across the roof. She knelt down, set the war hammers aside and reached out. She hesitated, looked at Marrah, who continued to sing while nodding once. Ash touched Idsiyushti's soft, smooth face, brushed white hair away. Then Ash reached out and touched Marrah's shoulder. The girl began to shake. She pulled Marrah close, held them both, held them tight.

Beyond the edge of the roof, down in the square, folk were beginning to show themselves. They dragged wounded and picked through the dead, smoky torches in hand, starting fresh fires here and there. Until they saw the standing stone. It was glowing, pulsing. Waiting.

The shackles that held Ashakarahad were tingling in time to the pulse of the stone, although their weight was diminishing, a dim pressure now rather than a painful clawing rending her existence. But the price—tears of sulfur, burning. She felt sick, wracked with something that seemed so broken and horrid that her head spun. Yet the presence of the shackles lessened even further as Marrah sobbed into her shoulder.

Ashakarahad wanted to scream. Wanted to lash out. Wanted to slam her hammers, her fists, her teeth into Ceàrain. But no. No, it was her fault. Not the hobgoblin's. She had accidentally called the dead forth. She had asked for Idsiyushti's aid, she had dismissed the writings in the old texts. She had drawn the attention of the old mage-lords, of the denizens of the city of chrome and glass. She, one of the Eld, who should have known better. The anger she felt now was the anger of coming to her senses on that cracked stone floor centuries ago, amidst a snow flurry in a ruin she could not name. In a circle that had been her cage for countless years before that.

Ashakarahad sobbed once and then Grendl touched her shoulder and squeezed. In the square below, the mud, the wood, the smoking fires and the remains of the undead and the townsfolk shimmered in the hot light of the day as, overhead, the thick clouds gave way to blue. The stone pulsed, calling.

After a time, Marrah's tears turned to sniffles. Gently, oh so gently, Ashakarahad and Grendl helped her carry Idsiyushti from the rooftop down into the tavern.

The endless city loomed, no longer receding with each step, no longer merely a feature of the horizon. Details were becoming clear, movement, sound, smell, a heat that was not the swamp. A cold heat, a detached heat, the heat of millions of exhalations on streets that were black and mazelike and fluid.

Ashakarahad looked behind her. The plain stretched out and she could see the lone standing stone, whole once more, as if carved new only moments before. The breeze from the plain, sweeping up past the stone, running its course towards the city still hinted at some distant charnel house far out beyond the black mountains in the distance, across the churning river. The pink sun was crawling up from the far horizon, opposite the city, just above the mountains, pulling itself as if from the grave of night, reanimated by sinew and blood and the dark sorcery of the mage-lords.

She looked back down at the thin sliver of the distant river and then to the standing stone but that portion of the plain was suddenly in deep shadow, as if it were in the process of being excised, cut and removed like a strip of unwanted, misshapen leather. Then the shadow narrowed and vanished, the edges coming together with what Ashakarahad imagined was a violent crash, as if the edges of the plain, to either side of the excised patch, had been drawn together by unseen hands. What was left was a smooth stretch of earth marked by patches of blue-green scrub grass. The standing stone was gone. In its place, a distant, silver-haired figure stood. An eye blink and the figure was gone as well.

Back in the swamp, they'd lit the pyre atop which Jak and Valen, both solemn, torn, bandaged, had laid Idsiyushti. The witch had been dressed in simple finery, if finery it could be called—a dress of threadbare silk that Marrah had found in a chest in Idsiyushti's hut. Marrah had stood back, tears dried up, her face tight and distant, while the flames ate her lover. Seran and Kel, in clean mourning dresses, had stood to either side, arms around Marrah's shoulders, crying into kerchiefs. Jak had said a few words, Jonath a few more. Peler began a low funerary song on his lute. Jak's legion sang tearful songs. Ash had stood beside Maeve, the young falkr, still mostly naked aside from helmet and gauntlets, wounds freshly bandaged.

Maeve would be leaving soon, leaving with Sigiswinth bundled in sailcloth, tied with rope, scented with herbs and spices for the journey, tucked into a wood box atop a cart drawn by a scrawny pony bought from Drag. The other falkr, Aeldreth, conscious now, would travel in the back of the cart too, propped up on a rug and some old blankets. They were headed for Esgen, a week and an eternity away, where they would hire a barge to take them up a long, twisting river back to Drilithae—where they would honor their fallen sisters and inform someone that the town needed a new judge.

After the funeral, while the others turned to their own dead and wounded, as even more pyres were lit, even more songs and prayers were offered up to swamp gods no one was sure they wanted to believe in anymore, Ashakarahad had walked with Marrah back to Idsiyushti's hut. The hedge maze and the ruins of the Winall house had both been untouched by the march of the dead. Idsiyushti's hut had been unharmed as well. But the herb garden was dried and withered. Marrah was silent and stoic until they came in sight of the ruined garden. She sobbed once and then Ashakarahad led her into the dark hut.

Marrah had stared at Ceàrain for a long time. Ash had stared too, ducking beneath the low ceiling. But she'd known that the hobgoblin would be there, had known it from the moment she'd help carry Idsiyushti down from the tavern roof. She wanted to hate Ceàrain, but her anger was dulling, somehow replaced by an ache that was more depressing than vitriolic. And the look in Ceàrain's yellow eyes during that shifted moment in the stone maze, before a ruined fountain, the look of violence and fire, was no longer there. Instead, there was compassion. Or what Ashakarahad assumed was compassion. In Ceàrain's goblinoid eyes, the look could simply have been amusement.

After a long time in the cloying smell of herbs, Marrah had stopped sniffling and simply demanded to know what was going on. Ceàrain gestured at the hut's door.

"Go out and touch the plants in the garden," was all she said. Marrah had started to balk, but then something snapped in the hut and she simply nodded and went outside.

Ashakarahad watched Ceàrain.

"It is past time for you to go, child of the Eld," Ceàrain said.

"Marrah?"

"This town will need a new witch. And that witch will need a teacher, as Idsiyushti had. But Idsiyushti had been so young, mayhaps too young, when she set out on her path. So much power—her spirit had burned so brightly. We'll see about Marrah."

Ashakarahad said, "You sound like you were there, when Idsiyushti—" She stopped, the pieces finally falling together, slowly, reluctantly, as it seemed they always did eventually, always just a little too late. She wondered why she hadn't seen through the illusion until now.

"I said it is past time you were gone, demon," the silver-haired elf said.

Outside, a single red rose bloomed on a withered vine and Ashakarahad watched Marrah remove her hand, fingers trembling, and start to sob once more.

Later, she felt Grendl's eyes from the porch of his tavern while Jonath shook her hand in the still-muddy square. Around them, the Legion of Queers gave a ragged cheer. Jak stepped forward and wrapped his arms around Ashakarahad's waist. She patted the top of his blond head. Ceàrain's words echoed back to her as she walked over to the standing stone. How many of these people would still feel the pull towards the swamp after all that had happened? How many more from out in the world would feel that draw still too? The stone was still glowing, still pulsing. The townsfolk had avoided it since the end of the battle. Now Ash approached it, the few belongings she'd been able to salvage from her dead-ravaged camp in a large pack slung across her shoulders. Her invisible shackles were light and vibrant, humming like Jak's now-silent amulet had. She reached out and felt the power of the stone. She knew the words now. Could see them scrolling behind her eyelids whenever she closed her eyes. It was indeed past time that she was gone. But she would miss this place, this swamp with its heat and weight. She would miss the libraries and academies of Drilithae too, the wide expanse of the Empire built on the bones of so much that was lost and forgotten, under the shadow of a distant, otherworldly city whose denizens still held the same sway over this world now as they had millennia ago. In a strange way, she would almost miss the heavy weight of the shackles that tied her to this land, had tied her for centuries. Without looking back, she touched the stone and stepped through the gate.

Out on the plain, the excised shadow, the standing stone, the way back to the swamp, was gone. The plain stretched out seamlessly now, stretched out to the river, now shining like tears, roiling towards the crimson, boiling sea. The sun continued to crawl up from the charnel wastes beyond the black mountains. Ash looked down at her own hands, made fists, relaxed her fingers. The weight of the invisible shackles was slight, drawing her on now with the light touch of a kiss by a fleeting, teasing lover.

Behind her, the city beckoned.

The End

Acknowledgements

Special thanks to Tommy and Geoffrey for discussing this project extensively and pushing me to get it out there, and to Rose for hours spent editing and commenting.

About the Author

David Alan Bennett is a writer, visual artist, and applied mathematician who teaches math, physics, and physical science on California's Central Coast.